The Day That Saved Us

MINDY HAYES

The Day That Saved Us

Published by Mindy Hayes

Cover Design and Photography by Regina Wamba

www.maeidesign.com

Edited by Madison Seidler

www.madisonseidler.com

& Samantha Eaton-Roberts

Book design by Inkstain Interior Book Designing

www.inkstainformatting.com

ISBN-13: 978-1544037851

ALSO BY MINDY HAYES

Kaleidoscope

Ember

Luminary

Me After You

Me Without You

CO-WRITTEN WITH MICHELE G. MILLER

Paper Planes and Other Things We Lost

For Michele—

The Day That Saved Us

BEFORE

PEYTON

The Day We Wore a Cap and Gown

IF GRADUATION IS one of those rites of passage, this monumental event that miraculously means we've officially joined the real world, then why is it so long and boring? Just give us the diplomas already and we'll be on our way. That would make everyone happier. No one wants to sit through this entire thing. Listening to dull speeches, an off-key "Star-Spangled Banner," and Principal Neiman slowly annunciating and fumbling over everyone's names.

If I'm being honest, what I really want is for today to be over so we can be on our way to Hatteras. That is where my summer will begin. If I can manage to survive this ceremony, I'll be one step closer.

None of my friends have a last name close to mine in the alphabet, so I search the auditorium toward the front and see my best friend, Harper Day, staring at the ceiling like she can't take one more second of this torture. Her dark pink curls drape over the back of the chair. At least I'm not the only one who finds this ridiculously mind-numbing. Almost as if she feels my eyes on her, she turns around and winks at me.

My eyes glide over the rest of my graduating class, trying to figure out where the F's are. I find Brodee easily because he's already looking at me. He has his fingers pointed at his head like a gun. I laugh. He flashes one of his charming grins that make all the girls fall head over heels.

Our parents have been best friends forever. They rarely spend time apart, so when they all graduated from college together, it only seemed logical to have houses built next door to each other. But they couldn't just do that together. Our moms *had* to get pregnant together. When Tatum found out that she was pregnant with Brodee, my mom was sure to follow. Brodee and I are only three months apart.

I think back to our freshman year when the three of us started going to school together. While Brodee and I have known each other since birth, Harper and I met in eighth grade when she moved here from Minnesota. Brodee had gone to a different middle school, so they'd only heard of each other through me. On our first day at Hilton Rock High she'd noticed him. It was hard not to.

"Don't look now, Peyton-Parker." She said my name like it was one word. Always. "But there's a McHottie at two o'clock watching us."

Even though Harper tried to stop me, I had to see who she was talking about. When I turned, Brodee smiled and gave a head nod. "Oh." I tossed a wave.

"Wait." Harper grabbed my arm, yanking me to face her again. "You know him?"

"It's Brodee, Harper. My best friend, Brodee Fisher."

"Holy crap. That's Brodee? Why didn't you tell me he was so hot?"

"You never asked." I shrugged.

"You seriously have nothing going on with him?" Her eyes grew wide. "You're crazy."

Crazy would be considering the possibility and ruining our friendship forever. "I've known him my whole life." I'm not willing to wreck that.

"So, then you wouldn't hate me if I took a whack at him?" Harper wiggled her eyebrows.

"Took a whack at him?" Did she really just say that about my Brodee? It didn't matter that technically he wasn't my Brodee. In my mind he kind of was. Not romantically speaking or anything, but if someone were to ask who my best friend was, I wouldn't say Harper, I'd say Brodee.

Harper giggled uncharacteristically. "You know, try to see if there could be something there? He's gorgeous."

There was nothing else I could say except, "Be my guest."

"I'll talk to him at lunch. He won't know what hit him." She smirked at me and let her laughter fly.

Brodee really hadn't. Harper has that way about her. She's about as subtle as a hurricane, but once she launches herself into your world, you cling to her for dear life because you feel alive having her near, no matter the chaos she leaves in her wake.

While Harper didn't hold anything back, for some reason Brodee didn't bite. She let go of her fascination when she took one look at his friend, Skylar. Skylar and Harper have been together ever since.

I peer back at Harper in the auditorium and see Skylar loop his arm around her neck. His top teeth graze his lip ring before he tugs her over to plant a kiss on the top of her head. Harper Day and Skylar Dalton,

Hilton Rock High School's sweethearts. Knowing them, they'll probably get engaged as soon as the diplomas are in hand.

Finally, Principal Neiman announces that it's time for the diplomas and everyone cheers. *Two hours later.* Well, maybe it hasn't been that long, but it feels like it.

When Harper is handed her diploma she curtsies and lifts a rock-on hand gesture while sticking out her tongue. Her dark pink hair flows over her shoulders in thick waves. That girl refuses to be predictable, and I love her for it.

You know that one guy at school who everyone likes? Not the popular jock or the biggest flirt, but the loveable guy? The one who's nice to everyone and can immerse himself into any group because he's laid-back and easy to get along with? That's Brodee Fisher. So when he walks coolly across the stage, like it's a regular day and there aren't thousands of eyes on him, he gets the loudest cheer out of everyone in our graduating class.

Normally when you've known someone your whole life and know everything about them, there are things that drive you insane. But for some reason with Brodee, everything he does is cool. It sounds so lame, I know. But it's the best way to describe him, to encompass everything that he is. The way he handles himself and can make anyone laugh. The way he casually paces a room when he gets a little anxious. The way he treats others and doesn't allow others to be treated. The casual way he dresses and styles his hair with surf wax. He really doesn't care about what people think. He's just Brodee Fisher. He's endearing without even trying.

All he does is smile when he's handed the diploma. I shout out his name and cheer as loudly as my voice will go. He nods his head like he's tipping the brim of a hat and walks off the stage.

When we're outside of the auditorium our group of friends congregate under a big oak tree for pictures. Our moms are the queens of picture taking. If they didn't have cameras in their hands for memories like this, I'd be worried about their mental state.

Brodee jumps on my back and gives me a noogie. Yeah. A noogie. *Who still does that?* Brodee Fisher. Then he lets out a Chewbacca howl, which he's surprisingly good at. Makes me laugh every time.

"Pete! We graduated!"

"Yeah," I laugh and shove him off me, rubbing the tender skin where his knuckles were digging into my skull. "I was there. And you're a dork."

I couldn't count the number of times I've been called Peter Parker in my lifetime, even if I tried. *What were my parents thinking, right?* Brodee was the first. When we were six, he had a huge obsession with Spider-Man, and I was the perfect target for teasing. Though at that age, he thought it was kind of cool, and I was embarrassed. I wasn't the type of girl that wanted to be associated with a boy superhero, especially one that has to do with spiders.

He's been calling me Pete ever since. It used to drive me crazy, but over the years it's grown on me. Dare I say that I even like it because he's the only one that does. Which makes it kind of special—personal to us.

"Peyton," my mom says, "I want one of just you, Harper, and Brodee."

"Oh, good idea," Tatum says, encouraging us to separate from the group. "Get together, you three."

When we branch off, Brodee stands on one side and Harper takes the other. For some reason, it's this moment that makes me teary. Not sad tears, but I realize how grateful I am to have these two in my life. They've always been there for me, and I know they'll stick by my side no matter what.

When I lost my dad last year, Brodee and Harper knew when to leave me alone and when to stick around even if I pushed them away. They knew when I was pretending to be okay. And they knew sometimes I just needed to cry. On nights when my bedroom window was cracked open, and Brodee could hear me crying from his room, he'd climb up the tree outside my house and crawl into my open window to hold me until I fell asleep. Sometimes I'd feel his tears mingling with mine. Other times all he did was hold me, clinging tightly, so I wouldn't feel alone.

Brain aneurysms suck. One minute my dad was there, the next he was gone. I know I'll never be fully healed, but I have Brodee and Harper to try and make up the difference.

Stupid monumental moments making me reflect.

When Brodee and Harper notice my glassy eyes, they laugh and reach around me in a group hug.

"Cry baby." Harper chuckles.

"I was wondering when you'd crack," Brodee says, nudging his head against my temple.

I laugh and shove them away, wiping my face. "I'm fine. Whatever. I just got something in my eyes."

"Suuuuuuure," Harper croons. "It wouldn't be like you if you didn't shed a tear, but no more. We have an entire summer ahead of us!"

"That's right, we do." I smile at her.

"Now, Brodee and Peyton," Tatum, Brodee's mom, says, motioning us to get closer together. "Our babies have graduated," she says to my mom.

"Don't remind me." My mom has tears in her eyes. No one has to guess where I get my sensitive side. Though, I know it's more than graduation. It's him. She wishes he were here with us.

I do too.

As if Brodee knows I'm about to cry all over again, he throws his arm over my shoulder, tugging me close, and murmurs wryly into my long hair, "They're going to be unbearable this summer."

"Save me," I mutter, chuckling under my breath, grateful for his distraction.

"But The Amazing Spider-Man doesn't need saving." He squeezes me.

I laugh so hard; I know that picture is going to be *really* flattering.

As my mom and I are walking to our car after all the picture taking, she places her arm around my shoulders and hugs me close to her side. "He would've been so proud of you today, Peyton."

I nod, unable to open my mouth to respond without crying. *Gosh*, I miss him. He would've squeezed my face with one hand, kissed my forehead, and said, "Peyton Jane, it's time to start a new chapter."

Every big event was a new chapter to him, a clean slate with a blank page to create new memories and adventures. As a writer, that analogy made the most sense for him. I want to go back and rewrite the chapter where we lost him, change the ending so he could be here now, with me today.

"I know he's with us today." Mom rests her head atop of mine. I hear the raw emotion in her voice though she tries to conceal it. "I feel it. He wouldn't have missed today for the world."

A couple tears fall down my face, and she leans down and kisses my cheek. "I love you, baby girl."

"Love you too."

SKYLAR IS HAVING a graduation get together at his house. We all want to ditch grad night anyway, so the whole gang heads to his house after we do dinner with our families.

"Hey, McLean, you know the point of ping-pong is to hit the ball onto the other side of the net, right?" Skylar taunts from the beanbag he and Harper are occupying. Harper thumps him in the chest with that back of her hand.

"Shut it, Dalton," Mike retorts, concentrating on not only hitting the ball, but also trying to fend off Robby, who's doing everything he can to distract him. "I'd like to see you do better with this moron in your way." He elbows Robby in the ribs, but all Robby does is laugh and move just out of reach.

"Oh, he's just making it more interesting," Skylar says as he and Brodee strum their guitars.

I'm really going to miss this, hanging out with this group, laughing and never having a dull moment. After spending four years with them, I'm comfortable with them. I don't want to lose this.

We've talked about making sure we get together in between semesters or on breaks, but they're all heading out of state for college. Since Skylar, Harper, and I are the only ones going to University of South Carolina together, it feels like we're grasping at anything we can to not lose what we have.

"Go ahead, Sky," Brodee interjects, pausing their guitar playing. "Show Mikey how it's done."

"Only if you take the place of Dickerson."

"Bring it," he challenges, setting down his guitar, and springs off the couch from beside me.

With all the boys in on the rousing game, I crawl onto the beanbag with Harper and lay back.

"I'm gonna miss this," she says with a soft smile on her face.

"That's exactly what I was just thinking."

Around eleven we call it quits. Since we live next door to each other, Brodee agrees to take me home. As we're making the fifteen-minute drive home, Brodee turns down the music.

"You and I need to make a pact."

"A pact…" I slowly repeat.

"Yes, a pact," he says in all seriousness. His eyes remain focused on the road. "No matter what happens after this summer, we won't drift apart."

I chuckle. "We won't drift apart, Brodee. Our lives are so tangled together there's no way that's even possible—like our families would even let us."

"I know, but Jackson and Isaac were talking earlier, and it got me thinking."

Oh great. Any sentence that begins with 'Jackson and Isaac were talking' never ends with anything intellectual or significant. "What could Jackson and Isaac have said that was so thought-provoking?"

"What they said doesn't matter. I just…" Brodee fidgets, keeping one hand on the steering wheel and rubbing the fingertips of his other hand over his mouth. "There are so many variables at play: different colleges, distance, the unknown future—I don't want things between us to change. You're my best friend. I never want what we have to go away."

"It won't," I assure him, "because we won't let it."

"You promise?" He glances my way, the lights of oncoming traffic flashing across his face.

"Pinky promise." I lean over, my elbow resting on the center console, and hold out my pinky toward him.

Brodee gasps, mocking. "Not a pinky promise. That's the most sacred of all promises."

"Shut it, clown, and pinky promise me." I keep my hand firmly between us, waiting.

He laughs, but reaches over to interlock his pinky with mine.

"So, it's solidified," I say. "We'll never change."

The Day Summer Began

MY HEAD TAPS on the car window, jostled by the pavement on the drive to Cape Hatteras. I listen to my mom talk to Tatum in the front seat. We left at five this morning for some cruel reason. Leaving Skylar's when we did didn't make much of a difference. If I weren't so excited about leaving I might have been able to fall asleep earlier, but my mind wouldn't stop forming every possible memory that we might make this summer. This summer is all we have left. And with it being the first summer in Hatteras without my dad, I'll need Brodee more than ever.

We won't get to the beach house for another six hours, and my body is begging to sleep, but I can't get comfortable. I keep repositioning my pillow beneath the curve of my neck, but it doesn't help.

"C'mere, Pete," Brodee's soft voice encourages. "You can't be comfortable. Lay on my shoulder."

I peer over at his reassuring smile. He nods his head to the side, persuading me to lean into him. He's always been more like the brother

I never had, so snuggling up to him isn't all that weird. I gradually move, curling around the side of his body. He shifts so we fit comfortably together. It *is* much better. I inhale his soothing scent and fall asleep within minutes.

THE HEAT OF the sunlight beams through the passenger window, slowly waking me. The engine is still purring, so I know we haven't arrived yet. I'm not sure how long I slept, but hopefully we'll be there soon.

As my brain fully wakes, I feel warmth resting on my thigh. My eyes gradually open to a familiar masculine hand curved around my bare leg. Brodee's head rests atop mine. During the course of my nap our arms intertwined. I feel his tight abs through his T-shirt and reign in the urge to run my fingers across them. That wakes my brain instantly. *Why do I want to rub my hands all over his body?*

I remain frozen, too afraid that I'll wake him and he'll read my thoughts. Then his fingertips gently stroke the inside of my thigh, drawing continuous circles. Maybe if I were wearing jeans, it wouldn't feel so intimate, but I'm in shorts, and Brodee is doodling on my skin. *Is he doing that in his sleep?* Goosebumps instantly spread across my flesh. Stunned, I shift my head from under his. Our eyes lock, but his are not dazed by sleep.

"Hi," he whispers.

"Hi," I repeat back, lost in his light green eyes. *Lost? Get ahold of yourself, Peyton.*

"Did you sleep okay?"

I nod.

His hand retreats from my thigh. He stretches his arms out in front of him like nothing happened. I guess it isn't a big deal. He was merely giving me a more comfortable position for the long drive, and his hand got bored. He's a doodler. I've never seen a homework assignment of his that didn't have some sort of drawing in the margins. That's all it was. His restlessness kicking in.

"We should be there soon," he says, slipping me a glance and leaning away. "The first thing I plan on doing is grabbing my surfboard. If you can keep up, I'll let you come with me."

I look at him, feigning annoyance at his challenge. "Like that's even a question. I could surf circles around you."

A slow grin turns the corner of his mouth. "I knew that'd wake you up."

WHEN WE REACH the Outer Banks and drive down the 12 toward Hatteras, I roll down my window to feel the salt air in my long blonde locks. This part of the drive is my favorite. It never lasts long enough. Seeing the Atlantic to our left and the Pamlico Sound to our right, and knowing it's just me and that ocean for the next two months, is a promise of living. Life begins on that water. Our home in Charleston might not be far from the ocean, but there's something different about The Cape. It feels worlds away from the real world, like being in a dream. Everything is better. Brighter. Magical. We don't live by clocks. We live by moments. And every moment counts.

We drive through all the beach towns on our way down, watching their colorful, weathered shingles and wraparound porches as we pass by. The lanky palm trees sway in the wind. Sea grass sprouts on the side of the road.

I once heard that salt water is the cure for everything. I couldn't agree more. When we're in Hatteras, the ocean heals our family. We don't fight. We don't stress. We relax and have fun. This summer we need the healing more than ever.

Though, I fear it may feel less like home without my dad. Since losing him, my mom hasn't been the same. How can she be? There have been times I've caught her standing in the middle of a room staring into space—so quiet and reserved with her feelings and thoughts. For the last eight months it's felt as though she's crawled inside her head to keep from projecting her grief onto me, knowing I have my own heartache to work through. Her silence is deafening.

Only recently has my mom begun to come out of her shell and smile again, becoming the woman she once was. Now I worry that maybe the beach house was a terrible idea. What if we don't continue to heal? What if being here is worse than being at home without him? What if I lose her completely? I push the thoughts away. I have to believe Hatteras is the key to making us whole again, or at least a step in the right direction.

It doesn't hurt that I'll get to see Tyler Hamilton. Our summers together for the last three years have never been anything serious, but who doesn't want a summer fling? We haven't talked since last summer, but I know he'll be there. He's always there.

My stomach flutters with anticipation the closer we get. The light gray shingles of our two-story beach house come into view, and the white Bahama shutters on all the windows have been propped open. It's like the house is welcoming us back. *I'm ready for you*, it says. My fingers itch to pull the car door handle and jump out. I need to be there already.

When we cruise into the circular driveway, there are two cars already parked up front: Brodee's Patriot—which I'm assuming his little brother, Carter, drove up—and his dad's Lexus. Tatum said they drove up after graduation yesterday to air out the house and get everything ready for us.

Once our car is in park, I fly out of the passenger's side. Before going inside, I stop, look up, and absorb it all. The tall front stairway of the cozy wraparound porch and the glass double front doors are the perfect greeting. There are hundreds of beach houses here, but not one compares to ours. It's the perfect mixture of beach and home. Big enough that we have our own space when we need it, but not so big that it feels like more of a hotel than a home.

I hear Brodee's feet on the gravel as he runs at full speed, vaulting off my shoulders, nearly knocking me to the ground. He runs past me. "C'mon, Pete! Let's get changed and go!" He runs up the wooden staircase of the white front porch, his backpack tossing from side to side, and busts through the front door.

Well, at least I had a second of peace to take it all in. Here we come, summer.

The Day I Kept Him My Secret

WHEN BRODEE AND I wake up the next morning, we drive a couple towns up to Rodanthe for the surf. We stand in the parking lot at the back of his black Patriot, sliding on our wetsuits. He turns his back to me and stands there. "You mind?" he asks. I don't catch on at first because wetsuits are made specifically with long enough zippers to zip up your own, but I don't question it.

"I'd do it myself, but my zipper has been giving me issues. I think I need to get a new one. It's time for an upgrade anyway."

"It's cool," I say nonchalantly.

His back is tan and muscular with freckles speckling his shoulders just like they kiss his face. I push away thoughts I shouldn't have about him. Thoughts I haven't stopped having since yesterday morning. I don't know why they're assaulting me all of a sudden.

Once I'm done, I turn my back to him so he can return the favor even though I've always zipped up my own wetsuit. "I always get my hair caught in it," I reason. It only seems fair. I sweep my long blonde hair to one side.

His fingers graze my bare back as he pulls up the zipper, and I have to suppress a shiver. *Did he notice?* It might be warm, but I know I have goosebumps covering my entire body.

Get ahold of yourself, Peyton. You're being ridiculous. This is Brodee. The boy who used to give you covered wagons and wet willies. The boy who tugged on your braids and burped the alphabet in your face while holding you down so you couldn't get away.

Sure, Brodee has grown up. I'm not blind to the fact that he's not a pubescent boy anymore. He hasn't been for years. So, why now? Why, during our last summer together before we're separated, am I looking at him differently? It goes against our pact. We can't change. I can't be having these thoughts.

"YOU GOT THIS one, Pete!" Brodee hollers. As I lay on my stomach with the water splashing my face, I stroke swiftly. I push myself as hard as I can toward the oncoming swell. "Take it!" I hear him yell from a distance. "Now!"

It's not as though I don't know what I'm doing, but it's nice to hear his encouragement, to know he has my back out here.

I pick myself up on my board, but can't keep my balance. I hit the water faster than I can think to balance. The water whirls around me, pounding me under until my surfboard finally pulls me to the surface.

I paddle back out to him, determined to catch the next wave. I'm off my game. He's in my head, making it too hard for me to concentrate. Others are surfing closer to the pier, but Brodee knows how much I hate to surf that close to it after nearly decapitating myself last year. The wave had it out for me, and the pier was its partner in crime.

"You'll get the next one. Just relax," he says.

"It's been like a month since I've gone."

"Yeah. What's up with that? Robby and I wanted you to come with us last weekend."

I shrug. "I've been busy with end of the year stuff."

He nods. "It's cool. I know my parents were hounding me to keep focused so my grades didn't slip. '*Duke could still check your grades,*'" he mimics Tatum's voice. "'*They want to know you're not going to slack off just because you've already been accepted.*'"

I chuckle. "I think I've heard your mom say that a couple times."

He stops. I feel his eyes on me, but I keep mine on the water. "Can I tell you something, Pete?"

"Always."

He pauses and quietly says, "I don't think I want to go to Duke."

My face whips to him. "What? What do you mean you don't want to go to Duke?"

"I mean…" He rubs his hand along the back of his neck. "I do, but I don't."

"You've been working your butt off for years so that you could get in. It's your dream school."

He scoffs and squints at the sun. "It's my dad's dream, and I've gone along with it. It's ingrained in me. Don't get me wrong, getting into Duke it awesome, but…" he trails off with a shrug. "I just don't know if it's me."

"You're just now saying something? Brodee, this is a big deal. Why haven't you said anything before?"

He tugs on his bottom lip before he says, "I can't disappoint him, Pete. You should've seen the look on his face when he found out I got in. It was like *he* got in. And it's not like it isn't an incredible opportunity. I just…"

Why is he telling me this now? "Are you thinking of not going?"

"I don't know. What do you think?"

This is my opportunity to discourage him. Red lights flash. Neon arrows point to him. It's like the Las Vegas freaking strip inside my head. *Opportunity: Take it.* From the moment we knew we were going to different colleges, it's been different. I've felt the place in my heart where he resides gradually empty the closer we get, like it's preparing for a new resident. I don't want a new resident. But it wouldn't be right to push my agenda. It would be completely selfish. No matter how much it hurts my heart to be separated from my best friend, I need to put those feelings aside. This about more than me.

"If it's what you want, absolutely. After years of preparing, there has to be a part of you that wants to go. You didn't work this hard for nothing. It's *Duke*, Brodee."

For a second he looks at me as if he sees right through my answer, but then he nods, peering beyond my shoulder with a distant look in his eyes. "You're right. I did work my butt off."

"Heck yeah, you did! So, you're not second guessing it?"

His eyes shift back to my face. "I am, but you know me. I'm not going to disappoint my parents." He shakes his head and squints at the sun again.

"I just needed to say that out loud. To someone who would listen to me."

My heart rate picks up. I honestly thought just *maybe* he was going to tell me he was going to USC with me instead. He applied there just in case, but it was never a serious consideration. It's always been Duke. I kind of hate Duke.

Over the last few summers, when Brodee wasn't on the water with me, he was studying or working on college prep assignments. His dad, Nick, meant business. *Summer isn't a time to take a break.* It's like he thought if Brodee weren't consistently keeping up with schoolwork, he'd lose his intelligence and a future with Duke. Brodee hardly complained about it though. He's always wanted to make his dad happy. But now I wonder if *Brodee* is even happy.

We sit straddling our boards for a little while in silence as we wait for the next good wave. I feel his eyes on me again.

"What?" I say without meeting his gaze, still trying to process his lack of interest in Duke.

"If your heart was a prison, I would like to be sentenced for life."

My head falls back as I laugh. "It took you a week to come up with *that*? C'mon, Brodee. You can do better."

He chuckles to himself. "For real? I thought it was pretty good. So, I guess you've got a better one?" He raises his left eyebrow, challenging me.

A couple years back, our cheesy pick-up line challenge started when we were at Folley Beach and this guy tried to hit on me. *I seem to have lost my phone number. Can I have yours?* Brodee laughed in his face and said he could have come up with a million different pick-up lines that would have been more original than that one. And so I challenged him, and he hasn't given up since. After all these years you'd think we'd be better at it by now.

I clear my throat. "There must be something wrong with my eyes because I can't seem to take them off you."

"*That?*" he says with a laugh. "That was not better than mine."

"It at least has to be a tie," I dispute. "There's no way yours is better."

"We'll call it a tie, but I expect better from you next time."

It takes me a few more tries, but finally, about three waves later, I get up and stay. I can hear Brodee screaming, "That's my girl!"

I almost scream back, "You wish!" But there's a part of me that wants to revel in a make-believe world where we're together. It'll be my little secret.

The Day She Met the Gang

I'M READING AT the kitchen counter when my mom and Tatum come traipsing down the stairs the following morning. They take turns kissing the top of my head as they pass.

"We're going shopping." Mom grabs her keys off the mermaid hook on the back wall. "If you need anything, you can reach me on my cell or on Tate's. Nick will be working upstairs today, so try not to bother him unless it's an emergency."

"Yes, ma'am."

Tatum says, "And tell Brodee to load up on sunscreen, because that kid only tans he thinks the sun doesn't affect him." She shakes her head with that motherly concern in her eyes.

"I'll take care of him." I smile.

"Thanks, Peyton. We should be back in a few hours."

"Have fun." I wave. "Bring back something good."

Brodee makes it downstairs just as they close the front door. "Where are they going?"

"Shopping, I guess."

He heads for the fridge. "Of course they are."

"Also, I'm supposed to make sure you're lathered up with sunscreen before we go out to the beach."

Today he's dressed like he always is—khaki shorts and a T-shirt. But I see him entirely different. His navy blue shirt is just tight enough that it hugs his back muscles and cuts perfectly into his biceps. I gulp. And blink. Hard. *What am I doing? Stop checking out Brodee!*

He turns around with a glass of orange juice in his hand and groans, flicking his unstyled hair to one side. "She's so paranoid. I'm not going to burn, but whatever. You'll just have to help me. I can't reach my back very well."

Back muscles. I'll get to touch his back muscles. *Oh gosh.* Get *to? Have to, Peyton.* Have *to. Change the subject.* I chuckle nervously. "Do you remember that summer—?"

"Don't remind me," he grumbles and wipes the back of his hand across his mouth. "You called me Zebra Skin the entire summer."

"I just don't understand how you could have missed that much skin." I can't stop laughing, picturing his brown and white striped back—a much easier image to visualize.

"You'll never let me live that down," he says before gulping down the rest of his orange juice.

"Never," I pledge, grinning.

HARPER DAY SHOWS up at the beach house around three o'clock, squealing and pumping her fists in the air. "The party's here!"

I get her for two weeks before she has to go back home, and there won't be a single dull moment. After I help her put her bags in my bedroom, we lean against the white railing of the back deck overlooking the beach—our own private solace. I breathe in deep. The air feeds my soul. With the ocean at our fingertips every day, nothing could put a damper on this summer.

"I can't believe this is where you guys come every year, and I've never been before." Harper takes a deep breath, inhaling the sea breeze.

I don't know why I've never invited Harper.

Well, yes I do.

Hatteras belongs to Brodee and me. It's the only place where I get to have him all to myself, and our real lives can't intervene. When Brodee invited Harper and Skylar, I was excited, but a little annoyed, and I know that's selfish and immature. But Skylar, Harper, and I will have USC. We're going to be spending every day together for the next however many years. After this summer, Brodee and I will go in different directions, and we'll never have this again. Who knows where we'll be a year from now. When we do come back to The Cape, it may not be the same, but I get that Brodee won't have USC with them, so I don't say anything.

"Yeah, relaxing, isn't it?" I finally say.

"This summer is going to be perfection." The wind whips her long hair around. She ties the strands back to tame them.

"When's Skylar coming up?"

"He'll be here next week. Tuesday probably. He had to take care of some stuff for his grandparents."

I nod. "All right, all right. So we get some girl time before he gets here."

"If you want to consider Brodee a girl for the next few days. Yes."

I laugh. "I doubt he'll mind."

"Well, let's get this party started!" Harper throws off her shirt, exposing her white bikini top, then runs down the boardwalk toward the waves. I copy her, my tank top and shorts joining hers on the deck.

We play in the ocean for a couple hours, bobbing up and down with the tide, basking in the summer sunlight. I can't remember the last time I felt this carefree. Hatteras has that effect. Brodee eventually makes a splashing entrance. He flings his dark, wet hair to the side and smiles brightly at us.

"Ladies," he greets. His toned, freckled shoulders speckled with water float above the waves. After a couple hours in the water, the three of us watch the sunset from the shore. The colors reflect onto the water as they tint the sky with orange and pink. I hear the bell ring in the distance. Brodee and I share a look and go running.

"What was that?" Harper asks, jogging closely behind us.

"The bell," I tell her over my shoulder.

With Brodee and I spending the majority of our summers in the water, the bell is the only form of communication we have with the landers. The landers being our parents—they rarely go in the water. One time we didn't listen to the bell. It was so quiet in the distance we pretended we couldn't hear it. The surf was too good. We didn't want to miss a single wave. I'll never forget it. We got lectured for an hour about the hazards of the ocean and how they'd thought we drowned. We never missed the bell again.

"This time of night it can only mean one thing," I say.

"Dinner," Brodee answers with a hungry smile. "And I'm starving."

Tatum's salmon is the best thing I've ever put in my mouth. When I saw her seasoning it this morning before they left, I wanted it to be dinner, not breakfast. I don't know what she does to cook it, but it's always perfect.

"Tate, this is incredible," my mom says after her first bite. "I don't know how you do it every time."

"Well, thank you." Tatum smiles. "There's plenty, so eat up."

"It's just so flakey and…*moist*," Harper says, eyeing me impishly from across the table.

I groan, knowing what she's trying to pull. "Harper, you could have picked any other word."

"But it *is* moist," Brodee agrees. A sly grin turns the corner of his mouth. He sits at the head of the table, watching me cringe, and laughs. I throw a roll at him and he bats it away, sending it across the hardwood floor.

"Why do you keep saying moist?" Carter asks.

"Oh my gosh," I gripe under my breath. "Say it one more time. I dare you."

"Children," Mom scolds, but she's laughing too. "No more. Stop wasting food. Just eat the *moist* salmon already."

"*Mom*," I warn with a chuckle. "I have another roll, and it has your name written all over it."

"I've got a palm, and it's got your butt written all over it." She gives me a sideways glance with a grin she's suppressing. "But seriously, Tate," Mom continues, "You have to tell me your secret. I've tried making it for Peyton at home, and it never measures up."

"I'll never tell." Her laugh sounds like the Evil Queen from Snow White.

Nick takes Tatum's hand on top of the kitchen table. "She won't even tell me. Good luck getting it out of her, Liv."

After we eat dinner, Brodee, Harper, and I relax on the rooftop lookout, lying back on beach recliners as night falls. Without the city lights, the stars are fully visible. The sky feels close enough that I can reach up and grab one.

"First person who sees a shooting star gets the last piece of chocolate mousse pie," Brodee challenges.

"But one other person has to witness it," I add. I know his games. Cheater.

"What, we can't go off the honor code? You don't trust Harper?" he teases.

"Psh. I don't trust you. I saw you eyeing that last piece. And you'll be lucky if you get to it before Carter does."

"Well, my odds are better than yours," he says. "Harper will share with me. Won't you, Harp?"

"Speak for yourself," she replies, scouring the skies. "If I win, that piece of pie is all mine."

I laugh. That's my Harper.

I win the pie. Harper backs me. But I share a bite with Brodee. Because I'm a nice person. Not because I have feelings for him. Stop judging me.

As we're getting up to go inside, a bonfire blazing in the distance catches our attention. *They're here.*

"What's going on down there?" Harper jerks her head in the bonfire's direction.

"It's probably the Hatteras gang," I say. Excitement pools in the pit of my stomach.

"As in *the* Hatteras gang. The one you've been talking about since you were fourteen?"

"That would be them," I confirm. I was wondering when they'd pop up.

"Well, let's go! I want to meet all the people you hang out with every summer without me. Especially *Tyler*," she says his name in a singsong voice to tease me.

I look to Brodee. I have a feeling there will be a certain someone there he'll want to avoid.

"Under one condition," he says, holding up his index finger.

"What's that?" Harper asks.

He eyes her, leaning over his armrest. "You've got to pretend to be my girlfriend."

"Why?" we ask him at the same time.

"Do you really want to deal with Rylie?" he asks me. *I don't.* "*I* don't. If she thinks I'm with Harper, she'll let it go. We won't have to deal with her snide comments and smug grin."

"Let what go?" Harper asks, looking between the two of us.

"You know we'll deal with them anyway." I sigh and explain to Harper, "Rylie and Brodee have had a thing going on the last few summers—kind of like Tyler and me." Though Tyler and I actually really like each other. We aren't just make-out buddies. "Last year she was convinced Brodee and I had something going on behind her back. Her jealousy became too much for Brodee, so he broke it off halfway through the summer."

"If she thinks I'm with you, we can prove to her once and for all there's nothing going on," he explains to Harper.

Why does he care so much? "Are you really that repulsed by me that you can't stand the thought of her thinking you might like me?"

"What?" Brodee frowns. "No. I just figured it'd make it easier for you and Tyler, right?" he tries to reason, but his eyes shift. A tell tale sign he's lying, but I don't know what about. "She'll lay off, and he can be reassured there isn't anything going on."

"How gentlemanly of you." I snort.

"Well, this should be fun." Harper smiles and rubs her hands together before she drapes her arm over Brodee's shoulder. "All-righty, stud, let's get this show on the road." She winks, and he laughs.

"You have to make this believable, Harp. If you joke about it, Rylie will catch on."

Harper lifts her hands in the air. "Oh, I've got this. Don't you worry your pretty little face." She taps the tip of his nose. "I'm an impeccable actress. I'm pretty sure I walked the red carpet in another life."

WE GRAB SOME light jackets and walk along the shoreline. As we draw closer, there are about twenty people dancing and hanging around the fire. That's more than usual. Party music drifts up toward us. I don't know how there hasn't been some sort of noise complaint to shut them down.

"So, everyone comes here to hang out?"

"Just those who vacation here every summer, yeah. Most of the time it's just a few of us. I've never seen this many people before." I look over at her, walking between Brodee and me, holding his hand. It's a strange sight to see and makes me…jealous? That can't be right. "There's not much to do at night so we chill and listen to music."

"Peyton!" The male voice is familiar even if I haven't heard it since last summer. I turn back to the Hatteras gang to see Tyler Hamilton jogging over in all his tall, muscular beauty. His T-shirt stretches across his fit chest, almost like he can't fit into it anymore.

Has he gotten even bigger?

He flashes his pearly whites before sweeping me up in his arms and hugging me so tightly I can't breathe. My feet don't touch the ground.

"Tyler," I giggle. I hate that I giggle, but he brings out that side of me. The silly, flirty, ditzy side I never knew existed until I was in his presence. I hate myself for it. He turns me into a breathless, giggling fool. It's embarrassing.

"Dang, Peyton. You get more beautiful every year." He sets me on the sand, looks me up and down, and smiles appreciatively. His subtle Southern drawl is just as charming as it's always been.

"*This* is Tyler?" Harper half-whispers, half-gasps into my ear.

I discreetly shove her away and speak over her the best I can to disguise her innuendo. "Tyler, this is my friend, Harper. And you know Brodee." I motion to them at my side.

"Yeah. Hey, man. Good to see ya." Tyler holds out his hand and they do that hand slap/shake/fist bump thing that guys do.

Brodee smiles tightly. "What's up." It isn't a question. It's a greeting.

"It's nice to meet you, Harper." He holds his hand to her for a regular handshake, and she smiles with stars in her eyes. Yeah, he has that sort of effect on women.

"Did y'all just get into town?" Tyler asks.

"Early yesterday, yeah." I nod and roll back on my heels. "Long drive."

"How long do I get you this year?" He smiles down at me with his ever-changing hazel eyes. The last year has treated him well. I find myself being especially nervous around him after all this time. He seems...different.

"Until the beginning of August."

"Almost three weeks longer than last year? Sweet!" He grabs my hand. "C'mon, let's grab y'all some drinks."

When we get closer to the fire, Tyler offers to go to the coolers and get me something. "Dr. Pepper, if they have it."

"All right. Harper, can I get you something?" Tyler offers politely.

"Oh...umm—"

"I can get you something," Brodee interjects, stepping forward, remembering his role as dutiful, fake boyfriend.

Tyler looks at Brodee, puzzled by his abruptness.

"Diet Coke, please," she asks.

"Sure thing. If there isn't any DP, Pete, you want a Coke?"

"Yes, please."

"You got it." Brodee nods.

After they're out of earshot, Harper can't hold back the interrogation any longer. "Ohmygoshheissofreakinghot. Peyton-Parker, why didn't you tell me he was so hot? And why in the world have you toned that relationship down? He so does not seem like someone you just 'hang out' with a little bit every summer. That kid is smitten."

I have a hard time hiding my smile. "He's a player, Harp. Not smitten."

"He's smitten. I don't care what you say. He may be playing the field while you're gone, but you have his full attention now. He never took his eyes off you. And when he did, it was only to be polite, not because he wanted to."

I have to laugh. "He's a good distraction." *Ugh*. Did I just say that out loud?

"Distraction? Girl. He is not a distraction. He's the full show. Take this like the gift it is and enjoy! Have fun for goodness sake! It's our last summer before real life begins." The boys are walking back so she quiets down. "Live life, Peyton-Parker. You only get one shot, one life."

AS THE NIGHT wears on, the four of us have circled the bonfire. Some people have tapered off to walk along the beach or headed home. About ten remain—the usuals. I've talked to most of them, and it never fails to feel like I've come home when seeing all of them again, like no time has passed at all.

Harper and Brodee are snuggled together, sitting on the sand with their knees pulled to their chests and a blanket wrapped around them, while Tyler sidles up next to me on some driftwood. It's weird watching them like this. So unnatural. Skylar should be in Brodee's place, flicking his lip ring and gazing affectionately at Harper. He's going to get a kick out of this story though. Thankfully, he's not the jealous type.

I keep peeking across the bonfire at Rylie who's been giving Brodee the stink-eye all night. Looks like his plan is working. He hasn't seemed to notice, or maybe he's just ignoring her. I laugh to myself and look down at my soda can, the brown liquid pooling at the top of the lid. I bring it up to my lips and sip it away.

When I zone back into the conversation, Tyler's talking about college plans. "I'll be heading to USC in the fall."

"For real?" I shift my body to him.

"Don't tell me you are, too."

"Yeah. I am." I smile. "Harper and I are rooming together in the dorms."

His arm drapes across my shoulder. "Well, look at that. This doesn't have to end when summer does this time." He says it teasingly, but it feels like anything but teasing.

My stomach curls into a tiny cluster of nerves, but I smile back coyly and say, "I guess not."

Tyler pulls me closer, squeezing me once before relaxing. His arm stays, surrounding me in a cocoon of warmth. He's like my own personal heater. When I look back to Harper and Brodee, Harper is biting her lip, holding in a squeal, no doubt. Brodee's expression is unreadable. Then I think about it. Since he's going to Duke, it can't be easy for him to think about being away from everyone. I smile gently, and his features soften.

"Hey y'all!" Rylie plops beside Tyler in her short denim skirt and red halter-top. *Isn't she cold?* "It's good to see you two, but I don't think we've met yet." She reaches her hand out to Harper.

Harper rocks forward on the balls of her feet and takes it, smiling. "I'm Harper."

"Rylie." Her smile is so fake I'm surprised it doesn't crack.

Even before last year, Rylie was so certain Brodee and me had a secret thing going on. *Because how can you spend every day together on a summer vacation and not fool around?* Easily. I could have told her that.

"'Sup, Rylie," Tyler says, scooting closer to me, giving her more room on the driftwood.

"I'm having a little get-together tomorrow night, and I was wondering if y'all wanted to come. It'll just be the normal people, not all these randoms who were here tonight. I want to catch up with everyone!"

Again, I look to Brodee for confirmation. I'm not going to accept anything until I know he's okay with it. Who knows if she has any ulterior motives? Clearly, she can see we *still* don't have anything going on since he's cuddling with Harper. Or awkwardly huddling together, I suppose is a better term. They could at least pretend to like each other. Though, if they were too convincing, I might be a little worried.

"Sounds like fun!" Harper says before anyone else responds. I can't tell if she's being fake, too, or if she honestly wants to go. Brodee doesn't dispute it, so I agree too. Maybe I'm misreading Rylie or overthinking it.

"You can count me in," Tyler joins in.

"Great! Okay. I'll see y'all tomorrow." She flashes a sultry smile at Brodee and saunters away, her hips sashaying from side to side as she walks across the sand in her tall wedges. *Who wears wedges at the beach?*

"Well," Harper laughs, "isn't she a treat?"

Brodee and I share a look and bust up laughing.

"What did I see in her?" he mutters as he shakes his head and takes a swig of his Mountain Dew.

"Beats me," I say.

"Yeah, man," Tyler says, chuckling. "Rylie is a handful."

"It was fun while it lasted," Brodee replies, shrugging.

Tyler gives him a funny look, like he can't believe he's talking like that in front of Harper.

"Harper and Brodee aren't really together," I explain quietly. "He just wanted Rylie off his back. For obvious reasons."

Tyler nods with understanding and laughs. "Smart move, man."

"We won't be able to keep it up for long. Skylar's going to be here next week?" Brodee asks Harper.

"Yup!" She smiles dreamily as if they just started dating—not four years into the relationship. "Skylar's my real boyfriend," Harper explains.

"And my good friend," Brodee interjects as if that explains everything.

Tyler looks at them like they're crazy.

TYLER WALKS ME home, while Brodee and Harper follow slowly behind us, dragging their feet. Harper's probably making Brodee give us space.

"It really is good to see you, Peyton," Tyler says, sliding his hand into mine, lacing our fingers together. "I'm glad you're here."

When I peer up at him, it feels like my eyes trail up for hours. He's taller than he used to be. What a difference a year makes. It makes me feel…dainty. And that isn't a word I would normally use to describe myself. I'm five-seven. Looking up at Tyler, he has to be at least six-three. Thank goodness for tall boys; I'm used to being around Brodee, who's only a few inches taller than me, so I mostly feel level with him.

"Me too." I smile.

When we reach the back of the beach house, Tyler looks to see if Brodee and Harper are there. They must have stopped along the way because they are nowhere in sight. It's too dark to see very far though. When Tyler turns back, he doesn't waste any time. He leans down, taking my face in his big hands, and kisses me. It's soft, tender. I definitely don't hate it. I wouldn't mind if it lasted longer. When he pulls back, he flashes a shy grin. He could make me forget *anything* for the summer.

"A year of waiting is worth it," he says, "just to be able to do that."

A short, nervous laugh escapes me. "Yeah," is all I can think of to say. *Why couldn't I be cleverer?* I feel like a cartoon character stammering, 'Duh, duh, duh.'

"So, I'll see you at Rylie's tomorrow night? Yeah?"

I swallow. "We'll be there."

"Cool. Goodnight, Peyton." His voice is deep and tingles my entire body. He kisses my cheek and starts to walk away.

"Night." I smile bashfully and wave. It's not just a tossed wave into the air. It's one of those four fingers curl forward waves, and it makes me want to punch myself.

The Day of The Dare

LEAVING HARPER IN bed to sleep in a little longer, I head downstairs to grab some breakfast. She doesn't do mornings like I do, and I'd rather not wake the beast.

"Morning, sunshine," Nick greets me as he sips his coffee from the kitchen nook next to Carter.

"Morning." I smile.

Carter gives me a head nod as he eats his cereal. He grunts his morning greeting.

"How'd you sleep last night?" Nick sets down his mug and focuses on me.

"Good."

Trying to pick a cereal from the plethora in the pantry is like trying to pick a favorite book. Impossible. I decide on Captain Crunch Berries and pour myself a big bowl.

"If you could survive off cereal and cereal alone, you would try."

"Yup." I sit across from Nick and smile with my mouth full.

He chuckles and shifts his attention to his laptop, tap-tap-tapping away, probably working on some lawyer stuff. Whatever is it they do.

"You're going to eat all my cereal, aren't you?" Carter says, teasing in his raspy, morning voice.

"*Your* cereal? I hadn't realized the Captain was claimed. But if it is I'll have to fight you for it."

"I'll accept that challenge." His eyes light up cheekily. He wiggles his eyebrows. "Wrestle for it?"

I chuckle and shake my head at him. Only sixteen and he's growing into such a flirt.

Nick speaks up. "Peyton, Brodee's out on the water already. He told me to tell you when you woke up."

"Cool." I'll head out when I'm done eating.

Nick has always been like a second father to me, but when my dad passed away he stepped up—never missed a soccer game or gymnastics meet. He even taught me how to change the oil in my car and made sure I was equipped with pepper spray (just in case). Things my dad never got a chance to do. Nick said he didn't want me to feel the loss of a father figure. Though he'll never ever be able to replace my dad, I'm grateful to have him.

My mom rounds the corner from the stairs. "You made it up before me this morning." She kisses the top of my head as she passes by.

"I hadn't realized it was a competition," I say, chewing. "In that case I'd definitely win. I'm always up before you to go surfing."

"Yeah, yeah. I don't know how I raised such an early bird. If it weren't for you, your father and I wouldn't have gotten up until noon every day." Her eyes drift out the window above the kitchen sink, overlooking the beach. "He always did write better at night," she says distantly.

That's exactly how I remember him. Hunched over his laptop, reading glasses perched on the end of his nose with only the light of the laptop illuminating his face as he wrote his next best-selling novel. Because of course it would be. He wouldn't settle for anything less. If I ever walked downstairs in the middle of the night, there he would be, behind the French doors of his office, letting his creativity flow.

A couple minutes pass by when there's nothing but silence. My mom doesn't move or say a word. She holds tightly to the edge of the sink and never blinks once.

"Olivia." Mom doesn't respond to Nick. "Liv, you all right?" Still nothing. Her chest rises and falls with her breath, but that's all that moves. He stands up and walks over to her. "Liv," he prompts, gently rubbing her shoulder. She startles and looks up at his face. I now see the streaks in her makeup. "You okay?" he asks softly.

"Yeah. Yes," she corrects. She smiles brightly—too brightly—swiftly wiping away a couple tears that leak down her cheeks. "I'm good." She nods unconvincingly and steps around him, heading back upstairs.

Nick stays at the kitchen sink—watching her retreating figure, concern marking his face.

"She'll be okay," I say to assure him. She does this sometimes. She'll be great for days, sometimes weeks. Then one day she'll have a bad day. Some bad days are worse than others. I expected this. I knew she couldn't be here for long without feeling the loss of him. I felt it the moment I walked through the door.

"I know," he accepts and turns to me. "It's hard for all of us. You know you can talk to me, right, Peyton?"

I nod, feeling grateful we at least have Nick. He lost his best friend, too, so at least he sort of gets it. "I know." And thank him with my eyes.

He squeezes my shoulder once before sitting back down and burying himself in work again.

RYLIE HOLLOWAY HAS the biggest beach house on the block. I don't know that you can even call it a beach house. It's a mansion on the beach, but it's perfect for big parties and hanging out if we want our own space away from the parentals.

About ten people show up to Rylie's thing, so it's more of a chill hang out. We congregate in their movie room upstairs with some action flick playing in the background, but no one is paying attention to it.

"Let's play truth or dare!" Rylie stands in the middle of the room so everyone will focus on her.

"Yes!" Harper cheers beside me on the couch. "We haven't played truth or dare since, like, eighth grade." She bumps my shoulder with hers and claps her hands together.

"There's a reason for that," I mumble. A collective agreement circles the room, and I chuckle to myself. "This should be interesting."

"Scared, Pete?" Brodee taunts from the floor across the room. He's leaning against the wall, his knees pulled to his chest with a smug grin on his face.

"What makes you think that?"

"You've never been much of a daredevil."

My eyes narrow. He knows exactly how to push my buttons. "Are you saying I don't know how to have fun?"

He lifts his hands in surrender. "I didn't say that."

I give him a bold stare, a look that I hope comes across as bring on the truth or dare, and we'll see who doesn't know how to have fun. Maybe I'm not much of a daredevil, but when Brodee challenges me, I'll do everything in my power to win or prove him wrong.

Nearly thirty minutes in, Brandi has confessed to her crush on Larson's dad, which is slightly uncomfortable considering she's dating Larson. Darren has downed an entire bottle of sprinkles, and now he can't get the chalky, waxy taste out of his mouth. He'll probably never have another sprinkle in his life. Tyler was dared to give Marcus a lap dance that turned out to be even more awkward when Marcus didn't seem to mind it. And Rylie confessed to cheating on her ex-boyfriend, which must be the reason why he's no longer a current boyfriend. *Hypocrite much?*

Now it's my turn, and I'm determined not to chicken out. No matter what. What can Rylie possibly come up with that I can't handle?

"Dare," I say, glaring at Brodee. *Yeah, who's a coward now!* I look back to Rylie for the price I know I'm going to have to pay.

She smirks like she's hiding a juicy secret. "I dare you to kiss Brodee."

Instant regret sets in, and the blood drains from my face. *Bingo*. Why did I expect anything less? *Meddler*. "That's just awkward." I try to think of a reason. "I can't kiss my best friend's boyfriend." Even if it *is* only pretend.

"Oh, c'mon. You make it sound like you haven't spent *every* summer together for years. Don't tell me you're not curious." Rylie eyes me. She knows my thoughts. She's been in my head. *She's* the reason I'm thinking of him that way. Her accusation has weaseled its way into my brain. It's being here in Hatteras! That's it! I almost laugh to myself. I can hear how crazy I sound.

"It'll be fun!" she says. "And it can't just be a little peck. I'm talking like ten to fifteen seconds at least. Real kiss action here."

"He's like my brother," I try, straightening my features. Rylie is only trying to prove herself right. And that won't happen. All it'll do is torment me. Maybe that was her intention all along. "I've known him since we were babies."

Her eyes resemble every evil fairytale stepmother—scheming and wicked. "Fine. Let's even the playing field then. You kiss Brodee and, Harper, you kiss Tyler."

My attention darts to Harper for confirmation that that is *not* going to happen. We're not about to kiss each other's flings—make believe or not. She actually has a *real* boyfriend, but Harper lets me down.

"It's just a game, Peyton-Parker. Why not? I've been curious to know how your boy-toy works his magic." I know she's kidding, but it annoys me nonetheless. She's supposed to back me up. *Unless she's trying to meddle, too.* Does she know what I've been thinking? No. I haven't told her. She's just being Harper Day—daring and adventurous. She lifts her eyebrows playfully at Tyler and crawls down to the floor where she pulls her hair into a low ponytail.

Harper's not afraid of any dare. When we were in eighth grade, Mike

McLean dared her to go skinny-dipping in Becca Adler's pool, and you would have thought he dared her to kiss Ryan Gosling. Of course, I made all the guys stay inside and kept them from looking through the blinds, but Harper didn't have a single qualm.

I look at Brodee and see right through the image he's trying to uphold. Chill, tough guy looks just as uncomfortable as I feel. We both know this will be awkward as all get out.

"It's just a dare, not a lifetime commitment," Rylie taunts, rolling her eyes. I'm *this* close to smacking her.

Brodee shrugs like he's over it and walks casually to the couch. "All right. C'mon, Pete. I won't bite."

I peer down at Tyler who chuckles. "It's just a kiss, Peyton. I won't be mad at you if you don't get mad at me."

Just a kiss? Sure, to everyone else, maybe. To me, it's *so* much more, but I can't ever say that out loud, and by dragging my feet, even more pressure is brought upon me. My hesitation is going to reveal why I'm so apprehensive. *Good work, Peyton.*

"What happens with the Hatteras Gang stays with the Hatteras Gang." Rylie snickers. I'll get my revenge. Just you wait, Rylie Holloway.

I watch Harper and Tyler lean into each other as if in slow motion, assessing how they're going to fit together. Then I'm suddenly aware that Brodee is only inches from my face.

This isn't happening.

This is happening.

"It's okay, Pete," he whispers, shifting his green eyes to my mouth. My stomach flutters. "It doesn't have to mean anything."

That's what I'm afraid of.

His eyes hesitantly travel around my face like he's committing me to memory, which is silly because he looks at me every day. He doesn't need to memorize my face. I nod my reluctant approval, swallowing my nerves and freeze until his lips gently meet mine.

Brodee's lips are kissing mine. It takes me a second to process that. I shut my eyes tightly as his lips press a couple long kisses against my mouth, taking my bottom lip between his. The unexpected move steals my breath. When he presses more firmly, I can't help but lean into the kiss with a sigh.

Under the surface everything shifts off its axis, altering the make up of my being, splitting everything like an earthquake, swallowing me whole. If he can kiss me like this and not have it mean anything, I'm not so sure I could handle what it would feel like if it meant something.

Whether the ten seconds are up, or Brodee just can't take it anymore, his hands grip my shoulders, shoving me away. He inhales, his eyes widening when he meets my stunned gaze. The moment flashes between us, a palpable tension I know he can't be immune to. Even though his lips are gone, I still feel them on mine. I want them back on mine. Then Brodee blinks and scoots away from me, back to the floor.

I touch my lips and turn swiftly to Harper. *What was that?* But Tyler and Harper are laughing and shoving each other like kindergartners on the playground.

"What was *that*?" Harper giggles.

"Me? You *bit* me!" Tyler laughs and pushes her shoulder.

What the…?

"Oh, it was only a nibble. That's my signature move. Don't go sharing my seduction tactics!" They break out into laughter again.

Apparently I missed something.

And so did they.

I shift my gaze to Brodee for some guidance, but he's staring at the floor with a blank look. When he feels my eyes on him he lifts his gaze to me, shakes his head, and shrugs. I don't know if it's his reaction to our kiss or to Harper and Tyler's.

When they quiet down they look around at the mixed emotions in the circle. Some laugh hysterically, while others look utterly baffled.

"Did we miss something?" Harper asks, attempting to control her amusement.

"Well," Rylie answers, "while Peyton and Brodee are totally confused and disgusted with one another, you two seem to be thoroughly enjoying yourselves."

Disgusted and confused? Is that what we look like? Because that's far from what it feels like. Confused, maybe. But disgusted? *Is that what he feels?*

"Well, you both will be happy to know we are laughing at how bad we were at that together." Tyler smiles at me and moves to the empty space where Brodee was on the couch. "I am much more compatible with you." His arm loops around my neck and tugs my mouth to his, kissing me in front of everyone. He's never done that before. His lips press fervently, but the swell in my stomach and lightheaded feeling I normally get when he kisses me is non-existent.

"Much better," he says when he pulls away. "Don't you agree?"

I nod mechanically.

When I turn back to Brodee, he's moved closer to Harper, his arm around her shoulder, tugging her to his side. He doesn't spare me another glance. Obviously, that kiss affected me a lot differently than it did him.

I will never be able to look at him the same.

The Day We Took the Climb

THE NEXT MORNING I get up around ten and head downstairs to eat breakfast. I didn't mean to sleep in, but we were out kind of late last night.

"So, how's Tyler?" Mom asks over her shoulder as she puts the dishes away from dinner last night.

"He's good," I say, taking another bite of my Lucky Charms.

"You guys have fun last night?" She smiles like she's living vicariously through me. She seems to be doing better than yesterday morning. Thank goodness.

I think about the kiss and want to find a cave and never come out. Fun isn't exactly what I'd call last night. Things are going to be so awkward today. Maybe if I stay in my room all day we'll never cross paths. Brodee can go his way, and I'll go mine. Problem solved.

"Yeah. We just hung out at Rylie's with everyone."

"Rylie's the one that liked Brodee, right?"

I hum my response as I chew and swallow. "I'm pretty sure it's *likes*, but she'll have to get over it."

The back door opens. I turn to see Brodee closing it behind him. His hair is damp, but he's fully dressed. When our eyes meet he ducks his head and I think he blushes, but it's gone so fast I probably imagined it.

When we got back to the beach house last night we went straight to bed. With a brief "'Night," he bolted to his room before I could even say goodnight back.

"Good morning, Brodee." The warmth in my mom's smile is such a contrast from yesterday. I'm so grateful today is a good day.

"Mornin', Liv." Brodee plops on the barstool at the counter next to me. He glances at me, and I nod a hello. I wait to see where this will go. Who will crack? "Lucky Charms," he says. "Good choice."

"I left the marshmallows for you," I joke, hoping to lessen the tension. I show him the remaining marshmallows floating in my blue milk. "Have to save the best for last."

"That's all right. You can have them," he teases with a scrunch of his nose. Holding my gaze, he doesn't say anything more, and a pregnant pause swells between us. I feel him drifting further away as he looks at me. I want to tether a rope to him and wrench him back, pressure him to tell me every thought. *Are we okay? Did that kiss ruin us?* Please don't let it. Finally he says, "Where's Harper?"

Diversion. Thank you. I blink. "Where else? She's asleep," I say and drink the remaining milk in my bowl.

"Still? Man. She's going to sleep the summer away. I've been up since six."

"Any good waves?"

He shrugs, not looking at me. "Decent. We'll have to head up to Kitty Hawk early tomorrow. There's supposed to be a storm heading in tomorrow evening. Surf is supposed to be ten to twelve feet. It'll be perfect."

"Sweet."

"Is your dad still here, Brodee?" Mom asks.

"Nah. I think he had a deposition pop up, so it looks like he'll be coming back some time next week."

"All right. More girl time for us old gals." She winks. "What are you three doing today?"

"I think we're going to head over to the lighthouse," I say. "Harper's been dying to climb it since I showed her pictures."

"Sounds like a good plan."

I sit there with my empty bowl, my mom continues putting dishes away, and silence ensues. And it's certainly not our usual comfortable silence. That kiss did change us.

"Well, I guess I should go wake up Harper so we can head up there." Brodee can't hop off the barstool fast enough before jogging to the stairs.

Mom hollers over her shoulder. "Oh, no you don't. No boys allowed in the girls' room."

"Ahh…c'mon, Liv," he calls back.

"You've never had a problem with Brodee being in my room before," I say, confused.

"That's because you're like siblings." *Rub it in, Mom.* "I don't know what kind of undress Harper may be in."

Brodee sulks back into the kitchen and hops up beside me again.

"I'll go get her." I place my bowl in the sink and head up the stairs. I'm not enduring this awkwardness any longer.

IT'S A TWENTY-MINUTE drive before I stand at the base of the black and white candy cane striped lighthouse and look up, the vivid sky as a picturesque backdrop.

"I haven't been here since we were kids." The nearness of Brodee's soft voice in my ear startles me. Looking over my shoulder, I see his smirk inches from me. I've seen that smirk a million times before, but this time feels like the first time. My chest seizes, and my legs wobble, and my heart jumps, and nothing makes any sense. "Geez, jumpy." He chuckles.

I try to control my breathing as my heart races. "Sorry. I wasn't expecting you so close."

Did I read him wrong this morning? He appeared so uneasy before. Now he looks completely at ease, like he has the upper hand. But the upper hand in what?

"Well, you're kind of blocking the path." He motions to the walkway in front of us, leading to the entrance of the lighthouse.

Duh. *He's not just trying to get close to you, Peyton.* As much as I want him to. I can't get the feel of his lips on mine out of my head. This *has* to stop.

"What are you guys waiting for? Let's go," Harper rushes us. For a brief moment I want to tell Harper to suck it and go home so I can have Brodee to myself. And then I realize how juvenile and ridiculous that sounds.

"My bad. I'm going. I'm going."

There are 257 steps. I know because I counted as I gripped the wrought iron railing on the strenuous climb. Heights are not my thing, especially in the narrow stairwell of a 200-foot tower. There are small platforms along the way to take a breather, but that just makes it worse. I want it to be over and done with. Brodee follows closely behind, reassuring me that he has me in case I trip and fall down all 257 steps. His hand occasionally brushes against my lower back, encouraging me forward. Just the touch of his hand is making me dizzy. Forget the compact space filled with fifty other people. I'm going to pass out from his proximity.

"Oh my gosh, this is beautiful!" Harper exclaims as she leans over the balcony, peering down to see how high we are. She stretches her arms out like she's flying. I press my back to the wall at the top of the lighthouse, staying clear of the edge. Maybe it isn't so much the height as it is the irrational fear that the railing will fail, or the deck supporting us will suddenly collapse and we'll plummet to our death. I prefer my feet safely on the ground.

Brodee chuckles. "What's your deal, Pete? You seriously scared?"

"I'm not scared," I counter indignantly. I'm lying. "I just like the view better from here."

"You have to look over the edge though," he coaxes. "It's not so bad. It's really pretty cool."

"No, thank you. I can see just fine from here." I smile, but it's strained.

He holds out his hand. "C'mere. I'll keep you safe."

Whether it's his words or his hand, I give in. The thought that I would go anywhere with Brodee crosses my mind. My hand slips into his, and I grip him tightly. A quiet chuckle passes his lips. I stare at him like he's my anchor. He'll keep me secure. He won't let anything happen to me.

A gust of wind blows through my hair. I inhale and feel myself relax a fraction. The view is indescribable. Miles and miles of bright blue ocean against the vibrant green landscape. It's so strange to think we're at the edge of the country. I've never really thought about it like that before. From here on out there's nothing but blue.

"See. It's not so bad."

I shrug coolly, not wanting to prove him right.

"You're fearless in the water, with waves crashing all around you, and the possibility of rip currents and sharks and other sea creatures or even drowning, but a little bit of height freaks you out?" Harper remarks, shaking her head with a snarky smile on her lips.

"We could all plummet to our death in a matter of seconds," I retort. "Then we'll see who's laughing."

"No one. We'd all be dead."

I want to shove her, but I realize that's the dumbest idea at the top of a 200-foot structure with only a metal railing to stop her fall.

It isn't until we're ready to head back down that I notice Brodee hasn't let go of my hand, nor have I attempted to loosen my grip on him. His touch alone was enough comfort to help me through my fear. Or maybe it was just enough of a distraction.

"Here." Brodee steps in front of me, squeezing my hand once before letting go. "I'll go first, so in case you trip I'll cushion your fall on the way down." Then he winks, and I try to find my stomach. The butterflies must have hauled it away. *Has he ever winked at me before? How have I never noticed how hot it is?*

Brodee smiles and steps into the lighthouse. Gosh, I'm gonna miss that smile.

It hits me. That's it. I'm having these unexplained feelings because I'm getting sentimental. I've been reading into things. That's all it is. We're splitting after this summer, and it sucks. It's just my sensitive hormonal womanhood reacting to being separated from my best friend. Boom! Problem solved.

The only way I'm going to be able to survive Brodee leaving me behind is getting used to not relying on him. I need to distance myself. Focus on Tyler. It's the only way I'll know how to live without Brodee. I'll stop having these baffling thoughts about us being something more, and we can move forward like normal.

AS HARPER AND I crawl into bed that night, she asks, " How was that kiss?"

"What kiss?" I pull back my side of the blanket, avoiding eye contact. While she could be talking about Tyler, I highly doubt it. If I answer her honestly, I'm not sure I'll be able to keep my voice steady.

"What kiss." She snorts. "With Brodee, dummy."

I'm tongue-tied. Do I tell her that it was surprising and amazing and kind of perfect? And all I want is to do it over and over again? *No. Wait. I don't.* That's just my sentimental, hormonal womanhood taking over again. *Stop that!*

"I know you two have never kissed before, so how was it?"

"It was awkward. I mean…good, but awkward."

She sighs. "I really don't understand why you never tried snatching Brodee. After all the time you guys spend together, I always thought it was inevitable."

I shrug self-consciously and slide further under the covers without looking at her. Harper might be my best friend, but I can't even confess to her how Brodee is slowly inching his way into my thoughts. If I say it out loud, then it becomes real, and nothing can ever happen between us.

"You know how weird that would be?" I deflect.

"I don't think it would be as weird as you think," she says. "But what do I know? I just watch you guys together all the time."

"What's your point?" I ask, finally turning to my side to look at her.

"You're perfect together. Duh."

I laugh like it's the most absurd thing I've ever heard. Because it is. Sure, we get along, and we can tell each other anything, and I know he'd never do anything to hurt me. We have tons in common, and I trust him more than anyone else in this world, but no. I don't know why I'm even contemplating the thought.

"Oh stop. He's gorgeous. You're gorgeous. You both love surfing. You love spending time together. You make each other laugh. I don't see a downside here."

"Aside from the fact that we don't feel that way about each other," I say dryly. Nothing has been defined. I'm not technically lying.

"And it's a dang shame," she says, clicking her tongue and shaking her head as I turn out the light. "Such a waste."

"Goodnight, Harper," I say as a way of shutting down the subject.

"Nighty night, Peyton-Parker."

The Day I Cheated On Him

AFTER I CHECK the surf report when I get up at seven, I throw on a swimsuit, leaving Harper in bed. We were up until one last night, so I'm not messing with that bear. For a second I stop outside of Brodee's bedroom door and think of asking him if he wants to go with, but I decide better of it. I grab my surfboard from the deck and head for the front door. As I'm opening it, Tyler has his fist raised, mid-knock.

"Hey." A slow smile curves his lips. "I thought you might be up. Glad I took my chances."

I smile back. "Hey, I was just heading to Salvo."

He's in a light green tank top that looks like it came straight out of the '80s and gray board shorts. Brodee always says only tools wear tank tops. I laugh to myself and feel a little guilty. Tyler isn't a tool. Not to me at least.

"Care for some company?" I look over his shoulder at his red jeep parked in our driveway with his surfboard strapped to the top.

"Yeah, okay." I smile.

"I'll drive."

Tyler drives with the top down and his radio turned up. The wind whips my wavy strands around. I stretch my hand out the window and let the salty air sail through my spread fingertips. Tyler reaches over and squeezes my hand resting in my lap. I shift my gaze to see him grinning widely at me. His teeth really are perfect, but I guess that's inevitable with a dentist for a dad.

With Tyler's aviators, chiseled jaw, and the wind blowing back his caramel locks, it's hard to deny how good it feels to be liked by someone as good looking as him. I know how shallow that sounds, and I kind of hate myself for thinking it, but it's the truth nonetheless. Maybe it's because of the kiss Brodee and I shared, the encouragement I feel knowing someone wants to kiss me.

Tyler takes his hand off mine and turns down the music. "How have you been since Rylie's house?"

Aside from the uncomfortable tension that's built up between Brodee and me? "Been doing good. Just been surfing and hanging out with Harper and Brodee. We went to the lighthouse a couple days back. I forgot how exhausting it is to climb that thing."

He laughs. "Oh man. I haven't been to the lighthouse since you and I went."

For a split second I don't remember. And then my stomach flips. *How could I have forgotten?* The first time Tyler kissed me. I was so caught off-guard I hardly kissed him back, but if Tyler is anything, he's determined. I wasn't saying no, so he kept kissing me in the stairwell. I finally caught on and it turned into one of the best kisses I've ever had. *Until Rylie's house.* I shake away the unexpected thought bomb. I'm getting really tired of those.

WHEN TYLER AND I paddle out, I can't help but feel like I'm cheating on Brodee. I never go surfing alone with any other guys. It kind of feels weird. Brodee and I have a groove. We know how to surf together—our techniques and limitations. I stop thinking and just paddle.

Tyler didn't bother putting on a wetsuit, not that he really needs one. The water's warm, but it's distracting. Without a shirt, my suspicions are solidified. He must do nothing but work out because his muscles are ridiculous. And by ridiculous, I mean huge. Not body builder huge, but he's got one of those bodies found in gym selfies. *You know the ones.* The kind where the sweaty hot guy poses in the mirror in all his pumped up glory with his backward baseball cap and earbuds. *Yeah, that.*

When we reach a good distance out and straddle our boards, Tyler shifts his gaze and catches me staring. *Dangit.* He smiles like he knows, but doesn't mention it.

"Did you hit Kitty Hawk the other day? I heard it was pretty awesome."

"Yeah," I reply after clearing my throat. "The three of us made it out there pretty early. Got in a few good hours before the storm hit. You didn't go?"

"Nah. I had to work. College won't pay for itself, though I wish it did." There's a legit twinkle in his eye, I kid you not.

When I first met Tyler I assumed he was just another entitled, rich kid who had everything handed to him—as most of the Hatteras gang does—

but then I got to know him. His parents make him work every summer out here. I have a feeling they'd help him out with college expenses if he couldn't pay for it all, but they don't give him a whole lot of slack. It's one thing I like about him. He's never complained once. It's just the way of life for him. Work hard, play hard, and it will pay off.

"Where are you working this summer?"

"At Lee Robinson General Store. I tried getting a job at Kitty Hawk Kites again, but they weren't hiring."

"Well, one job is better than no job, yeah?"

"Yup." He continues to smile, and I have to keep my blush in check. I hate that he makes me so flustered.

We're out on the water for a couple hours. There's not much conversation, but it's nice to be out here with him. Tyler's the kind of surfer that obviously only surfs in the summer time. He's okay, but he's not as good as Brodee. Like me, Brodee lives and breathes the ocean.

Oh my gosh. Can you hear yourself, Peyton? I need to stop thinking about him, comparing him. *Distance yourself.* If I don't let him go now, it's only going to get harder. *No more, Peyton.*

"DANG, PEYTON." TYLER nudges my shoulder as we're walking back up the shore. "You've gotta stop making me look so bad out there."

"What. You can't handle being shown up by a girl?" I tease.

He laughs and shakes the wet strands from his eyes. "It's not that at all. I was just trying to pay you a compliment in a roundabout way. I remember you being good, but I think you're even better than you were last year."

I shrug. "I guess it's one of the perks of not living far from the beach. I go probably two or three times a week. Most of the time I go before school." What I don't say is that half of the time I don't surf. I sit on my surfboard and let the waves crash around me. I'd rather be on the water than on land, whether I'm surfing or not. When all I have are my thoughts, I breathe in the ocean.

"Must be nice. I don't normally go unless I'm here. The downside of living inland."

When we get to Tyler's jeep, he checks the time on his phone. "It's only ten o'clock. You wanna grab some breakfast?"

I check my phone. No texts. No missed calls. Guess they aren't missing me. Or maybe Harper isn't even awake yet, which is most likely the answer.

"Yes. I'm starving."

WHEN TYLER DROPS me off, he waits until I'm inside before he waves and takes off.

As I walk through the kitchen, Harper is perched on a barstool at the counter. "Hey." She smiles above her bagel and cream cheese. "Where were you?"

"I went surfing with Tyler." I make my way to the back door with my board. "And then we got some breakfast."

"Ooo," Harper croons. "How's Mr. Right doing?"

I snort, but don't correct her. "He's good. We just talked about his job and USC and stuff. It'll be fun having him at school with us." As I shut the back door, I ask, "Where's Brodee?"

"I told him it was a Harper-Peyton day. No boys allowed. I mean… if you're cool with that. I just want to spend some time with you before Skylar gets here."

I pause. That shouldn't bother me as much as it does. *It's one day out of sixty, Peyton.* I'll have plenty more days with him before the summer ends. *And how easily you forget your promise to distance yourself.* "Sounds good to me."

"I practically had to kick him out. He was kind of offended." She rests her head on her propped up hands, elbows on the counter.

Can't say I blame him. I would've been too. "He'll get over it."

"So, what do you want to do today?" Harper bounces on the barstool. "We should go on an adventure. Search for buried treasure or some really cool seashells."

I laugh lightly. "Buried treasure for sure."

"And then we can do makeovers. I can curl your hair and make it all pretty."

My nose scrunches up. "What's wrong with my hair?"

"Nothing. You just *never* do anything with it. It'll be fun. I brought some of my wig collection. Oh! Oh! We should dye it!" She gets really excited about that prospect.

"No dyeing," I say flatly.

"Your virgin hair will need to be deflowered someday."

"Today is not that day."

"Fine," she pouts. "Then we can do a fashion show, make a runway out of the boardwalk in the back."

I chuckle. "Like we used to do on your back deck? And your mom would video tape us pretending like we were supermodels."

"Yes! Let's play dress up. I already have the perfect wig in mind for you."

"Did you seriously bring your wig collection to the beach?"

"Hey." Harper stops. "You never know when a good wig opportunity will present itself. I'm like a boy scout. Always prepared." She salutes me with three fingers.

"DON'T FORGET TO cover these." I point to the freckles on my nose and cheeks.

"Patience, grasshopper."

Harper has placed me on the stool in front of my vanity to do my makeup. "We'll, get there," she teases, "Has Tyler proposed to you yet?"

"Nope."

"Will you say yes when he does?"

"Nope."

"You should."

"Nope."

She sits back. "Peyton-Parker, I thought you liked him. Are you having second thoughts?"

"Nope."

She sighs. "If you say 'nope' one more time, I'm gonna smack you."

I laugh. "I'm sorry. Being obnoxious felt necessary in that moment."

She pauses, pulling back the eye shadow brush. "Seriously. I want to hear about your morning with him."

"It was good. We surfed and chatted."

"Thanks, Captain Obvious."

I laugh again. "What more do you want?"

"Did he kiss you?"

"I never kiss and tell."

"Why are you being so difficult?!"

I don't know. I should want to talk about Tyler and excitedly squeal over his kisses and affection and our possible future. Instead, all I want to do is talk about Brodee.

After applying mascara, she leans back with a satisfied smile. "Done." She holds up a mirror.

I've worn makeup before. I wear mascara and lip gloss every day, but I don't do blush and eye shadow and eyeliner and all that junk. So when I see myself in the mirror, I gasp.

"You hate it."

"No." I shake my head, taking it in. "It's just different." She's done the whole smoky eyes and dark eyeliner. I look exotic.

"You look beautiful! Okay. Now for the wig."

She pins a black blunt cut wig on me. It's such a contrast from my natural blonde hair; I look like a completely different person.

"Va-va-va-voom." Harper smiles with her hands on her hips. "I done good. You're like an undercover cop. Or a pin up model!"

THAT NIGHT WE all gather for dinner. My mom cooked up some shrimp boil and spreads it across newspaper covering the kitchen table. Brodee keeps giving me funny looks that I shoot right back like I'm five years old. There comes a point where I almost stick my tongue out at him.

"What's up with all the makeup?" he finally asks.

I took off the wig because it made my scalp feel like there were a million ants crawling all over my head, but I kept on the makeup. I figured I'd wash it off when I showered before bed.

"Oh." I laugh. "Harper and I had a fashion show today. You missed out."

"Looks like it." Brodee closely examines my face. I immediately want to run upstairs and wash it off, but I also don't want him to know that I care so much about what he thinks. Then he turns back to the food on his plate.

"Doesn't she look so pretty?" Harper says, beaming proudly from across the table. "That would be my handy work, thank you very much."

"Peyton's always pretty, but she knows that." Brodee looks at his plate as he says that. He starts shoveling food in his mouth, like he just commented on what the waves are going to be like tomorrow.

No. No, I didn't. I mean…No, I didn't know Brodee thought I was pretty. Not that I think I'm pretty. I mean…I know I'm not ugly. Okay. It doesn't matter. Brodee Fisher thinks I'm pretty.

"I think it looks like nice, Peyton," Tatum says. "But I think you're a natural beauty. You don't need all of that to be beautiful."

"It was just for fun," I mutter and take a bite of my dinner. I don't know why I feel like I have to defend our girl time. Or why everyone is making such a big deal out of it. It's just some eye shadow and lipstick. "Even if I wanted to, I couldn't do all this. I don't know the first thing about makeup."

"She looks hot," Carter comments casually as he eats.

Everyone else stops and shoots him a look, then we bust out laughing. Except Brodee.

"Carter," he says, stunned. Brodee looks like he wants to say more, but doesn't. If I didn't know any better, it almost looks like he wants to punch Carter.

He looks at Brodee and shrugs. "What? She does."

Gotta hand it to the kid. He's not afraid to say what he thinks. I chuckle, feeling my cheeks heat up from the attention. "You're sweet, Carter."

He lifts a crooked smile and adds more shrimp and potatoes to his plate.

"You wear whatever makes you most comfortable, Peyton," Tatum says.

I will. "Thanks." I don't like that the attention is all on me, so I keep my mouth shut for the rest of dinner and let our moms carry the conversation.

The Day She Caught Me

I'VE BEEN CATCHING some five-footers behind our beach house while Brodee and Harper have been playing in the waves. The surf hasn't been great, but it's better than being the third wheel. I realize I'm not actually a *third* wheel, but for some reason today it feels like it.

Some of the Hatteras gang is hanging out on the shore near our beach house. Unfortunately, Tyler had to work, so while most of them are playing in the water or lying out on the beach, I distance myself. I just want to surf, but the pitiful waves don't make me feel very fulfilled, and I don't feel like driving anywhere.

Eventually, I give up and head inland. I set down my surfboard and curl my toes in the sand. Rather than going inside, I watch Brodee and Harper dunking and splashing each other. It's not like I couldn't go out there and join in. I'm sulking, and I know it. I'm only the third wheel because I'm acting like it.

"It must suck."

I turn to see Rylie sitting down beside me.

Ugh. *What does she want?* Sighing, I ask, "What must?"

"Watching the boy you love fall in love with your best friend."

I nearly tell her the truth, but it'll be kind of fun to watch her confusion when everything comes to light. With Skylar coming later today, the truth will come out eventually.

"I mean…it sucked for me last year when I figured it out, but at least you and I were never close. You have to sit by and suck it up because you love them both. Brutal." She shakes her head with an almost laugh.

Nothing I say will help this situation. "You're delusional, Rylie."

"Oh please. From one lovesick fool to another, it's so obvious it's painful."

I glare at her. I'm not lovesick. And I haven't been acting any differently than I normally do around Brodee. *Right? RIGHT?*

"Don't worry," she says sardonically, looking out at Harper and Brodee in the waves. "Your secret's safe with me. If I hated you, I could make your life hell, but you're in luck."

I purse my lips, unconvinced. "Since when do you not hate me?"

She laughs like I'm an idiot. "I've never hated you, Peyton. Have I been jealous? Yeah. Resentful. Of course. Intimidated. Heck yes."

I laugh. "Oh, c'mon. I'm not intimidating."

"Yes, you are. You try getting the best friend of the boy you like—who's beautiful and cool and funny, who you know he has a history with—to like you. Then come back, and tell me that's not intimidating."

I'm not all of those things. I'm just me. "Brodee and I have always only been friends, Rylie. I was never your competition."

"Au contraire…" She gets to her feet, dusting the sand off her butt.

"You're the worst kind of competition." Rylie pauses, peering down at me. "You're the one." She says it so matter-of-fact I nearly laugh, but she doesn't give me the opportunity before she turns and walks back up the beach.

I glance at Brodee and Harper bobbing in the water, diving under and over the waves. Harper sees me and motions me in, but I shake my head and hold up my hand to say no thanks. I'm just going to lie back on my towel and breathe in the sun. Pretend I'm the only one on this beach. Because Rylie is crazy. And I'm certainly not "the one."

I SHOWER THE beach off after our long day and settle in next to Brodee on the couch. He's plucking out notes on his guitar; I tell him not to stop. I love hearing him play. There's something comforting about watching his quiet concentration on the music and hearing him occasionally hum along. It doesn't matter what he plays, I could listen for hours, but he tells me he's done playing anyway as he sets down his guitar and grabs the TV remote.

Harper is taking her turn in the bathroom before Skylar gets here. He should be here soon. I snag the remote from Brodee and flip through channels, finding nothing eye-catching.

"Do you teach lessons?" Brodee's voice is uncharacteristically sultry.

I look at him in confused anticipation. "Lessons?"

His eyes are doing funky things to my stomach. Before, when I looked at him, it was simply looking into the eyes of a friend, but now there's a… spark. It feels like the longer I look at him the more he'll be able to read my mind. But I can't look away. I love the warmth and ease in his eyes when our gaze is locked.

"Please tell me you do, because you have to teach me how to steal your heart as fast as you stole mine."

For a split second I think he's serious. My breath catches. Then I realize it's only a cheesy pick-up line. But it feels so real. I give him an approving nod and force a laugh. "Clever."

"Came up with that one all on my own." He folds his arms across his chest and nuzzles further into the couch with feigned smugness lining his face.

"You're so full of it. No, you didn't," I call his bluff, nudging him with my shoulder.

"So quick to doubt me?"

"I might be blonde, but I'm not an idiot."

He chuckles. "Okay, so I overheard Robby use it at Sam Hardy's party a few weekends back."

"Oh my gosh, he did not. Did it actually work?"

With a shake of his head he says, "He had Tara Schumacher practically eating out of the palm of his hand."

"*Wow*," I exhale. "Lines like that just would not work on me." I hear the lie and hope Brodee doesn't. I actually didn't hate that line. At all.

"No? I think maybe with the right guy and the perfect delivery, you'd be begging for more." He's challenging me. A part of me wonders if he's referring to himself or if he's just running his mouth. "Maybe if Tyler laid it on thick, you'd melt at his feet." Brodee raises one eyebrow suggestively, wiggling it a little.

"If Tyler delivered a line like that, I'd laugh," I retort.

"I thought you liked Tyler."

"I do."

I did? I do.

"But..." He hears the uncertainty in my voice before I can cover it up. Brodee bites him bottom lip, and I'm suddenly tongue-tied. *He's not trying to seduce you, Peyton. He's just chewing on his lip! He's done this a hundred times before in front of you when he's waiting anxiously or bored.*

I clear my throat and say with a surprisingly steady voice, "There's no buts. I do. Why did you wait so long to pull that one out if it worked so well for Robby?"

Brodee gives me a look, but doesn't get a chance to answer.

"He's here!" Harper comes bounding down the stairs, her wet, pink hair flopping around her. "He's here!" Her feet tap the wooden floors as she runs straight for the front door. We get up and follow.

When she opens the door, Harper flies down the stairs and into Skylar's waiting arms. You'd think it'd been years since she last saw him. Not five days.

He kisses her like he'll never get enough of her before setting her back on the ground. Tucking his long, shaggy hair behind his ear, he shrugs his backpack further up his shoulder. "What's up, guys?"

Some guys could never pull off long hair, but Skylar has the features for it. Even though it can get unkempt, as if he only washes it in the ocean, it's dark and thick enough that he makes it work.

"You're finally here. It's about time." Brodee lifts his hand for a high five. "The estrogen levels were getting out of control."

Skylar chuckles. "'Sup, P Parker." And high fives me, too.

"Oh, you like it," Harper taunts Brodee. "It's not every day you get to hang out with two pretty girls on a beach for a week."

Brodee opens his mouth to respond, looking at me, but closes it and laughs. "That is true," is all he says.

What did he hold back?

"What's for dinner? I'm *starving*," Skylar rubs his flat stomach.

"Our parents went to get some pizza. Should be back soon." Brodee motions us to follow him back inside. "C'mon. You can put your stuff in my room."

"SO, SKYLAR," NICK says as we're gathered around the dining table, eating the pizza they brought from Rocco's. "You're heading to USC with Peyton and Harper?"

"Yes, sir." Skylar wipes at the corner of his mouth, biting on his lip ring nervously. I can already see where this is headed.

"Have you decided on your major?"

Oh, the dreaded major talk. As soon as we decide to go to college we're automatically supposed to know what we want to do with the rest of our lives? I plan on changing my major at least three times. Maybe four. Maybe even five just because I can. How am I supposed to know at eighteen years old what career path is the one for me? It's too much pressure.

"Uh, right now I have it as computer science. I'm pretty tech savvy, so I'll see where it takes me."

"Good choice. Maybe you can do some web design for Brodee when he gets his law degree and opens his own firm. He'll need a tech savvy guy like you to help him out with all his computer issues." Nick winks at Brodee while chewing his food.

Nick and I get along. I love the guy like family, but sometimes the way he talks about Brodee's future like it's his own, or like Brodee doesn't have a say, rubs me the wrong way. Especially when I look at Brodee and can't read his expression. Is he agreeing with Nick? Does he resent him ever? Does he even want to be a lawyer? Duke was a bit of a joint decision. How about law? Does he want to follow in Nick's footsteps? I can't picture Brodee being a lawyer. He's too laid back for that. Too much of a peacemaker. I don't want him to choose a career that will change him.

"All right." Mom pushes herself away from the table and stands, clapping her hands together. "Enough with the college talk. I'm done thinking about my baby leaving home. Shall we play a game of cards?"

"I'll go get a few decks, and we can play Hand and Foot," Tatum says and points to us. "Children, clear the table, please. It's about to get competitive."

THE SKY IS clear tonight. Hardly a cloud in sight. I feel him. Cloudless skies make me feel like it's a little easier for my dad to watch over us. Nothing is there to hinder the pathway.

After we played cards with the family, the four of us decided to veg on the roof.

"That's cool that your parents are so close," Skylar says, looping his arm around Harper on the recliner they share.

"Oh, yeah," I say, blinking away the moisture in my eyes, grateful for a distraction. "My mom and Nick go way back. They grew up together in the same church and went to the same schools. Even went to college together. Nick is actually the one who introduced my mom to my dad."

"Really? That's sweet," Harper says. "How come I didn't know that?"

I shrug and look back up into the night. "I guess I never mentioned it. My dad and Nick were roommates their freshman year of college. Just fell into place from there. And Nick met Tate shortly after that. So, they all go way back."

"Pete and I were doomed from the start," Brodee says. His tone is light.

I shove his shoulder. "You're *blessed* to have me in your life. You. Are. Welcome."

He laughs. "Yeah. I guess."

"We hitting the waves tomorrow?" Skylar asks Brodee.

"Yeah, man. There's going to be some sweet surfing in Buxton. It's only like fifteen minutes from here."

Brodee and Skylar talk over Harper and me in the middle. She leans into me. "You going to invite Tyler?"

"Why would I?"

"Oh, I dunno, because you're totally into each other."

"Well, yeah, but we don't have to do everything together. Should I invite him? You don't think it would be weird?"

"Invite who?" Skylar interrupts us.

"Peyton's boy toy," Harper replies.

"You have a boy toy?"

"Can we not refer to him as my boy toy?" I ask. "He has a perfectly acceptable name."

"Which is?"

"Tyler," Brodee answers for me. He says his name like a swear word.

"Tyler sounds like a tool."

"You don't even know him," I retort.

"He is." Brodee smirks at me.

I shove him again, but this time I'm being less playful. "He is not!"

"He's going to USC too, and he's smitten with our Peyton-Parker," Harper pipes up.

I want to bury my head with my tail feathers in the air. *What does that? An ostrich?*

"Well, let's meet him. If I have to play nice with him at USC, I might as well get to know him now."

"He's probably working tomorrow," I say, relieved. It's not that I'm embarrassed of Tyler. I just don't want whatever we are to be made into a big deal. Skylar has a knack for making things awkward on purpose. He does everything he can to make some people uncomfortable simply to see how they'll react. It's a test, really. If they can take it or dish it back, they pass. Something tells me Tyler won't pass. I'm not ready for them to meet yet.

"You won't know unless you text him," Harper says, and I want to slap my hand over her mouth and shush her. *Can't she tell I don't want to invite him?*

"I can tell you all you need to know about him, Sky." Brodee starts holding up his fingers one by one. "Gym rat. Wears tank tops, and not ironically. Football player—"

"All right. Enough said." Skylar stops him with one hand and looks squarely at me. "What do you like about this guy, P? Is he good to you?"

While I appreciate Skylar's interest in real answers, I disregard him and narrow my eyes at Brodee. "You say all of those things like they're cons. What's wrong with working out or playing football? Not all football players are dumb jocks."

"But I can tell you where he falls." Brodee chuckles, glancing at Skylar who shares a look. If their eyes could high five, they would. Then Brodee continues, "Tyler's a total kook, talks like he knows what he's doing on the water, but that's all he is. Talk. He's your classic rich kid. Son of a dentist."

Do I hear a hint of jealousy? While I know he's just teasing me, it pushes me over the edge. I'm not sure why I feel like I need to defend Tyler so fiercely, but it's really ticking me off that Brodee is tearing into him. Tyler's never done anything to him.

"Tyler's dad is no different than yours," I cut Brodee off. "Hounding him about schoolwork, riding his butt, making choices for him, except *his* dad actually makes him work for his school tuition. It's not just handed to him on a gold platter."

That shuts him up and not in a good way. Hurt flashes across Brodee's eyes. I wish I'd never said anything. *Why did I throw that in his face?*

"Tell us how you really feel, Peyton." Skylar laughs awkwardly.

The whole vibe shifts. Harper tries to laugh, but it falls flat. I've had enough of the rooftop talk. I move to get up from my recliner.

"I'm sorry, Pete," Brodee says genuinely. "I didn't mean to upset you."

I sigh. "I'm fine. It's fine." And it is. I just want to drop it. I don't want to talk about Tyler anymore. "I'm sorry, too. I'm gonna go to bed."

Brodee snatches my hand as I pass him. His thumb softly rubs the top of my hand. My thoughts jumble. I can't remember why I was so upset. "You know I was just playing, right? I didn't mean it, Pete," he whispers.

"I know." I nod and pull my hand away. Brodee's tender touch confuses me more. "G'night, guys."

The Day I Caught the Train to Crazy Town

WHEN WE GET up in the morning, all is forgotten. Or at least everyone pretends that I didn't have a little freak out moment. I slept horribly, though. Harper came to bed about twenty minutes after I did. I pretended to be asleep, but I couldn't have been less tired. A creeping ache filled my chest, but I couldn't place it. Until I did, and then I couldn't help but miss my dad like crazy.

Sometimes his loss hits me out of nowhere. I can be fine one minute and curled in the fetal position the next. Grief is funny like that. Not in the funny ha-ha way, but the unexpected, cruel kind. It feels like I'll never get a hold on mine.

So, when I finally fell asleep around three and was woken up at seven by Brodee to go surfing, I was less than ready to get out of bed. When I pulled back the covers, he tossed them off and wouldn't let me have them back. He nearly died.

The four of us are headed to Buxton now with Brodee at the wheel.

He's lucky I let him live. Skylar borrowed one of Brodee's millions of boards. That kid collects surfboards the way Harper does wigs. He has a different reason why he needs each one of them. And I get it. Each wave is different. Sometimes the surf requires a different kind of board, but I love my baby. I learned on her and can't imagine surfing on anything else. It's a miracle I haven't busted her with all the wipeouts I've survived.

The sun feels hotter today than most. We're out in the oceans for hours. It's been so long since the four of us have gone out together I think we want to soak up as much time as we can. By the end of it I'm wiped out. Lack of sleep, the heat, exertion from the waves. I want to fall asleep and never wake up.

After grabbing lunch, Brodee drives us back, and it takes everything in me not to fall asleep in the front seat. Even if I could sleep, he wouldn't let me. Brodee keeps poking me in the shoulder.

"Poke me one more time," I warn, only half-joking. My eyes are closed as I lean my head against the headrest. "I dare you."

Poke.

I pause. I hear him chuckling to himself. "If you weren't driving, you'd regret that."

"So, are you saying I'm safe while I drive?"

I level a stare. "After that, all bets are off."

"Noted." He bites his lips to hold back a smug grin. I nearly smack it off.

A minute later he sticks his finger in my ear.

"Oh my gosh." I throw my hands down and shift in my seat to get a good angle to punch him. "You're gonna get it."

"Don't poke the bear, Brodee. You know better," Harper says from the back seat. "Especially since you're driving, and I'd like to live to see tomorrow. I choose life!"

"But it's so much fun."

I hold back my punch. Rationally, I see how stupid it would be to punch the driver of the vehicle in which I'm traveling.

Harper says, "Not when the bear is tired and could tear your head off with one look."

He chuckles. "I just can't help myself."

"The big tormenting brother in him can't be suppressed," I murmur, leaning away from him, my head tapping on the passenger window. The tapping doesn't even bother me this time. I don't remember falling asleep.

"PEYTON." A LOW voice rouses me from my sweet *sweet* release as a hand rocks my shoulder. "Pete." I open my eyes to see Brodee's face above mine. "You slept the day away."

I blink, but I don't try to get up. I'm laying on the couch in the living room, but I can tell it's dark outside. "What time is it?"

"A little after ten." The corner of his mouth lifts up.

Seriously? "Where are Harper and Skylar?" I rub my eyes.

"They're just as bad as you. Tuckered out on me about an hour ago." He stands up and walks over to the TV, flipping it on. "You sleep like the freaking dead. You even slept through dinner. I was so tempted to jump on you, but Liv wouldn't let me wake you up."

"It must've been the sun. And I would have punched you so hard." I stretch my arms above my head.

He lets out a low chuckle. “I know. Let’s watch a movie.”

I lazily pick myself off the couch and head to the kitchen to get the taste of sleep out of my mouth. “You pick. I’m too tired to make any decisions.”

“You can’t be tired. You just slept for like ten hours, and we have a movie marathon ahead of us.”

I really did sleep the day away. “A marathon?” I laugh and walk back in with a glass of orange juice. “It’s ten o’clock.”

“The night is young. We can do whatever we want. Besides, we have to make up for the time you lost today. The summer is dwindling fast. We’ve got to soak up every minute before the semester starts.”

I don’t want to think about school starting. School starting means no more summer. It means no more Brodee. It means real life begins. And I’m not ready for any of that.

Brodee picks a comedy, and even though the couch is completely empty, he chooses to sit right beside me with the popcorn he popped. His thigh grazes mine, and it’s like my body has never felt his touch before, igniting a livewire that tingles every inch of my body. But it doesn’t seem to faze him. He doesn’t flinch or subtly try to move away. Neither do I. Because why should I? It doesn’t mean anything. We’re just best friends watching a movie like we’ve done millions of times before. I’m the one making it weird. It’s not weird. It’s nothing. *Stop making it weird.*

I ease more comfortably into the couch as the previews begin. Brodee gazes over at me. “You missed out on playing in the waves with us when we got back.” He lifts his arm along the back of the couch behind me. “Or I should say you were missed.” I can feel him looking at me, but I don’t have the guts to meet his eyes. I don't know what I'll see there. Or maybe I don't want him to see what my eyes may convey. I'm still trying to breathe through our touching thighs.

"We can play tomorrow. I'll feel better then. I just didn't sleep well last night."

"Yeah? Why not?" he softly asks.

"Just…thinking about my dad."

He reaches his arm around and tugs me close to his side. "I miss him too."

We don't say anything more because the movie starts. The popcorn bowl sits in his lap, so I have to lean into him every time and reach for a handful. He chuckles, carefree, at every little humorous part in the movie. Brodee's laugh echoes throughout the house. I want to bottle his laughter to savor it and release it when the world needs it most.

My nap didn't revive me. Or I guess it was more of a coma. My coma didn't revive me. If anything, it made me more tired. Halfway through the movie I feel my eyes closing, but I fight back for as long as I can.

"Here." I look to Brodee as he moves the empty popcorn bowl to the floor and shifts away from me. "Lay down." He places a pillow on his lap and pats.

I hesitate. It's not like we're cuddling. I'm just resting my head on his lap to sleep. We've done this hundreds of times before. *Calm your nerves, Peyton.*

"I can tell you're still tired, but I'm not finishing this movie alone. Lay down," he orders.

I'm too tired to argue, so I do the only thing I can. I nestle into the couch and rest my head on his welcoming lap. At first he doesn't know what to do with his arms until I feel a soft tug at my scalp. Brodee gently runs his fingers through my hair. Utter bliss. If he doesn't want me to sleep, this is not going to help matters. My eyes flutter closed, and the haze of sleep takes me away.

THE PILLOW SHIFTS under me, waking me.

"Sorry," Brodee murmurs. The TV is off now, and the room is dark. "I was trying to get up without waking you."

I sit up too fast and hold my head, sleep still heavily weighing it down.

Once he stands, he offers me a hand. I slip mine in his, but blackness flashes in my eyes when I stand up too swiftly, causing me to fall forward. Brodee grabs me, placing a hand on my arm and the other around my waist to steady me.

"Whoa there, Grace."

"Sorry," I mumble and let him hold me until I don't feel so dizzy and can see straight. It takes me longer than it normally should because I feel his touch all the way down in my ankles. They wobble and tingle. Stupid weak ankles. When I open my eyes, Brodee doesn't make an attempt to let me go. He's only inches from my face. His fingers touch the skin of my back between my shirt and shorts where the material has ridden up.

"You all right?" His voice is low, husky, and I can't stop the shiver that begins at the base of my spine. Our proximity and his hand touching my bare skin, mixed with the stillness of the night—the moon and stars as our only source of light—suddenly the air between us is too thick to breathe.

The words get stuck in my throat. "I'm fine." After "fine" passes my lips I wish I could take it back. Fine is the universal sign for women *not* being fine in *any* context.

His eyes unhurriedly drift over my face and land on my lips, leaving me defenseless. Ever so subtly he bites his bottom lip, and I'm a goner. Putty in his hands. If he leans in, my self-control cannot be held accountable. As of now, I have none.

"Peyton," he whispers. Our bodies are so intimately close I can feel his warm breath on my face. "We should go to bed." His words don't convince me until he steps back awkwardly.

I nod fervently. "Yeah." I back up out of his arms and rest my hands on my hips, attempting to act more casual than I feel. "I'm exhausted. I really need to go to sleep. I'm just gonna grab a glass of water first." I head toward the kitchen so I don't have to look at him.

"Night," he says hoarsely.

When Brodee disappears up the stairs I fall back against the counter, out of breath. HO-LY. CRAP.

It's not just me. He feels it too, right? Or am I just imagining things because I feel it so strongly? That has to be it. I've officially caught the train to Crazy Town.

How's the distancing yourself working out there, Peyton?

I need to try harder.

The Day Our Foundation Cracked

"WHAT TIME ARE you guys leaving tomorrow?" I curl onto my side in bed and face Harper.

She groans and stretches her arms above her head. I decided to wake her up earlier than normal today with it being our last day together.

"I think we're gonna get up early and go so we can make it home before it gets dark."

"I wish you guys could stay longer."

"Trust me," Harper says, flipping onto her side to face me. "I would much rather stay in paradise than spend a week in Minnesota with my entire family. This reunion might be the death of me. Don't forget to remember me if I don't survive."

"If you die, who am I supposed to hang out with at USC? It'll be *so* boring."

"Ha-ha." She lightly kicks my shins under the covers. "What are we gonna do today?"

"Let's go find out." We hop out of bed in search of the boys. "They've been up since, like, eight playing video games. It's going to be a struggle to pull them away."

"Morning," I greet my mom and Nick who are in the kitchen milling around. They weren't up when I came down earlier. Tate must still be sleeping.

"Good morning," they say in unison, offering a smile.

Brodee and Skylar are in the zone in the living room. I don't even think they noticed we walked into the room until Harper says, "Hey, bums, what's the plan today?" and squeezes beside Skylar and the armrest, leaning her head against his shoulder.

"The beach, beach, and more beach," Brodee replies, concentrating on the TV.

"Well, then let's go to the beach! Shut this off, and let's get out of here." Harper grabs the controller from Skylar and attempts to end the game. "You can play video games anytime."

"Hey! C'mon, babe. I was just about to annihilate Brodee," he groans and throws his arms up in defeat.

Brodee pumps his fist in the air with a Chewbacca howl. I can't help my giggle. Every time. He shoots me a smirk before shouting at Skylar, "Ha! Suck it!"

"Don't get too cocky, Fisher. I'd have killed you, if Harper hadn't intervened."

"And it's a good thing I did. The party will be leaving in ten minutes." She gets up and saunters toward me.

I have one foot on the bottom stair when my mom's voice stops me. "What are you doing with that?" Though it's quiet, her tone is sharp. At first I think she's talking to me, but it wouldn't make sense. I don't have anything. When I turn, I see her staring at Nick, her body rigid.

My eyes travel to him standing near the fridge, leaning his back against the countertop. He has a mug halfway to his lips, but it's not just any mug. It's a fairly significant mug. It's my dad's mug. The one I made for him when I was in eighth grade. The one my dad used every morning while we vacationed here.

Nick slowly lowers it and looks at the surfboard I engraved into the side of the ceramic with 'Dad' written inside of the shape. He opens his mouth, not understanding her distress at first. Then it dawns on him. They exchange looks I don't follow.

"I'm sorry, Liv. I didn't think." He holds it out to her, and she swipes the mug from his hands. "I just grabbed the first mug I—"

"No. You didn't think." Her voice is strained. She takes the mug to the sink and pours his coffee down the drain.

"You know I'd never…" Nick trails off; his eyes drift over to us watching the conversation go down. We all take that as our cue to quietly creep up the stairs.

Brodee and Skylar part from us at the top of the stairs with looks of apprehension as Harper and I walk into my room to change into our suits.

When I close the door Harper says, "Well, that was awkward. It's just a mug. Why is she so upset?" She sounds more confused than anything else, so I don't take offense.

Harper obviously couldn't see what I saw and doesn't understand the significance. "It was my dad's mug," I say quietly as I take my black bathing suit out of the top drawer of my dresser.

"Oh." She digs in her duffle bag for her bikini. Carefully, she asks, "Do you think she overreacted a little bit?"

I don't answer right away because I can't decide. My mom has never scolded Nick like that before. Come to think of it, I'm not even sure I've seen them argue openly.

"I dunno. Maybe. After the years of friendship they've shared, a part of me thinks Nick should've known better, but at the same time it's hard to gauge what's going to set her off. And I honestly don't think he was paying attention."

"Did it bother you to see him using it?"

I shrug. "A little, yeah."

"Maybe you should take the mug out of the kitchen. I wouldn't have known not to use it."

"No. It's fine." I see how silly it might sound to an outsider, being upset over a piece of pottery. And my mom didn't need to take it from him and dump his coffee down the drain. That may have been taking it a bit far. "It *is* just a mug."

"But it means something to you and your mom."

It does. "Yeah. She probably took care of it though. I doubt anyone will use it again."

Today is clearly leaning toward a not-so-great day for my mom if she let something like that affect her so easily. It's always hard to decide if she needs space or if I should go to her on days like this. I toy with idea of trying to talk to her. I'd understand if she wants to be left alone. I know there's nothing I can say to help her or make her feel better. I know because there's nothing anyone can say to me either. I've simply learned to live through the days, breathe through the pain.

There's nothing more that I want to do now than to get out of the house and relax on the shore all day.

AS WE LAZE around the beach in Rodanthe and surf, the only thing I can think about is how much I want this to last. It's not the big moments I want. It's this. Watching Brodee and Skylar skimboard and laugh as they biff it, looking to us to see if we witnessed it. And Harper reading a magazine beside me on her stomach, her feet swinging back and forth in the air, while I read one of my dad's old books. The comfort I feel with our solidarity.

Brodee and Skylar walk up the beach back to us with their skimboards in hand.

His heart-melting smile widens when he looks at me, and, for the first time, it scares me.

I want him more than anything else.

WHEN WE GET back to the house after Rodanthe, it's time for dinner. Tate is the only one around, and she's made us a pot of chili.

"Hey, where is everyone?" I ask.

"Your mom and Nick ran to the grocery store to grab a few things, but they should be back soon. And Carter went out with his friends. If you guys want to go ahead and eat, feel free. It's ready."

Hopefully, they patched up everything after this morning. I hate seeing my mom so upset. This summer was supposed to help her. And maybe that's why they went together. To have a moment to fix whatever happened this morning.

"How was the beach?" Tatum asks.

"Good," Brodee answers and grabs a bowl to fill.

I give her a more detailed reply. "It was beautiful. Surf was pretty decent. We just relaxed on the beach most of the day. The boys did some skimboarding. Harper and I read."

"Thank you, Peyton." She smiles, giving me a knowing look. *Boys.* "You guys look like you got some sun. I'm seeing some pink cheeks."

Harper pats her face. "I was afraid of that."

"It'll work in your favor in a couple days," Tatum amends. "You tan beautifully, Harper."

While everyone eats at the kitchen table, I revel in being together, taking in every second, trying to appreciate every moment the four of us have left. After dinner we squeeze onto the couch in the living room and turn on some music to play in the background.

Harper leans into me. "Hey, Peyton-Parker. You okay?"

"Huh?" I look to Harper.

"You've been really quiet today. What's on your mind?"

I know it's not the end of the summer, but with it being the last day the four of us have together, it almost feels like the end of our childhood in a way.

"I just don't want this to end. It's going to be so different without Brodee, you know? I want today to last forever." I wipe my eyes of the stray tears filling them.

"Oh no, you getting all sappy on us, P Parker?" Skylar asks, leaning around Harper.

Brodee wraps his arm around my shoulder and tugs me to his side. "Aww…Pete. I mean…I know I'm awesome, but you don't have to cry over me."

"Shut up." I laugh and shove him away. "Don't flatter yourself. I'm a crier. Leave me alone."

"Well, stop it." Harper gets up and throws her hair into a ponytail. "We're not ending today on a sad note." And then she's on a mission toward the back door.

"Harper, where are you going?" I ask over the back of the couch.

She looks over her shoulder. "I'm going for a swim." And then she's gone.

When we reach the open doorway, Harper is jogging down the boardwalk into the dark, shedding clothing down to her bathing suit. "C'mon, losers!" she shouts. So, we shrug and run after her—taking off layers as we go, stumbling and laughing until we're only in our swimsuits—and plunge into the sparkling moonlit ocean.

It's freezing and refreshing and exhilarating all at once. I duck my head under the water, slicking back my hair. When my head breaks the surface, I wipe my eyes, and I see that Brodee is watching me. There's an exchange. I'm not even sure I can explain it. The way he looks at me, his smile gradually disappearing. His eyes radiate heat, and my entire body warms by his stare. I'm not sure that he knows what he's doing to me. It's as though we're both trying to read each other's thoughts, but we're afraid to think too deeply for fear that the other will know too much.

Or maybe that's just me.

He swims toward me, and I stop breathing. I hear Skylar and Harper splashing and giggling, making a commotion near us, but that's all it is. Noise. Background noise. My focus is all Brodee.

"You remember our pact, right?"

I can only nod. There is no air in my lungs for words.

"I don't want you to worry about us, okay?"

Worry about what, exactly? That we'll drift apart? That we'll change? That I'll ruin everything with these feelings?

"You're my best friend, Pete."

"And you're mine," I whisper.

The grip of his hand on my waist surprises me for a few reasons. First and foremost, I wasn't expecting it. And I wasn't quite sure what it was until I felt his fingers dig into my skin and draw me closer. But, mostly, it surprises me because his touch feels different than it ever has. It's intimate, and dare I say…possessive.

Our pact is broken. I'm changed. We've already changed.

Does he realize it?

Without a second thought, I push his dark hair from his forehead to better see his eyes in the dim light. If eyes are windows to the soul, I want a better view. He blinks, and there's a hitch in his breathing. It's so subtle that, had I not already been so hyperaware of him in this moment, I may have missed it.

Suddenly, the background noise is gone. We're in silence, but not the in-our-own-world silence. I don't hear Harper and Skylar. I sever eye contact and look to where they were last playing around. They're gone.

Then I'm being pulled under. I thrash in the water and break free of the hold around my ankle. Rising to the surface, I gasp for air. Brodee appears above the water almost immediately after me, coughing up water. Skylar and Harper bust out laughing as they swim around us.

"You guys are gonna get it," Brodee warns, wiping the salt water from his eyes.

"You scared the crap out of me!" I shove water in Skylar's face, and he backstrokes away, laughing his head off.

"Peyton and I will get our revenge." Brodee gives me a conspiratorial glance and I nod, smirking back at him.

"Good luck!" Harper says. "We leave in the morning!" She giggles, treading water.

"Challenge accepted," I say with a laugh.

I wish we could always be this way, but I know this is the end of one chapter and the beginning of another.

The Day I Caught a Big Fish

A WEEK LATER, the jostling of my bed wakes me up early.

"Pete! Pete! Pete! Wake up, Pete!"

I groan and curl my covers over my head. While I'm normally a morning person, you better know how to wake me up the right way. And jumping on my bed and chanting my name definitely isn't it.

"Brodee, I will murder you."

He laughs, but doesn't stop bouncing at my feet. "C'mon! It's morning! Time to wake up!"

"If you want to live to see tomorrow, I suggest you stop jumping," I say from under the covers.

The jumping stops. The bed shifts slightly. When I remove the blanket from my head, Brodee is sitting at the end of my bed, grinning. "You want to go fishing?"

Even at… "What time is it?"

"Seven," he replies.

Even at seven o'clock in the morning, he somehow wakes up my entire body with one smile. I press my palms into my eyes, rubbing away the sleep. If only the pressure of my palms could detach my retinas so I'd never have to look at his beautiful face again.

Oh, stop being so melodramatic, Peyton.

I throw back my covers and slip out of bed in pajama shorts and Dad's old, oversized T-shirt. Then the strangest thing happens. Brodee's mouth slowly hangs open, not gawking, but definitely caught off guard. His eyes travel from my bare feet to my face, and it's highly likely that his eyes have magical powers because I can't the stop the tingling sensation in every part of my body his gaze caresses. *Did he just check me out? In an oversized T-shirt?*

I look down at myself to realize the shirt is so long it looks like I'm not wearing anything underneath. As I walk to my closet, I do my best to nonchalantly pull the shirt to the side and hold a wad of material on my hip, so Brodee can see I wasn't trying to flash him. I am, in fact, wearing shorts. There's nothing to see here.

He clears his throat. "I'll meet you downstairs." Brodee bolts out of my room so fast, when I turn around to tell him, 'okay,' he's gone.

I wasn't going to change in front of you. Geesh. I throw on a pair of jean shorts and a light yellow T-shirt, slip into my Rainbows, and head downstairs.

Brodee's flipping through the channels when I walk through the living room and head straight for the kitchen. The layout is basically one big, open room. The kitchen island is the only thing that separates the two, so Brodee and I can talk freely from one room to the next.

"You ready?" he asks.

"Let me grab an orange and then we can go. Have you seen my mom?"

"I don't think our parents are awake yet. The house has been silent since I woke up."

I write on the whiteboard on the fridge that we've gone fishing. "All right. Let's go."

Brodee drives us about an hour and a half up to Nag's Head. The drive up the 12 never gets old. I love seeing the ocean all around us. I roll down my window to breathe in the fresh, salt air. Out of the corner of my eye, I check out Brodee. His Ray-Bans perch on his tan, freckled nose, while the short strands of his dark hair flicker in the breeze. *Be still, my beating heart.*

I've ridden shot gun a million times in Brodee's car, but seeing him behind the wheel—sure of himself, in control—never gets old. We don't have to talk. He doesn't even have to acknowledge me. It's calming just to be near him. I love the comforting silence for what it is. Ours.

When we arrive, we walk down the pier and find a spot where there isn't anyone. Thankfully, it's early enough that the pier isn't too crowded yet.

We throw cheesy pick-up lines back and forth all morning. We've recycled some, but they're still funny.

"All right, all right. I've got one," he says. "Did you know they changed the alphabet?"

"Did they now?" I raise my eyebrows skeptically.

"Yeah, they put U and I together."

I laugh, rolling my eyes, and turn my face to him as I keep control of my fishing pole. "I'm pretty sure Mike tried to use that one on me at least once, if not more."

Brodee chuckles. "He would." His smile is warm. Brodee pushes his sunglasses on the top of his head to get a better look as he hooks more bait on his line. The sun hits his eyes just right, flickering the gold in his green pupils.

"I'm not a photographer," I say, "but I can picture me and you together."

He doesn't skip a beat. "Can I take your picture to prove to all my friends that angels exist?"

I smile. "I'm not drunk, I'm just intoxicated by you."

"Let's commit the perfect crime: I'll steal your heart, and you'll steal mine."

Little does he know, he already stole mine. I'm a goner. It's official. *No. You like Tyler. And Tyler likes you. And you're going to have a future at USC together. Keep the pact in tact.* I laugh to myself. That rhymed. *Dork.*

"If you were a Transformer, you'd be Optimus Fine."

Brodee throws his head back and laughs. "If I were to ask you out on a date," he says, "would your answer be the same as the answer to this question?"

I have to think that one through for a second. "Clever." I chuckle. "If someone were to actually use that on me, I might have gotten stuck."

He laughs. "It's good, right?"

"I'll give you that one." I continue, "I thought happiness started with an H. Why does mine start with U?"

As though Brodee can tell my pick-up lines are veering from the cheesy, he says, "If I had to choose between one night with you or winning the lottery, I would chose winning the lottery. But it would be close…real close…"

"Oh my gosh," I say, snickering. "What kind of pick-up line is that?" I shove him as he laughs. "Though, I can't say I'd blame him."

"Me either." Brodee throws out another fishing line.

My line snags. "Oh! I think I got something!"

"Reel it in!"

The tug is strong. I nearly lose my grip on the pole so I hold on tighter. It's been so long since I've been fishing I have to listen to Brodee's instructions or I know I'll lose it.

"Hold on. Let it drag. Tire it out for a sec."

"I feel like I'm gonna lose the pole."

"You need help?"

I want to do it myself. "No, I'm good."

"All right. Reel it in again. Okay. Let it drag for a sec. You got it. There you go."

His encouraging words continue until I've pulled it out of the water. Brodee says it's a Spanish mackerel.

"Way to go, Pete! We're gonna feast like kings tonight."

As I detach the mouth of the fish from the hook, Brodee brushes the tip of my nose with his knuckle. "You look better without all that makeup, by the way. You shouldn't cover up your freckles."

I automatically cover my nose. "You know I'm self-conscious about how much they show in the summertime."

He laughs. "I know. That's why I thought you should know. They look good on you. Don't hide them."

I hate it when he says stuff like that. I know he doesn't mean it the way I want him to. To him, he's just talking to his buddy, Pete, trying to pay me a compliment because he's nice, not because he likes me.

"Well, I hate them," I say.

He simply says, "I don't."

THAT NIGHT, WHEN I jog down the stairs into the kitchen, Brodee is stirring something on the stove, while my mom cuts vegetables and Tate sets the table.

"Well, don't you look pretty," Tatum comments as she sets down a plate.

"Thanks," I respond self-consciously and look down at my white dress. It's nothing special. Just a simple eyelet dress I've had for years. It only looks like I tried harder because it's a dress, but really it's much more low maintenance not to have to think of what top I'm going to pair with what bottoms. I can throw on a dress and be done.

Brodee looks over his shoulder and catches my eye. He blinks and gives me a once over. If I'm not mistaken, I think Brodee Fisher just checked me out again. I can't help feeling a little satisfaction.

"When's Tyler picking you up?" Mom asks.

"He should be here any minute."

"You're hanging out with Tyler tonight?" There's a weird tone in Brodee's voice. "You're not gonna eat the fish you caught?"

"Well, no. Tyler called when we got back from the pier and asked me out to dinner." There's a knock at the door. "And that's probably him."

I skip to the door because of course I can't gain control of my evil, giddy twin. Tyler stands on the other side of the door. My eyes trail from his face to the bouquet of calla lilies in his hand. My chest tightens. *I will not cry. I will not cry. I will not cry.*

"It's your favorite still, right?" he asks.

It's not, but I tell him yes anyway and smile. There's no way for him to know I haven't been able to look at a calla lily the same since my dad's funeral. They were everywhere. Tulips shortly after became my favorite. It doesn't change the fact that the calla lilies are gorgeous, and Tyler's thoughtful.

"Thank you." I take them and clear my throat. "Come in. Let me put them in water before we go."

He follows me to the kitchen, and I head for the cupboards to look for a vase. Brodee is looking at the flowers like he would beets. He hates beets.

"Well, hello, Tyler." Mom sets down the knife and wipes off her hands on a dishtowel over her shoulder before she goes in for a hug. "Look how handsome you've grown up to be."

Tyler's cheeks redden, and his eyes shift to the ground like he's embarrassed. "Thank you, ma'am."

"Please. We've gone over this," she says. "It's Olivia."

He chuckles nervously. "Okay, Miss Olivia."

Tyler's family is clearly a little more proper than ours. He's got the true Southern boy down pat. His politeness melts my heart.

"So, where are you taking Pete, Tyler?" Brodee asks. There's no mistaking the subtle—or not so subtle—over protective brother edge in his voice.

"I thought we'd go to The Wreck. They've got a live band there tonight. Should be fun." Tyler looks over at me as I arrange the calla lilies in the only vase I can find.

"I love The Wreck," I say. "Good choice."

Before my mom starts making more small talk, or worse, starts to get mushy about us going out on a date, I lead Tyler to the front door.

"You two have fun!" Mom hollers and waves from the end of the hallway by the kitchen.

When I turn as I open the door, Brodee's mouth is set in a straight line, and his eyes narrow. He looks angry, but then the corner of his mouth lifts, softening his expression. I wave. He waves back.

"Marcus is throwing a big party on Wednesday," Tyler says as he pulls out of my driveway. "You should go."

"Oh yeah? Any reason in particular?"

"I'll be there." Tyler flashes his thousand-watt smile.

"Well, if that's the case, then I'm definitely not going." I suppress my smile, but my eyes give away the teasing.

"Oh, is that so?"

"Yeah. I've heard this Tyler guy is kind of full of himself."

His head knocks back as he laughs. "I've got to find out who's feeding you these lies."

Tyler and I spend the night eating and listening to the music. A few different guitarists sing and play, and they're all pretty decent. Around ten they wind down and we head out.

Tyler intertwines his fingers with mine. "Take a walk with me?"

"Okay."

We dart across the empty street and have to sneak through someone's yard to get to the beach. A motion light flares on, and we bolt toward the sand, stifling our laughter.

"I still can't believe you're going to USC," Tyler says.

"I know. It's crazy. Are you staying in the dorms too?"

"Actually, my dad bought an apartment off campus as an investment property to rent out when I graduate, so I'll have my own place until then."

"Well, that'll be really nice. Do you have any roommates yet?"

"I convinced Marcus to come with me, so it'll just be us."

"How awesome. I'm jealous. I wish Harper and I had a place of our own."

"Why? The dorms would be so much more fun. You'll have so many more people to get to know and socialize with."

"Yeah, and that much more girl drama to avoid."

Tyler chuckles. "Something tells me you'll be just fine. Just don't forget about me once we get there." He nudges my shoulder with his.

"Me? Ha. Whatever. Girls will be swarming you. If anything, by the first day you'll be asking, 'Peyton who?'"

Tyler stops. My hand tugs to a halt. I turn and face him. His hazel eyes glimmer under the stars. It's easy to forget how effortless it is to be with him when we're not together all year. It's even easy to forget while I'm here and distracted. His gaze holds mine, and in this moment I don't breathe.

"You really don't know how amazing you are, do you?"

Through all of our summers together, Tyler's never been so forward with his feelings. Our conversations have always stayed casual and flirtatious, but the look in his eyes now tell me he wants to be anything but casual and flirtatious. He's earnest.

"You're *all* I think about, Peyton. Since I met you, I've counted down the days to every summer because I knew I was going to get to spend it with you. At least I hoped I would get to spend it with you. I've gotten pretty dang lucky so far. When I say, 'don't forget about me,' I might say it jokingly, but I mean it. Wholeheartedly. I'm kind of crazy about you, Peyton Parker."

I don't know what to say. I'm flattered and swooning, but when I process what he's saying, all the meaning behind it, all I see is Brodee. I don't want Brodee to forget about me.

"Peyton." Tyler's voice brings me back.

"Yeah?" My voice shakes. I cleared my throat.

He pushes a strand of hair behind my ear. "Sometimes I wish I could crawl inside that pretty head of yours to see what's going on."

No, you don't. "I'm sure you do, but then you'd be able to understand me perfectly, and what would be the fun in that?"

Tyler chuckles, holding my face. "None at all. You're right. But it sure would make my life easier."

To push thoughts of Brodee aside, I do the only thing I can think of that will leave those thoughts dead in the water. I lift up on my tiptoes to kiss Tyler. He wraps his arms around my waist, drawing me close as I loop my arms around his neck. We kiss under the stars, the waves lapping the shore. This is what summer romances are made of. Waves and sand and kissing and no other care in the world. Maybe our romance will change with the seasons this time.

WHEN I WALK in the front door, feeling lighter on my feet, it's dark except for a TV glow coming from the living room. Brodee is lounging on the couch with his feet propped up on the ottoman.

"Hey. What are you still doing up?" I plop down beside him, my head falling back on the couch. I didn't realize how tired I am, or maybe I'm just feeling dreamy.

"Hey," he mutters. "I got caught up in *Criminal Minds*." Brodee stares blankly at the TV. "Your mom wanted to go to bed, so I told her I'd wait up for you."

"She hasn't bothered staying up for me so far this summer. Why tonight?"

Brodee shrugs. "I guess because you were with Tyler, not me."

"Huh." I stare at the screen, not really taking in what's going on. Tyler's words replay in my head. I never knew he liked me so much. Our summer flings always felt like just that. A fling. Why hadn't he said anything before? Maybe because of the possibility of a future this time. Something more than a fling is possible now, and I'm kind of excited.

"Have a good night?" Brodee's voice is so emotionless I hardly think he cares enough for a reply, but I answer him anyway. He's probably just as tired as I am. We *were* up pretty early to go fishing.

"It was really fun. There was some pretty good music at The Wreck tonight. We stayed for a few hours just listening and talking."

"Classy joint he took you to," he says dryly.

I dart him a look. "What's up with you tonight?"

"Nothing," he says apologetically and shuts off the TV. It's pitch black, so he turns on his cell phone for light and heads for the stairwell.

"Brodee, c'mon. Did I do something to make you mad?" I click on the light of my cell to find the light switch for the kitchen. "You're acting weird."

When the light flickers on, he turns. I stop short. His brow creases. "You're just too good for him, Pete. I thought you'd figure it out by now."

"Oh, stop playing the big brother card." I roll my eyes. "Tyler's a good guy, and you know it."

"He didn't even know not to bring you those lilies. You can't even look at those things without cringing." Brodee works his jaw and shrugs. "I just think you could do better, Pete."

"There's no way for him to know about the calla lilies," I defend.

"Has he even asked about your dad?"

"Well, no, but it's not like we've had the opportunity. It's not a topic that gets easily brought up."

"You just spent like five hours with the guy, and not once did he think to bring up the most life-altering event in your life."

I don't answer.

His eyes narrow. "Does he even know about your dad, Peyton?"

I stop to think how to answer this. As nonchalantly as I can, I say, "I haven't told him yet."

Brodee's mouth drops. "Don't you think it's a little odd that we've been here a month, you're planning your future at USC with this guy, and you haven't once mentioned your dad to him?"

Well, when he put it like that…But I don't want to talk about my dad right now. "It's hard to bring up something like that, especially when I don't want to talk about it. I don't want the pity I get when people first find out. I don't want him to look at me differently."

"But that's just it—if you really liked the guy you'd feel comfortable enough to say something, to let him in. If he cares about you enough—knows you well enough—he won't look at you with pity. He won't look at you differently. He'd find a way to be there for you the way you need it."

This is not an argument I want to have right now. "Look. I like Tyler. I'm just not ready for that talk. And maybe I'll find someone else when I get to USC, but we're having a good time, and he's here now."

"So am I."

His answer is so automatic, so quiet, I almost don't catch it. "What?"

"Nothing. Forget I said that." He takes his first step up the stairs without looking at me.

I move toward him. "I don't want to forget it. What do you mean?"

"Nothing." He waves me off, rubbing his eyes. Something that sounds like a laugh, but is more self-deprecating, seeps out of his mouth. "I don't know what I'm saying. I'm so tired. I'm going to bed. I'll see you in the morning."

"Brodee," I call, but he's walking away with no intention of stopping.

I think about following after him, but what if I heard him wrong? What if he didn't mean it? What if he really *is* tired and isn't thinking straight? I'm not about to face the humiliation of confessing my feelings if he didn't really mean what he said. So, I don't stop him. We go to bed with the awkward tension heavy in the air.

The Day We Didn't Pick a Winner

BRODEE HAS BEEN gone all morning. Didn't even bother asking if I wanted to go surfing with him, but I know he went because his favorite board is gone. His Patriot isn't though, so I assume he's out back. I debate going after him, but I have a feeling he's avoiding me, and I'm going to let him until he's ready. I know he regrets what he said. He's probably so embarrassed or doesn't want me to take what he said the wrong way. Maybe I do need to go find him so that he knows we're cool. I don't want things to be weird between us now. I don't want to waste the rest of the summer.

Once I walk out onto the beach, I don't have to go very far before I see Brodee. He's coming up out of the water in his wetsuit. With his surfboard tucked under his arm, he uses his other to run his fingers through his wet strands, brushing the hair out of his eyes. It's the sexiest gesture he could have made. How many times have I watched him do just that and never noticed? I have to close my eyes for a second and focus. *This is not the time, Peyton. Get your mind out of the gutter.*

When I open my eyes, he's almost to me on the shore.

"Hey," he says casually with a head nod. "'Sup." He doesn't smile or act embarrassed. He seems indifferent, which is worse than I thought.

"Hey. The waves any good?" I ask to fill the cavernous space.

He shrugs. "I caught a couple good ones, but it's getting a little rough. Time to call it quits." Brodee sets down his board and sits beside it on the sand, propping his arms up on his knees, while facing the water. I take my place next to him and mirror his pose. There's a minute of looking out at the ocean crashing against the shore before anything is said.

"Look," he says at the same time that I say, "So…"

Our gaze meets and we laugh uncomfortably. I hate it. We're never supposed to be uncomfortable around each other. Everything is supposed to be easy with us. We have nothing to prove or hide. At least that's how it was before.

Brodee clears his throat before he begins, "I just want to apologize for last night. I was so exhausted I wasn't thinking straight. With the stress from my dad and college coming up fast, I think I'm just struggling with everything changing. You know? Can we just forget it happened? All of it?"

I try to hide the hurt. I don't want to forget it. Any of it. But isn't that why I was coming to him? Because I knew he regretted it or knew it came out the wrong way. Of course he's struggling with things changing, just like me. I don't want to lose him. "Yeah." I nod. "Of course. Already forgotten. What were we talking about?"

He smirks. "Thanks, Pete. I mean…anything between you and me would just be weird."

"Totally." I try not to sound breathless, even though I feel like he punched me in the stomach.

"Cool. Glad we're on the same page. Just smack me if I say anything stupid like that again. Or better yet, push me up the stairs so I can get a good night's sleep with a clear head."

"I got your back." I punch his shoulder, trying to use the most platonic gesture I can think of.

"Cool," he says again. "I'm gonna go wash up. You wanna go on a bike ride when I'm done?"

"Sure." I smile to ease the tension.

"'kay. I'll meet you downstairs when I'm ready."

Brodee gets up and walks away, and I watch him go. He doesn't walk like a tough guy, even though at times I know he wants to be one, but he still has a certain confidence about him in the way he moves—not cocky, just confident—never looking at the ground, eyes forward, shoulders square and relaxed.

With each step he takes, he stomps on another piece of my heart. I don't know why my heart hurts so much right now. Logistically speaking, it wouldn't make sense even if Brodee did have feelings for me. Love would only make things messy and complicated.

WHILE WE'RE RIDING our bikes side by side down the streets of Hatteras, our pick-up line challenge pick-ups where we left off.

"Do you have a pencil?" he asks. I look at him funny. "'Cause I want to erase your past and write our future."

I want to laugh, but my heart is too busy racing out of my chest. That one was kind of cute, and Brodee couldn't have picked a worse moment to say it. If only he were serious.

I snort to cover up my almost swoon moment. "Are you a camera? Because every time I look at you, I smile."

He smirks, but doesn't say anything. We don't pick a winner that round.

The Day I Rode Willem

A COUPLE MORNINGS later, I wake up to a text from Tyler. Rubbing my eyes, I blink at the screen.

Tyler: I need my Peyton Fix.
You up for some horseback riding?

Is that even a question?

Me: Yeah! What time?
Tyler: I'll come get you in like 45 min.
Me: Sounds good.

This is perfect after my day with Brodee. I could really use a break, implement that distancing myself plan, and a…Tyler fix? Is that what he called it? I laugh to myself. *Dork.*

As I'm shoving a bagel smothered with cream cheese into my mouth, Brodee strolls into the kitchen. "How about we go to Kitty Hawk today? Go jet skiing or something."

I swallow my bite. "I'm going horseback riding with Tyler. He should be here in like ten minutes."

"Oh." The disappointment in his voice is hard to miss, but I try to ignore it.

I look to Carter, eating his breakfast next to me. "Take Carter with you. You guys could use some brotherly bonding time."

While I was only trying to make up for telling Brodee no, he's hardly spent any time with Carter so far this summer, and I know Carter's been a little hurt by that. I've seen it on his face every time we've left him behind. He does what he can to make it seem like he doesn't care, but I know him better than that. When Carter was younger, being left out wasn't uncommon, but he wasn't afraid to voice his frustration, throwing tantrums and threatening to tell on us. Now that he's sixteen, he's too *mature* and *cool* to show the disappointment.

Brodee perks up, but it's forced, merely for the benefit of Carter. "Yeah, Carter. You game?"

Carter nods and shrugs, but I can tell he's excited because he shovels in the last bite and drops his bowl in the sink. "Sure. Let me go change."

When Carter's up the stairs, Brodee sits beside me and starts thumbing through a random catalog on the counter. I'm pretty sure it's Pottery Barn, but I figure I won't be obnoxious and point out he's reading his mom's mail.

"Horseback riding, huh?"

"Yeah, I think we're gonna go to that place here in Hatteras. So we'll have the instructors walking with us the whole time, but it should still be fun."

He nods and turns the page. I hear nothing but the swipe, swipe, swipe of pages going by. Brodee doesn't say anything else, and neither do I.

It never used to be like this. Awkward silences. Uninterpretable gazes. Words left unsaid. There wasn't anything left unsaid between us, because even if we didn't say anything, we knew. We always knew what the other was thinking. Now, no matter how much time we spend together, Brodee feels miles away. Maybe it's for the best. Soon we'll *actually* be miles away from each other.

Tyler comes to get me before Brodee leaves. I get a, "see ya" and a nod from Brodee as I walk out the door.

I DON'T REALLY know the first thing about horses, so I can tell you one of the horses is black and the other one is gray and white speckled. I can also tell you they're beautiful.

Tyler walks right up to the black horse and strokes his mane. "This is Shadow. He's a Percheron mare and Hackney pony cross." He nods to the gray and white one. "You'll be riding Willem. He's an Arab stallion and Percheron mare cross."

I'm impressed. "Wow. I didn't know you knew so much about horses."

"I don't." Tyler gives me a boyish grin. "I Googled them."

I laugh and lightly smack his shoulder.

"Just trying to impress you. Did it work?"

"It *did*," I say. "You should've kept Google to yourself. I never would have known the difference."

"I'm a horrible liar." He chuckles. "I'd have slipped up somewhere and made a real idiot out of myself."

"Well, since we're being honest, I've never ridden a horse before."

"Really? My family and I ride every time we come out here. Don't worry. They make it pretty easy on you." He points to the horses. "They're ridden nearly every day, so they're used to humans, and we won't do anything more than walk along the shoreline."

The ride is more relaxing than I expected, though it would be difficult not to be. Listening to the waves crash against the shore is enough to calm any nerves I might've had. Tyler is wearing a dark red ball cap and worn jeans today, making him seem more like a cowboy than a surfer as he holds the reins confidently. There's something tempting about a guy who knows exactly what he's doing on a horse. He exudes masculinity. I want to throw myself at him, but I don't, of course, because morals.

"You doing okay?" Tyler asks when he notices me looking at him.

"Yeah." I nod, feeling a tad uncomfortable in the saddle. "I think so."

"You *look* good." He smiles. I blush. "Though you should know...you'll probably be a little sore afterward. Might not be able to walk tomorrow."

"Thanks for the heads up," I say wryly, but smile.

"In my defense, I didn't know you'd never ridden before, but you're athletic. You might be fine."

"If I can't walk tomorrow, I know where you live."

"Good thing it'll take you a few days to get to me."

I laugh.

IT FINALLY HAPPENS—like it does every year at the beach. Mom, Tatum, Brodee, and I are watching *Beaches*. Tate went out and bought Junior Mints and white cheddar popcorn because she knows how much I love both.

Nick had to go back home for another deposition, and Carter had to take the ACT in the morning, so they left for the weekend, leaving just us.

Halfway through the movie, Tatum threads her fingers through my freshly showered hair. I rest my head on her lap and curl up on my cushion with my feet hanging over the armrest. She always refers to me as her favorite daughter. I was five when she first called me that, and I'd thought she'd gone crazy. *She knows I'm not actually her daughter, right?* And I'd nearly told her as much, but I'd loved how it'd made me feel, knowing she'd loved me enough to wish I was hers, so all I had done was smile.

Her fingers begin to braid my long strands, and I'm *this* close to falling asleep when a pillow hits me in the face. I immediately lift my head and shoot Brodee a glare. He raises his hands innocently, but I see the condemning evidence written across his face and throw the pillow back at him.

He catches it and says, "There's no sleeping in *Beaches*," While he chuckles to himself.

"Who are you, Tom Hanks? We're not in *A League of Their Own*, and I wasn't sleeping!" I hiss. "I was closing my eyes." I refuse to prove him right. Technically, I wasn't asleep, just almost.

"Shhh…you two," my mom says. "It's almost over."

I keep my eyes trained on him until Tatum tugs on my hair, coaxing me back into her lap.

"You're lucky they're here to hold me back, Fisher."

"Bring it, Parker." He continues to laugh quietly.

"Be quiet," Tatum scolds, and so I shut my mouth and look back at the screen. I feel Brodee's eyes on me throughout the rest of the movie, but I don't want to give him any more fuel, so I ignore him and focus on the screen.

When *Beaches* is over, and my mom and Tatum are wiping tears from their faces, Brodee says, "Pete and I will clean up so you guys can go to bed."

What's he doing volunteering me? I'm tired, man. Then I move. *And sore.*

It's begun.

"Thanks, Brodee." My mom bends down and kisses the top of his head. "You're a good son." Tatum does the same thing as she passes by him. They say goodnight and head up the stairs.

I carefully get up and waddle to the kitchen. I know I waddle because I feel like a penguin, but not just any penguin. A nine months pregnant penguin. *Wait, penguins don't get pregnant.* Whatever. I'm waddling.

Brodee clears his throat. "You all right there, Pete? You seem to have transformed into my nana. She's ninety by the way."

"Why didn't anyone bother to warn me that horseback riding makes you sore? How did I not know this? How have we not gone before so I could've been prepared?"

Brodee throws back his head, laughing. "C'mon. You can't be that sore. You went for like an hour."

His patronizing tone does not mesh well with my exhaustion or my pain. "You can clean this kitchen up all by yourself." I steer around the counter, heading for my room.

"Aww...c'mon. Don't leave me hanging. I was just giving you a hard time. Please help me? Pretty please?"

I turn my head over my shoulder because it's about the only muscle that doesn't hurt. He's giving me puppy dog eyes. *Not the puppy dog eyes.* They stupidly work.

"Fine."

After we've finished with the dishes, swept the floor, and wiped down the countertops, I make my way to the bottom of the stairs. When I look up, I think to myself, I've never seen so many stairs. It's going to take me an hour just to get up them. I hear quiet chuckling over my shoulder.

"Here," Brodee says. Before I know what's happening, I'm in his arms, and he's carrying me up the stairs like I weigh nothing. When we get to my room he stops. "Can you get your door?"

"You can put me down. I'm perfectly capable of getting myself into bed." I wiggle, but not convincingly enough because even that hurts. I'm already in my pajamas, so really all I have to do is crawl into bed, and that's exactly what I'll do. Crawl. Slowly. One knee at a time over my comforter.

"Just open the door, Pete."

I'm too tired and too sore to argue, so I oblige and turn the knob. Brodee walks me to my bed effortlessly. I knew he was strong, but I've never really experienced it firsthand. The most I've ever done is ride on his back. He sets me gently on my bed and helps me pull back the covers so I can maneuver under.

"Look at you tucking me in and stuff," I tease.

"Oh. I'm a pro at tucking." He starts at my feet, exaggeratedly shoving the covers around me, cocooning me. I chuckle. When he moves up to my waist and up around my shoulders, he comes face to face with me, and my laughter dies. He doesn't pull away like I think he will. He tucks slower and slower, avoiding eye contact until I'm completely wrapped up.

Brodee swallows, watching my lips. His eyes drift up to meet mine. "There you go," he says a breath away from my mouth.

I don't say a thing. There isn't enough air in my lungs to form words. For a second I think he's going to kiss me—and I'm pretty sure he's thinking hard about it—but then he pulls away and turns.

"G'night, Pete."

I still can't respond. He shuts my bedroom door after him. The closed door stares back at me, begging me to open it and go after him. Obviously, I don't. Because I can hardly move. And because it would be a completely irrational idea.

The Day With No Distractions

I CAN'T MOVE my legs.

My thighs are on fire. My butt feels like I'll never be able to sit down again. It's very possible that I won't be able to walk today. And if I do, it won't be normally. Brodee's going to make fun of me all day. He'll be enough of a pain in my butt; I don't need the additional soreness.

When my phone buzzes, I blindly feel for it on my nightstand. Holding it above my face, I see Tyler's name.

Tyler: I hope you're not too sore today. ;)

Ha. If only he knew.

Me: I can't move, but I'll live.

Tyler: Are you serious? Haha. Peyton I'm sorry.

Me: Don't feel bad. I had so much fun. :)

Tyler: I have to work all day or I'd come take care of you.

Well, isn't he sweet?

Me: Even if you didn't work, I wouldn't let you. I'm seriously okay!

Tyler: Okay good! Can't wait to see you tomorrow at Marcus's.

I stare at my screen, rereading the text. There's a knock on my bedroom door.

Me: Ditto.

"Come in," I holler.

Mom peers around the door. "You're not up yet."

I groan and settle further into bed. "I'm a little sore from horseback riding with Tyler yesterday."

She chuckles and sits down beside me.

"Okay. Well, I came up because I need to head back to Charleston for a few days, but I'll be back on Friday."

"Everything okay?"

"Oh yeah. Nothing for you to worry about. Just some odds and ends that I need to tie up with the insurance company."

"Dad stuff?"

She nods, melancholy, and runs her fingers through my hair. "Nothing you need to worry about."

"Okay."

She kisses my forehead. "Don't stay in bed all day. It's beautiful out. Not too hot. If nothing else, just go lay out on the beach."

"I will," I say to assure her, but I could contently lie in bed all day. The more I move, the more muscles I discover that I didn't even know existed. I'll see what my body will allow me to do. Maybe Brodee will carry me again. I'm not that heavy. He proved that last night. It'll be good exercise for him.

"Love you, Peyton."

"Love you too."

ABOUT FIFTEEN MINUTES later, I'm contemplating texting Brodee. I could holler, but I don't even know if he's inside. *Stop being such a baby and get up, Peyton.*

It's not without difficulty or pain, but I manage to get out of bed and make it out of my bedroom. As I stand at the top of the stairs, I think that going down can't be worse than coming up. It is. I consider sliding down the carpet on my butt, but I can hear Brodee strumming his guitar downstairs. If he catches me, he'll never let me live it down. So, I hobble down one step at a time, holding onto the railing, careful not to put too much pressure on either leg.

When I round the corner of the first set of stairs, I realize Brodee has stopped playing and is at the bottom with raised eyebrows. "I don't remember Nana coming with us this summer, but I guess I was wrong."

I peer down at him. "You like breathing, right?"

He laughs. "Let me help you." When he takes a step up, I stop him.

"You don't need to baby me. If I don't push through it, I'll only be stiffer. It's fine."

"So, I take it no surfing today." Brodee leans a shoulder against the wall and crosses his arms. It's such a casual move, and yet so sexy. *Sexy? Peyton!*

He gets the evil eye from me and laughs more.

"What are we going to do today with you like that?"

"We can still swim in the ocean. You can surf or skimboard. I'll just watch."

"Well, that's no fun."

"For today it'll have to be."

I still haven't made it all the way down the stairs. Just … I count the stairs in my head…five more steps. I wince.

Brodee doesn't stop chuckling. "I've never taken you for such a wimp."

"Have *you* ever tried horseback riding?"

He doesn't respond because he hasn't. I know he hasn't.

"Exactly."

"C'mon, Pete. At least hop on my back. I'll carry you around today. If I let you walk, we'll never get anywhere."

He's probably right. "Fine."

Brodee spends the rest of the morning helping me around the house, carrying me up and down the stairs, which really is much appreciated and kind of sweet, even if it makes me feel a little embarrassed. I know I'm not super heavy, but I think every girl feels uncomfortable when a guy knows exactly how heavy she is. Thankfully, he doesn't make me feel like I weigh a million pounds and never once fumbles when he's carrying me.

He helps me onto his back when we head outside and walks us down the boardwalk. It's more for his benefit than mine, because Brodee's too impatient to wait for my slow butt. This is also a bit more intimate because I'm only in board shorts and a bikini top, and he's only in his board shorts. We're skin to skin, my arms around his neck, my chin resting on his shoulder. I'm having trouble breathing. We've spent so much time at the beach I know every angle and curve of his body. There's no way he hasn't given me piggyback rides in our swimsuits before. This time is different, and I keep wondering if he feels it too.

Our afternoon is spent in the water. Thankfully, I feel weightless in the waves. We bob and float, dive and jump over waves. The only thing that doesn't occur is our pick-up line challenge. I can't think of a single one, and Brodee never mentions it; I'm not sure what that means.

When he skimboards, I lay out on the beach and let the sun dry the salt water on my skin. I watch him jump and ride the waves. When he spreads his towel out and lies down beside me, we joke and laugh and talk like we haven't all summer. Just Brodee and me. No distractions. No other friends. Nothing but the ocean and us. *This is how I wish every day was.*

The Day My Defenses Failed

AS SOON AS we walk onto Marcus's street, we hear the bass bumping from inside the house like it has its own heartbeat. The two of us walk up the mile-long driveway. It's a nice night, so Brodee and I decided to walk since Marcus is only a couple miles away. When we open the door, there are people everywhere. Where did all these people come from?

"Peyton!" Tyler throws his arm around my neck and pulls me to his side, planting a kiss on my temple. "Hey, gorgeous."

"Hi."

"I'm glad y'all made it. Hey, Brodee. Good to see you, man." He holds his hand up for a high-five, which Brodee reciprocates.

When Tyler opens his mouth to say something more, Marcus Surgett comes barreling through the entryway and nearly knocks Tyler over. I break away so I don't get caught up in their playful tussle.

"Dude." Tyler laughs and shoves him back. "Way to make an entrance."

"Just wanted to make sure you didn't miss me." Marcus grins, and his eyes go straight to me and my legs.

I am wearing a blue top and white shorts, but now I'm wishing I wasn't. "Seems to me that would be quite difficult," I say dryly.

"Same goes to you." His grin never falters. He's got 'flirt' written all over him. Always has. I can't remember a time that we have hung out where he hasn't hit on me. His dusty blonde hair is messily arranged on his head like he's been nervously tugging on it all night.

I find myself stepping closer to Brodee, then look to him and realize he's gone. "Where did Brodee go?" I ask, searching. It's a pretty open floor plan so I can see most of the rooms, but I don't see him anywhere.

"Huh?" Tyler looks around too.

Brodee was just here. How did I miss him taking off? Why didn't he say something?

"I don't know. Probably making the rounds to say hi to people."

Or doing his best to hide from Rylie.

"Let's get you something to drink," Tyler says, grabbing my hand, and guides me toward what I assume will be the kitchen.

I keep my eyes peeled for Brodee. When we pass through the living room I see him off to the side with Darren and Larson and some girls I don't recognize. They're really pretty. Tan, tall, good hair—a blonde, a brunette, and a red head. *Nice array to choose from, Brodee.* The girls are eyeing him, flirtatiously touching his arm and laughing at who knows what, but he only seems mildly interested. He's offering his half-smile, but not the cute one. It's the 'I'm only smiling because I'm trying to be polite' half-smile. A small sense of relief clings to me, and I want to ignore it. It doesn't matter who he smiles at. At least it shouldn't matter. But it does.

It really does.

Almost like he knows my eyes are boring into the side of his head, he looks my way, and his cute half-smile replaces the other, but there's something in Brodee's eyes I'm not completely familiar with. Disappointment? Hurt? *Did I do something wrong?* He almost looks annoyed. I raise my eyebrow in question, but he just smiles in return, ignoring my inquiring eyes. He's pulled back to their conversation when the brunette snatches his arm so he'll look at her. *Attention hog.*

Tyler keeps me pressed against his chest as we make our rounds, chatting with a bunch of people I've never seen before. Occasionally he kisses my cheek or the top of my head throughout our conversations like it's the most normal thing. Like we've always been a couple. And I have to think to myself, am I still with him for the summer because I actually like him that much? Or am I with him because it's the way it's always been?

My eyes drift over the sea of people to see who else is here and land on Brodee again. It's not as though I was seeking him out, but my eyes always know where to find him. His spine-tingling smile is spread across his face as he continues to talk to the attention hogs.

I take a minute to look at him while he's not paying attention. His brown hair looks like he styled it with eggbeaters tonight, and somehow he still makes it look good. Brodee's only wearing khakis, a white T-shirt, and flip-flops, but it's my favorite. He doesn't need to dress up to look good. He always looks good.

How much do I really like Tyler? Am I stringing him along now?

Tyler keeps referring to the future as 'we' and 'us'. Have we officially reached the 'us' status, where I'm not longer a 'me' and he's not longer a 'him'? When did I agree to this?

The future sinks in more and more—cementing how different life will be in the coming months. I'm not sure how ready I am for that change. Rather than Brodee and I going to parties and hanging out with people, I'll be with Tyler.

As I look at Tyler while he talks to Darren and Marcus, I take him in. His model status looks and perfect laugh that verges on overly practiced. His tan skin and light brown hair with sun-bleached tips. And that jawline with a faint shadow of facial hair. It's perfection. I listen to his topics of conversation that I don't care much about. Football and his workout regimen. Granted, they asked since he's doubled in size from last summer, and Darren wanted to know his secret, but I realize…I don't care. Even if it's not a topic I know much about or have interest in, shouldn't I care a little bit because it's what he loves?

Why am I with him?

Tyler has to leave early—work at 7:00 in the morning.

"Dang responsibilities." He smiles and kisses me goodbye. I don't care as much as I should that he's leaving.

That should be my answer, shouldn't it?

With Brodee acting especially pouty and distant, after Tyler leaves, I go in search of him and find him sitting alone on the beach out back. I plop down beside him on the sand.

"This party is such a drag," I say jokingly and nudge his shoulder with mine.

He lifts a small smirk in return, but stares back at the black ocean without responding. I nearly start twiddling my thumbs, trying to think of something to say to make him laugh, or figure out who peed in his cheerios.

"Are you ready to head back home?" I ask.

He pauses. I almost think he's about to give me the silent treatment when he says, "Yeah. Let's get out of here," and gets to his feet.

We decide to take the beach route back. Brodee isn't any more talkative than when we were at the party. I thought maybe it wasn't any fun for him, but he's not acting any different now that the party is just noise in the distance. So, maybe he is mad at me.

"You okay?" I hesitantly ask.

He shrugs and nods, but it's so subtle I almost don't catch it.

"You sure about that?" I press. Holding my sandals in one hand, I bump his shoulder with my other.

"I just didn't picture our last summer panning out this way." His eyes remain forward as we walk.

"What way do you mean?"

Brodee silently sighs. "You and I barely getting any time together as just us. We've been hanging out with Harper and Skylar, our family, and the other Hatteras gang. You've also been spending a lot of time with Tyler. In August, we're going in different directions, and who knows when we'll get another chance to do this again. If ever. Our lives will be so unpredictable. Doesn't that bother you?"

"Of course it does," I scoff. How could he not know that? I've been trying so hard to get ready for what life will be like without him. I wanted Brodee to notice me this summer, but now, more than anything, I want to be able to see myself without him, knowing I can survive without him. And I think I can. But each time it hits me that I won't get to see him every day, I feel like I can't breathe. It hurts to breathe. I don't want to think of life without him. But that's reality. Hatteras is a dream.

"You don't act like it," he mumbles, shoving his hands in his front pockets.

I stop on the shore, trying to figure him out, trying to understand where this is coming from. "You don't think I think about the future and you not being in it with me? Brodee. Do you know me at all?"

He stops when he realizes I have and faces me a few feet away.

How do I put this into words that won't make me sound like I'm crazy in love with him? Because I'm not. I can't be.

Am I?

"I've been trying so hard to detach myself from you, to move forward so that I'm prepared for when we won't see each other every day. We've hardly had a day apart in the last eighteen years. I think about you at Duke and me at USC, and it makes me wish that my grades were good enough, that my mom could afford a school like that just so I could go with you. I don't want to go a day without you."

Brodee's mouth slowly opens, perplexed. I failed. My heart is painted across the sand between us in streaks of red, trailing from my chest. He's attempting to figure out the underlying meaning, wondering if there is any. There is. I'm hoping I can play it off as a best friend missing a best friend, but he knows me better than anyone else. He'll call my bluff.

"You're my best friend, Peyton," he utters.

"I know." He doesn't have to remind me or rub it in to make it clear. I know that's all we are. "And you're mine."

"I just—" he motions between us. "I don't want to mess this up."

"It's just different colleges, Brodee. I remind myself of that all the time. We can still see each other on weekends and holidays, between semesters. We're not going to colleges across the United States. We're only a few hours away from each other."

"That's not what—" he pauses and shakes his head. He mumbles something that I can't hear and looks out to the ocean.

"What's not what?"

"Nothing."

"Stop doing that. Say what you want to say," I demand, taking a step toward him. "I'm tired of us not saying what's on our minds. We've always been honest with each other, but I feel like we've been anything but this summer."

"I was going to say that's not what I meant. I thought you—"

When he doesn't continue, I wait. I'm not going to try and interpret what he means. He needs to explain himself. I'm not a mind reader. I can only hope he means what I want him to mean. This is now a stand off. Whoever speaks next loses or wins; however you want to look at it. So, I wait and hold his gaze.

"Say it," I finally plea.

"Peyton." He says my name breathlessly, questioning. I want him to just know. Or forget what I said. Whatever way will make this situation less awkward. His pause extends. I hold my breath.

He takes two long strides until we're only inches apart. He hesitates for a second. When I don't step back, he takes my face in his hands. There's the briefest hesitation and then he kisses me. I gasp into his mouth and he deepens the kiss, infiltrating my mouth, infiltrating me. I am a city under attack, and my defenses have failed. He wins.

I wanted him to win so badly.

Instinctively, I drop my sandals, and my arms wrap around his neck, tugging him closer, as close as he can get. And it's still not enough.

Truth or dare comes rushing back to me, but this kiss is so different. He's not learning my lips. He owns them, like they were never mine. I suppose they never were. My lips were made to kiss his. Be his. How could I not know that? It's always been him.

"I'm still here," he says against my lips. "Don't leave me while I'm still here."

My breathing is unsteady. My heart is racing. My mind is jumbled. I blink up at him, waiting for clarification. *What just happened?*

"You just kissed me," I whisper. My arms are still laced around his neck, holding him in place. "You weren't dared to."

He releases a throaty chuckle and shakes his head. "And you kissed me back."

As if my mouth doesn't know how to function without his anymore, I press it back against his. I no longer want to remember what it was like to not kiss Brodee Fisher.

"What took you so long?" I utter between kisses. *What took* me *so long?*

"I didn't know. I figured it out too late. I'm an idiot." He pulls back and brushes the back of his hand against my cheek. "I didn't want to lose you."

I bite my lip to keep from grinning like a fool. "You're my best friend. Losing me isn't an option."

"Why didn't you say something?"

"Probably the same reason you didn't," I say. "Our friendship means everything to me. I didn't want things to be different or ruin us. But this summer, something changed. I think we both felt it the moment we kissed at Rylie's."

"Yeah." He nods. I'm so glad I'm not alone in this. My heart sings. His eyes travel around my face, taking everything in. "Things will definitely change. They're going to be better."

So many questions swirl inside my head. We're in uncharted territory. How long has he felt this way? Where do we go from here? "How are we going to make this work?" I ask.

That question scares me more than anything. "Let's not worry about that right now."

"We've got the rest of the summer," I agree. "That's what matters."

"Tyler gets USC," Brodee mutters.

"You get Hatteras."

Brodee knows.

Hatteras is everything.

The Day He Never Glanced Back

HARPER SQUEALS IN my ear.

I could hardly sleep last night, thinking about what happened, so when a phone call from *Harper* is what wakes *me* up—a first—she knows something is going on.

"Shhh…you're screaming in my ear." I chuckle.

"Peyton-Parker, it's eleven o'clock. You should not be this tired."

"What?" I sit straight up and look at the alarm clock on the nightstand. 11:03 AM. I can't remember the last time I slept in that late. Maybe never.

"Obviously, you were having some nice dreams." I can imagine her suggestive eyebrow wiggle. "I wouldn't want to wake up either."

I groan. "You cannot make a big deal out of this, Harp. I don't want Brodee to regret it. Oh gosh. What if he regrets it? What if he woke up this morning and second-guessed the kiss?"

"Chill out. I'm sure he's downstairs waiting for you. He's already talked to Skylar this morning. Why do you think I called you?"

"He did? What did Brodee tell him? Was he acting weird? Did he say he regretted it? What does Skylar know?"

Harper laughs at me. I can hear myself. This isn't me. *Take a chill pill, Peyton.* I take a deep breath. Then bolt out of bed to throw on some clothes and brush my teeth.

Harper continues her amusement. "I've never heard you like this before. I like it."

"Like what?"

"Flustered."

I roll my eyes. "He could tell me he regrets it. If he does, I have to keep my cool. This cannot ruin us, okay? You have to help me. Help me be rational, Harp."

"Oh em gee, Peyton. You need to *calm* down." Harper chuckles. "It's going to be fine."

"Yes. Yes, it will," I attempt to reassure myself. My nerves are haywire. It's not working.

"What are you going to do about Tyler?" she asks, and the whole situation comes into view like a panoramic picture.

That nauseating, sinking feeling sets in my stomach. I hate hurting people. I especially hate hurting people who don't deserve it.

"I need to talk to him. Brodee and I don't know where this will go, but I can't be with Tyler."

"Obviously," she says dryly. "You and Brodee didn't talk about it last night?"

"There wasn't much talking going on last night."

"I bet there wasn't." Her innuendo makes me sigh.

I pause and reconsider my phrasing. "We're not talking about the future."

"Living in the now."

"I can't think past that."

"Well, maybe you should slap on some mascara and chapstick and head downstairs to face your Now."

I take a deep breath. "Right. I'll call you later."

"You better!"

I begin to jog down the stairs, but I don't want to appear too eager, so I take a deep breath and slow my pace. By the time I reach the last step I feel like I'm moving in slow motion. Brodee is sitting on the couch, feet propped up on the ottoman, flipping through the channels.

When he sees me, his feet immediately meet the floor and he sits forward on the edge of the couch, setting the remote beside him. He slowly stands, not taking his eyes off me. I can't read him yet. This could go either way. He's not smiling, but neither am I. First, I want to know last night meant the same to him as it did to me.

When it's quiet for too long I cave. "Hey."

"Hi." There's his heart-stopping smile. I take a breath, but I don't move. I want him to say more. *Gosh, I don't want this to be awkward.*

"I was wondering when you'd wake up," he says. "I almost came up."

"Why didn't you?"

"I don't know."

Silence. We stand. We stare. We don't move.

"Screw it," he says under his breath and strides toward me. His arms are around my waist, and his mouth is on mine in seconds. My smile can't be stifled. He kisses my teeth.

Brodee laughs. "Sorry. I didn't want to wait any longer."

"You made a good decision." I bite my lip to stop my silly grin.

"It feels so good to finally be able to do that."

"Yeah?" The smile can't be suppressed any longer. "How long? Before truth or dare?"

"Oh yeah."

"Really?" The flutters are rampant in my stomach. "Are we talking weeks? Months? Days?"

"Years. Two or three give or take."

My eyes grow wide.

His throaty chuckle sends my heart into overdrive. "I'm a guy, Pete. I'm dumb, not blind." I laugh. "I didn't want to ruin us for one kiss. It just took me too long to realize it was more than just a kiss I wanted." I press my lips to his again and dive my fingers into his hair.

"*Finally.*"

Brodee and I jump apart. Carter walks from the stairs toward the back doors with a cheeky smirk. "I can't believe it took you guys *this* long." And then he's out the sliding glass door, closing it behind him.

We laugh. My face is hot. I cover my cheeks, wishing my hands were ice packs.

"Guess the secret's out," Brodee says.

"Where are our parents?" Suddenly, I'm mindful of our out-in-the-open affection and look around downstairs like they're hiding, spying on us.

"On the beach," he says, tugging me back to him and kissing me. I don't want him to stop, but…

I pull away just enough so that our lips don't touch. "Before we do anything more, I really need to talk to Tyler."

He groans his consent. "This is going to be awkward, isn't it?"

"Yup," I reply. "And we'll never hear the end of it from Rylie."

"Screw her. I don't even care anymore. She can think whatever she wants. We didn't do anything wrong."

I agree. "Tyler's working right now, and I don't want to do this over the phone, so we just need to slow it down a bit until I talk to him."

Brodee doesn't look too happy about that, but he gets it. We unhurriedly break apart. We have years to make up for and only a little over a month to do it.

I wait for guilt to set in, but it doesn't. Not in the way it probably should. I don't feel bad about kissing Brodee. I feel bad about giving Tyler hope for a future, for pursuing something I wasn't fully committed to. But I can't, would never, take back this chance we have. Hopefully, Tyler and I can remain friends, but something tells me he won't want to be.

MRS. HAMILTON ANSWERS the door. When she sees me, her face lights up. "Oh, hi Peyton. It's so good to finally see you!"

"You too." I smile, though uncomfortably.

Mrs. Hamilton is the epitome of class. Even though we're at the beach, it looks like she just left the salon. Her light blonde hair rests effortlessly on top of her shoulders, flipping out at the ends. And her entire outfit is probably J. Crew or Lilly Pulitzer. She has better taste than I do. That's for sure.

"Come, come." She opens the door wider. "Tyler was just washing up.

He should be down in a minute."

"Okay." I wring my hands and drop them to my sides to keep myself from fidgeting.

I don't know why I'm so nervous. It's not like we're in some serious relationship. It's not a legit break up. Just two people not kissing anymore. We're not that close. Right? *I'm lying to myself.* It's more than that. I know it. Tyler wants more. I wanted more.

I thought I wanted more.

I've never broken someone's heart before. Not to say I think so much of myself that he'll be heartbroken, but if I do, I'm well acquainted with what it feels like. I don't want to be the heartbreaker.

"I just need to pop dinner in the oven." Mrs. Hamilton says as she leads me into the kitchen. She grabs the big roasting pot on the island and pushes it into the oven behind her. "Tyler says you'll be attending USC in the fall as well. That's just wonderful. It's such a fabulous school."

"Yeah. I'm excited," I lie.

"I know Tyler is very excited you'll be there." She looks knowingly at me. A twinkle in her pale blue eyes. Maybe it's a hereditary gene. "You two will have so much fun together. I can't wait to hear all about your adventures."

I'm a horrible person.

And then I hear Tyler jogging down the stairs. *Saved.* When I turn, he's striding toward me with a big grin on his face. *Or not.* My stomach drops, but I try to smile. I worry it looks more like a grimace. His arms loop around my waist as he picks me off my feet in a bear hug.

"Hey you." He squeezes.

"Hi," I say breathlessly because I'm literally having a difficult time getting air into my lungs.

"Your ears must have been burning," Mrs. Hamilton says.

He puts me back down. "What was she saying about me? Don't listen to a thing she says." Tyler walks over and slings his arm around his mom's shoulder. "She's a liar."

She smacks his chest and chuckles. "Oh stop."

Seeing them stand side by side makes me realize where he got his height, and it definitely wasn't his mom. He towers over her. Her petite frame barely comes to his chest.

"We were just talking about y'all going to USC," she explains. "And what a wonderful time you two will have."

Tyler nods, and his eyes trail to me. "Ah. Yes. We'll have *such* a wonderful time." He mimics her voice.

"Knock it off." Mrs. Hamilton laughs and slaps his chest again.

I need to talk to him now. Like right now. "You want to go for a walk?" I ask.

He kisses the top of her head. "We'll be back, Ma."

He takes my hand and tugs me toward the back door that leads to the beach.

"Peyton, you're welcome to stay for dinner. We'd love to have you."

I don't have the heart to tell her no. Tyler can explain it all. "Okay. Thank you, Mrs. Hamilton."

"Please. Call me Claire."

I pause and clear my throat. "Thank you, Miss Claire."

Once we're on his deck, the door shut behind us, he asks, "Is everything okay? You seem off." Tyler steps in front of me and loops his arms around my waist, tugging me against his body.

My hands press against his pecs to put some distance between us, but I drop them instantly when I realize how intimate that feels. "Umm…" I say to his chest because I can't meet his eyes yet.

"That doesn't sound good." He loosens his hold and drops his arms to his sides.

It's almost worse that he knows it's coming. "I know. I'm sorry," I mumble. "You know these last few summers have meant so much to me. We've had a lot of good times. Umm…but I think we need to put the brakes on this now." *Put the brakes on? You mean slam the dang brakes and never take the foot off.*

My eyes lift up and up to meet his. I was right. Looking at him makes this so much harder. The hurt hidden there is more than I was expecting. *Why can't this be easy?*

"Oh." Tyler blinks and he runs his fingers through his hair, taking a step back. "Okay." His shoulders sag in defeat. "Right…" he breathes.

Tyler is perfect. Just not perfect for me. But that doesn't mean I'm okay with hurting him. "Tyler, I'm sorr—"

"No, Peyton." He lifts his hands almost in surrender, stepping farther away from me. "It's fine. I don't need an apology." I don't know what else to say, so I watch him put everything together, letting the pieces fall where they may. "Do I at least get an explanation? Did I come on too strong? Did I scare you with all the talk of USC? We can slow it down. Just see where this goes."

He deserves so much more than an explanation. And it's not like he won't see Brodee and me together at some point. I swallow back the lump of tears. I don't have the right to cry.

"No. This isn't your fault at all. I haven't been fair to you." I lick my lips nervously, reining in the courage to tell him the truth. "I thought if I just liked you enough, everything would fall into place, and I could move forward in a relationship. I thought we could be happy. And you have made me happy. I just..."

"Just say it, Peyton. I can't take it," he says stoically.

"I have feelings for someone else."

He nods and looks to the ground like he knew that's what I was going to say. The knots in my stomach coil tighter. Why does this have to be so hard? In the grand scheme of things, this will be a blip, but right now it feels so much bigger.

"Brodee," Tyler says his name with such certainty, no room for question.

I suck in a breath. "How did you know?" Gosh, that's a stupid question. I regret it the instant it leaves my lips. It's not as though I spend time with any other guy. Everyone has been speculating for years. Of course, it's Brodee.

Tyler's sad eyes peer back into mine. "Give me a little credit, would you, Peyton? No one pays attention to you more than I do. I've seen the way you look at him when you don't think anyone's watching. Or maybe you're just so lost in your own world that nobody else matters...but I see that look in your eyes. I've seen it in his too."

I look at Brodee differently? And Tyler saw it? Brodee looks at me differently?

"You look at him like you'd be content looking at him and only him for the rest of your life. But you've always been so adamant that nothing was going on. I thought maybe I was misinterpreting it." He pauses. "Deep down I knew I didn't stand a chance, but at least I tried, right?"

I open my mouth to respond, but all that comes out is air. I hate that I hurt Tyler. He was never meant to get hurt in any of this. This wasn't supposed to happen this way. I've wanted Brodee, but not at the expense of Tyler's feelings.

"Nothing has been going on, just so you know. Last night, after the party, it sort of clicked. The last thing I want is for you to think we've been going behind your back all this time. Rylie has never been right. We haven't. I promise you." He needs to believe me. "I never would've started anything with you if there was something going on."

Tyler nods and looks away. Pauses. "I don't want this to end with you thinking I'm bitter or feel betrayed." I attempt to interrupt, but he holds up his hand. "Let me say this. I don't want any regrets."

"Okay," I concede. I stand with my arms hanging at my sides, unsure where to put my hands if they can't find solace in his.

"Yeah, this began as a fling, and I was hoping it would grow to be something more... Maybe someday it will..." He's still holding out hope. He quietly sighs, and my heart clenches. "But you've made my summers so much better. We've made memories that I'll always remember. Thank you for that."

I don't know what to say so I hug him. I hug him as tightly as my arms will go. Even though I know this is what needs to happen, I feel so bad. I know he probably doesn't want to hug me, but I selfishly need this, and I'm taking it. He finally brings his arms around me, hugging me back, but it already feels like goodbye. His touch isn't the same. It's filled with sadness. *Can a hug feel sad?*

I ruined this. Everything that we built over the summers is ruined. Tyler lets go of me suddenly and won't look me in the eyes.

"Bye, Peyton." He walks back into his house without even one glance back.

The Day We Created Something Better

WHEN I WAS little, before my dad taught me how to surf my summers away, I spent my days on the shore with him building drip castles. Hours and hours were put into crafting fortresses with spherical towers and drawbridges and moats. We'd make them far up on the shore so the waves couldn't wash them away.

For good measure, I'd ask my dad to build a tall, protective wall between the ocean and our masterpieces, so the castles would remain for the summer. But every morning when I'd wake up and run out onto the beach to check on the castle we'd created the day before, the waves had always taken away all our hard work.

When I'd run back inside with tears streaming down my face, he'd say, "Peyton Jane, there's beauty in a new beginning. It brings the opportunity to create something more, something better."

I was too young to understand the deeper meaning I'm sure he was intending, but it brought me small comfort knowing I had him to create something better with. He'd always be there.

At least I thought he would.

TODAY, I SIT on the shore with a bucket of sand and water, holding my fist above the sand, drizzling the mixture back and forth to build the base of a castle. This time I have Brodee with me. He's got crazy, ambitious ideas and is excitedly running up and down the beach in search of driftwood and shells that he can use to build "the biggest, coolest drip castle there ever was." I smile.

I'm creating something better with him now.

IT'S HARD TO keep myself from touching Brodee all throughout dinner. I have urges to kiss his cheek, to take his hand in mine. I want to rest my head on his shoulder and feel his arm around my waist. How did we ever function before?

He keeps giving me secretive sideways glances that I can't help but reciprocate. My foot brushes against his, and his toes curl around mine. I discreetly nudge his shoulder, and he nudges me back. With one hand, Brodee eats. With his other, he squeezes my thigh and keeps his hand there for the remainder of the meal, drawing doodles on the inside of my leg. I realize now he knew exactly what he was doing on the ride up here.

"There's something different about you two tonight," Tatum says, pointing at Brodee and me with her fork. He subtly takes his hand back into his lap.

We share a look. *Are we that obvious? Do we tell them?* It's not like we'll be able to keep it a secret for the rest of the summer when we're all in the same house.

"They kissed," Carter outs us.

"Thanks, Carter," Brodee says dryly.

He smiles while finishing his last bite. "I'm here to help."

"You *kissed*?" My mom is the first one to comment as her fork drops on her plate with a clink.

"We're going to need new house rules," Nick says authoritatively.

"Oh c'mon," Tatum interjects. "They've resisted doing anything stupid for the first eighteen years of their lives. I think we can trust them. Besides, they're old enough. If we can't trust them now, we never will."

"How long has this been going on?" Mom asks. She seems dumbfounded. *Aren't parents supposed to be the intuitive ones?*

I answer, "Just…since…the other day." I peer over at Brodee beside me. He smiles like we're the only two in the room. I wish we were.

"But you're going to different colleges. This has 'bad idea' written all over it," Nick says, massaging his chin, and sighs heavily. "What do you two plan to do?"

Of course, Nick has to make it about the college.

"Don't worry, Dad," Brodee appeases him. "I'm still going to Duke, and Peyton is still going to USC."

"So, you're going to have a long distance relationship?" Mom pries, anxious.

Why the third degree?

"Well, we haven't really talked about it." I look between the three parents. "We're still trying to figure out what this is." Brodee takes my hand under the table and squeezes. It makes me feel better.

"Long distance relationships are really difficult," Mom says, like we don't know that already. "I hope you two are thinking this through."

"There's only a month left in the summer," Nick backs my mom. "Don't let this cloud your judgment. You two have so much going for you. Don't mess it up."

Tatum comes to our defense again. "Okay, okay. That's enough. This isn't the end of the world. Let the kids just be kids for the summer. They'll figure it out when the time comes."

I thank Tate with my eyes. She smiles like she has a secret.

I hadn't realized what a family affair this would become. Brodee and I kissed. We're not engaged. I'm not pregnant. This shouldn't be huge news.

"I think it's cool," Carter chimes in as he pushes away from the table with his dinner plate. "Peyton could finally officially be my sister."

Nick chokes on his water. Tatum laughs. And my mom looks like she can't breathe.

"What did I say? It's not like we weren't all thinking it." Carter walks up the stairs like Brodee and I getting married is no big deal. "We're basically family anyway. Might as well make it official. I thought it was kind of inevitable."

"Well, let's not get ahead of ourselves," Tatum says. "You two still have a long way to go."

Brodee and I look at each other with open mouths. Neither of us knows how to respond. "We kissed," I answer for us. "You guys are the ones getting ahead of yourselves."

She chuckles. "Right."

"Good," Nick says.

And then Brodee and I get up from the table as fast as we can to escape before anything else is said. I can imagine my mom saying, *I'm too young to be a grandmother.*

"CAN YOU BELIEVE them?" I laugh. We leave our flip-flops on the boardwalk and head down the shoreline hand-in-hand. "Had I known they were going to react like that, I would have done everything in my power to keep this a secret."

"Ooo…secret lovers." Brodee stops me and grabs my waist. He kisses me once. Twice. "I like the sound of forbidden lovers. We can always pretend."

I playfully smack his chest. "We might not have to pretend. I have a feeling this is going to take them some getting used to. *I'm* still trying to get used to it."

"Really? Maybe that just means we need to do more of this." His hands run up the side of my body to hold my face. This kiss is slower than all the rest. Brodee takes his time, as patient as he is with the waves. He delves his tongue into my mouth, but it's so tender. His tongue tells me all that he never did before.

"I could definitely get used to kissing you every day for the rest of our lives."

My stomach jumps. "Brodee..."

He shakes his head, his lips brushing mine back and forth. "We don't have to go there yet. Just kiss me."

And so I do.

The Day He Became a Magician

"I'M NO ORGAN donor, but I'd be happy to give you my heart."

Brodee and I walk hand-in-hand through town with our ice cream cones. The only place the surf was any good was up in Kill Devil, and we didn't feel like driving all the way up there today. Instead, we decided to take the ferry to Ocracoke Island this morning and walk along the beach for new scenery. We talked. We laughed. We soaked in every minute together. After the ferry dropped us back off on Hatteras, we stayed in town.

"Do you have a sunburn or are you always this hot?" I lick my chocolate ice cream cone, staring at him from under my eyelashes.

He tugs on his bottom lip and smiles at me. "Where do you hide your wings?"

"Are you calling me an angel?" I give Brodee a flirtatious side-glance. "Or an insect?"

"Hmm…so I take it that was a pick-up line fail."

I nod once with laughter in my eyes and take another lick. "Nice try."

I continue, "If you were a triangle, you'd be acute one."

Brodee doesn't shoot back another line right away. He just watches me with a subtle smile as we walk. "You're so beautiful you made me forget my pick-up line."

I tug on his hand, stopping us on the sidewalk, and pull him to me so I can kiss him. Tilting my face to him, we meet in the middle. It wasn't meant to be more than a peck, but I can't help melding into him the moment our lips meet. I sharply inhale when he breathes a possessive grunt and takes my bottom lip between his teeth. *I think I love you.*

"I knew I was right."

Brodee and I jump apart, startled by the voice. Rylie eyes us with a satisfied but crestfallen expression. Perfect timing. She's the last person I want to see right now. Brandi is standing beside her, shifting her uncomfortable gaze between Rylie and us.

Brodee sighs heavily like he was waiting for this to happen and feels the same way I do. He doesn't want to deal with her. The last thing I want is to hear is an 'I told you so' from Rylie. Even if Brodee and I didn't have anything going on before, I think deep down we always knew we could someday become something, even if we didn't think it or say it aloud.

"You caught us, Rylie," Brodee says wryly. "Secret's out of the bag."

"What did I tell you, Peyton? You're the worst kind of competition." Rylie's tone isn't at all condescending like I expect it to be. She sounds like she didn't want to be right. My heart aches a little for her. She really does like Brodee. It should make me want to lift my fists in the air and shout 'I win,' but it was never a competition. And she's trying to cover up the hurt, but isn't doing a very good job. I'm not her. I won't gloat.

"But how will you guys last? You guys are going to separate colleges," Brandi says, as if we're unaware of this fact.

"That is true," Brodee says slowly like it's hitting him for the first time, and he squeezes my hand once in his.

"What are you going to do?" Brandi asks like it's her business. She's not being nosey. She honestly doesn't understand what would possess us to take this kind of risk now. "You broke things off with Tyler so you could be with someone you won't even see every day?" Brandi has never been good at being tactful.

At that moment, Tyler and Larson walk out of the marina store that we're stopped in front of, holding two drinks. I cringe. This just keeps getting better and better. Though I knew seeing him was inevitable, I was hoping we'd be able to avoid him longer. He stops in his tracks when he sees us all standing together.

Almost instantly his demeanor changes. "What's up, guys?" He lifts a smile, showing his pearly whites. Either he's really good at faking a smile or he's genuinely happy to see us. Something tells me he's really good at faking a smile. "Here," he says, handing Rylie a fountain drink. After Larson gives Brandi a drink, he does a guy handshake thing with Brodee.

We can hardly get through the awkward small talk fast enough. When we say our goodbyes, Rylie laces her fingers through Tyler's as they all walk away. It makes me wonder if it's a tactic or if they're riding the end of the summer fling.

That was quick. Okay, so I'm not really *that* surprised. Rylie is definitely an opportunist.

"Well, that was fun," I say when they're out of earshot.

"I honestly thought it was going to be worse. I half expected Tyler to be a fighter. I really didn't want to have to give his pretty face a black eye."

I nudge Brodee's shoulder and chuckle. Like he could give Tyler a black eye. But I don't dare say that out loud.

"So, you're the worst kind of competition, huh?" I was hoping he wouldn't bring that up.

"Apparently."

"What did she mean by that?"

I roll my eyes. "It's kind of embarrassing."

"I like embarrassing."

Groaning, I answer, "When you and Harper were pretending to date, Rylie cornered me on the beach, and we had a little heart-to-heart."

"Uh-oh. What did she say to you?"

"Just some stuff about you and then said I'm the worst kind of competition because I'm 'The One.'" I use air quotes and laugh at the ridiculousness of her insinuation.

"Why is that so funny?" Brodee looks at me seriously.

It's hard for me to answer him when his eyes hold no humor. "Just... because it sounds so...I dunno ..."

"So, while Brandi doesn't think we'll make it because of our college choices, Rylie thinks we're the real deal."

"Yeah." I chuckle mostly to myself. "Crazy, right?"

Brodee's expression stays earnest, the most sincere look in his green eyes. "I don't think it's that crazy."

It takes me a second to say something. I'm not ready for this talk. It's only been a week.

"Brodee, we've been avoiding this for a reason. I think you and I both know how this will play out at the end of the summer. Let's not go there yet."

He nods. I can tell he doesn't want to think about it either.

"Let's just forget about everyone else. Stop focusing on what will happen and do what we came out here to do. Savor the summer. So we go to different colleges. So what?" I shrug. "Things will work out, Brodee. No one knows us like we do." I kiss him, hoping my pep talk will rub off on me. "We'll always come back to each other."

He throws his arm over my shoulder and draws me to his side. He kisses my hair and we walk toward his Patriot.

"Are you a magician? Because whenever I look at you, everyone else disappears," I say.

"Did you fart, cause you just blew me away," he responds.

I die. I can't stop laughing. "Gross!"

"C'mon," he says, laughing with me. "It's funny."

The Day We Sang in the Rain

A FEW DAYS later it begins to rain, and it doesn't stop. We've been stuck in the house for two days straight with nothing but *Singin' In The Rain* on repeat. My mom's a sucker for a good classic. When I tried to turn it off, I thought she was going to decapitate me.

While the Fishers have all sought shelter in their rooms—including Brodee who has been up in his room spending his time studying who knows what—I've stayed downstairs with my mom. I think I have every word memorized now. I'm *this* close to crashing his study session.

I have a feeling being cooped up isn't any easier for my mom. Idle time equals idle thoughts, which transform into a wandering mind that takes her to places she doesn't want to go. Today is a bad day for Mom. While the movie has been on she's done nothing but clean.

I do my best to stay out of her way, but stay close by in case she needs me. I've nestled myself into a chair in the corner near the large window facing the beach. It's surprising how quickly time flies when watching rain trickle down glass, and how mesmerizing the droplets are as they tap the surface of the ocean. Plunk, plunk, plunk. The sound alone induces a trance. Pitter-patter, pitter-patter. Hours could pass by, and I wouldn't even know it. Today my time is measured by scenes and how many times I've seen them. It's the fourth time I've seen "Make 'Em Laugh," so I know it's probably around three o'clock. I've yet to hear her laugh.

I stare longingly at the ocean. My mom and Tatum won't let Brodee and me surf when the weather is this bad. Not that the waves would be any good. They're too choppy. But still. I'd take anything over being cooped up for one more day.

Around six, I'm lying on the couch with a book when Brodee finally comes traipsing down the stairs.

He nods at the TV. "Still watching *Singin' In The Rain*, I see."

Gene Kelly is swinging around a lamppost as we speak and twirling his umbrella. I whisper so she can't hear me from the next room. "In some strange way, I think it's comforting to my mom. I don't know why."

"Come play in the rain with me."

"Seriously?" He nods. Even if it means heavy, wet clothes, I'll take anything over staying inside for one more minute. "All right."

"DO YOU KNOW what my shirt is made of?" Brodee flicks his wet sleeves as he walks backward down the beach. His soaked white T-shirt is suctioned to his chest. "Boyfriend material," he finishes.

I roll my eyes, but he gets a good laugh out of me. "I may not be a genie, but I can make your dreams come true," I say.

We share a look and agree, "Yeah. Okay. You won," I rel

"C'MERE, PETE. DANCE with me." He grabs my hands and swings me around. He spins us in circles as he bounces around like a five year old with too much sugar in his system.

I feel infinite. We're the only ones in Hatteras. We own this cape and this rain is ours. Anything is possible.

I chuckle until he tugs me closer. Faintly, Brodee sings in my ear as he sways us back and forth. Only a note or two is off key. He doesn't really know the words, so he fills in the gaps with humming. I'm not sure what awful dance moves he was thinking about before because nothing about this is awful.

All at once, I feel myself falling. Or flying. I feel feather-light—as if I could blow away, soaring high into the sky. I would be content riding his tune in the wind forever.

Brodee whispers the end of the song, tapering off. No words, just 'do, do, do, do.' The moment is ending. I think I might be falling in love. *How will I recover? How am I supposed to look at him the same?*

As soon as he pulls back, he peers at me with the rain dripping off the tips of his eyelashes. They bunch together into soft peaks. I brush the back of my fingers across them. I'm not sure why. My fingers are just as soaked. I want to touch him. He blinks and leans in. I meet him halfway. The tips of my fingers graze his jawline. He smiles.

Kissing in the rain is a much better way to spend our time than singing. Maybe I'll change the words.

I'm kissing in the rain.

Just kissing in the rain.

What a glorious feelin'.

I'm happy again.

Yup. It works.

He pushes away with a goofy grin. "Now you can't say I never danced with you." He's jogging backward away from me. "Race you back to the house!" And then he takes off.

Oh, no you don't.

I bolt after him, determined to win.

The Day He Wasn't Going to be a Rock Star

THE RAIN DECIDES to give us a break after three days. *Finally.* We'd be flooded here if it hadn't stopped. Brodee and his parents needed to get out of the house, so they take the night to go out as a family and grab dinner. My mom and I stay at the beach house for a girls' night in. We ordered enough Chinese for an army.

Mom grabs the nail polish and suggests pedicures. It takes some persuading, but finally I convince her to let us watch *Dan In Real Life* instead of *Singin' In The Rain* while we do our nails.

While the movie quietly plays in the background, Mom starts talking as though I asked her a question.

"It was our first summer at the beach house." Her voice is soft, solemn. "You probably don't remember. The Fishers didn't come—the one and only summer—because of prior family obligations that they couldn't get out of. You were four, and the rain hadn't stopped for a week." A reminiscent smile traces her lips as she stares forward, yet to make eye contact with me. "We were running out of options to entertain a four year old. Back then we didn't have the Internet or even cable in the house, so we couldn't turn on cartoons for you. Our movie collection wasn't what it is now. Your father figured there wasn't a better movie to watch than *Singin' In The Rain*, so he drove across town in search of it for me. He had to drive all the way to Avon, but he finally found it." She chuckles behind her hand.

"We didn't leave the house once that day. You kept singing and dancing for us—wouldn't let us turn the movie off. So, it played on repeat for the rest of the day. It was the best day out of the whole summer." Tears fill her eyes and she swallows.

It all makes sense.

"You've never told me that story before."

"I nearly forgot about it until the rain started," she talks through her tears, but she smiles and peers over at me.

I whisper, "I miss him too."

On an exhale, she whispers back, "I know, baby."

"We can watch it again if you want."

She shakes her head with a sad smile.

I've been preparing for this all summer. I knew the breakdown was coming. We've been avoiding the heartache for so long, but neither of us can pretend any longer. He's not here with us when he should be.

Mom takes me into her arms, and I cry on her shoulder like I've done so many times before over failed tests and rejection letters and broken hearts. She kisses the top of my head, resting her head there and says what she always does. "It's all going to be okay, Peyton. You'll see. We're going to be okay."

This time, her reassurance doesn't comfort me because if my mom doesn't get a happily ever after, how can anything be okay? How could I ever deserve one?

ON MY WAY to bed after the movie ends, I hear Brodee softly playing his guitar, so I knock on his bedroom door.

"Yeah?" I hear him say.

I peek inside to see Brodee sitting on the edge of the mattress with his guitar resting on his lap. "Just wanted to say good night." I smile.

"Come in," he says, tilting his head to the side, encouraging me in.

I secure the door behind me. "I thought maybe you'd be asleep, but I saw your light on."

"Yeah, I'm not quite tired enough yet." His fingers toy with the strings on his guitar, plunking out notes to a melody I don't know, but it sounds like something I'd love, creating a song of his own.

I sit down beside him and appreciate the strength of his fingers and the way they methodically stroke the strings. For a brief moment I think about what his fingers would feel like if they touched my body in the same way. With precision and care. I feel my face flush.

He presses his hand flat against the base of the guitar, stopping the captivating tune. "So, I kind of wrote you a song."

"You what?" I blink, struggling to clear away my thoughts.

With a nervous smile, he says, "It's nothing special, don't get too excited. Just a little something I've been working on."

"You going to play it for me now?"

"It still needs some tweaking," he tries to explain, or possibly get out of playing it for me, but if he wasn't going to play it, he shouldn't have told me about it yet. "You might want me to wait."

"I won't judge you." I place my hand on his leg, trying to persuade him. "Play it for me. I want to hear it."

He reluctantly nods, and then begins to strum the melody he was playing moments ago. When he begins to sing, my heart sighs.

When you're here with me,
There's no other place I'd rather be
Than in your arms so tight,
Holding your hand, you're holding mine.

What did I do?
To deserve you
I'm so lucky
That you're with me.
What did I do?
To deserve you
I'm so lucky
That you're with me.
My Peyton.

On cold Hatteras nights,

I hold you so tight.
Then I stare into your eyes,
And that's when I realize…

What did I do
To deserve you?
I'm so lucky
That you're with me.
What did I do
To deserve you?
I'm so lucky
That you're with me.
My Peyton.
You're with me…

So, I wrote this song
For you.
I wrote this song
For you.
I wrote this song
To tell you,
I love you.

Brodee repeats the chorus and ends with one last strum. He anxiously chews on his bottom lip, looking at the floor before he unhurriedly lifts his eyes for my reaction. I can't speak right away, so he covers up the silence, "So, the lyrics need some work, and I know some of the chords are a little off..."

While he isn't going to be some professional songwriter or a rock star someday, his voice is perfect, and he wrote this song for me, and I love it. I don't say I love you back because I'm not ready yet, but I take his face in my hands and kiss him hard on the mouth. I let our lips and tongues do all the talking.

The Day We Stopped Pretending

BRODEE AND I spent our day on the beach. We surfed this morning and spent the rest of our afternoon making drip castles and basking in the sunlight.

"I need to run inside real quick," Brodee says. "I'll be right back."

"Okay." I roll on my stomach, changing positions to read. I put my nose back in my book to get lost with my newest book boyfriend and drown out thoughts of everyone else.

Why hello, West. You can be my anchor during a tornado any day.

I'm not sure how much time passes before I look up and let my eyes drift down the beach. When I squint, I notice Brodee in the distance sitting with his knees to his chest, looking out at the waves. *What's he doing all the way down there?*

I place a bookmark to hold my spot and close my book before I make my way to him. Brodee doesn't move when I approach. When I say, "Hey," he startles.

I chuckle. "Sorry. I didn't mean to scare you."

Brodee's laugh is different, strained. His eyes remain on the water.

"What are you doing all the way down here?"

He leans back on his hands. "Just took a walk."

I sit down beside him, mirroring his position. "Did you even go inside?"

"Huh?" He peers over at me, puzzled.

"You went into the house. Did you do what you needed to?"

"Oh." He nods, clipped. "Yeah. Just decided to go for a walk when I saw you were still reading."

This is it. With only a week left, he's doing exactly what I tried to do. Brodee is distancing himself. I can't even blame him. I get it. It's going to be hard enough as it is. Maybe it's time we stop pretending the end of the summer isn't nearly here and that whatever this is will end.

"Brodee." He has to pry his eyes away from the ocean. It's painful to look at me. "I get it. This will all be a dream in a week, but don't leave me yet. Don't leave me while I'm still here. Isn't that what you said?"

A layer of tears coats his eyes. "I won't." He shakes his head adamantly. "I won't." His voice is certain, firm. And then he latches onto me, clinging to me like it's the end of time, not the end of the summer. His face burrows into the crook of my neck and his arms squeeze tighter.

When he pulls back, it's merely enough to kiss me. Brodee holds my face to his. His fingers tangle tightly into my hair, desperate. I don't know what's gotten ahold of him, but it scares me. Scares me enough not to ask. All I can do is kiss him back and make every touch count. Make sure every kiss leaves such an imprint on our hearts that the only thing that could affect the mark is another kiss, deepening the imprint, branding our hearts as one.

The Day He Made a Choice

THE NEXT MORNING, I walk by Brodee's bedroom door and notice it's cracked open, inviting me in. I knock lightly and peer around the door, expecting to see him lying on his bed, but his room is empty. He must be eating breakfast.

I jog down the stairs and find Carter playing video games and Tatum doing dishes. "Morning, Peyton. How'd you sleep?"

"Really good." I smile and grab a bowl from the cupboard to pour my cereal. "Where's Brodee?"

"He didn't tell you?" Tatum asks, turning from the sink. "He left for Kitty Hawk about an hour ago."

"Oh." I look at the clock on the microwave. 8:35. I stop and think. *Did he mention that?* No. He didn't. "Did he leave a message for me?"

"Sorry, darlin', he didn't. I'm surprised he didn't tell you. You two have been inseparable lately." Tatum has a mischievous glint in her eyes.

"Yeah. I guess I'll just text him." I take my bowl of cereal out on the deck to listen to the waves. "Thanks, Tate."

"Anytime."

Me: Hey. You left without me.

Fifteen minutes go by with no response. It's possible he's already in the water. In that case I won't hear from him for a couple hours, so I busy myself.

A few hours come and go. I surf. Go on a bike ride. Walk the beach searching for shells. When I check my phone at 12:15 there's still no contact from him.

Me: How's Kitty Hawk?

Nothing. Carter left to go hang out with Chelsea, so I take advantage of the TV and watch a movie.

Two more hours pass.

Me: Are you alive?

Another twenty minutes goes by, and I'm about to call the cops. This is so unlike him. Instead of resorting to such drastic measures, I go out back where my mom and Tatum are relaxing on the deck.

"Hey, Tate, have you heard from Brodee?" She looks up at me from below her sunhat.

"Yeah. He touched base about an hour ago. Should be home before dinner."

"Oh. Okay." I try to disguise the hurt, but it's really hard.

Brodee is avoiding me. For the first time since whatever we are began, he went surfing without me. I don't mean to sound needy. It's fine if he wants to go alone. It's just weird that he didn't mention it to me or respond to me when I texted him. He's never ignored me before.

With the end of summer drawing closer, I know it's hard to think about what will become of us, but it feels like it's more than that. He didn't think to leave a note to say where he was going so I could meet up with him. Clearly, I wasn't wanted.

Sure enough, Brodee walks through the front door right before dinner. He doesn't say a word. Not to me. Not to Carter. Not to his parents. He gives his mom a kiss on the cheek and sits down at the table across from me. I try to catch his eye during dinner, but he won't look me in the eye for long. When I smile, his lips turn up, but it's nothing like a smile. It's a crescent moon on a stormy night. It wants to gleam, but darkness hinders it. *What did I do wrong?* I thought we fixed this yesterday. He's not supposed to leave me yet. He's already backing down on his promise, and it hasn't even been twenty-four hours.

Whenever Nick makes a comment, Brodee makes a nearly silent noise of annoyance or snarky comment under his breath. I'm not even sure anyone else notices, since no one says anything. *So, maybe Nick did something? Did they have a fight about Duke?*

After Brodee finishes eating, he heads straight to his bedroom. I give him a few minutes, help with the dishes, and then follow him up. It's quiet. Hesitantly, I knock and wait for his reply.

"Come in." He doesn't sound like he actually wants me to come in, but I go against my gut instinct and open the door. Brodee is lying on his bed with his arm draped across his face, only his nightstand light creating a glow on the pale blue walls.

"Hey." I pause. He doesn't move. "Are you mad at me?"

"Huh?" Brodee lifts his arms from his face and peers at me from beneath his thick lashes. "Nah. I'm just tired."

That sounded really convincing. "Are you sure?"

He slowly sits up on his elbows, looks at me for a moment, and nods once. I waver in the doorway. *Should I leave him alone? Should I press for more details?* With a wave of his hand, he motions me in. I close the door behind me and crawl onto the bed beside him. He tucks me into his side.

"Sorry I've been out of it today," Brodee murmurs, nuzzling his head against mine. "I just needed the space to clear my head. Been thinking about the future and stuff."

I nod into his chest. "You worried me."

"I know."

As we lay there silently, rain starts to tap on the window. "What did you come up with?" I quietly ask.

"I want to go to USC."

I sit up so fast my head knocks into his. "What?"

"Ouch." He holds his jaw with a quiet chuckle.

"I'm sorry." I gently touch where I hit, brushing my fingers tenderly against his skin. "What?" I repeat.

He leans into my hand. "I've been thinking a lot. You make more sense than Duke. I want to be wherever you are."

"Brodee," I utter, shaking my head. "Don't make a rash decision. This is not something you can take back. I don't want you going to USC just for me."

"Why not?"

"You have to want this. I don't want you to wake up one morning months or years from now and wish you'd gone to Duke. That kind of regret can never be reversed. It's *Duke* for heaven sake's. People dream of going to that school, and you're willing to give it up so easily."

"Pete, I know what I'm doing. I know what I want, and what I want is you. If that means going to USC, so be it. I don't want Duke that badly. But I do want you. If I've learned anything this summer, it's discovering what's most important to me and seizing it."

"No." I shake my head. He's not thinking straight. What if we don't last? What if tomorrow he decides we're over? Anything can happen. "College shouldn't be decided based on who you're going with. That never works out. It causes fights and resentment. I don't ever want to be a source of your bitterness. I care too much about you to let you throw away Duke for me."

Brodee sits up, taking my shoulders in his hands. He holds on so tightly. "I'm not throwing it away. USC is a great school, too. It's not like I'm throwing away my future to work at McDonald's for the rest of my life. I'm just choosing a different school, Pete. This is a good idea. It solves everything."

"Sleep on it," I say and kiss him lightly. "Tomorrow, if you feel the same way, we'll talk about it." I maneuver off of his bed.

"I won't change my mind," he says, resolved.

The Day I Was Scared

THIS TIME *I'VE* been avoiding Brodee all day. I can lie to myself and say it's because I wanted to give him enough time to think things through, but truly I'm just scared of his answer.

While I realize most girls would think him following me to USC is a romantic gesture, I'm not most girls. There's too much history between us. This new chapter is only just beginning. He can't push the climax of our story already. It's not time.

Though I hadn't sat down and contemplated what would happen to us, I think I always assumed we'd take this for what it is, and then go our separate ways. Maybe we'd last. Maybe we'd date other people and then find our way back to each other. Maybe we'd go back to being just friends. But I never once expected Brodee to give up Duke for me. It's too much pressure.

If he slept on it and gives me a valid reason for wanting to go to USC, I'll accept it. If he slept on it and tells me he had a lapse in judgment and will still be going to Duke, I can't be upset about that. That's what I want—for him to choose for himself and no one else. *You can't have it both ways, Peyton.*

Brodee once again ignores everyone at dinner, which makes me nervous, like he's officially decided to ditch Duke and he's avoiding telling Nick. He only acknowledges me and even then it's stolen glances as he tries to read me or communicate through eye contact. Sometimes he smiles. Sometimes he merely watches me. I look away every time.

After dinner, the family disperses. Carter heads out to meet up with Chelsea and their friends, while Nick slips away to the study and our moms follow each other upstairs. I sit on the couch, ready to face Brodee. Or not so much ready as I am exhausted from avoiding him.

"So, I slept on it. Slept long and hard, even slept in a little bit," Brodee says lightly and plants himself beside me on the couch. He offers a heart-stopping smile. "I haven't changed my mind."

My heart flutters. I take a deep breath. "Why do you want to go?"

"We went over this, Pete." He takes my face in his hand. My face loves his hands. I feel adored and cherished. "For you."

Wrong answer. I want to cry.

"Peyton, we're it," he whispers as his thumb grazes my cheek. "Can you feel it? We're the forever kind. I'm not going to take my chances. The thought of not seeing you every day *kills* me. I think of not hanging out or surfing, not being able to throw cheesy pick-up lines back and forth every day, and I regret ever mailing in my application to Duke."

I try really hard not to cry. I don't know if I want to cry because I'm scared or angry or because I'm grateful, and I realize I might love him. Everything is too much to take in.

But what if we aren't the forever kind? What if he breaks my heart?

What if I break *his*? He'd have followed me for *nothing*. You can't force a destiny. Isn't there a saying? If you want to hear God laugh, tell him your plans. I bet the big man upstairs is rolling on the floor right now. We'll put on an entire improv show for the heavens.

I can't have that kind of weight on me, on us. For us to succeed. As soon as we set this in stone, something will shatter it. Our plans will disintegrate, and the only thing left will be our broken hearts. I can't risk losing him forever.

I shake my head, pulling away from his touch. "You're just scared." I make up crap. "You don't think you'll do well at Duke, that you'll let everyone down. This isn't about me." *Why am I doing this?*

"Well, I mean sure, there's a lot of pressure to succeed. You can't go to Duke and flop."

"See?"

"No, stop it. That's not why I changed my mind. We talked about this before you and I began. At the beginning of the summer, I told you I had doubts."

"Which you said was bogus, that you were still going to go. You can't have it both ways, Brodee."

"I was second-guessing it because of us then, too. I just didn't admit it to myself because I hadn't accepted my feelings for you yet. No matter how you look at it, whether we're together or just best friends, it all comes back to you. It will suck to be apart no matter what we decide. We've already started experiencing it this summer. Neither one of us want to be left while we're still here. It's not going to change when we're miles away from each other. I feel like that will be worse. It's less salvageable that way.

We have the chance to be together. We shouldn't squander it."

He's making so much sense and none at all. I can't listen. "I can't do this." I get up. "You can't give up Duke."

"Pete." Brodee gets up to follow.

"You can't."

"Peyton!"

I hold up my hand to stop him, but don't look back as I walk to the back door. "Now *I* need space." I need to drive the 12. I grab my mom's keys from the rack and leave. Brodee doesn't follow me.

AT THE BEGINNING of the summer this was exactly what I wanted. Him. Any way that I could get him. And now I realize how hypocritical I sound by pushing him away. Far away. I'm scared. I know it. He knows it. But it's a logical argument. Life is unpredictable. Anything could happen. I know firsthand. One day I had my dad, the next day he was gone. An instant. That's all it takes.

A thought sinks every organ inside of me. *What if he's meant to go to USC and meet someone else?* The mere image of him kissing another girl churns my stomach. I hate that thought more than any other. The irony. Following me to USC only to fall in love with another. *Wouldn't that be my luck?*

I end up driving the 12 for hours. Brodee calls and texts, but I don't respond. When I've been gone for three hours I get a call from my mom. I tell her I'm alive and that I'll be back in a little bit. I take a deep breath and focus on the road under the dark sky.

It's after ten by the time I get back. No one is downstairs except for my mom, so I tell her I'm heading straight to bed and apologize for making her worry. We say goodnight, and I creep up the stairs and down the hall, safely making it to my room without any close encounters. Then there's a knock at my door, and it's opening slowly without my permission.

"Pete?" Brodee says around the door, peeking his head inside.

I sit on my bed, watching him enter.

"Do you know how worried I was about you? Why didn't you respond to me?"

"Sorry." I really don't want to keep talking about this right now. I'm too tired to argue. "I needed space. I told you that."

"A simple text back would've sufficed." He sounds like my mom when I forget to text her back.

"I was driving. And what part of 'I need space' means, 'Call me incessantly, and text me until I want to throw my phone out the window'?"

He grimaces. "Wow. Just a little childish, don't you think?"

"Childish," I spat. I can't believe he called me that. "Excuse me?"

He crosses his arms over his chest. "Yes, childish. Running away, rather than talking about this with me. I poured out my heart and you bolted."

"Well, then I can't image why you'd want to be with such a child. It's little inappropriate, don't *you* think?"

He tenses and takes a step toward me. "That's not what I meant. Don't twist my words."

"No, I'm a child for wanting space. It's fine. I get it. I'm the one trying to be logical and not just think with my heart, but *I'm* the childish one."

Brodee groans in frustration and tries coming closer to me, but I hold up my hands. When he touches me it only muddles my thoughts, and he knows it. This is no time for distractions.

"Pete, c'mon. You know what I meant. You're being ridiculous."

"So, I'm ridiculous *and* childish. Cool." He rolls his eyes. I exhale.

"I just want to go to bed, Brodee. You should too."

He grunts, but doesn't argue with me as he nearly slams the door behind him. I grab a throw pillow from my bed and hurl it at the door with a thud. I fall back on my bed and stare at the ceiling.

Stupid, stupid, stupid.

The Day It Was Up to Us

BRODEE MADE SURE to give me space the following day. I couldn't reach him on his cell phone because he'd turned it off. Tatum wasn't even allowed to tell me where he was. *Now who's the childish one?*

The house is so quiet. Tate is the only one home, but I don't want to bug her while she's relaxing and has the house to herself. With no car, all I can do is surf, and so that's what I do. I stay out in the ocean for hours. I don't come inside until I hear the bell.

Brodee doesn't even come home for dinner. Tatum can't tell me when he's coming home. I guess he's getting his payback. Jerk.

While I'm finishing helping my mom and Tatum with the dishes, I say, "I'm gonna take a walk up the beach."

"Bring your phone with you," my mom says.

"Good idea," Tatum says. "The sunset is gorgeous tonight. You should go watch it. Head to the tip of the cape. It's always best from there."

And so I do. I walk the shoreline as colors paint the sky above the ocean and night falls.

I think more about Brodee going to USC. I think about what a comfort it will be to have him with me—the adventures we'll have and the new memories we'll share. I think of never having to say goodbye. I hate goodbyes. The more it sets in, the more I accept it. The less upset I am, the happier I am.

"Pete?"

My heart jumps at the sound of his voice in the dark. I search the shore and find Brodee sitting on a blanket spread across a small sand dune. Tatum knew where he was. She knew where to guide me. It's only been a day, and I missed him so much. It's pathetic. I'll never be able to lose him to Duke.

"Have you been out here all day?"

"No, I've been around. I came here about an hour ago. The ocean air helps clear my head, and you know how much I like watching the stars."

I nod, but I'm not sure if he can actually see me.

"Will you join me?" I hesitate. Though I'm annoyed he ditched me today, I don't want to fight anymore. With only days left in Hatteras, I don't want to waste it.

He scoots over on the blanket to give me room to sit beside him, and then he lies back, lifting his arms under his head like a pillow. I flip my hood up and tug my flannel shirt tightly around me before following suit. I stretch out beside him with one arm under my head, the other resting across my stomach.

We remain that way for a while. Gazing at the backlit sky in silence. Our bodies are so close, yet only the warmth radiating between us touches.

The calming swish of the ocean and Brodee's steady breathing are almost enough to put me to sleep.

"You said something to me once about the stars." His voice isn't loud, but with only the waves lapping the sand and the wind licking my ears, I jolt at the sound.

I hear his quiet chuckle of amusement at my expense.

"'When I'm at home looking at the stars and thinking of you, I wonder if you're at home looking at the same stars, thinking of me,'" he repeats the words as they scroll through my mind.

We used to lie on the trampoline in his backyard, looking for shooting stars and pointing out different constellations. We couldn't have been more than thirteen. I was in love with the idea of love. Brodee was hardly on my crush radar, but he was the only boy I was friends with, so he got the majority of my failed attempts at flirting. I thought I was so clever and romantic. He never made fun of me or took me seriously. Thankfully.

"I wish I could go back and change the past, Pete. I would have taken my chances sooner. You and I would've had longer to explore this." He drops an arm between us and he lifts himself to his side to face me. "Maybe if I had I'd never have applied to Duke in the first place, and we wouldn't have to be here."

I don't want to think about the what ifs. They do nothing but give you regrets.

"I think this is the longest you've ever gone without speaking," he says. "Normally, I'd say it was a gift to me, but right now it feels more like a slap across the face."

I only shift my eyes. "I'm not sure what exactly you want me to respond to first." He stays quiet. "You're forgiven if that is what you were looking for." My eyes go back to searching the bright speckles above us. I hate myself for giving in, but I don't have it in me to stay mad at him anymore, not when he looks at me like that.

"Pete." My heart sighs at his tender tone, as if my name is something to handle with care.

I swallow and brave the look I know I'll see in his eyes. His eyes are soft, pleading, yearning for answers. I can't tell him to give up Duke.

"You have to know I can never stay mad at you. That much has to be obvious." I sigh.

"Nothing's ever obvious with you."

"Speak for yourself."

"I would gladly make myself clear. Right now."

I place my hand on his chest before he can make me lose my mind. My words will fall right out of my head if he kisses me right now. "What if we don't last, and you give up Duke for nothing?"

Brodee's face falls. "Are you saying you don't think we'll last? Do you not want me to go to USC?"

"No, yes. I mean. I do...want you to go to USC if it's for the right reasons. Brodee, it's just...we can't make promises to each other that we can't keep. We made a pact at the beginning of summer that we wouldn't drift apart. What if you following me to USC causes us to drift apart? Or what if you go and you hate it, and you're stuck at a school you didn't want to go to in the first place? What if we lose what we have? I can't risk losing you."

"What if going to Duke causes us to drift apart? What if an asteroid falls from the sky and strikes me dead? What if the Earth opens up and swallows USC whole with you in it?" I snort a laugh. "Where I go to school isn't going to affect you and me. It's up to you and me. If we don't last, we don't last. But it won't be because we didn't do everything we could to make it work. You can't lose something you cling to. I'm willing to work my butt off if you are."

I can't speak. How I keep my breathing steady is a mystery to me. As if my heart hadn't been beating fast enough before, when he reaches up and brushes my bangs aside, leaving his hand resting in my hair, I think I might spontaneously combust.

"You do something to me when you look at me like that."

I know my voice will shake when I let the words out, but it suddenly doesn't matter anymore. "How exactly am I looking at you?"

"With this innocence and yet uncontrolled desire. You really don't know the effect you have on me."

I feel the grains of sand shift under the blanket as he moves to hover on top of me. His breathing is heavy. His heart races so fast under my fingertips I wonder if it's actually possible for a heart to beat out of a chest. Brodee lowers himself inches from my lips, watching my expression. *Do I have to beg?* I don't break my gaze even though my nerves are out of control.

When our lips connect, something happens in that moment. It isn't fireworks or an uncontainable fire igniting, but a deep burn that flows like lava, coursing through every vein in my body. I melt under his touch, and yet I can't keep my hands from twisting into the hair on the nape of his neck and securing myself as closely as possible to every inch of his body.

Brodee's hand grips my bare waist where my shirt has ridden up. His hand clenches so tightly as though it's trying to behave. It trembles, attempting to control the yearning to wander. He reaches one hand to my cheek and brushes his thumb along my jaw, quivering with every stroke. I kiss him with everything I've been holding back—trying to show him with my mouth everything I don't know how to put into words.

"Please let me keep you." His voice shakes.

I exhale against his mouth and pull back so I can look him in the eyes. "Okay."

"I'm going to USC."

"I know," I yield. I want him to look at my face. I want him to know how badly I need him. There isn't anything in this world that I would let get between us. I know that now.

"What about Nick? How are you going to break it to him?"

"Screw Nick." I'm so caught off guard by his response I chuckle. He doesn't smile back at first. "He doesn't get a say anymore. It's my life. And I choose you."

"I choose you back."

He closes his eyes tightly, inhaling deeply, then opens them momentarily before pressing his lips back to mine.

We kiss for hours…minutes…seconds? I can't keep track of time with his hard body against mine, his tongue intertwining with mine. We kiss as if tonight is all we have. When we slow down he softly touches his lips to mine once. Twice. Three times.

"I love you, Pete," he breathes against my mouth.

My mind awakens from the kissing haze. A couple breaths pass my lips.

Do we really know what love is? Of course I love Brodee because he's my best friend. But am I *in* love with him? I've never felt this way before. It's more than infatuation. It's more than what I felt for Tyler. I want to spend every moment with him. It guts me to think of not spending every day with him. I want what's best for him, for him to be happy. *Is that love?* Maybe it is.

"I love you, too."

His eyes glisten under the moonlight. I know his eyes better than my own. The subtle creases in the corner from squinting against the sun as he waits for a wave. The little brown flecks scattered across the green, matching the freckles dusting his nose. I could live in his eyes. They are my home. I realize that now. Wherever he is, I am home.

Brodee kisses my lips gently once more and rolls back to lie beside me under the stars, which we watch silently until I fall asleep with his arms around me.

The Day That Changed Us

I WAKE UP to a dog barking, which is weird because we don't own a dog. My sleeping fog is drifting away as I feel a breeze rolling over my body, my body pressed up against another body. Brodee's arm drapes across my stomach as his face nestles further into my neck. I lift my head to see the sun has just begun to rise above the horizon. A jogger with his dog acknowledges me with a head nod, passing by across the sand.

Instantly, my brain wakes up. "Brodee, wake up! We've been out all night! Get up now!"

He sits up quickly, then puts his palms into his eyes as if to keep from blacking out. "What time is it?"

"I don't know. Morning. Five? Six?" I pull my cell phone from my back pocket. Fifteen missed calls from my mom and Tatum. *Crap*. "We have to get back to the house. Our parents are *freaking* out."

We scramble to our feet. Brodee snatches the blanket, and we book it to the beach house. We don't even have time to concoct a story before sneaking across the back deck and in through the back door.

"Peyton?" A voice comes from down the hall when the back door clicks shut. When I don't answer, another voice calls out, "Brodee?"

Our parents round the corner, and relief washes over their faces as they rush to us standing guiltily in the kitchen.

"Morning," Brodee and I timidly say at the same time.

"Where have you two been?" my mom demands, worry tainting her face. It pinches her forehead and tightens her mouth. "We were about to call the police!"

We hadn't technically done anything wrong. I try to calm my mind. "We fell asleep on the beach," I explain. "We were watching the stars and lost track of time."

"We're just grateful you're okay," Tatum says, relieved.

"That is unacceptable behavior," Nick scolds, wagging his finger like we're children again. "You're old enough now that sleeping together is completely inappropriate. You two should know better. We're not old enough to be grandparents. You need to be more responsible. You're not children anymore."

"Nothing happened—" I try.

"Oh, you're one to talk," Brodee retorts snidely. It's so unusual for him to talk back; we all flinch.

Nick's eyes are wide with disbelief. "What did you just say to me?"

"You heard me." The venom in Brodee's voice scares me. My eyes widen, taking in his stance. He stands a little taller, fiercer. I almost don't recognize him. What happened to the boy on the beach?

"*Brodee*," Tatum reprimands.

Nick takes a step, narrowing his eyes. "Watch your mouth, son. I won't say it again."

"Like you're watching yours?" Something breaks inside of Brodee. I see it in his eyes like a dam rupturing, flooding with animosity. "Tell me. Does Mom know where it's been?"

Nick goes white. What is happening? What am I missing? And that's when I hear Brodee's jaw crack as Nick backhands him.

"Nick!" Tatum screams and pulls him back. My mom grabs Nick's other arm securely, holding him back.

I wrap my arm around Brodee's waist to steady him. Brodee spits blood onto the wooden floor and holds his jaw. "Class act, Dad," he breathlessly says. He's not letting this go. "She doesn't. Does she?" There's no question is Brodee's eyes. He already knows the answer. But none of us do.

What is going on?

"Nick, what is Brodee talking about?" Tatum tugs on his arm so he'll face her.

My mom drops his other arm and steps away. Something in her eyes is off, registering the situation. *Does she know? Are Tatum and I the only ones in the dark?*

"Tate," Nick begins, placing his hands on her shoulders, at the same time as my mom says, "How about we have this conversation in private?"

When Tatum looks at my mom, the questions are circling. *We? Why would my mom be in on this conversation?*

"Liv?" Tatum whispers, and everything falls into place. Like glass vases being knocked over one by one. *Smash. Smash. Smash.* Each second ticks by, exposing more and more of Tatum's recognition.

"No, no, no, no..." she murmurs, shaking.

Guilt. That's what I see in my mom's eyes. I thought my world had already come crashing down, but betrayal is just as lethal as grief. *What has she done?*

Tatum starts to cry. So does my mom. Nick's trying to reason with them both, while I stand stalk still next to a shattered Brodee.

"How could you?!" Tatum cries.

"We can explain!"

"I trusted you! You're my best friend!"

"Tate, please!"

Brodee finally drags me away when picture frames and treasured memories go flying across the living room, shattering against walls and wooden beams. Once we're upstairs, Carter comes out of his room.

"What's going on?"

"Go back inside your room, Carter," Brodee orders.

"Why? What's happening down there? Is Mom okay?"

"Carter, now," Brodee barks, shutting him up. The yelling and crying carries up the stairwell, clear as day.

"Why! WHY! All of this time!"

"Tatum, please! It's not what it looks like. Let us explain."

"Explain? How! What is there to explain? I think it's exactly what it looks like!"

Without another word, Carter shares an uneasy look with Brodee, then backs into his room and shuts his door. I inch away, drawn to the security of my bedroom. I can't listen to them any longer. The animosity. The accusations. The anguish.

Brodee follows me and closes the door behind us. I walk straight to my bed and lie down on my stomach. I'm in shock. That's the only way to explain my silence and tangled thought process. My brain is still trying to work through the scene. I curl into the fetal position, tucking my arms into my chest. My fists close in tightly. I know Brodee's in the room with me, but he doesn't lie down beside me.

I stare at the wall, at the canvas painting of a sand dollar on the shore with a receding wave. I've stared at it hundreds of times before. It's never been anything more than a watercolor of the beach. All I see now is the wave washing the sand dollar up on the sand, abandoning it, leaving it to dry up and die alone as the wave returns back home.

Betrayal.

How can something so simple—one act, one decision—cause everything to shatter? Like our bonds were never strong to begin with. Made of paper, not steel. So easily torn apart.

I now understand why walls are built, cages are locked—so no one and nothing can penetrate the soul. Hearts remain unbreakable that way. If you have the right armor, are shielded from the pain, nothing has the power to hurt you.

"You knew?" I utter.

"Yeah."

The emotions plastered on my sleeves want to crawl back inside to seek solace inside of my chest. *Sorry to break it to you.* It's not any better inside.

I close my eyes, begging dreams to take me away. I want sleep, to wake up and for this to be one big misunderstanding. It has to be. My mom would never do this to Tate. To my dad. Nick is madly in love with

Tate. He'd never do anything to destroy their marriage. They simply need to explain what happened, and everything will be okay. Everything will go back to normal. We'll finish this summer, savor the last few days we have, and appreciate our time together. Yes. It'll be okay.

AROUND TWELVE O'CLOCK Brodee wakes me with the touch of his hand on my shoulder. "Pete," he whispers. It's a whisper that's afraid to be heard. His eyes tell me he's nervous to wake me. The beach house is silent. "I think they're gone."

He convinces me to follow him downstairs to get something to eat. I should be hungry. I'm not. It's so quiet, either we're going to stumble upon a murder scene or everyone did leave. Both options seem viable.

The wooden stairs creak with each slow step I take. When we reach the bottom it's empty. There's no blood, so that's a positive sign. Even Brodee's blood and spit mixture has been cleaned up.

"Are you hungry?"

"No," I say, but it sounds so far away I'm not sure I actually said it.

"We need to eat, Pete. I'll make us some sandwiches."

While Brodee moves around the kitchen, I leave him and go outside to the back deck to lie in the sun. I'm not sure how much time passes before I hear the back door open and shut.

"Peyton." I can count on one hand the amount of times Brodee has called me Peyton. He says it with a quiet caress that tingles my skin, but I don't want to feel that tingle. I want to rub the tingle with sandpaper until it rubs me raw so he can no longer affect me. Until I bleed him out of my system. I lift my head from the reclining beach chair as Brodee sets my plate on the table next to me. "Can we talk?"

"I don't really want to talk right now, Brodee." I lay my head back down and close my eyes. And I certainly don't want to eat.

"This feels like something that we should talk about."

I hear the sliding of chair legs as he moves to be next to me. I keep my face blank and breathe.

"Will you please look at me? We need to talk about what happened this morning."

"No, we really don't."

"I didn't mean for it to come out then, but I couldn't stand watching him get away with it, being so hypocritical, when he's the one the finger should be pointed at."

Abruptly, I sit up. "And you thought outing our parents like that in front of Tate was a good idea? Do you really think that's how your mother deserved to find out? Why didn't you tell me? How could you keep that from me?"

I watch the pain settle in his eyes, but can't bring myself to feel guilty. Everything is ruined. All I can think now is that everything we were, everything we are, will become a memory.

"You betrayed me," I say.

"I know. I know!" He roughly rubs his hands down his face. "It was stupid. *So* stupid. After I walked in on them, I should've gone straight to you, but I was still trying to process it. I didn't know what to say. I didn't know what to think. Your mom and my dad have been affectionate before.

They're best friends. Like you and me. That's all I thought it was at first… until it wasn't."

No. NO. I shake my head and cringe. "Stop. I don't want to picture it. I don't want to think about it. I don't want to talk about it. I just want to be left alone. Please, Brodee." I lie back down and drape my arm across my eyes, shielding me from the brightness, from him.

He takes a deep breath. I'm not sure if it's out of aggravation or determination. "Have you ever wanted something so badly you were afraid of it? You didn't want to believe it could be possible because it could be taken away or be just out of reach? Or wanted something, but the timing was off? You knew that it was the end game, not the starting line or even the right course."

"Say what you mean. Stop talking in riddles," I mumble.

"I want us to work so badly. I knew their affair would ruin everything. That it would tear us apart. That it would tear our families apart. So I kept it to myself. This morning I snapped. I wish I could take it back. I wish I never said anything. Then you and I wouldn't be here."

I remove my arm from my eyes. "Whether you said something or not, it eventually would've come out. It was only a matter of time. We were destined to fail from the beginning."

"Don't say that. You don't mean it."

"How long have you known about them?" I ask.

A few seconds pass before he responds, "A few days."

"Unbelievable. I *knew* something was off! On the beach, when I found you sitting alone after you'd gone inside. You saw them then, didn't you?"

He nods.

"You looked me in the eye and lied to me, over and over. What else can you lie about?"

"That's not fair, and you know it!" He glares at me. "I couldn't just drop a bomb like that on you. I was trying to find the right time."

I sit up. "Right time? Right time! There *is* no right time! Nothing about this is right! Your dad and my mom are having an affair. In what world would that kind of information ever have perfect timing?"

"This is exactly why I kept it from you! It's already destroying us, and you and I didn't even do anything wrong!"

I keep my voice low and surprisingly steady. "You think it was easy for your dad, preying on a woman who's already at her lowest?"

Brodee's jaw clenches. "Your mom is just as guilty as my dad. It takes two, Peyton."

"Your dad didn't lose his spouse less than a year ago. My mom is probably desperate for any kind of affection. She wasn't thinking straight enough to say no."

Why am I defending her?

"My dad would never have done anything with someone who wasn't willing."

"Of course she was willing! Nick's the closest thing she has to my dead dad!"

Quit defending her!

Brodee flinches. "Stop! What are we even doing? Why are we fighting about who's more in the wrong? This isn't our fight!" He breaks. Softly, he says, "You and I didn't do this."

I stop. He's right. The only sound is our labored breathing as we try to calm down. There's nothing left to say. This isn't something you can come back from. This wrecked us, smashed us to a heap of unfixable parts. There is no salvaging the pieces.

As the pieces fall to the ground, they find new homes, new revelations. "This is why you want to go to USC, isn't it? It had nothing to do with me at all. You just wanted to get back at him."

"Don't twist that, Peyton. Of course I want to go because of you. I *love* you."

As I bring my legs to the side of the lounger, I grip the edges on either side of my thighs. "Then tell me. Please enlighten me. How long after you saw them together did you decide you no longer wanted to go to Duke?"

He can't respond.

I shake my head—fight back tears. "That's what I thought."

"What can I do to make this right?" he desperately asks.

"Nothing." I don't mean for it to come out as bitter as it sounds. It's the simple fact. The truth hurts. Nothing will ever be the same. Nothing can fix this. I'll never be able to look at him the same. Or Nick. Or my mom. Or even Tate. Not because Tate did anything wrong, but because it's *my* mom who destroyed her marriage. Her best friend—aside from her husband—she's one person Tate should've been able to count on. We're family. Family doesn't do that to each other.

"I can't lose us." Brodee's voice cracks.

"Right now there is no us."

Silence tugs and stretches the reality until it's the only thing between us. What we built is gone. It's over.

I watch his retreating figure on the boardwalk and regret what I said, but I can't take it back. I can't take back what our parents did. I can't change what happened to us. Even as my heart softens, I can't even call him back to me. I don't know where to go from here.

AFTER A COUPLE hours of lying there I go back inside. When I close the door quietly behind me, my mom is coming down the stairs. I halt and nearly backtrack. The waves and their security are calling to me.

"Peyton," she tries and takes a step toward me.

I shake my head to stop her. I can't look at her, let alone have her touch me.

"Stop where you are." She nods. Tears fill her eyes as she hovers below the last step. "I want to hear it from you. Tell me what Brodee saw was a misunderstanding—that it was a moment of weakness or not what it appeared to be at all. Tell me you'd never do that to Dad, to Tate, to us."

"Honey…" Her hands fist against her mouth. "I…I…"

"You can't, can you?" I choke. "You and Nick?"

"It's so complicated, Peyton." Her hands drop to her sides, and she tries to move toward me again. I put up my hands, stopping her. She stays put. "You know Nick and I go way back. We have this history that was never dealt with, never explored. It just happened. We're in love. I know that's hard to hear, but if this wasn't something real, we never would have risked it."

"So what, Dad dies, and Nick thinks he can take a shot with you now? All bets are off now that the husband is out of the picture."

Her sad eyes transform to fury. "*Peyton Jane*."

"No," I snap. "You don't get to reprimand me right now. *You* screwed up. Not *me*!"

"I am still your mother, and I deserve respect."

I nearly choke on my laughter. "Just like you respected this family? Like you respected Tate and her relationship with Nick? You don't get to reprimand me about respect. You're such a hypocrite! How do you think Dad would feel about this?"

"Don't," she warns.

It's as though I don't even hear her. That, or I don't care. More likely the later. "You think he'd understand? That he'd give his blessing."

"Stop," she says.

Nothing can stop the truth. "You think he'd be okay with you sleeping with his best friend?"

"That's enough!"

I bite my lip, holding back more words, more truth. "Truth hurts, doesn't it? I think I've had enough too." I shoulder past her, up the stairs and slam my bedroom door behind me. I lock it for good measure.

I can't be here for one more second. Racing around the room, I snatch up my clothes, anything I can find and pull out the duffle from under my bed. Then I grab my phone from my nightstand.

Me: Where are you?

I fling open drawers and empty their contents. I yank clothing off hangers and grab my sandals from the floor. I sweep my arm across my vanity and swipe my makeup into my makeup bag. Anything and everything ends up in my duffle in a jumbled mess of material and cosmetics.

Brodee: Walking back to the house.
Me: Let's go. Please. I need to get out of here now.

I think he might tell me no, but within seconds I get his response.

Brodee: Okay.

The Day We Played Pretend

BRODEE AND I drove all night. The majority of our drive was in silence. I read while he drove, or rather pretended to read while all I saw was black ink on cream paper. The only topic of conversation was food, gas, and bathroom breaks. It took us eight hours, but we made it back a little after midnight.

My mom isn't home, and I don't know when she'll show up. I don't want to be at home when she does, so Brodee lets me stay at their house for the night. Being neighbors has its perks. I'll know when she gets home—more precisely when it's safe to go home and when to stay away.

Tatum and Carter are already at the Fisher's, as we figured they would be. Carter's room was cleared out when Brodee and I left the beach house, and Nick's car was gone as was my mom's. My guess is she let Nick take it to go after Tate, but he obviously didn't get very far. Tatum has locked herself in her bedroom, and it's unlikely we'll see her before morning. Nick is MIA, and I hope he stays that way. If Brodee has any power, he'll make sure Nick stays far away from their house.

The house is still as we walk up the carpeted stairwell to Brodee's room. We pass Carter's closed bedroom door and peer down at his parents' closed door at the end of the hall. Tatum's pain practically leaks from beneath the door, soaking into the house.

I drop my duffle at the foot of his bed and sit down on the edge. The mattress squeaks as I sink into it. When we used to have sleepovers, Brodee would let me have his bed, and he'd take the floor. I hated sleeping on the floor. He'd get a sleeping bag and tell me he didn't mind, that it was cool because it felt like he was camping. I learned later on Brodee hates camping.

The mattress squeaks again as Brodee sits beside me. Out of the corner of my eye, I see him run his hand down his face and rest his elbows on his knees as he leans forward. I can tell he's exhausted—physically and emotionally. I napped earlier and was able to sleep in the car, too. I'm not sure if he's gotten much sleep since we fell asleep on the beach. It all seems like a lifetime away. Hatteras. Happiness. Hope in the future.

"Tonight, can we forget about it? Can we pretend that nothing has changed?" he asks desperately, watching me from the corner of his eyes. "When we wake up, we can let reality set in, but tonight I just want to hold you."

It will only hurt more in the morning, but the pain is inevitable whether we prolong our time together or not. I want him to hold me, too. I nod. I don't say anything. We crawl up his bed and lie on our sides, my back toward him. Brodee curls behind me. His arm wraps around my torso, tugging me snugly to his body.

I ask, "Do you remember my eleventh birthday when all I wanted was a telescope?"

"And the subtle hints you left for your parents." I can hear the smile in his voice.

I softly laugh, recalling the magazine telescope clippings I'd left all around the house. One on my dad's pillows, one under a magnet on the fridge, one laying on his nightstand, one slipped under his laptop in his office so it peeked out just enough from beneath it.

"I remember you making me cut out every telescope we could find from any magazine you could get your hands on."

"And I was so mad when, on my birthday, I woke up to a new surfboard and not a telescope." I chuckle before I pause. "Do you know why I was so upset?"

"Because you really wanted a telescope?"

"Because the telescope was something you and I could do together, star gaze the right way. You didn't know how to surf yet, and I was so mad at my parents for getting me something I couldn't share with you."

Brodee holds me tighter. "Why do you think the very next weekend I asked your dad to teach me how to surf?" he asks.

"It wasn't because you wanted to learn how?"

"I wanted to learn how so I could do it with you."

I twist my face to look at him. "Really?"

"Don't you get it, Peyton? Every obstacle that we've faced, threatening to distance us, has lost. More than friends or not, we've never let anything stand in our way before," he whispers.

Until now, I think and turn away, hiding the tears in my eyes.

He buries his face in my hair and exhales. "I love you so much."

A tear falls and wets my hair on the pillow. "I know," I say, because saying it back will only make this more difficult when we wake. I tuck one arm under my head and tangle my other with his over my stomach, settling further into him to savor every last touch. I breathe out. *I love you, too.*

THE SUN WAKES me. It takes a second before I realize I'm in Brodee's room, not my bedroom in Hatteras. Everything from yesterday crashes into me like an asteroid. I don't feel Brodee around me, so I look to the left side of the bed. He's gone. Stretching, I get up and let myself out of his room in search of him and some breakfast. I forgot to charge my phone, so I don't even know what time it is. It could be lunchtime for all I know.

When I get to the end of the hallway I hear him and Tatum talking downstairs, so I pause. Not because I want to spy, but so I don't interrupt their conversation. And maybe to listen for a little bit.

"I don't know where he is, Brodee."

"Does Carter know? He was standing outside of his bedroom door when we walked upstairs. He had to have heard something. You guys weren't exactly quiet."

"He knows we got into a big fight, and that's all he has to know for now. I didn't tell him more than that. Your father can do that."

There's a pause.

"Mom…" Brodee utters. It sounds like he has tears in his voice. "I'm so sorry. I shouldn't have said what I did, broke the news like that."

"Brodee, son, you have nothing to apologize for. If you hadn't, I don't know how much longer it would've gone on without me knowing."

"But I feel so awful. I hate to see you hurting. I should've told you in private. Or talked to Dad and made him tell you himself. That's what I should have done."

"Oh, sweetie, this is not something I want you to beat yourself up over. Crap happens. It wouldn't have mattered how I found out. You did *nothing* wrong. Okay? You hear me?"

"Yeah." He's unconvinced. It's my fault he feels so guilty. I opened my big mouth in the heat of the moment when I wasn't thinking straight. If I were in his shoes and I walked in on them, I would've snapped too. But I wouldn't have been able to wait. I'd have yelled at them right then and there. Or maybe I would've done exactly as he'd done and kept it to myself, trying to process it.

"Okay?" she asks more adamantly, but I can hear that she's tearful.

"Okay," he concedes.

"This should never have involved you in the first place. I'm sorry that you had to find out first."

"You don't have anything to apologize for either, Mom. I'm a big boy. I can handle it."

I decide this break in conversation is the best time to go downstairs before I get caught eavesdropping. As I walk, I can see them talking at the kitchen counter. Tatum is wrapped in a bathrobe, her hair damp and hanging over her shoulders. Brodee looks just as disheveled as he did last night, wearing the same rumpled T-shirt and jeans he slept in. Their heads turn to me when they hear me coming down the steps.

Tatum's the first one to move. She glides across the hardwood floors to meet me at the bottom of the steps and pulls me into her arms. "Oh, Peyton."

I'm so caught off guard it takes me a moment to reciprocate. *Why is she hugging me? Shouldn't I be consoling her?*

She pulls back and kisses me on the cheek. "Did we wake you? You look so tired, honey. Are you okay?"

"I'm fine." Why is she asking *me*? "Are *you* okay?"

"I'll be fine," she assures. It's a lie. We both know it.

I bite my lip. "Tate, I'm so sorry. I'm so sorry she did this to you."

"Why are you and Brodee apologizing for things you can't control, for things you shouldn't even be worrying about? This is not your fault."

"Because she's my mom, and she hurt you. You're my family too, Tate."

"Oh, baby." She pulls me back in, hugging me closely. "Yes, we are. We're going to get through this. We're going to be just fine."

I catch Brodee's sad eyes over her shoulder. He shrugs and offers a small close-lipped smile. Apparently he doesn't agree, but he's going to smile because there's nothing else he can do.

The Day He Was More Important Than Me

I STAYED AT the Fisher's again last night. Tatum said I could have one more night, and then I would have to go home. My mom hasn't stopped texting and calling me. I acknowledged her to let her know I was safe, and that was it. She's too much of a coward to come and get me herself.

Nick has yet to show his face. I'm not even sure if he wants to. And if he does, Tatum must be turning him away because we haven't heard anything from him. I wouldn't be surprised if he's staying at my house with my mom, which makes me want to stay away that much longer. It's made it easier for Brodee and me to continue pretending for another day. Or avoiding it. However you want to look at it. But now it's time to go back to reality.

I stand on my front door step, staring at the handle like it's a poisonous snake. I don't want to touch it. Brodee must be watching me because my cell phone sounds off from inside my pocket.

Brodee: You've got this.

I turn toward his house and see him standing in the center of his front porch. He nods encouragingly. I know he gets it. He wants to see his dad about as much as I want to see my mom. I nod back and head inside.

My mom is sitting on the couch in the family room with her head down when I round the corner. She lifts her gaze. Her eyes are bloodshot, and her face is all blotchy. It looks like she hasn't stopped crying in days.

"Why did it have to be Nick?" I ask from where I stand. She remains seated. "I get you may be ready to move on—trying to date—but Nick? Why did it have to be Nick?" I don't want to cry, but I can't help it.

She stands. "Peyton, I know it's hard, but I didn't do this to hurt you." She reaches out to me, but I shy away. I'm not ready for her to touch me. She settles back on the couch. "I never wanted to hurt any of you. Any of you. It just happened."

"That's a horrible explanation," I say.

"I can't explain why. You wouldn't understand."

"No, I don't understand." I take a bold step forward. "I don't understand how you could be so callous, to hurt your best friend like this." And another. "I don't understand how you could disrespect Dad by sleeping with his best friend." My voice quivers with pain. "I don't understand how you could destroy the only family we have left!"

"I know." She cries. "I'm sorry."

"Sorry doesn't fix this, Mom. Why Hatteras? The one place that's sacred to us. You took that away from me. From all of us. Everything Hatteras was will be tainted by your unfaithfulness."

She sniffles. "Honey, I'm sorry. We knew what this would do, that everything would change. We were going to come clean when we got home.

We waited so you and Brodee could enjoy this last summer together."

"Waiting wouldn't have made a difference. The summer would have been tainted no matter what. There were still lies and secrecy and betrayal. Whether you told us during or after, you ruined everything!"

My mom grits her teeth. "I get that you're upset. I don't expect you to accept this right away, but everything isn't ruined. It's messy right now, but we'll work through it."

"Work through it?" I snort. "With or without Nick by your side?"

When she doesn't respond right away I think I have my answer. "Are you going to get married?" Please say no. Please. *I'm begging you.*

"It'll be quite some time before any of that is discussed." She stands and comes closer to me. "We'll take it slow. We understand what a shock this is."

I scoff. *Shock?* Is that what this is called? Every part of my insides hurt. I've been dragged behind a horse on a desert road for miles. There isn't a part of me that's untouched by her deceit.

"You don't get it, do you?" I shake my head, so disappointed in her. Our roles are suddenly reversed. I feel like the adult in this situation. "You're so flippant about this, like you didn't take one second to step back and think about what this would do to all of us. You wrecked it all, Mom! Brodee's and my relationship will never be the same. Ever. I'll never be able to look at Nick the same. Tate…Tate is *devastated.* Our families will *never* be the same. And it's your fault. Because you and Nick couldn't keep it in your pants!"

My mom shoots forward, her hand raised to smack me, but she stops herself. "You think this has been easy for me? Every day of the summer it's weighed on me, and how it will affect every one of your lives. You don't think I haven't thought about how it will change the way you'll look at me, how it'll change you and me. What your father would think of me. You don't think I regret what this will do to my relationship with Tate? It *kills* me, Peyton." Her hands take my shoulders as the tears stream down her face. "It kills me," she whispers.

"Am I supposed to feel bad for you?" My voice cracks.

"I'm not asking for your pity or your forgiveness. I'm asking for your understanding, for your acceptance."

"I can't give you that because I don't understand this. I don't understand how you could do this. I don't understand why you thought he was more important than the rest of us." Tears sting my eyes.

"He'll never be more important than you, honey." Her voice is desperate. "*Never.*"

"If you felt that way, we wouldn't be having this conversation. You'd never have started this or you'd stop it now. You'd get on your hands and knees to beg for forgiveness and never consider being with him for one more second."

She swallows. "I can't do that. It doesn't change how we feel. I wish it happened differently, but I can't change that now. Nick and I have thought long and hard about this. We love each other. And you'll eventually have to accept that we're going to move forward."

I can almost hear her tack on in her head, "Whether you like it or not." That's essentially what she's saying. She doesn't truly care about how this is going to affect everyone. She knew it would destroy us, and she did it anyway.

I'll never be able to look at my mom the same.

The Day We Said Goodbye

WHEN I WAKE up the next day, all I want to do is be near Brodee, and then I remember that I can't run into his arms for comfort. I can't waltz into his house like it's my own or share cheesy pick-up lines with him. We can't pretend anymore. We're over.

I spend my day locked in my room, packing up everything I won't need at USC. Moving day can't come fast enough. There comes a point when I can't stand being in the house any longer so I grab my board and head for the beach. I don't check the surf report. Even if the waves are crap, they'll be better than staying in that house with her. I just need to be in the ocean.

When I've spent a few hours away, I pull back into my driveway and see Brodee. He stands from the steps and waits for me on my front porch. He's got a key to my house, so I'm not sure why he's not inside.

"Hi," he says.

"Hi." I amble toward him.

"Your mom is inside."

Duh. There's my answer. I haven't gone to his house for the exact same reason. I can't bear the thought of seeing Nick. The man who was supposed to be my loyal father figure. I was going to ask him to walk me down the aisle one day.

I nod. Brodee steps to the side, and we both sit down on the top stair, overlooking the street we grew up on.

We don't say anything for a few minutes. We sit, resting our arms over our knees, studying our hands in our own laps.

"I'm leaving for Duke tomorrow morning," Brodee quietly speaks up.

I nod. I hoped he'd change his mind. There's no way I'll be able to see him every day, knowing we can't be together. He made the right choice, even though it hurts. It needs to happen this way.

"But I want you to know I'm not giving up on us."

"Brodee…" I sigh.

"No," he cuts me off. "Listen to me. This sucks now. Everything is messed up, but it's not that much different than before. We weren't going to do the long distance thing before anyway. We'll work through this when the time comes."

"Not that *different*?" I nearly choke on a laugh. "Don't you get it? You and I will never be what we were. What we had is broken. It's gone. There's no way you and I can ever be together."

"Our parents screwed up, Peyton. *We* didn't."

"Brodee." I punctuate his name. "Our parents are in love. Do you realize that? This wasn't just some heat of the moment affair that happened once. This has probably been going on a lot longer than we realize. *Everything* is different. We'd be some twisted form of stepbrother and sister. You might be okay with that, but I'm not."

He runs his fingers roughly through his hair, standing it on end. "We made a pact. We weren't supposed to change."

"It's a moot pact. There's nothing we can do. It's not your fault. It's not mine. It was broken for us."

"I can't lose you, Pete," he says softly. "I don't know how to live life without you. From day one, you've been by my side. Every memory I have has you. I don't know what a memory feels like without you in it. And I don't want to."

And that's exactly why we shouldn't be together. I don't want to be his crutch or just some comfort. We need to be on our own, away from each other, to discover who we are without each other. Nothing in this life is certain, even relationships. Especially relationships. That truth is shattering when it's the only truth you believed in. Love, friendship, marriage. Every relationship I knew—believed in—was solid. How easily a truth can be obliterated.

I rest my hand on his cheek, and he leans into it, closing his eyes as he inhales. He places his hand over mine and turns in, kissing my palm.

"You could never lose me for good, Brodee. You'll always be my best friend. That will never change. But you have to see we'll never be the same. You have to feel it, too. What we built in Hatteras is dead. We can't change that or fix it. Right now we need to let each other go and get past this, but it's going to take time."

"Our story isn't over yet," he insists.

Tears roll down my cheeks. "Our story never got the chance to begin."

His jaw clenches. He exhales, fighting against the emotion inside of him. He loses. A tear streams down his cheek. Angrily, he swipes it away.

We stand, and he takes me into his arms. I cling to him. His lips caress my cheek over and over. Each kiss I savor more than the last. Each kiss marks a goodbye.

Goodbye, once upon a time. Goodbye, Hatteras. Goodbye, happily ever after.

Goodbye, Peyton.

Brodee lets me go. He doesn't smile when he looks me in the eyes. He tries to, but the muscles in his face revolt. "If I were a stoplight, I'd turn red, just so I could stare at you a little bit longer."

I know he's trying to bring levity and light into a crappy situation. I know the pick-up line is supposed to put a smile on my face. All it does is make me cry. I try to smile through the tears.

Brodee kisses me one last time before he steps down off the porch and doesn't look back.

The Day I Sought Solace

THE OCEAN IS my solitude.

Whether I'm on the water or listening from a distance, the waves whisper to me. They call me home. It's why I need to be here today. It's the only home I know now.

As I straddle my board and wait for the next wave, the sun pauses on the horizon, peaking softly above the seamless ocean line as it rises. The beach is pretty quiet this morning. Only surfers occupy the water. It's too early for anyone else to be here. I take the time to appreciate the stillness. With all that's changed in the last week, it's been difficult to find a moment of peace.

Brodee left this morning. I didn't see him off. I didn't have it in me, but I was up. So, I watched from my bedroom window that faces his bedroom, the way I've done so many times before. I watched as he looked to my window. I stayed in the shadows so he wouldn't see me. Seeing me watching—caring—would only make it harder. I watched as he frowned and looked down, dejected, as he walked out of his room. I watched as he shut off his light switch and darkened the light in my heart.

I believe we're made of bits and pieces. Pieces of everyone we know that make us who we are. We go throughout life giving and taking pieces of each other, building the basis of ourselves. We grow and transform. Some people get bigger pieces than others. I'd never realized how large of a piece Brodee was. Without him, half of me is missing. And I'm not sure I'll ever get it back.

"Peyton-Parker," Harper says, paddling up next to me. She says my name like it's meant to be one word. Always. "Are you going to take the next wave? You've been sitting here for like thirty minutes. You've missed so many good ones."

Looking to her, I slowly blink. I know she's talking to me, but my brain hasn't caught up to answer. Time doesn't exist on the water. Hours could pass and the only reminder I'd have is the progression of the sun in the sky.

"I guess I just zoned out. It's going to be nice out today."

"Yeah. Should get up into the seventies later." Harper squints as she looks out for the next wave, straddling her surfboard. The tan skin creases at the corner of her eyes. Water leisurely drips down her neck.

"How many have you gotten?" I ask.

"You've seriously been in your own world, huh? That was my third one, babe." She pauses. "Have you ridden any yet?"

"I caught one." I shrug.

To think, the summer is over and in one day we'll be on our way to USC; it makes me more than melancholy. As ready as I am, this summer changed me, changed us. I'm terrified to live in the real world without the crutch of my home, though it feels less like a home now. A home should be a solace. Instead, mine's broken chaos.

We float just beyond the break, the water gently rocking our boards until we see a good one coming.

"Oh, oh," Harper exclaims. "Get ready for it. Go, go, go."

I paddle hard until I reach the wave and stand, making the drop. With the wind in my face, I ride the wave. Just when I think it's going to be clean sailing to shore, I wipe out. Tumbling under the water, I can't find the surface. The waves keep crashing down over me. I'm starting to lose air, but I tell myself not to panic. I think of the only thing I can to calm down. *Brodee.* I repeat his name over and over. He's my solid ground. He has the power to save me. I stop struggling and wait until I feel myself begin to float to the top. I finally break through, gasping.

Stumbling up the beach, I cough and spit out salt water. My throat burns. Once I reach our towels, I drop my surfboard on the sand and peel off my rash guard. It's suffocating me.

I lay back on my towel in my bikini, letting the sun dry off my skin and breathe. Then I hear Harper jogging up. She sets down her board.

"Are you okay?" she asks with concern, kneeling down. "You took a pretty rough spill out there. I wasn't sure you were going to surface."

"Yeah. I'm good," I say, clipped. "I just need to catch my breath for a second."

Instances like this are a good reminders that, as much as the ocean is my home, sometimes it doesn't want me to get too comfortable. It doesn't have my back. I'm on my own out there. How metaphorically true of my life. I'm all on my own now.

After lying there for a few minutes, Harper asks, "Do you want to talk about it?"

"What makes you think I have something to talk about?" I keep my eyes closed and my arm shielding my face.

"You can't hide anything from me, Peyton-Parker. You've been really quiet this morning." I hear her shift down, lying down beside me. "Over the years I've surfed with two different Peytons. There's pumped, motivated Peyton who's like a kid on Christmas morning when she gets good waves, and then there's pensive, quiet Peyton who's trying to solve world peace while on the water. I thought when you called last night about surfing, it was because these waves were supposed to be perfect, but something tells me it's more than that."

I turn my head. The sand shifts beneath my towel. "Am I that transparent?"

"Just to me." She smiles gently. Her lips are pink from biting them.

After taking a breath, the pit in my stomach grows. I'm hollow. "Nothing will ever be the same."

Harper's eyes grow sad. "Maybe it's for the best. It's time to learn who you are, to take charge of your life, and live for you."

"Yeah," I say distantly. "Maybe."

"You have me, you know? I'll always be here to remind you of your strength and your worth. No matter what happens. It's going to be okay."

"I want it to be okay with him."

"And maybe someday it will." For some reason I doubt that. My brain has tried over and over to strategize ways to keep us from tearing apart, but not one solution gives me Brodee.

I hear my dad's voice then, *Peyton Jane, there's beauty in a new beginning.*

I hope he's right.

FOUR & A HALF YEARS LATER
AFTER
BRODEE

The Day I Invited Her

THE BLARING SOUND of my alarm clock wakes me. The room is still dim, my dark curtains blocking out most of the morning light. I reach over to shut it off, but another arm beats me to it. A more feminine arm. I look over at Brooke, who curls into my side and hums. With her apartment flooded, I forgot I let her sleep over last night.

"Why did you set an alarm on Saturday morning? It's too early," she sleepily groans with her eyes closed. Her long brown hair falls across her face. I brush it back and gently remove her arm from my chest before sitting up.

"I'm going on a run."

"On Saturday morning?" She curls her arm around my waist, trying to pull me back into bed. "Run later. Sleep now."

I stand up, untangling myself from her and the temptation. "Gotta keep my routine. You can stay here. I'll be back in a little bit."

She groans, but rolls over and falls back asleep. It's six o'clock. Brooke won't come back to life until around noon.

I throw on a T-shirt, grab my iPod, slip into my running shoes, and head out the front door. Plugging in my ear buds, I make my way around the first block. With each pounding step, I turn up the volume of my music to drown out my thoughts. Thoughts of the past, thoughts of the future, thoughts of my tangled life.

I do this every day like clockwork. It's a new day, fresh start. The goal is to go an hour without thinking at all. Nothing but music, heartbeats, and the pounding of my feet. Just how I like it.

ABOUT AN HOUR later I make it back to my apartment. It wasn't a very successful run. My thoughts of her were relentless today. One after another, they knocked into me like flashes of light, in time with the beat of my feet on the pavement.

Beat. Her laugh.

Beat. Her smile.

Beat. Her kiss.

Beat. Her tears.

Beat. Her goodbye.

I give up to return to Brooke. She doesn't erase them, but she helps to conceal them. The flashes become dim flickers when we're together. The ones you can't tell if you actually saw or if your mind just imagined them.

When I walk into the kitchen to get my protein shake, I'm surprised to find Brooke standing on the linoleum next to the coffee maker, waiting for it to heat up. She's pulled her hair to the side in a low ponytail and wrapped herself in one of my zip-up hoodies.

"Did you have a good run?" Brooke asks and stands on her toes to kiss my cheek.

It's no ocean wave, but since I'm not close enough to the beach for that, it'll have to do. "Yeah. Thanks." I turn my head and kiss her mouth. "Morning," I say against her lips.

My phone buzzes in my shorts pocket.

Skylar: When do you plan on getting in?

Me: I'm leaving after my last final on Wed. Should be there around 6 or 7.

"Who else is awake at this painful hour on a Saturday?" She pours herself a cup and cradles it between her hands against her chest like it's her personal heater.

"Skylar. He just wanted to see when I'd be home."

"Oh." The disappointment in her voice is not lost on me.

I've done everything I can to avoid 'the talk.' Brooke is a Durham local, and we haven't exactly determined what will happen to us when we graduate. I'm moving back home next week for a month before heading to Boston for a job. And she's…well…not.

We've been together for a year, and I know she's waiting for me to either ask her to go with me or end it, but I'm not ready for either. The only thing I can think about is the fact that in less than one week I'll be graduating. In one week my best friends will be getting married. In one week I'll see...*her*.

Four years doesn't seem that long in the grand scheme of things, but these years at Duke feel like a new lifetime. Everything is different. Everything, that is, except for Skylar and Harper.

I've thought about asking Brooke to be my date to their wedding, but I don't know what Peyton has planned—if Tyler will be her date or if they're even still together. Though, if that status had changed, I'm sure Skylar would've said something to me by now. I don't want to make things any more complicated than they already are.

My phone buzzes in my hand.

Skylar: Cool. Excited to see you, man.
Harper misses you, but she'll never own up to it.

I chuckle.

Me: I miss her too. Hey.
Is Peyton bringing Tyler to the wedding?
Skylar: Harper says yes.

I tuck my phone back in my pocket and turn to Brooke. "So. I have this wedding coming up next week."

"You don't say." She flutters her eyelashes and smirks, showing the dimple in her right cheek.

"I was wondering if that's something you might be interested in going to with me."

She presses a hand over her heart and gives me her best Southern accent. “Well, I do declare, Mr. Fisher. Are you asking me to be your date to your best friend’s wedding?”

I laugh lightly and wrap my arms around her waist. “Is that a yes?”

“Of course. Will I finally get to meet your family?”

I internally cringe. “They should be there, yes.”

“Good.” She gives me a peck. “It’s about time.” My unease doesn’t go unnoticed. Not that I was trying to hide it, but it’s impossible to mask. “I know you don’t really like talking about them, but it’s going to be fine. Parents love me.”

It’s not Brooke I’m worried about. It’s me. I have a hard enough time being around my dad and Olivia in their new life. I’m not ready to introduce Brooke to the dysfunction that is my family.

“Yes, they will.” I smile and pull back. “I’m gonna go shower. Get ready so we can go do something.”

“I’m going to need a new dress for the wedding,” she calls to me as I walk down the narrow hallway to the bathroom to get cleaned up.

“I’m not going dress shopping,” I holler back. “Take Deanna.”

“Oh, c’mon.” Brooke follows me into the bathroom. “I want your opinion. This is for *your* friend’s wedding, and I’m meeting *your* family. Please. I need to know how I should dress.”

“My friends are pretty easygoing. You’ll look good in whatever you wear, Brooke.”

“You always say that.”

“Because it’s true.” I turn on the water, remove my shirt, and turn back to her in the doorway. She pushes out her bottom lip in a fake pout.

"Fine," I chuckle and shoo her out of the bathroom. "We'll go pick out a dress. Go get ready."

WHEN WE GOT back from Hatteras all those summers ago, Peyton and I promised to stay in touch, and we did at first. We saw each other every few months, in between semesters or on random weekends. But our every few month visits eventually became the occasional holiday: Thanksgiving, Christmas, and New Years. The last time I saw her was Christmas Eve. Twelve months ago. I think about how long it's been, and the faded aching in my chest comes to the forefront. I wonder where we'll go from here. When I see her will enough time have passed so the possibility of an 'us' becomes an option? Will she look at me the way she used to, or will too much time apart make us nothing but strangers?

This time I make a pact with myself. If nothing has changed, I stop this for good. I'll give my heart fully to Brooke. I'll ask her to come with me to Boston. Maybe I'll propose. All I know is I can't keep waiting for something that will never be. I refuse to be my father, waiting my entire life for my opening. If it's not meant to be, I need to move on. I have to let Peyton go.

The Day I Picked Spider-Man

FOUR YEARS AGO

WHEN I REACH their dorm room I knock twice. Harper opens the door and looks startled; not quite the reaction I expected. *Surprise?* "Brodee, hey!" She opens the door wide enough for Peyton to see me. "Look, Peyton," she slowly says with strained enthusiasm. "Brodee's here." I don't like the sound of Harper's voice. Peyton's eyes widen, but she stays on her made bed as I enter the room.

"Hey," I say, nervous that this surprise visit was a bad idea. We haven't seen each other since we said goodbye a month ago.

Peyton gradually crawls off her bed—still not smiling—and uneasily walks up to me. Not even a hint of happiness crosses her lips. This was a very bad idea. *Why did I come?* It's too soon. I should have called first. She isn't ready to see me. But I was ready to see her. I couldn't go any longer. I missed her too much. I needed a cheesy pick-up line. I needed one of her half-smiles that always illuminated her eyes. I needed her comforting silence.

We stand toe-to-toe for an exorbitant amount of time, staring at each other. I see so much in her eyes—too much. Sadness. Regret. Fear. Pining. It all jumbles together, forming one overwhelming ache in my chest. Then she flings her arms around my neck and it instantly diminishes. Her body shakes. At first, I think she might be laughing—manically—but then she gasps, and I know that sound. I've heard it enough to know she's crying. I hold her tighter. I hear the door quietly open and close, Harper most likely leaving and giving us some time alone.

"Shhh…Pete, why are you crying?"

She shakes her head, unable to answer me, or refusing to. I can't tell which. Her face is buried in the crook of my neck, soaking my skin. If her tears were a hurricane, I wouldn't survive. I hate to see her pain. I lift her trembling body off the ground, walk to her bed, settling her in my lap, and intensify my grip around her. Her inability to form words is scaring me.

"Pete, talk to me." I run my fingers down the back of her head, over her long blonde hair. When I try leaning away to look into her eyes, she holds on with more strength. "Okay," I quietly say. "We'll just sit here. I've got you now."

When I think about the last time she clung to me like this, I worry more. She hasn't cried like this since her Dad died. I'm not sure what that means for us. It can't be anything good. Her tears feel desperate and broken. What hurts most is that I can't do anything to take away her pain. So I sit without a word, clutching her to my chest.

After a few minutes, she calms down, rubs the back of her hands against her face, and slides off my lap to sit next to me. When she looks up at me, black streaks stain her freckled cheeks. I take the sleeve of my hoodie and wipe it across her face.

"I've missed you," she says softly, batting her wet, clumpy eyelashes and sniffling. She wipes her hand under her nose.

"Is that why you're crying? Because you missed me?" I try not to laugh. Because *that* I can handle. Heartbroken crying? Bad news crying? Death of a loved one crying? No thank you. But tears because she missed me as much as I missed her, I'll take it.

She nods.

"Oh, Pete." I take her face in my hands and try to kiss her, but she turns away, pulling out of my grasp.

Her head shakes. "That hasn't changed."

Her rejection hurts, but I accept it. I knew it was a possibility. She'd made it clear on her porch that we were over. If I wait, if I have patience, our time will come. I don't want to fight. I just want to be here. With her.

"Okay," I say. "That's fine. When you decide I'm the one, I'll be waiting. But for now, can I at least hold you until you stop crying?"

She nods again and leans into my shoulder, allowing me to wrap her in my arms again. If this is all I can get, I'll take it until she can give me more. Or until she takes it away altogether.

Harper comes back about twenty minutes later, and they've been decorating ever since, pretending Peyton doesn't have the remnants of black makeup dotting her face and eyes so puffy she can hardly open them.

"Do you think we need curtains?"

Peyton looks confused. "We have blinds. Why would we need curtains?"

"I don't know," Harper says. "To add character. Our dorm is so bare and dull."

Skylar should be meeting us soon to go see a movie, but he's late, so

I'm stuck listening to things a man should never have to worry about.

I was hoping Peyton would be alone when I came to her dorm room, but since Harper answered the door, that squashed my envisioned reunion. I wanted to come the first weekend after school started, but I knew I needed to give her space. I was hoping the month apart would have given her enough time to get over the notion that we can't make this work.

"Brodee, what do you think?"

"Huh?"

"Robert or Chris?" Harper asks.

I'd stopped listening to them ten minutes ago.

"Huh?" I repeat, even more confused.

"Robert," she holds up a poster of Iron Man. "Or Chris," she holds up a poster of Captain America. "Peyton will only let me hang one."

"Because you don't even like The Avengers," Peyton argues with a sigh that tells me they've had this disagreement many times before.

"But they're hot. What does it matter if I like the movies or not? I like looking at them."

Peyton face-palms. Literally. Palm to forehead. I laugh.

"Andrew," I answer.

"Who?"

"Andrew Garfield. Spider-Man."

Peyton giggles and continues hanging pictures on a string across the wall above her bed. Scanning the pictures, I notice not one is of our summer together. However, I made the wall in a couple other pictures from high school, so at least she doesn't want to erase our entire history.

Harper groans. "You're no help. Of course you'd pick Peter Parker.

Prejudice," she grumbles.

There's a knock at the door. "Skylar!" Harper drops the posters, jumps off her bed, and lunges for the door, flinging it open as she leaps into his arms.

Yeah, that was the reunion I'd hoped for with Peyton. Too bad it didn't happen quite like that.

When Harper lets Skylar go, he comes in and hugs me. "It's about time you got your butt in town."

"Ha. Yeah. Just needed to get all settled in first."

"Took you long enough. I thought I was going to have to drag you here for a weekend. So, are we going to a movie or what?"

I look to Peyton whose eyes are still a little puffy and red as she sits cross-legged on her yellow bedspread. "Let me just fix my mascara, and then we can go," she says. Awkwardness settles in the room as she moves toward her desk.

"Aww…P Parker, you miss me that much?" Skylar teases to lift the tension. He must know.

"So much, Sky. I don't know how I survive with you all the way across the parking lot," she says dryly, lifting her makeup bag out of her desk.

"I'm here now. Big Sky is here. No need to fret."

She cracks a smile and shakes her head at him. Our eyes meet briefly. There's something in them that tells me we're going to be okay.

We're going to be okay.

We have to be.

The Day I Played Her the Song

I MAKE IT into Charleston just in time for the Christmas party, because I promised my mom I would. The Christmas party used to be a Fisher/Parker tradition, but now only my dad and Olivia put it together. My mom hates going, but she's too classy of a woman to decline an invite after all these years. They might not be best friends anymore, but she refuses to be anything but gracious and civil. She's a better person than I am. I don't even want to be here, but I am for her. Well not *her* her, but her too.

I pull into the driveway I've parked in hundreds of times, behind all of the other parked cars, and slowly make my way up the pathway to the front door of the Parkers' house—or I guess I should say the Fisher's house since it's my dad and Olivia's now—and let myself in.

It doesn't matter that there are a hundred other people here—when I walk in I can feel her. It doesn't require sight of her to take my breath away. Just knowing we're only feet from each other makes my heart race and all the air leave my body.

As my eyes roam around the house for her face, I see Peyton talking to Harper in the back corner of the living room. She's already looking at me. I was hoping I'd see her first, so I could watch her uninhibited for a moment, but she'll just have to be aware that I'm checking her out. The first thing I notice is her hair is gone. Her long, beautiful blonde hair is chopped up to her chin. And it's lighter, almost white. I blink, taking it in. It's such a shock I don't know what to think at first, but Peyton could be bald and still be gorgeous.

She's wearing a little red dress that hits her above the knee. I don't think I've ever seen her in red, because she never liked herself in red, which I've never understood. It looks incredible on her.

I know I'm supposed to act unaffected—that what we had is gone and can never be again—but she's so beautiful, every wound that was once scabbed over is now raw. It takes a few seconds before I make a move.

A timid smile spreads across her face as I approach, and my smile is automatic. I've gone twelve months without her smile, and I don't know how I lasted that long. Seeing it now makes me realize I had a gaping hole in my life, but as soon as she smiles at me, the hole refills.

Peyton hands Harper her champagne glass without breaking our gaze and walks with purpose toward me. I nearly forgot how good it feels to touch her. When we hug, it's a silent exchange. It seems it always is now. I'm filled with so many emotions it's hard to identify them all. The love. The regret. The comfort. But most of all, the longing. And by the feel of her arms wrapped firmly around my neck, I know she has to feel it all, too.

"Hi," she says when we break apart.

"Hey." I take my bottom lip between my teeth to keep from grinning.

"What's it been? A year since I've seen you?"

Almost to the date. "Something like that." I notice her freckles are gone. She completely covered them with makeup.

"You went to Brooke's house for Thanksgiving, right?"

"Yeah." I nod and shove my hands in my front jean pockets. They're having a hard time keeping to themselves. *She's not yours to touch,* I tell them.

"Tyler and I decided to do Thanksgiving here with my mom."

I heard. It was why I went to Brooke's. Seeing her with Tyler isn't any easier now than it used to be. It's worse, in fact. I notice Peyton doesn't say Nick, though I know my dad was there, too.

"How is Brooke?"

"She's good. She'll be coming to the wedding, so…"

"Oh good. I'll get to meet her finally." Peyton smiles. It's hard to tell if it's genuine or forced. She's mastered hiding emotions over the years. Better than I have. I wish it were as easy for me as it is for her. Somehow it feels like a competition, and, if it is, I've already lost. "Tyler will be here a little bit later tonight."

Though I haven't seen Peyton in the last year, the occasional text or email has been exchanged. And, of course, there's social media, where Brooke plasters pictures of us all over. I do what I can to avoid seeing Peyton and Tyler in pictures on her profile, so I rarely go online. All I know is that I want to be long gone by the time Tyler gets here.

"Don't tell me my son decided to seek out his friends before his own mother."

I turn and see my mom maneuvering around people, acknowledging them as she goes. She's all smiles, and I hug her when she gets to me. "Hi,

Mom." I kiss her cheek as I pull away.

She touches her fingers to my face, and I know exactly what she's going to say. "You haven't shaved."

"Finals have kept me a little preoccupied." I rub my palm back and forth against my stubble.

Her face softens. "Well, you look very handsome with a little scruff. Makes you look so grown up. You haven't called in a week, though. Just because you're a grown man doesn't mean you don't have to call your mother. Don't you turn into Carter on me."

"I'm sorry." I chuckle. "Studying for finals was seriously a nightmare. Where is the punk anyway?"

"Oh, he should be here soon. He had a date with…what's her name?" she asks and wags her finger at me like I'm supposed to know.

"Veronica?" I offer.

She shakes her head. "No, the redhead."

"Leah? Nichole?" I honestly have no idea who she's talking about. I'm just spouting out names. "Alexis?"

"No…The curly redhead. Short. Wears too much makeup."

"Oh," I say with a laugh. "You're talking about umm…" I actually do remember that one. I snap my fingers, trying to recall her name. It was different. "Aniessa? The one he met at rush last year."

"Yes! Goodness, I can't keep track of them. I don't know why I try."

Me either.

"I knew he'd grow up to be a heartbreaker," Peyton says, laughing to herself.

Mom puts her arm around Peyton's waist and tugs her to her side. "I don't get to see you enough." She kisses her temple. "Will Tyler be here soon?"

Peyton flashes the light on the screen of her cell and looks at the time. "Should be here in about an hour."

"Oh. Well then. I'll let you two get back to chatting. Just wanted to see my son before he leaves me for good."

"Mom." I sigh. "I'll be here for another month, and then I'll only be a flight away."

"I know, I know." She smirks. "I'm just giving you a hard time. Massachusetts is so much farther than North Carolina. But I'm so proud of you. You deserve the position."

When she walks away, Peyton questions, "Massachusetts?"

"Yeah." I rub the back of my neck. It's weird we don't know these kinds of details about each other anymore. Before, she would have known about the application I sent in. I would have called her as soon as the interview was over. She'd have been the first call after I heard I got the job. Now, I have Brooke. "I got a job at John Hancock in Boston as a financial analyst."

"Oh." Again, I can't read her expression. I think there's sadness there, but she blinks it away and replaces it with excitement. "Congratulations! That sounds like the perfect place for you!"

"Dude!" Skylar claps me on the back as he comes up and tugs me around for a hug, briefly patting my back before letting go. "You're home! Finally! Where's Brooke?" He looks over my shoulder like she might be hiding behind me.

"She'll be here in a couple days. She wasn't able to get off work to come earlier." I leave out the part where it's my fault. Had I not procrastinated and asked her to come to the wedding earlier, she would've been able to ask for more time off.

Harper squeezes between Peyton and Skylar and hugs me. "She's coming to the wedding?" I pat the top of her head because I know how much she loves it. She ducks away, smoothing her hair. I think it's the first time I've seen her hair without some bright color. It's light gray. *Is that a thing now? Or did she just want to see what she'd look like when she's eighty years old?*

My hand instantly finds the back of my neck again. I don't want Peyton to know I asked Brooke so late in the game. This is such a stupid, one-sided competition. "Yeah, Skylar didn't tell you?"

Harper looks over at him, and I beg him with my eyes to play along. I still hadn't mentioned to him that I was for sure bringing Brooke.

"Oh, yeah. Sorry, babe. I just figured you would assume she was coming."

"Perfect!" she says too brightly. The last time Brooke and Harper were in the same room, I thought I was going to suffocate from the awkwardness. It was clear Harper didn't like her, and Brooke was oblivious—still is—and I'd like to keep it that way. Though I still don't know why Harper doesn't like her. Everyone likes Brooke.

"Is she going to Boston with you?" Peyton asks.

I don't know why I wasn't expecting that question. If the rolls were reversed, I'd have asked her if Tyler was going with her, though my reasoning would be different. "Uh, we haven't really talked about it, but it's a possibility."

Skylar interjects, "I thought you weren't sure you were going to ask her to go with you?" Realizing too late it was info I wanted him to keep between us, the last few words come out slow and awkward.

I shoot him a look. He's killing me. He's supposed to make it look like Brooke and I are happy and in love. Which, of course, we are. But Peyton needs to know that. It needs to be plastered across the walls in bold, vibrant letters.

"I haven't outright asked her, which is why it's only a possibility right now."

Skylar realizes his mistake and shuts up.

"Are you nervous to ask her?" Peyton prods. "Worried she'll say no?"

I smile tightly. "Just haven't gotten a chance yet."

Harper saves me. "Will she be here in time for the rehearsal dinner on Friday?"

"Yeah, she'll be here Friday afternoon."

"Skylar has your shirt, bowtie, and suspenders for the wedding, so don't let him forget to give them to you."

"Babe, I won't forget. You gave me one job. I think I can handle my groomsmen."

"He says that," Harper leans into Peyton and me, "but someone is going to go without something the day of. I'll put money on it."

"Well, it won't be me," I say to appease her. "I'll get my stuff from him tomorrow."

"Thank you. Robby and Mike already have theirs," she says, "but Jackson isn't back from Utah until Thursday night. And no matter how many times I remind Skylar to give Isaac his stuff when he sees him, he never does."

"Cut me some slack. We still have three days. I think we'll be okay."

"Whatever you say, babe."

"She will be the death of me," Skylar mutters in my ear, and I snort.

"I heard that."

"Have you seen our parents yet?" Peyton whispers to me. I love the way she says it conspiratorially, like we're still in this together—against them.

"No, where are they?"

She nods her head toward the archway that connects the entryway to the living room. They're kissing. Mistletoe dangles above them. When they pull back, my dad smiles down at Olivia. Even though it been four years, it's still unnatural to see them do that. I don't know that I'll ever get used to it.

"You'd think they would have more respect for Tate. It doesn't matter how much time has passed, they don't have to parade their marriage in front of her."

"Respect?" I scoff. "They lost that a long time ago."

Peyton laughs without humor. Olivia notices us, says something to my dad, and they make their way over.

"Incoming," she mumbles.

"We're going to get something to eat," Harper excuses her and Skylar, timely enough.

"Hey, son!" My dad claps his hand on my shoulder and pulls me in for a hug I don't go into willingly. "We didn't see you come in. How long have you been here?"

I offer a stiff smile. "Like twenty minutes."

"Have you seen your mom yet?" His eyes dart around the room, looking for her.

"Yeah. She came and said hi to me a few minutes ago."

"What about your brother? Is he here yet?"

I'm not the host. Shouldn't you know these things? "Not that I know of."

Olivia stands beside him, almost like she's waiting her turn. "Hey, Liv," I say. We've been trying to figure out our dynamic ever since they began. It's strange, considering she's my stepmom now, but she acts less like a mother than she used to. While she's not blameless in any of this, I've always held more resentment toward my dad.

Every time we're together Olivia walks on eggshells. I can tell she wants to hug me, but doesn't want to make things more awkward, so I make the first move.

"It's good to see you, Brodee." Her genuine personality hasn't changed. She squeezes me once before letting go. "We really missed you at Thanksgiving, but I hear Brooke's family took good care of you."

"Yeah, they did."

"When are we going to meet her?"

"She'll be here for the wedding."

"Oh good!" Olivia exclaims. "It's about time."

"I was beginning to wonder if she was merely an excuse to get out of the holidays." My dad's joke falls flat, forcing laughter and tight smiles from all of us. *Good one, Dad.*

"I've seen pictures," Peyton interjects. "She's definitely real, and she's beautiful."

"Pictures? What pictures?" Olivia asks her. "Why haven't you shown me?"

"They're online, Mom."

"Oh, I hate the social media." I snort. "That's all anyone ever does anymore. No one ever carries on conversations without their phones. It's all gossip and propaganda."

"It's just social media, Mom. Not *the* social media."

"Whatever." She waves Peyton off. "I hate it."

I do my best to stifle my laughter. Peyton pinches my arm. "Ouch," I mutter and cover my smile.

"Where are you staying while you're here?" Dad asks.

"I'll be here for a month, so I'm going to stay with Mom."

"Well, you're more than welcome to crash here for a couple nights if you want to," Olivia offers.

"Thanks," I offer, though I won't.

"Hey." I lean into Peyton, "Come with me to my car?" With a head nod, I gesture for her to follow me outside. "I have something I want you to listen to."

She nods rapidly. We're both grateful to be saved from this hell. I only have thirty minutes until Tyler shows up, and I *will* duck out before then.

We grab our coats off the hooks and walk out the front door. It's not snowing, but it might as well be. It's freezing. Peyton tugs her coat a little tighter around her frame and speed-walks to my car.

"Gosh!" Peyton shivers. "What is it? Ten degrees out here?"

"Feels like it, but it's probably thirty." I chuckle. "There's this new band that I think you'd like. I want you to hear them."

"Cool. You know how much I love your recommendations."

I can't remember the last time we talked music. It's one more thing I miss about us.

My heart speeds up at the thought of being alone with her again. It's been so long. I open the passenger door for her and then I hop in on the other side. I start the car so we can have some heat, and turn on my stereo. When I say the band's name, I can tell she hasn't heard of them yet. I flip through the songs, stopping long enough so she gets a taste of each song.

It has your typical rock band instruments, but what I love most about this band is the unexpected sound of violins. It never struck me as an instrument used for anything outside of an orchestra before, but it blends so well with the drums and guitars.

Peyton smiles the way she does when she's into a band—a hint of a smile, absorbing each song. It feels good that I still know her. I stop on the last song of the album. The song I wanted her to hear most—the reason I wanted her to hear the band in the first place.

It's a slower paced song. The guitars strum gently but upbeat.

"I listen to this one a lot." I turn up the volume a little.

Peyton sits quietly, and I watch her. She shifts in her seat and tilts her head as she stares at the dashboard. I wish I could read her thoughts. She feels so far away, though she's only a couple feet from me. I want to reach out and take her hand, but I know I can't do that.

The male vocalist sings of falling into old memories, into things they used to do together, and going back to a beautiful place they could share. How he wouldn't forget how he felt. I feel it every time I listen to the song. I feel his need to remember, to be able to hold onto whatever he can to get him through every day. The only thing pulling me through is memories of her. What we had can't be forgotten. Maybe it faded for her, but it's still so vivid in my mind, I'd do anything to remake it.

I continue to watch her as the song plays. I want her to look at me, but she stays focused on the dashboard, lost in her thoughts. Her smile gradually fades. If only her thoughts were constellations that I could gaze into and explore.

Once the song is over, there's only silence. My breathing and time stop as I wait for her to feel everything I feel. For her to fall into memories with me, and come back to me.

She lifts her eyes and the corners of her mouth, but it's not the smile I want. "Yeah, it's a good band," she says. It's like she's trying to appease me.

Did she even listen to the words? Is she ignoring them? Is this her way of telling me she doesn't feel the same way?

"I'll have to get their album. Thanks for the recommendation. You still know my taste in music." She smiles, but it's only a fixture on her face. It's not filled with any emotion. Even if she doesn't live in those memories with me, isn't she at least a little sad that what we had is gone? Her face is all wrong. It's false, filled with fake emotions and empty eyes.

I take a deep breath and pull the key from the ignition. "You ready?" I ask, motioning back to the house. She blinks like she's confused. *Does she really not get it?* I don't want to have to explain it to her. She should get it. She should know me.

Peyton doesn't respond the way I expect her to. "Tyler proposed last night."

My heart tightens in my chest.

"And I said yes."

I can't breathe.

"We don't have a date set yet, but I don't think it'll be a long engagement. We've been together long enough and just want a small wedding. Just close family and friends."

I don't even know what to say. It hurts too much. *Am I having a heart attack? Is this what it feels like?*

"I wanted you to be the first to know before we announced it to everyone else tonight."

How thoughtful.

She pauses for a reply I can't give her. She said yes? I've never hated three letters more. They are the worst letters in the alphabet. *How could she say yes?* There are feelings churning inside of me that I can't keep down. I think I'm going to be sick. Peyton is staring at me, waiting. I have to pull myself together.

"Are you going to say something?"

I have plenty that I want to say. *Don't do it. Come back to me. Forget him. You were always meant to be mine.* But I can't get my mouth to form the words. We haven't talked about our feelings in so long, about what we are or could've been. I know it's over, but I can't seem to let her go.

Smile, Brodee. I do. Forcefully. "Congratulations."

"Thanks." She smiles back. It's not one of her Peyton smiles. It's sad, apologetic even. *Does she pity me?*

I take a deep breath, but it burns to breathe. I can't get enough air in my lungs to feel any relief. Suddenly, my car feels too small. Claustrophobia is setting in. I need her out of it. There isn't enough room inside for the both of us.

"He should be here soon then, huh? We should get back inside, so you can make the big announcement."

Softly, she says, "Okay," and nods.

I lock up the car and walk the short distance back to the house. I stop before going inside. Tyler could be in there already. I can't go in and hear her announce it all over again and pretend everything is fine. I don't even know the meaning of fine.

"I think I'm actually gonna head out."

Peyton blinks. "Already?"

"Yeah. I came straight here after I got into town, and I'm super tired." I scratch the back of my neck, faking exhaustion. "The three-hour drive kinda took it out of me. Plus, Brooke will be calling me soon, and I want to be able to answer it when she does so we can finalize the plan for her coming down." I motion for Peyton to head inside without me. There's no way I'll be able to hang around and hear everyone cheer and congratulate them. "Tell my mom I headed home. We'll catch up later."

Peyton reaches out and hugs me. I reflexively stiffen, though her touch quickly softens me. I wrap my arms around her like it's the last time. I breathe her in, and I'm punched in the gut with a dose of reality. She's not mine, and she never will be. I pull back first—and swiftly—because it's too painful being this close to her with so much distance between us.

"See you later?" she asks, hopeful, but uncertain.

"Sure." I turn with a strained smile and wave.

"Brodee?" Her questioning voice stops me. Peyton takes a step toward me, but I take a step back. She takes another step, like she wants to see if I'm trying to get away from her. I move back again. I have to. I can't be close to her any longer. I have to go.

Her eyes hold the question: *What are you doing?*

"I just can't, okay?" I can't hide the pain in my eyes any longer. We've been pretending for too long.

Tears start to sting her eyes. “Brodee,” she nearly pleads. “Can’t we talk—?”

I shake my head and walk away without a backward glance. It hits me even harder as I walk away.

I lost her.

I really lost her this time.

The Day She Lumped Me with Him

FOUR YEARS AGO

I FIND PEYTON exactly where Harper said I would, walking out of the building where she had her last class. It must have been a lazy morning. Peyton has her hair up on the top of her head and is wearing one of those thick stretchy bands around her head to push back her bangs. She looks cute, cozy. I wait for her to pass me, lingering under an oak tree before I stealthily walk up behind her on the sidewalk.

"I'm new in town. Could you give me directions to your dorm room?"

Peyton spins around, nearly knocking her head into mine. "Brodee!" She punches my shoulder before engulfing me in her arms. "You stupid creep, you scared me!"

"Point for Gryffindor."

She chuckles. "Since when do you like *Harry Potter*?"

I nudge her shoulder with mine as we walk through the grass on campus. "Who doesn't like *Harry Potter*?"

"What are you doing here?"

I shrug and say, "Harper told me you finished class at two, so I figured I'd come surprise you."

She blinks in confusion. "No, I mean, you were just here a couple weekends ago. I thought I was supposed to come see you next month."

"I couldn't wait that long."

My roommate, Greg, is a sophomore who has a new girl in his bed every day. Yeah. Day. Not night. I've walked in on him like ten times. He doesn't even care, and neither do his conquests. They just keep doing their thing, and I'm left scarred and bolting out of the room faster than I can count to one. I hate it. All I can think about is how much I wish Peyton were around, so I could seek shelter in her room and vent. She'd get it. We could joke and laugh about my misfortune and then come up with solutions to save my eyes.

There's a shift. Peyton's no longer smiling at me or laughing. "Brodee…"

The way she says my name…I hate it. There's no gold and fire in her eyes. There's no playfulness or affection. I'm no longer a person. I'm a sadness.

I sigh. "Peyton. Stop making this so depressing. A guy can't come and see his best friend?"

"I just don't want you to get false hope in us."

"I'm not," I counter. *Why does she have to bring that into this?* "It's hard adjusting to not seeing you every day. I wanted to hang out with my best friend. Am I not allowed to do that? Can we do that?"

Her stare is solemn, almost condescending. "Can *you* do that? Just hang out, I mean."

The way she asks makes me feel two inches tall, like this isn't nearly as difficult for her as it is for me. As if I'm so pathetically in love with her that I can't control myself, that I'll fling myself at her any minute. She can disregard her feelings for me like she would shoo away a fly. I wish I could do the same.

One part of me wants to shout at her and ask her how she can shut me out so easily. Another part takes it as a challenge. *Of course I can do it, but if I turn on my charm and shut off my desperation, can you?* The other parts shut up. They're already tired of this argument.

"I can, if you can."

Peyton smiles with a light laugh like she wants to call me out on my crap, as if she knows me or something. "Let me text Harper. See if she and Skylar want to meet us to get some food."

Chaperones. She really doesn't trust me.

"How is this so easy for you?" I ask. I let it go last time, but if this is going to be an ongoing battle, I want to end it now. "How can you just shut off your feelings like that?"

She puts down her phone and sets her stare. There's no light, no more laughter. "Because I have to," she whispers. "You think this is easy for me? If I don't, then I'll be a puddle. I'll be nothing but tears and heartbrokenness, and that's not how I want to live."

I take one of her hands in mine. "If it's so hard to let us go, it can't possibly be right, Pete."

Her eyes break away, following the tree line on the open lawn in the middle of campus. Her silence is suffocating me. Whatever she's going to say isn't going to be what I want to hear.

"I've thought the same thing, you know?" she says, her voice faraway.

"If it hurts this much, maybe we made the wrong decision. Maybe I pushed you away too soon." Her eyes lock with mine. "But making the right choice doesn't always feel good. If it did, it would never be hard to choose what's right. We'd always just go with what makes us feel good."

"What's wrong with being impulsive? Living in the moment? Doing what feels good? Being with the one you love?" I let go of her hand and take her shoulders in my hands, brushing my thumbs back and forth. "Why can't we have both? We feel right. We feel good. It's okay to do what feels good sometimes."

She puts distance between us. "Because we're not right. We're twisted."

It couldn't have hurt more if she'd slapped me across the face. I choke, "Twisted?"

"Please don't look at me like that, Brodee. You *know* it's true. And every time we see each other, the harder it gets to make the distinction between friends or more. We have too much *more*. It's blurring the lines and only making it more difficult for us to move on."

"We're not twisted. That's your own insecurity." I straighten. "And maybe I don't want to move on."

She shakes her head. "It's not just that. Someday I want a happy marriage, a solid family. How can I have that with the son of the man who harbored feelings behind my dad's back all those years, and then took advantage of my mom when the timing was right?"

A knife in my chest cuts off my air supply. "You're lumping me with him?"

I want to punch something. Too bad the closest thing is a tree trunk. I don't need a broken hand *and* a broken heart.

"I want you in my life," she says, inching into my space again, peering up at me. "I need you as my best friend, Brodee. Just my friend. If we keep holding on, this will turn into a bloodbath. The only thing that will remain of our hearts is the tissue. We seemed like a good idea once upon a time, but you have to know, you have to see that ship is long gone."

Why do I feel like she's breaking up with me all over again? All I wanted was to seek comfort in my best friend, to spend time with someone who knows me better than anyone else. All I wanted was to come and be with the one person who could make me feel better. Now, all I feel is worse—worse than I've ever felt.

I can't open my mouth to say anything. She takes my silence as her cue to drive the nail into the coffin. "I can't handle you constantly reminding me of the summer. It's hard enough as it is. And you looking at me like that and touching me the way you do…it makes it so hard to think straight, to make the right choice. I need you to go back to what we were before Hatteras. If you care at all about my happiness, I need you to be the over-protective brother. The platonic, carefree best friend." Tears glisten in her pale blue eyes. She doesn't blink once. "I'm begging you. If you love me…Let. Me. Go."

When she begs like that, looking so desperate and distraught, what can I do but nod. And if she's going to lump me with my dad? Why would I want to be with her? Why would I want to be a constant reminder of betrayal?

The Day I Implemented My Pact

WHEN I WAKE up I don't get out of bed. I stare at the ceiling of my old bedroom with my arm behind my head. It baffles me—and everyone else—that my mom never sold this place and moved far away. Every day she has to look next door and see the love of her life with her ex-best friend. But she refused to lose the house my brother and I grew up in. And I don't think she wants them to think they won. Though I don't think anyone won in this situation. Everyone lost something.

"Just because this house holds memories with him, doesn't mean I should have to move. It's ours. I won't give up a part of my history because he decided it wasn't what he wanted," she once said to me. "It's what I wanted. I'll cherish this house until the day I die."

At first, I thought she kept the house because she hoped he'd come back, but now I know even if he did attempt to come crawling back, she wouldn't let him. She's done with that period of her life. She asked him to move out. She served him with the divorce papers. All things he did willingly.

Our last summer in Hatteras plays like a broken record in my head all the time. Sometimes my brain gives me the good parts—the parts where Peyton smiled at me, the times when she kissed me, the feel of her arms wrapped around my body, the sound of her laughter—but days like today, all I see is the bad.

When I had come up the boardwalk and into the beach house that day, I'd nearly walked in on my parents kissing, but it hadn't been right. It'd been my dad, but not my mom. It had been Olivia. I'd stopped and quickly, but quietly, taken a step back. They had been too wrapped up in a passionate embrace to even notice I was there.

"Stop," Olivia said, pushing him back. And I slipped behind the corner, out of sight. "Nick, we can't do this right now. It isn't right."

"Liv, it's our time."

"I know, but this summer...this summer is all we have left, and it's almost over. Tate's not just your wife. She's my best friend."

"You know, I loved you first."

She groaned. "It's not some competition. You might have loved me first, but you gave me to him. I moved on with my life. You moved on with yours. Just because Jon is gone doesn't mean that it's paved the way for our future."

"Then why do you keep kissing me back?"

"Because I miss him! Because you've always been there for me. Because I'm so lost without him I don't know what to do with myself!"

"It's more than that, and you know it, Liv. You're lying to yourself. You love me. If you didn't you wouldn't keep kissing me back."

"Stop it, Nick. You're taking advantage of the situation, and you know it."

"So what if I am? You love me, and I love you, Olivia. I always have.

I've waited twenty-five years. I've regretted not taking a chance since the day you met Jon. "

"You introduced us!" she bellows.

"He was my roommate. Of course I introduced you. So we could all be friends! Not so you could fall in love with him!"

I couldn't listen any longer. I'd bolted. I'd taken off down the beach and had dropped onto the sand, needing the waves to bring me back, to center me. My mind had to catch up with all that I'd witnessed.

He destroyed everything.

I knew from that day forward everything would change. Peyton and I would never be the same. I had been so furious after seeing them—after what he'd done—I'd wanted to hurt him the only way I'd known how. By not going to Duke.

So much for that revenge. I thought I'd finally forgiven him. It took me a few years, but I thought I'd gotten over it. I understood on some level what my dad felt. I couldn't imagine watching Peyton love another man, marrying another man, and having to spend every day knowing I did nothing. It hadn't excused what my dad did, but I'd understood it.

After last night, I hate him all over again. I fought for Peyton and she still wouldn't be mine. I'd have to watch her marry another man, have his children, grow old with him…all because our parents fell in love. Life can be so cruel and perverse.

So, this is it. Time to implement the pact I made with myself.

"HEY, TURD BISCUIT." Carter knocks once before barging into my room. "Wake up. Mom wants to talk to you."

"Well, good morning to you too, snot nugget." I yawn and stretch before sitting up on one of my elbows. "What does she want?"

"How am I supposed to know? She just told me to come get you. So get your lazy hiney out of bed." I throw a pillow at the wall by his head as he laughs and ducks out of my room.

When I walk downstairs, she's in the kitchen, sipping her coffee. I sit up on a barstool at the counter.

"Morning," I greet.

My mom passes me a cup of coffee. "How are you holding up?" She leans over the countertop with her coffee mug in hand and a robe tied around her waist.

I raise my eyebrow in question. "Fine. Why?"

"I mean with Peyton and Tyler."

I run my hand down my face, desperately not wanting to have this conversation right now. I'd rather plan my own funeral than have this conversation. *How does she think I'm doing?*

"It's great. I'm really happy for her." Even I can hear my big fat lies. I know I should be happy for Peyton. I know I should be long over this. I know Brooke is a future any man would be lucky to have. *I'm* lucky to have her. And yet, my heart feels like a steamroller has leveled it.

"Don't underestimate my instincts. I'm your mother. I know all."

Resting my elbows on the countertop, I lean forward. "What makes you think it bothers me?"

"When Peyton made the announcement, and then told me you'd gone home after I asked where you were…I knew."

We don't talk about us. Peyton and me. It was clear after that summer anything to do with Peyton was off limits. My mom had been rooting for us then, but how could you continue to root for your son and the daughter of the woman who had an affair with your husband?

"I don't know how I expected this to all pan out, but it definitely didn't end with losing her to him."

She nods her understanding. "Do you think she still loves you?"

I wish I knew. That would make this so much easier.

"She won't allow herself." Mom's eyes turn down and her head tilts. I hate the sadness in them because I know it seeps out of mine. "She refuses to be with the son of the man who betrayed her dad and destroyed her family. And she's too afraid of what everyone else would think."

"Do not tell me she holds you accountable for the things your father did." Her eyes narrow. Mama Bear is emerging.

Wrong move. I shouldn't have said that. "It was enough that she wouldn't be with me, but not enough to sever our friendship. She said it a long time ago. Forget I mentioned it. I don't even know why I said it."

She sighs deeply, not wanting to let it go, but moving on. "And the other part? Do you care what other people might think?"

"Psh. I couldn't care less. No matter what the law says, she's not my… *sister*," I choke on the word. "I *hate* calling her that. We're grown adults. Harper's closer to being my sister than Peyton is."

"You know we would never judge you two, right?"

"It doesn't matter even if you did," I mutter.

"I was really rooting for you, brother." Carter claps his hand on my shoulder before walking to the fridge. I'm not even sure when he came downstairs.

My mom smiles, but it's the smile of someone who knows it won't make a difference, so it sits gloomily on her face, trying to look happy and encouraging. Pity. That's all I see. This conversation needs to end.

"Whatever. I'm fine. I am. I love Brooke. I really do." I didn't believe it was possible to love two people. And then Brooke came along. I've held onto an impossibility for far too long. It's time I move on. Brooke has made me realize it's okay to open my heart to something more.

"I'm really excited to meet this Brooke Whitaker you've spoken of for months," she says, optimistic. "If she's lasted this long, she's obviously something great."

"She is," I agree. "She's smart and fun and beautiful. I think you'll love her."

"I know I will."

"If she's hot, you know I will," Carter says as he swipes the back of his hand across his mouth and sets the milk carton back in the fridge. *Gross.*

"Don't pretend like your standards are high. If it's a female with legs and a good butt, you're sold."

"Don't forget that she has to have a nice rack." He burps.

Mom smacks him upside the head. "If you talk like that about another girl again, you'll wish I never gave birth to you."

He ducks away from her, chuckling. "Yes, ma'am." When he passes me, he pretends like he's grabbing two gigantic melons over his pecs.

"Carter Nicholas!" Mom maneuvers around the counter, but he bolts for the stairs before she can lay another hand on him, snickering all the way up. "I'm sorry! I'm sorry!"

"What am I going to do with that boy?" she groans.

I shake my head and laugh to myself. "When he falls in love one day, he'll learn."

"If he makes it to that day. He'll be lucky to make it until tomorrow."

The Day She Needed Me

FOUR YEARS AGO

I'M WORKING ON my accounting homework, debating on whacking my head against my textbook when my phone lights up on my nightstand. My heart tightens when I see Peyton's smiling face staring up at me. I took a picture of her when she caught a fish in Hatteras. She's standing on the pier, grinning from ear-to-ear, so proud of herself.

Unhurriedly, I pick it up and run my finger across the screen, hovering over the accept button. I debate answering. If I had the volume up, I'm sure the ring would be on the last one when I finally do hit accept. "Hey."

"Hi." Her voice is a mixture of relief and hesitation. I imagine her having the same battle as me, and regretting placing the call in the first place.

A beat of quiet passes before I ask, "How's it goin'?"

"It's okay." Her voice is very soft, very un-Peyton like. There's something on the tip of her tongue, but she stops herself. "We haven't talked in a few weeks."

Meaning: *We haven't talked since I told you I hold our parents' affair gainst you.* Clearing my throat, I lie, "Yeah, I've been swamped with midterms and stuff. Haven't had much time for anything but school." Technically, it's only a partial lie. I have been busy with all those things, but I've never been too busy for Peyton before.

She tries to make her tone light. "Yeah, work is kicking my trash, and my sociology class is so much harder than I thought it would be." It falls flat.

"Yeah."

When more silence carries on between us, she says, "Brodee, I'm sorry about what I said."

I fiddle with the pen in my hand, running it up and down the tops of my fingers. "Sorry that you said it? Or sorry that you meant it?"

I can hear her breathing, attempting to think of the right thing to say. "I shouldn't have said it. It's just difficult. You know? I know you're not him. You could never be Nick."

I restrain my snort. "What a relief."

She hurries on, "That came out wrong. That's not what I meant. There's just so much connecting us. I needed one of the strings to be severed. One that I could control. I can't manage all the strings. They strangle me." Peyton pauses. "Does that make any sense?"

I'm a string that strangles her. Her insults keep getting better. "Yeah, maybe some distance would do us some good."

She doesn't respond right away. I want to hang up. I don't want to hear her answer, because I already know what it will be. The distance we've had over these last few weeks was torture enough. But then her silence lengthens for so long, I want her to say anything. Anything would be better than nothing. "Maybe…I dunno."

"Right."

"Can I still come to see you next weekend?"

"I don't think that's such a good idea." I thought I could do it, put a hold on my feelings until the timing was right, but it sounds so much easier than it is. I need more time.

"Brodee, we talked about this. You knew when you left for Duke this wasn't going to go anywhere. Why are you changing on me now? I still need my best friend. I need you so badly. You're the only other person who understands what I'm going through. Why can't we still be there for one another?"

"Because if I thought time was all you needed, it would be different, but I know you. I know it won't change anything. I want so badly for time to heal all our wounds, but it's going to take a lot more than that to fix what we've been through."

She pauses. When she speaks, I hear the tears in her voice. It shakes. "I just want to go back."

If only that was an option. I would do so many things differently. A piece of me thinks if I knew what I know now, I'd never have kissed her on that beach. I would have walked away and never thought twice about it. But another piece knows not everyone gets the opportunity to have what we did. There are people who dream of having what we did, if only for a moment.

"Me too. Good luck with your sociology class, Peyton."

"Wait, Brodee." Her breath trembles. "I *need* you today."

I can't handle the whiplash. "Well, I really need you every day, but I can't have that. You can't have it both ways. Make up your dang mind, Peyton."

"I'll let you go then." She hangs up before I can say anything else.

When I see that she disconnected the call, I throw my phone across the room. I regret it instantly. *Never take it out on the expensive stuff, Brodee.* I cross my room to pick it up. There's a crack across the screen, right through the date. October 3rd. *Son-of-a…* I don't know what a gunshot to the chest feels like, but I imagine it's similar to this. It's the one-year anniversary of her dad's death.

I'm the world's biggest prick.

My finger hits SEND. She doesn't say a word when she answers, but I know she's there because I hear her quivering breath.

"I'm so sorry, Peyton. I didn't even realize…it's today." I hear her sniffle, but she remains silent. "I'm *so sorry*. I take back everything I said. I'm a selfish jerk who doesn't deserve your forgiveness."

She chuckles through her tears, but it sounds more like she's choking. "Yeah, you are."

"Sorry doesn't even cover it. If only I'd been thinking more clearly. I would've picked up on it sooner. I would've known."

"It's okay."

"It's not." There's nothing I can say to make it okay, but I remain on the line and let her cry. If that's all she needs from me, I can give her that much. My stillness.

The Day She Met Her

AFTER BROOKE ARRIVED and spent a couple minutes meeting my mom, we had to head straight to Harper's house for the rehearsal thing. Brooke was running behind, like always, so the hour I thought we'd have in between her arriving and getting to Harper's was cut short. Harper will kill me if I'm late to this thing.

"Is your mom not coming?" Brooke asks as we get in my car.

It's one thing for my mom to be in the same room as my dad and Olivia with a hundred other people. It's another for her to be at a low-key dinner in Harper's parents' backyard. She's stoic, but not a glutton for punishment.

"No…she'll just be coming to the wedding tomorrow." I try to casually say it, but even I hear the hesitation in my voice.

"Is there a reason she's not coming?"

The only detail about my family history Brooke is familiar with is the fact that my parents are divorced. That's it. She never asked for more information, and I never offered it. Not because I was trying to hide it from her. I don't share my dysfunctional family with anyone, if I can help it. With her here in Charleston, the rest of the details are bound to come out, and I know Brooke will be more upset if she doesn't hear it from me. "You know my friend, Peyton Parker?"

"The beautiful blonde, how could I forget?"

I ignore the mocking in her voice. "My dad is married to her mom."

As I peer at Brooke from the corner of my eye, she blinks, and then looks straight forward. I give her a minute to let it all fall into place. I know it eventually will.

"The girl you grew up living next to," she says slowly. "So, Peyton's your stepsister. Not just your friend."

"Well…" I clear my throat, wanting to throw up after hearing that reference. "Technically, yeah."

"Why did you take so long to tell me that?"

Because I hate calling her my stepsister. Because I hate to relive that part of the summer. Because I hate how warped my family is. Because I hate that what they did destroyed my mom and the future I wanted. *Which answer do you think she would prefer?*

"It's complicated. I hate talking about it." I give Brooke the basics of my family history, but I intentionally leave out the part where Peyton and I fell in love the summer our parents decided to do the same.

"So, they'll be there tonight because Harper and Peyton are best friends."

"Yeah, and my mom would prefer the least amount of contact as possible."

"Understandable." She nods. I keep looking at her, thinking she'll see through something. Like she'll somehow know Peyton and I have a history, even though I've never mentioned a word of it. She smiles and looks relieved, which confuses me. "Okay."

"Okay?"

Brooke peers over at me. It's like I gave her good news. "With how uncomfortable you were to talk about your family, I always knew there was something off, but I imagined it being so much worse."

How could it get any worse? It's clear she doesn't understand the gravity of the situation since she didn't witness all that was lost. Not just the love I'd lost, but the relationships our families had. Even though I'd told her Peyton was a close family friend, and our families had done everything together growing up, Brooke doesn't seem to get it. She doesn't understand what we all lost.

When I don't say anything back, she says, "People cheat, Brodee. It happens. If you're worried I'll dislike your dad or judge him, I won't. Not that I condone the cheating. At all. But I won't make any judgments until I meet him. You don't have anything to be worried about. All families have baggage."

That's what she thought I was worried about? That she would judge my family's baggage? *Judge my dad all you want,* I nearly say. *I do.*

BROOKE AND I walk hand-in-hand through the open gate into Harper's backyard. She gasps. "It's like an enchanted forest."

I focus in to see what she sees. Harper's yard is a lot bigger than I remember. They've already started setting up for the ceremony tomorrow.

Tall logs are placed upright around the Days' yard. Not sure what they'll be used for yet. Flowers, maybe? Lights have been wrapped around all the tree trunks, and crystal chandeliers hang from the branches. It's pretty cool.

Harper comes from money, but you'd never know by looking at her. Peyton once told me her parents wanted a sweet Southern belle, but got opinionated, free-spirited Harper instead. I liked her more after hearing that. I think I might have felt a kindred spirit in her, wanting to defy parents' expectations. She was brave enough to do what I never could.

Harper is barking orders at everyone, instructing them where to stand. Peyton, Skylar's little sister, and some girls I remember meeting at USC are lined up on one side of the back fence while Skylar and all our buddies are lined up on the other. Peyton catches my gaze first. Her initial response is a smile, but it quickly falls.

"Fisher!" Jackson shouts.

"Heeeey!" Issac and Mike holler.

Robby breaks out of line and comes barreling at me, and the rest follow suit. I let go of Brooke's hand before they tackle me. We haven't all been together since the night of graduation. I feel shenanigans on the horizon. Before Harper kills us all, I break away, laughing, and look to her.

Her arms are crossed over her chest with her hip popped. "You're late, best man," she says like I may be next in line to receive a whooping.

"I'm know. I'm sorry," I apologize with a smile, but don't out Brooke for being the reason. "Tell me where to go."

She points next to Skylar, keeping her look of annoyance until I walk past her and wink to soften her up. She rolls her eyes, but the corner of her mouth lifts. When I take my place and look back to where I left Brooke,

I see Tyler standing a few feet away, talking to Harper's older brother, Ethan, and her dad. When we make eye contact, he gives me a head nod. I hate it when he does that so casually. As if we're old friends. We were never friends.

It's not a secret that I've never been a fan of Tyler. He's rubbed me the wrong way since the moment we first met. I don't know why. He's never done anything to me personally, and it doesn't have to do with the fact that he was with Peyton all those summers, because I didn't always feel this way about her. Peyton was charmed by his good looks and Southern boy charm, but I've always seen something more. I've never been able to pinpoint it. And now that they're engaged, I'll never be rid of him. Bile rises up my throat. He'll be *family*.

I'M WITH BROOKE, talking to Mike and Robby after we finish the ceremony rehearsal, when Peyton walks up.

"You must be Brooke." She smiles cheerfully and leads with her hand outstretched.

Brooke takes it and returns the smile easily. I have a feeling her expression would be different had Brooke not known what she knows now. "Yes, and you must be Peyton. It's really nice to meet you." She sounds so genuine, and I have to hand it to her, after all the times she's cringed at the mention of Peyton's name—without even knowing what we used to be to one another—I'm surprised she's being so friendly.

"You're even more beautiful in person," Peyton says. Brooke looks confused, nearly accusatory until Peyton explains, "I've seen the pictures you've tagged of Brodee and you together."

I stand silently, unable to figure out how I feel about this conversation.

"Oh, duh," Brooke says with a laugh.

When Brooke and I first started to hang out, she saw a picture of Peyton and me on my nightstand. It was the last picture we took together. We were sitting on our surfboards on the sand with the boardwalk and the beach house behind us. Her head rested on my shoulder as we smiled at the camera. I saw the wheels turning in Brooke's head then, wondering if I was unattached, why did I have a picture of such a pretty girl by my bed. That was when the white lie began. *We were best friends growing up.* And it actually wasn't a lie. It just wasn't the whole truth.

As she laughs and talks with Peyton, I realize Brooke no longer feels threatened by my beautiful friend, Peyton. She looks at her like they might become best friends someday. *If our parents are married I can't possibly have anything going on with her.*

And I don't.

And I never will.

Tyler sneaks up behind Peyton and possessively wraps his arms around her waist, burrowing his face in her neck. *We get it, dude. She's yours. Why don't you beat your chest while you're at it?*

"Hey, sweetheart." He kisses her cheek, and then looks at me. "Long time no see, bruh." *Bruh? Who talks like that?* Does he think I talk like that? Because I know he doesn't talk like that. He sounds so dumb. Tyler holds up his hand for me to high-five. To keep from causing tension, I return the high-five and smile as cordially as I can manage.

Tyler's eyes roam to Brooke, and his smile widens. *No, no.* I grab her waist and pull her to my side as discretely as I can. *You can't have them both. This one's mine. I'll beat my chest right back at you, if that's the only language you understand.*

"Brooke, this is Tyler. Peyton's fiancé." It feels like I've swallowed glass every time I say it. "They got engaged this week."

"Nice to meet you." She shakes his hand and inches closer to me. I like it. It's almost as if she catches the same vibes I do.

And then, because I said fiancé, I look to Peyton's left hand to see a rock on her ring finger. It's the size of my fist. The thing has to be like two or three carats.

"Oh!" Brooke exclaims, delayed. "Congratulations! Let's see the ring!"

Peyton looks uncomfortable, but smiles and lifts her hand anyway. When I get a closer look, I see that it's a huge oval with more diamonds circling it. I'm surprised her finger can tolerate the weight of it. It looks nothing like Peyton. *Did she even pick it out?*

I look at her, and she's gnawing on her lip. Peyton meets my eyes when she feels me staring. All she does is shrug, like she knows I'm asking if she likes the ring. She should be beaming. She should be excited to show it off. Instead, she looks self-conscious and embarrassed. But is she embarrassed because she likes the gaudy thing or because she realizes I know the truth? Tyler doesn't know her at all.

HARPER SEATED MY dad and Olivia across from Brooke and me. Peyton and Tyler sit next to Olivia, while Skylar and Harper sit next to me. My dad won't stop asking Brooke questions. How did we meet? *Through my roommate, Scott. Her ex-boyfriend, ironically enough. And now my ex-roommate.* What is her degree in? *Engineering.* How many siblings does she have? *Two sisters, both older. And a little brother.* What do her parents do for a living? *Mom is a nurse. Dad is an orthopedic surgeon.*

The questions don't stop. She's answering them all like a champ, trying to be gracious. Although, I can tell Brooke is starting to feel interrogated. As a lawyer, my dad has that affect on people.

"Dad, how about we focus on the couple we came here for," I interrupt when he starts asking her where she sees herself in five years. *Is this an interview to date your son?* If it is, I want to inform him that he doesn't get a say in that. We're already solid, and he's not going to change that.

My dad chuckles when he realizes he's gone too far. "I'm sorry. This is the first girlfriend you've brought home since high school. I simply wanted to know what's special about this one. And, after talking to her, I know." He winks at her. "She's a keeper, Brodee."

"Thanks, Dad," I murmur. Not that I was waiting for his approval. I know Brooke is incredible. I'm not dating her because I think he'd approve. I'm dating her because I want to. Because she was the first girl to catch my eye in years. Because she's independent and selfless and makes me want to be a better man. No matter how cliché that sounds. She does.

"I'm the first?" she whispers to me. I'm not sure if she's surprised or concerned.

I nod once.

"I don't know if I should be worried or flattered."

She doesn't have to know why. "Definitely flattered."

Brooke squeezes my hand under the table, and I place a kiss on her dimple as she smiles at me. When I pull away, I catch Peyton watching us from across the table. I didn't mean to look her way. She's in my line of sight. Her expression is unreadable. She may be assessing the relationship I have with Brooke, or she's shocked, or maybe she's jealous. Perhaps it's none of those, and I don't know how to read her at all anymore. But then she blinks and offers a thin smile that I return before focusing on the meal in front of me and ignoring her for the rest of the night.

The Day He Didn't Care

FOUR YEARS AGO

"IT'S REALLY NICE to have you, Brodee," Olivia says. We sit at their kitchen table, after eating dinner. "It's been so long since Peyton visited. I was really hoping she'd accept our invitation this weekend and take a break. She's just so busy."

I can't imagine why. I bite my tongue. I remember the manners my mom taught me. "Yeah, with work and school, she's got her plate pretty full. Speaking of, dinner was really good. Thank you, Olivia."

"You're so welcome." She takes my plate and my dad's to the sink. "I know salmon is your favorite. I wanted to make sure you got a good home-cooked meal while you were here." She's never been more over the top in my entire life. And she could never make salmon as good as my mom if she tried. "Not that Tatum wouldn't make you one. I know my salmon probably didn't live up to hers."

When I don't respond, my dad covers it up with, "How is Peyton?" He stretches back in his seat. It doesn't surprise me that I'd know more about her than them. While I don't talk to Peyton as much as I used to, I know I talk to her more than she's willing to talk to them.

"She's good. I saw her last month. But most of my time was spent with Harper and Skylar. Peyton had to work a double at the restaurant."

He nods. "Hopefully she's still putting school first. It's important she doesn't let other things get in the way of her education."

"Well, she does need a job to eat and live, so she's probably found a good balance." Honestly, I don't know how she manages both. I feel like I'm drowning in schoolwork, and I don't have a job. That's one thing I can thank my dad for—the money to pay for the cost of living, so I can focus on school and not stress about making ends meet.

Olivia sits back down after putting our dishes in the dishwasher, and Dad says, "We were hoping Peyton would come home this weekend, too, because we wanted to talk to you both, but who knows when she'll make it home."

A boulder sits in the pit of my stomach. For them to want to speak to us in person, and together…

"Olivia and I have decided to get married."

I've been waiting for this. Peyton and I make snarky comments about it all the time. We joke and make light of it because we know the reality of it is so much worse. But hearing him say it out loud…I feel like I'm on an airplane, falling from 35,000 feet, praying I'll die before we hit the ground.

"We're not going to have a big reception, just a small courthouse ceremony, dinner downtown afterward. It feels pointless to wait any longer, so we're hoping you'll be willing to come back next month. And maybe you can talk Peyton into coming with you this time. You could pick her up on the way."

Everything is said so casually. *How was the surf today, Brodee? Did you catch any good waves? It seemed like it would be a perfect day for the beach.* Except we're not talking about the ocean. We're talking about my dad marrying his mistress. I don't like to refer to Olivia as that. I cared about her once. She was my mom's best friend, my best friend's mom, my second mother. But now that's all Olivia is to me—the mistress who tore apart my parents' marriage.

"You really don't care about what this is doing to us."

"Brodee," he warns, and the space between his eyebrows pinches together. My response wasn't exactly stellar, but it was definitely called for.

"I have a phone call to make," Olivia excuses herself quickly.

I don't stop before she's out of the room. "You're joking, right? You honestly think Peyton and I want to be there? In what realm does that make sense?"

"Well, yes." It's not even a question in his mind. He's so hardheaded and oblivious. "I know it's hard, but you two are part of this family. I expect both of you and Carter to be there to support us. To support this fresh start. This new life for our family."

"If Peyton has a hard enough time being around me, what makes you think she'll even set foot in that courthouse?"

He looks at me as though I'm speaking a foreign language. He really is oblivious. I want to shake him. Bash his head into the table. But I know that's my irrational anger.

"Do you realize you're the reason Peyton won't be with me? *You.*"

He calmly tries to say, "Well, it's probably for the best. It might be a little strange since you'll be related soon…"

I snort. "Don't even go there, Dad. It has more to do with what you did to her father. To his memory. She won't be with me because I'm a constant reminder of you and what you did to her family. To our family. She can avoid you with distance, but I'm the one who suffers the consequences. So, thanks. Thank you for not only ruining our family and hurting Mom. Thank you for taking away the only girl I've ever loved."

"You're being a little dramatic. It's time to move on. It's been more than a year. We've given you plenty of time to get used to the idea of us. You two are old enough to accept it and stop acting like two rebellious teenagers."

My hands clench into fists. If he weren't my dad, I'd punch him. Right in the face. "Funny thing I'm only nineteen, so forgive me if I still act like a *rebellious* teenager."

I shove my chair back from the table. He calls out my name as I storm toward the front door. He keeps shouting at me to come back, hollering about how childish I'm being.

"I'm not finished talking to you!"

Oh, yes you are.

"Brodee!"

I slip into my flip-flops in the entryway.

"Don't you dare walk out that door!"

I not only walk out the door, I slam it behind me with satisfaction.

The Day I Said Goodbye

WINTER IN CHARLESTON is not like normal winters. One day it can be thirty degrees, the next it can be in the sixties. It's bipolar.

Today, Harper and Skylar lucked out. We're in the high sixties. The girls can still wear their dresses, and we don't have to hear Harper complaining about how their jackets or sweaters don't match.

Harper and Skylar say *I do*, and as they do, Peyton and I find each other like a gravitational pull. Our eyes smile. At first it's out of happiness for our friends, but it changes. The smile remains, but longing shades it. For a moment, the ravine between us isn't as vast as it normally feels. She's really looking at me. It's only a moment, but everything fades and leaves only us. I get a glimpse of the Peyton in Hatteras, who loved me in the rain and kissed away my worries. But then she blinks, and I lose her. She looks out at Tyler in the crowd, and grins, like she wants me to see it's *him* she wants. Not me.

As we follow Harper and Skylar up the aisle, arm-in-arm, Peyton quietly says, "They actually did it."

I whisper back, "They did."

In reality, it feels like we're saying, "*They did what we never will.*"

AFTER THE HAPPY couple cuts the cake, my buddies stand around the dessert table with Brooke, Peyton, Tyler, and me. I grab a plate for Brooke, and she thanks me. I take another one and hand it to Peyton, but before she can thank me, Tyler stops her.

"You don't really want to eat that, do you?" he asks her quietly, but not quietly enough. "You have a wedding dress you'll want to fit into soon."

"Oh." Peyton puts the plate down on the table. "You're right. I have a dress fitting next week."

I'm dumbfounded. *Is my hearing working correctly?*

"Did he just say what I think he said," Brooke hisses into my ear, low enough so only I hear.

I have to replay it in my head because I can't believe he did. "I think he did." I eye Tyler up and down in his tan suit and perfectly combed hair. *That smug douche is trying to control her weight?*

Harper must have heard Tyler, too, because her eyes nearly sear the side of my head. I look. They say, *you have no idea.* It makes me wonder what else I've missed and what Harper and Skylar haven't been telling me.

The DJ starts playing music. Peyton takes Tyler's hand and guides him to the middle of the yard where there's a black and white checkered dance floor.

The guys have been hitting on the USC girls, whose names I still can't remember, so they all make their way to the dance floor as well.

I turn to Brooke. "You dancing?"

"You asking?" She bats her thick eyelashes and cocks her head to the side. Coy little flirt.

I smile. "I'm asking."

She smiles back. "Then I'm dancing."

This woman deserves my whole heart. Any man would be lucky to have her. Brooke is quick-witted and laid back. For every joke or dig I give, she can shoot one right back. When she dances, her hair falls in her face and she laughs. It's contagious. I take her into my arms and sway with the music, letting our eyes and bodies do all the communicating.

After a few songs, a slow song begins; I lean into Brooke's ear. "I need to talk to Peyton. Do you mind dancing with Tyler for a song?"

Brooke grimaces, but agrees. I know the grimace isn't aimed at Peyton, but Tyler. "As long as you're asking her why the heck she didn't stand up for herself."

I chuckle. "I'll say something like that. Don't say anything to him, though, okay?"

"I'll do my best to bite my tongue." She scowls.

We hold hands as we walk across the dance floor. Tyler and Peyton seem to be deep in conversation with their heads close together. I almost feel bad for interrupting, but then I remember what he said to her, and I ask, "You mind if we cut in?"

Their eyes flash to us. It takes a minute for what I asked to register. "Yeah, sure," Peyton says with a smile. They break apart, and I take Peyton's hand, drawing her against me. Tyler wraps his arms around Brooke's waist as she tries not to sneer. I feel guilty for asking her to dance with him.

I'll have to make this quick.

"You know," she says, meeting my eyes, "this is only the second time we've ever danced."

I laugh. "You've really got to stop keeping score. This might be the last."

I don't know why I said that. She was trying to keep things light, and I shut it down. Her gaze turns away. I try to think of how to approach carefully what I came to ask. "You missed out on that cake. Harper's cousin sure knows how to bake."

"Oh." She laughs uncomfortably. "I know. I hate that I'm cutting back."

"To fit into your wedding dress?" I lift one eyebrow.

"Well, yeah. I mean…I've got to maintain my weight before the wedding so I don't have to do any last minute alterations. I don't want to deal with that. Such a pain in the butt."

"And that's why Tyler was so concerned about you eating a piece of cake?" I try to laugh, pretend like I'm teasing her.

She rolls her eyes. "He knows my goals. He was just trying to help me keep them."

Don't be stupid, Peyton. This isn't you.

"Gotcha."

The comfort I used to seek in our silence is absent. It stretches and grows strained the longer we dance. It seems like the more time we spend together, the further apart we grow. Will we eventually become two people who are in the same family, but no longer know each other at all, who dread going to family functions and avoid family time so we don't have to ever see one another?

Peyton steps closer, but it's more like she doesn't want to look at me and is closing the distance so she doesn't have to anymore.

"Brooke seems nice."

I could take that statement several different ways, but it seems most like an olive branch.

"Yeah, she's pretty great."

"She's really pretty, too."

My eyes are drawn to Brooke as she dances with Tyler. Their movements are stiff and painful to watch. I know it's Brooke's doing, and I feel a little satisfaction knowing she's not tempted by his charm. Okay, *a lot* of satisfaction.

She spent hours curling her long hair this morning. It cascades around her, covering her bare back in chocolate waves. Her airport blue dress—at least that's what she calls it, airport blue—brushes her thighs and hugs her hips. I'm regretting asking her to occupy Tyler. I don't like that his hands are touching her. "Yeah," I agree, debating on cutting this dance short and taking back Brooke.

"Do you ever think about that summer?" Peyton's voice is so soft. It's almost inaudible, but I hear her so loudly.

Is it even possible to forget that summer? If so, I feel like I would have done it already. I've tried hard enough. But there isn't time long enough, substances strong enough, hobbies consuming enough to drown out the memories of that summer.

"Yes."

The song comes to an end.

In the space between I ask, "Do you?"

She lets me go without a glance. "No."

And just like that, the world I built in my head—a world that disregarded black and white and painted the landscape in shades of gray, where we couldn't be judged for our feelings and our so-called twisted love was accepted as it is, a world where we ignored our pride and took a risk to be together—came crashing down.

This was her final goodbye.

As well as mine.

Goodbye, world of gray. You were my best dream.

The Day I Won

THREE YEARS AGO

"I CAN'T BELIEVE I let you talk me into this," Peyton grumbles from the passenger's seat. I practically had to drag her out of her apartment on my way to Charleston, but I wasn't going to take no for an answer. Not this time.

"Look. I don't want to go to this stupid ceremony any more than you do, but my mom really thinks we should. We're doing this for her. I don't want to disappoint her. So, if I have to be there, you do too."

"I can't believe Tate is siding with them." Peyton sinks further into the seat, crossing her arms over her chest. She's wearing a black dress with her hair in a messy ponytail. It's not that I know much about girl's hairstyles, but I can tell Peyton didn't give a crap about what she looked like when she did her hair. I'm not even sure she brushed it. Of course, she's still beautiful, but if I didn't know any better I'd think we were going to a funeral. I see pouty five-year-old Peyton all over again. Her bottom lip pokes out, and her eyebrows squish together.

I drag my hand over my face. "I think it has more to do with the fact that she wants our relationships mended. If we ditched the wedding, it would only cause a deeper wedge, and it doesn't only affect us. It affects her, too. The more we push away, the more the backlash falls on her." She would never tell me that, but I know it does. Which is so messed up in it's own right. She's the one who got screwed over, but if we don't want to be a part of this ridiculous new family, it gets blamed on her, as if she's forcing us to side with her. Never once has she asked me to be on her side. There are no sides. It's not an us-against-them battle. Everyone lost. But if there were an us-against-them, Peyton and I would be aligned against the world and its cruelties. That's right, world. We're fighting.

My mom wants me to regain a good relationship with my dad, but that's not her decision. He obliterated any chances of that when he decided his happiness was more important than she was.

"That's so stupid," Peyton says. "She hasn't done anything wrong. If anything, your mom has been a saint. They should be thanking her for not blowing this out of the water and slandering their names." She mumbles, "Not that people couldn't figure out what happened."

I can't help but laugh. Not that Peyton's animosity is humorous, but it kind of is, because I get it. Everything she said is so true.

"Will Carter be there?"

"I don't know if my mom could convince him to go. I tried talking to him, but it's possible he's against this more than we are. And I can't blame him for that. He still needs time to work through his anger."

"If only drinking and girls could solve all of *my* problems," Peyton grumbles and looks out the window. I snort. "You know what I mean. Not girls, girls, just...forget it."

"I get it," I say with a laugh. "Loosen up, will you? We'll get through this a lot easier if we can keep our mouths shut and have fun together."

"You honestly believe today will be fun." She looks at me, deadpan.

"Well, not with *that* attitude." I smile as an idea comes to mind. "Let's play a game. Every time one of them calls the other 'babe' or 'sweetheart' we get a point. So, if it's my dad, you get a point. If it's your mom, I get a point."

Once their relationship became public, it was like pet names became their given names. They don't call each other by their actual names anymore. And every time I hear it, I gag.

A disgusted groan passes her lips. "And these points add up to…?"

"Whoever has the most points by the end of the day has to buy dinner."

"You're on."

OLIVIA, IN A short cream dress, is standing next to my dad on the sidewalk with tears in her eyes when she sees Peyton and me get out of the car in front of the Charleston County courthouse.

"Mom, I told you we were coming," Peyton says with a sigh and hugs her. It's not a usual Peyton hug. Hugging Peyton always makes me feel loved, important. She has a way of hugging so tightly it feels like she never wants to let go. This time her arms limply wrap around Olivia's waist, and she pulls away almost instantly.

"I know, but I still wasn't sure if you'd show up," she says. Olivia takes a second to appraise Peyton's dress. She thinks better of saying anything. "We're so grateful you came to support us."

Peyton meets Olivia's eyes and articulates her reply. "Us being here doesn't mean we're okay with this."

Olivia nods her understanding and wipes the tears from her face. "And yet, you're here anyway, so thank you."

Peyton nods, but she doesn't smile. It's clear their relationship is still strained. It's about as pleasant as my relationship is with my dad. I'm not sure we'll ever have the same bond we used to. There's too much pain and betrayal to be forgotten. Even if we do forgive them someday, I don't see how anyone could go back to normal. Nothing about their relationship is normal. Maybe we'll look happy on the outside, but I feel it may always be superficial, that we'll go through the motions so we can get by. We'll never truly get past this.

"Son." My dad steps forward and clasps me on the shoulder with a nod of thanks. I don't acknowledge it. "Where's Carter?"

"He won't be here."

He tightens his lips and nods. The disappointment isn't unexpected, but he should know better. Carter hasn't spoken a word to him since he left for college in September. He's going to school in town at College of Charleston, but he cut off communication as soon as Mom wasn't there anymore to encourage him to play nice. I wish I had the same luxury.

While we weren't exactly on speaking terms after I left for Duke, I eventually gave in and answered my dad's calls six months ago. Our relationship has been difficult and forced, but I manage to give him as much respect as I can muster when we're in person. I don't respect his decisions, but I respect that he's still my father. Carter, on the other hand, is taking his sweet time to patch things up. I pity Dad too much to shut him out completely.

PEYTON AND I sit toward the back of the courthouse. Olivia's parents come and sit in front of us, but my dad's parents don't show up. I'm not surprised. They love my mom. Whether there was a prior relationship with Olivia growing up or not, I know they aren't happy with him.

When I was home for the weekend a couple months ago, I overheard my mom talking on the phone with Grandma Fisher. It seems like my mom is trying to play peacemaker with everyone. I heard her say over and over again, "It's okay, Mom. Stop apologizing. I'm fine." I can imagine my grandma crying and apologizing for her son's behavior. My grandma knows he's obviously not sorry enough to fix it himself.

I sort of zone out during the whole ceremony. It's not long. The officiant says a few words, they repeat it. Yada, yada, yada. It all feels so meaningless. Small ceremony doesn't even describe the wedding. There are four of us here. Four. Shouldn't that tell them something? No one supports this.

They don't care.

When the officiant pronounces them husband and wife, I peer at Peyton sitting next to me in her mourning dress. As I take a closer look, I'm reminded of a crying Peyton standing next to her father's casket. It has to be the same dress she wore to Jon's funeral. This is her passive aggressive act of defiance to remind them who else they screwed over when they chose each other.

Tears fill Peyton's eyes with a look of devastation. There could be a number of things going through her head, but it doesn't matter what's making her cry. I grab her hand lifelessly lying in her lap. She squeezes my hand so hard I think she might break my fingers.

"All right, babe, you're mine now," I hear my dad say after they kiss.

"Point for me." Peyton smirks and dabs under her eyes with her free hand.

"Dangit," I hiss, but I smile at her.

The points don't start to tally up until after the wedding, when we walk down East Bay Street for dinner at Magnolias.

"Babe, will you hand me my purse?" Point for me.

"Sweetheart, did you grab the marriage license?" Point for Peyton.

"You look so beautiful today, babe." I inwardly cringe. Point for Peyton.

"Oh, sweetheart, don't forget about Mr. Lawson. He asked you to call him back." Point for me.

And it goes on and on. Peyton and I can only handle the hour at dinner before we get the hell out of dodge.

"Twenty-three," Peyton says.

"Thirty-seven." I sigh. "My dad sucks."

Peyton laughs a genuine belly laugh. And that's all I wanted out of today. So, I guess, in reality, I won.

The Day I Felt Content

I TAKE BROOKE to Botany Bay where seashells hang from bare trees and perch on driftwood along the shore. As a preserve, nothing in nature is allowed to leave the beach, so it's covered in full-size conch shells and sand dollars. It's one of my favorite places in Charleston. It might not be much for surf, or even for wading in the water, but it's peaceful to sit and relax under the seashells and the shade of the palm trees.

As we listen to the waves crash on the inclining shore, Brooke settles between my legs. I lean back on my hands and dig my palms into the sand.

"This place is so beautiful. I bet it's going to be really difficult for you to leave all of this for Boston."

"It'll be hard, but I'll manage. Boston will have its own charms." I sigh, keeping my eyes set on the ocean. "The hardest part will be leaving my mom. At least for college, it was temporary. I could come home on the weekends whenever I felt like it. Now, I'll have to plan around my work schedule, and plane tickets aren't exactly as cheap as a couple tanks of gas."

She nods against my chest. "Understandable, but she's a strong woman. I'm sure she'll be okay. I really love her, by the way. She's really sweet. I see where you get your good heart."

"I'm pretty sure she loves you, too." I know she does. She told me as much.

"I could get used to Charleston." Brooke's fingers run along the tops of my legs. "I really wish I didn't have to drive back tonight."

I tug her closer to me, and she nestles into my chest. I nuzzle her neck with my nose and press my lips against her warm skin. "Mmm…me too."

"You seem different."

"Hmm?"

She turns her head to peer up at me. "You. You seem…free. If that makes any sense."

I think about that for a minute. It's hard to relax when I'm around my family. If I were to describe myself in one word, when I spend long periods of time with them it would be *tense*. Maybe because I've been tormented by thoughts of that summer in Hatteras for years, and now that I know Peyton is moving on, I have to, too. There's nothing restraining me, tethering me to the hope of maybe someday. I've been tortured long enough. Now I can look at Brooke and be…free of Peyton Parker.

"When I'm by the ocean I feel free."

She nods and hums her understanding. With the calming sound of the ocean waves, and the sound and smell of the fresh sea breeze, it's impossible not to feel limitless.

"Come to Boston with me."

Her eyes jump to me. "What?"

I don't want to be without Brooke. Not because I can't be with Peyton, and Brooke is the next best thing, but because I see Brooke with fresh eyes, and I can't imagine a life in Boston without her. She's supposed to be there with me.

I brush the strands of hair blown across her face away from her green eyes. "I want you to come to Boston with me. It doesn't have to be right away. I know we haven't really talked about this, and it's a little sudden, but I don't want to be there without you."

Her face, like a dimming switch being turned up, gradually lights up. I think I said the right thing. Her dimple deepens, and she nods. "Okay."

"Yeah?"

"Yes." Her nod is eager, vigorous. She flings her arms around my neck and matches her lips with mine.

This kiss is unlike all the rest. And it's not because she's kissing me any differently. It's me. All this time I don't think I was truly kissing her back. Not that I was imagining Peyton, but I just don't think I allowed myself to fully be consumed by Brooke Whitaker. There was always a piece, no matter how big or small, that resisted the love that was growing for her. So, I kissed her, but I never knew what it felt like to be in love with her and appreciate the kiss for more than physical contact. It's no longer only lips pressed together in affection. It's a heart-pounding, soul-changing, out of body experience. She's everywhere.

I lower us onto the blanket and let Brooke fill every chamber, every crevice of my heart.

And I'm finally content.

The Day It Ended

TWO YEARS AGO

AFTER SPENDING CHRISTMAS Eve with my dad and Olivia, they head to bed, but Peyton and I decide to stay up for a little while. It's been several months since we've seen each other. I don't know exactly when the time between visits lengthened, but it seems like over the last year I only got to see her a few times. There was some weekend in February, then my birthday in June, and her birthday in September. While I promised to win her back, it seems like we've only drifted further.

The strands of white lights on the Christmas tree illuminate the family room. We've turned off all the lights because Peyton loves the way the tree looks when it's the only lighting in the room. I can't take my eyes off them as they twinkle. I wonder what it would look like from below. I crawl across the carpet.

"What are you doing?" Peyton laughs.

"I want to know what the lights and ornaments looks like from underneath." When I reach the tree, I turn on my back and look up at the shadows and colors. "It's pretty cool. C'mere."

I feel Peyton come up beside me and lay down on the tree skirt, easing her head right next to mine. "I read about this in a book once. They'd made it a tradition. Every Christmas, they'd lay under the tree together and ponder the last year."

"Well, maybe we can make it our tradition, too." Considering that's kind of what I was doing. While under the tree, it feels like we're isolated from the world. The house is quiet. It's only the two of us. Uncertainly, I let my hand rest on top of hers between us, giving her the option to take it or pull away. I don't want her to pull away. I want her to feel the deep need to be close to me as much as I feel it for her.

Peyton hums her response, almost in a way to avoid saying yes or no. She doesn't remove her hand, but she doesn't take mine either. It's a step, so I keep my hand where it is. My heart beats fast. Before I can intertwine my fingers with hers, she draws her hand back and places it over her stomach.

I thought we'd been having a good night. The first in…I can't even remember. The tension between our parents and us was nearly nonexistent. Carter even showed up, and he's made it his life's mission to avoid my dad at all costs. Only, the real test will be the deciding factor on where we stand.

"Can I follow you home? 'Cause my parents always told me to follow my dreams."

"Ha." Her stare is glued to the branches above.

No rebuttal. Not even a real laugh. Crash and burn.

I can't help it. I have to ask. "Did I do something wrong?"

She's quiet when she says, "No."

"Are you sure? I thought we were doing okay. You and me." I roll onto my side to face her. I bump the branches, but I still manage to fit.

"We are."

Her reassurance isn't very reassuring. "There's something else you want to say."

"I just..." She exhales and turns her gaze on me. "I thought you'd given up on us. I thought we agreed that's what was best. We were on track to becoming us again."

And I thought all you needed was time. My voice cracks. "You once said we would always come back to each other."

Her mouth sets into a line. "That was different. That was before."

"Before what? Before our parents *ruined* it all?" I'm so tired of that excuse.

"Pretty much." I know the attitude in her eyes isn't aimed at me, but it feels like it.

"Stop," I snap. "Stop blaming them. It's an excuse, and we both know it. That was two years ago. It's water under the bridge. They've moved on. My mom moved on. I've moved on. Why can't you?"

Her eyes cut me. "So, what they did is excusable now?"

"*No*," I retort. "Of course not. But at some point you have to stop holding it against everyone. Do I agree with what they did? No. Do I wish it never happened? Yes. But it did. And they're married now, and they're happy, and my mom is happy, and I just want to be happy with you. We have to stop letting this come between us."

She clenches her teeth the way she does when she's trying not to cry.

"You can't let what happened that summer define us. We're more than that summer."

"I wish that were true," she whispers.

I know this will end with me losing again, so I stop before it gets that far. Once I return to my back, the Christmas tree is no longer magical from underneath. I never want this to be a tradition. I feel trapped by the low hanging branches and bright ornaments. I'm about to get up when Peyton speaks. "Tyler and I started dating again."

If I thought the night couldn't have gone further down hill, I was wrong. I didn't even know they started to hang out again. Last thing I heard, she'd seen him once on campus, and he not only ignored her, but turned in the opposite direction just so he wouldn't have to talk to her. Granted, that was a year ago. Clearly, anything can happen in a year, but I hoped she was past him, that he was a memory we would talk about someday.

"Remember those few summers when I dated that one guy?" she'd ask. *"What was his name?"*

And I'd say, *"Travis? Tommy? Who cares? He was a tool."*

And Peyton would laugh and say, *"Yeah. What did I see in him?"*

I feel the dream collapsing to rubble and a new one rises from the ashes.

"You remember my friend, Brodee? Brodee, you know my husband, Tyler?" And then I'll puke all over his leather Sperrys. He's not even on a boat. *Why is he wearing those?* He'll only have to get news Sperrys; I'll have to get a new dream. But it'll be worth it to see the look of disgust on his face.

"Brodee?" Peyton pulls me from my trance.

I haven't said a word to her in a few minutes. *What does she want me to say?* Either way, I lose. I can pretend to be happy and then head straight to my bedroom to cry like a girl. Or I can pour my eyes out in front of her and beg her to reconsider. One will hurt my core. The other will damage my pride.

I choose neither option. "Tyler, huh?" My voice remains indifferent, even with its greatest efforts to shatter.

"We ran into each other at a party a few weeks back and got to talking. We kind of just…fell back into place."

"You can do so much better than him."

I don't pretend to be happy. I don't begin to sob like a baby in front of her. I get up and walk away. She doesn't call for me. I don't expect her to.

The Day I Taught Him Respect

PEYTON WENT TO Asheville to spend Christmas with Tyler and his family, which is a catch twenty-two. She won't get to be a buffer on Christmas day when I have to spend half of the day with our parents. On the plus side, I don't have to spend the day with Tyler, and I'll be in Boston with Brooke before I have to deal with either of them again.

As I open presents with my mom and Carter, I find myself wishing I'd asked Brooke to stay for the holidays. There's a feeling of incompleteness—if that's even a word. If she were here, I wonder if our family would feel whole.

"Why do we have to spend half the day with *them*," Carter asks once the last present is opened, lounging back on the couch in his traditional Christmas pajama pants and hoodie that Mom got us this year. "They have each other. What are you supposed to do with the rest of your day, Mom?"

"Enjoy a quiet, relaxing evening without hearing: *What's there to eat in this house? When's dinner? Do we have any snacks? Will you make some brownies?*" She mimics Carter so well, and winks at him.

"You love me," he says. "You miss me when I'm not here."

"Of course, son. Every day." She looks at me and subtly shakes her head. I laugh and don't even attempt to make it subtle.

"Laugh all you want, dipstick. She was grateful to be rid of you too," he taunts as he walks toward the stairs. "Once we're both married, she'll be halfway to the Bahamas."

"Maybe, but she'll take *me* with her," I holler as he turns the corner upstairs.

Mom chuckles and asks, "He doesn't really think I'm grateful he's gone, does he?" She's genuinely worried. Carter is her baby.

"Nah, you know Carter. He's just being a pain in the butt. What are you going to do with the rest of your day?"

"I thought I'd make some sugar cookies. Maybe take a bubble bath. Pop in *Miracle on 34th Street*. I haven't seen that one this season yet."

I have to say, I agree with Carter. We shouldn't have to leave her alone on Christmas. It's hard to tell if she wants the peace and quiet or if she truthfully doesn't want us to go. She'd never tell us not to. "You'll really be okay?"

"I'm fine, Brodee. It's not like you two will be far. You're next door. I think I can manage a few hours alone."

"You could come with us," I offer, though I'm not sure it's a good or bad idea.

"No, no. I'm perfectly content staying home. Go. Go get ready and head over there. I'm going to clean up the kitchen from breakfast, so I can get it ready to bake. By the time you boys are done, you'll have freshly baked sugar cookies to come home to."

I kiss her cheek. "I love you, Mom."

"Love you too, son."

THE AFTERNOON WAS going surprisingly well with Dad and Olivia. Better than it's gone in years. Carter was on his best behavior, only making five snarky comments within the last couple hours as opposed to every other sentence. Then present time came.

They'd splurged on gifts for us, which wasn't the first time. Every Christmas since they'd became a couple they've bought us something that used to be financially out of reach. Not because my dad couldn't afford it, but he felt spending that kind of money on presents was frivolous. Everything needed to be invested and saved for more important things like college and retirement.

Carter used to be ecstatic about the extravagant gifts. The first year, Carter got a brand new Land Rover. My mom's cars have never been that expensive. But Carter didn't see what was happening then. He saw a new car and didn't care about much else. It made him the top man on campus. The manipulation actually worked, buffered Dad's mistakes for the meantime.

When we open up a fourteen-day cruise for the *family* to Aruba, the bribe must finally register, or maybe it no longer cushions the past.

"A cruise?" Carter asks, straight-faced.

"Yeah." Dad smiles a little sheepishly. He's aware of the game he's been playing, and he thought it could still work. We're not children anymore.

I almost step in before Carter blows, but Dad keeps talking. "I know it'll be…different. But we thought it would be a good bonding experience right before Peyton gets married for all of us to go on a final family vacation."

"Do you two think you can just buy our allegiance?" Uh oh. "Do you think money and vacations and expensive gifts are going to make us choose sides in this irrelevant game of which parent we love more?"

My dad tries to interrupt him, but there's no stopping Carter now.

"We will never forgive you for what you did. Ever. I've tried to be civil because Mom asks it of us, but I'm tired of pretending I can stand you. We're done. Take your cruise and shove it up your—"

"Carter!" I interrupt. He throws the brochure in Dad's face and heads for the front door.

I spare a glance at him and Olivia. My dad looks guilty. Olivia is about to cry.

"I'm sorry," I say and follow Carter out. "We'll be back."

I gently shut the door behind me. Carter is halfway across the Parkers' driveway when he hears me coming. "I don't want to hear it, Brodee."

"Well, too bad because you're gonna listen. I get the anger. I get the bitterness. There are still moments when I wish I could punch the man in the face, but there's a level of respect we still need to uphold."

Carter spins around and shoots his index finger at their house. "He doesn't deserve our respect. He's the epitome of disrespect. How can you even defend him?"

"I'm not defending him," I amend. "I'm just saying it's been long enough. We're better than he is. Mom brought us up to be better. We don't have to spend time with him or call him on the phone to chat. Hell, we don't even have to like the man, but it wasn't just Dad you spoke to like that. It was Olivia. And she deserves more respect than that. It's time we stop going in there guns-a-blazing. It just makes things worse. Aren't you tired of being angry all the time?"

"You're siding with *them*?" Carter staggers back. "You actually *want* to go on that B.S. family cruise?"

"Heck no. I was going to *respectfully* decline. I'll have to work anyway. I can't take that kind of time off, but that's beside the point. There are two ways we could've handled that. The way you just did, like an immature, thoughtless teenager. Or we can go in there, be men, and just say, no thanks, we'll pass."

Carter crosses his arms over his chest. "So, I'm just supposed to accept what they did because it's been *long enough*?"

"No, I'm saying you need to stop being such a punk about it. It's called deference."

"Huh?"

"Read a dictionary every once in awhile."

Carter grunts. "When did you become such a grown-up?"

I snicker. "I'm pretty sure it happens in spurts. That just happened to be one of those moments." I point back at the house.

"You really think I should apologize to them?"

"Not for his sake, but for yours. The anger you've got going on will rot you from the inside. He doesn't win just because you forgive him. You can still keep your distance without all the hate."

He sets his jaw. "I don't forgive him. I'm not going on that cruise."

"Neither am I."

He nods at me like we shake on it, sealing the deal.

I'm suddenly very grateful Brooke isn't here. I barely introduced her to my dysfunctional family. That scene in there would've been a baptism by fire, and I highly doubt she's ready to commit to that much crazy yet.

AFTER CARTER AND I go back inside for him to apologize and say, thanks but no thanks, we head back home. Dad didn't take the news very well, but I didn't expect him to. Olivia seemed to expect it. In a way, she looked relieved. The cruise was probably his idea, and she was going along with it.

When we walk in the front door, Mom is pulling a cookie sheet out of the oven. The house smells like sugar and warmth.

"You're back already?" There's a mixture of a smile and a frown on her face. She's happy to see us, but is obviously concerned as to why. "I thought you'd be at least another couple hours."

I shoot Carter a look. I don't want Mom to know about his outburst. She worries enough about us.

"We just wanted to be here with you," Carter says as he hops up on the barstool. "They understood."

"Well, good. When these cool off, you two can help me frost and decorate them. Go get comfortable. I'm about to put on *Miracle on 34th Street*."

Carter groans. "The old or new one?" he asks as tries to sneak a cookie.

She smacks his hand with her spatula. "The new one."

"Ouch." Shaking his hand, he concedes, "Okay," before jogging up the stairs.

"What did he do?" she quietly asks when his bedroom door shuts.

"Nothing for you to worry about. It's been fixed. No stress."

Her eyes fill with tears. "I will worry. I'm your mother."

"I handled it, so you don't have to worry. I think he'll be okay." I saw a change in his eyes when we talked in the driveway and even a little remorse when he apologized to Olivia and Nick. If nothing else, it's a step.

The Day I Got Lost in Peppermint

ONE YEAR AGO

"SHE DOESN'T EAT Kit Kats right. It's sinful."

"What?" Peyton asks. She heard me, but she thinks I'm crazy.

"She eats them all wrong—just takes a big bite off the top, not breaking them apart as they were intended."

"Are you telling me you can't be with this Brooke girl because she eats Kit Kats wrong?" Peyton is laughing now.

"That's precisely what I'm saying," I tell her, trying to keep a straight face. "How can I be with someone who can't take the time to break them apart? So lazy. So careless." I crack and start to laugh.

"You realize how silly that sounds, right? She's beautiful. She's obviously smart if she's graduating with an engineering degree. She's willing to put up with you, which is no easy feat. How are these things getting overlooked?"

Because she's not you.

It's like Peyton can hear my thoughts through the phone. She's immediately quiet, but not because she's waiting for my response. Her silence is uncomfortable. *Fix it, Brodee.* "Oh, and she's definitely not a morning person."

That gets a chuckle. "Yes, that's a definite deal breaker."

I laugh with her. "You'd think so."

"I hear a 'but' in there…"

"She's the real deal, you know? So, I'm gonna try. We're going to see where this goes."

"I think that's a great idea." Peyton's voice is strained, but only a little. Anyone who doesn't know her might not detect it, but I can. It's off just enough. I also know that even if my new relationship bothers her, she'll do nothing about it.

So I ask, "How are things with Tyler?"

She clears her throat. "We're going strong. We just passed the one-year mark. Crazy, right? It's weird to think it's been that long already. I feel like I just bumped into him at that party."

"So, nothing's changed?" I let that sink in, to make her think I'm asking something deeper. It's cruel and immature, but I want to make her squirm. "He still the same Tyler we knew in Hatteras?"

She grunts. "Just a grown up version. Did you know Rylie transferred to USC after her second semester to be with Tyler?"

I nearly choke. "Whaaaaat?"

"Yup. Apparently, after their month-long fling at the end of the summer she thought he was going to be *the one*."

"Ha. Imagine her disappointment when you came along."

"Oh, no. Tyler broke things off with her a year before we met back up. So, the poor thing transferred back to UNC soulmate-less." Peyton pauses. "I do feel kind of bad for her though. I want to know what kind of support system she had that let her make that kind of a mistake. Following a boy to another college. That's just poor decision-making skills."

"Did Tyler ask her to?"

"Nope. At least not that he told me. He said one day she showed up on his doorstep. *Surprise!*"

"Wow." I snort. "That's something."

"Yeah." Peyton's laughter fades along with mine.

It was nice. For a moment it felt like we were us again, our banter covering up all the awkward bullcrap. I'm so tired of it. I want us back.

There's a soft knock on my bedroom door. None of my roommates would knock that quietly. I pull the phone away from my mouth and holler, "Yeah?"

Brooke's head peeks around and she lifts a small wave. "Hey."

I sit up on my bed. "Oh, hey!"

"Is someone there?" Peyton asks.

"Brooke just showed up. I gotta go. We'll talk later."

"Oh, yeah. Okay. Sounds good."

"Bye, Pete."

I hang up and motion for her to come in. Brooke sits on the edge of my bed as I scoot forward, setting my feet on the floor beside her. I brush the hair from her green eyes, tucking it behind her ear, and kiss her. She smells like peppermint, as always. I'm not sure if it's the stuff she puts in her hair or a perfume or what, but it's becoming my favorite scent.

"Who was that?" Because she doesn't sound accusatory, only curious, I answer honestly. Not that I wouldn't tell her the truth, but I feel comfortable being honest.

"Oh, that was my friend, Peyton."

She motions to the frame I have on my nightstand. Her smile is faltering. "The beautiful, blonde one."

"That would be the one. But you can just call her Peyton. Most people do." That gets Brooke to laugh. "We were just catching up. She was telling me about her boyfriend, and I was telling her about my girlfriend."

"Oh, yeah? You have a girlfriend? Should I be worried about her?" She shyly bites her bottom lip. It's not coy or flirtatious, which makes the gesture cuter and more tempting.

"Maybe. She's kind of territorial, but she has this really cute dimple that makes it difficult to take her seriously." I softly poke the little indentation in her right cheek.

Brooke swats my hand away and bubbles with laughter. Her laughter is throaty and sexy. It's the kind of sound that isn't forced. It's genuine and makes me feel like the funniest person alive. "Shut up." Her hand covers her dimple as she flushes red.

"Don't cover it. It's my favorite." I remove her hand, kiss her palm, and then press my lips to her right cheek. The blush on her cheeks deepens.

When she looks at me she asks, "So, you call her Pete?" The nickname has a tendency to throw off anyone who doesn't know us.

"Peyton Parker. Peter Parker. Spider-Man," I explain the progression. "So I call her Pete. I started calling her that when we were really young, and I was obsessed with superheroes. Spider-Man in particular."

"Ah, yes. As most young boys are. So, I hope you were telling her all good things about that girlfriend of yours." She sucks on her bottom lip nervously, and my eyes are drawn straight to her mouth. She's got to stop doing that or I won't be able to control myself.

"Well, aside from the way she eats her Kit Kats and hate mornings, only good things." I grin. Brooke smacks my shoulder. I pull her face to mine and get lost in the peppermint and a new life.

The Day We Got to Begin Again

I'M STRAPPING MY surfboard to the top of my Patriot when I hear the Parkers' garage door open. I don't care that it's technically my dad's and Olivia's now; that house will always belong to the Parkers. It's too early for either of them to be up on a Saturday. Then I spot Peyton walking around Olivia's brand new Audi before sliding her surfboard into the open trunk. She turns around and stops when she sees me standing in my driveway, watching her.

I don't know why I was assuming she would stay in North Carolina with Tyler after Christmas. No one told me she was coming back. They probably assume Peyton and I talk all the time. As her best friend, I should know these things.

"You're staying with our parents?" I ask. While we're all amicable now, I know that's the last place she'd want to stay for long periods of time. It occurs to me that I have no idea what she has planned until she gets married.

"Just until the wedding," she calls back and walks across her driveway toward the bushes at our property line. I meet her there, at the edge of my driveway. "I needed to be home with my mom to plan. And Tyler is helping in his dad's office to gain some experience until we get married. We figure the more money we can save before the wedding, the better."

I don't know what I thought, but I didn't expect Peyton and me to ever live next door to each other again. It might only be three weeks, but I'm already dreading it.

How does my mom do it?

"That sounds like a party," I say, and she laughs.

"Every day. You heading out on the waves?"

"Yeah, I thought I'd check out Folley. Surf looks pretty decent."

"Care if I join you? I was heading that way too."

We haven't talked since Harper and Skylar's wedding. I don't know if she hates how we ended that night as much as I do, but to me, it feels like she wants to make it right. Our lives are infinitely connected, so we might as well try to make it work. We couldn't do it before, but maybe this time will be different. She has Tyler. I have Brooke. Maybe we can go back to the beginning.

"Yeah," I say. "Grab your board. I'll drive."

THE DRIVE TO Folley Beach isn't as uncomfortable as I imagined it might be. We talk about the last year and all that we've missed. The things short phone calls and texts to make sure the other is still alive don't cover. She tells me about all the classes she's relieved to be done with and the teachers she was sad to leave. She talks about her borderline sexual harassing boss who she is incredibly grateful to be rid of. If he weren't in Columbia, I'd put this surfing trip on hold and walk right into that restaurant to kick his trash. She never mentions Tyler, and it's the best part of the conversation.

Peyton asks me about Boston, and we talk about all the things I would've told her about the job had we been on better terms. We talk about Carter and what a mess he is, though I say it with all the brotherly love that I have for him. He'll find out quickly or the hard way that partying through college won't get him very far in life. She asks about Brooke and how things have progressed since we last talked about her. Gosh, I can hardly remember the last time we talked about Brooke. It could've been when Brooke and I very first started dating.

They would get along better than I think either of them realize. I'm not sure I'm ready for that. I'd never win with them together in a room.

I clear my throat. "She's coming to Boston with me. I mean, since I kind of sprung it on her before Christmas, it'll be a month before she can get out there with me, but I think it'll be good for us."

"Oh. Yeah. That'll be great for you two." Her tone is difficult to decipher. If I didn't know any better, I'd think it was hard for Peyton to hear the news, but I know I'm misinterpreting it. This must be her excited voice now. Maybe Tyler has changed that too.

"I think so. We need a fresh start. Since neither of us has family or any connections in Boston, it'll be an adventure for us both."

"What's Tate going to do?"

"What do you mean?"

"Well, with you in Boston and Carter out of the house. Is she really going to stay in that house?"

"She hasn't told me otherwise."

"She's braver than I am." Peyton's voice drifts off as she stares out the passenger window. There was a time when I could ask her anything and she'd answer. *Honestly*. I want to ask what she means by her comment, but I know she'd never tell me the truth.

ONCE WE'RE OUT on the waves, we fall right back into the groove we once had. Salt water is our cure. There are no words. We don't need them. Only ocean waves and wind lapping against our ears. When I look to Peyton, straddling her surfboard on top of the water, and she smiles, it feels like all our bitterness and distance is washed away. Her face is free of makeup, letting her freckles show. We're back to being Peyton and Brodee. Best friends. We get to begin again.

HEARING BROOKE'S VOICE reminds me how excited I am to move to Boston with her. It's easy to fall back into the comfort of Charleston and home, especially after being on the water with Peyton today. I was beginning to second-guess my decision to up and relocate. Boston is pretty far away, and my mom could use the support here, but I know it's the right decision.

Maybe these next couple weeks won't be so bad with Peyton next door after all. If I can keep my focus and forget about the past, Peyton might let me back in. We can pick up the pieces of our deteriorating friendship.

"So, I gave my two-week notice to my boss."

"Already?" I ask.

"Yeah, I'll be able to move to Boston at the same time as you."

"Brooke, that's awesome! I really wasn't looking forward to trying to figure out what to do in the city until you got there." I laugh.

"And now you don't have to. I've done some research. There are tons of places I want to visit and explore. There's this place called the Back Bay, and Jamaica Pond, and the Esplanade. Did you know Cape Cod is only an hour from Boston? We *have* to go. And I think a Red Sox game is a given. Promise you won't judge me for being a tourist in the beginning." It's likely she hasn't yet taken a breath while talking.

I laugh again. "We can be tourists together. You just name the places, and we'll make it happen. So, your family is good with you moving to Boston with me?"

She pauses briefly. "It's taking my parents a little getting used to the idea, having me so far away, but they'll be okay. Honestly, I don't need their approval. I want to be with you."

Those words are the only ones I need from her. "I love you, Brooke."

"I love you, too."

The Day It Became Clear

I'VE JUST FINISHED helping my mom fix the garbage disposal when Harper's number lights up my screen. *Why is she calling me?*

"Hey, Harp, the honeymoon phase can't be over yet." I tuck my phone between my shoulder and ear as I dry off my hands. "You miss me that much?"

"Ha. The honeymoon phase will never be over."

I chuckle. Sounds about right. "Well, to what do I owe the pleasure of your call?"

"Oh, you know..."

I wait. "No, I really don't. Is everything okay?"

She sighs heavily into the phone. "I tried keeping my nose to myself, but she's my best friend, and her business is my business." I think I know where this is going. "Peyton can't marry Tyler, Brodee."

I exhale and release my humorless laugh. "Tell me something I don't know."

"Tyler's no good for her. He's such a jerk, and she doesn't even see it.

He's not the same guy from her summer flings."

I toss the dishtowel onto the counter and begin to pace. "Again, you're going to have to be more specific. I agree with you one hundred percent, but I have a feeling my reasons are a smidge different than yours."

"Didn't you notice how different she was when you came home? Cutting off all her hair and dying it platinum blonde. Not to say it isn't cute, but I tried getting her to dye her hair for years and she refused. Then all of a sudden she's engaged to Tyler, and she gets a hair makeover after twenty-one years? She looks like a freaking Stepford wife."

"Maybe she just wanted a change. We've all needed a little bit of change recently."

"It's not just that," she counters. Once Harper is on a roll, there's no stopping her, so I listen patiently. "Did you notice how she quietly remained by his side all night long. Or how about the amount of food she ate. Did you see how he talked her out of that piece of cake? I nearly punched him. And that's not even the first time I've seen him do something like that." I can hear her noises of disdain on the other end. She sounds like she ate a bad piece of seafood. "He doesn't want her to gain any weight. The man needs the *perfect* trophy wife since he's going to be *Doctor* Hamilton, you know. I once heard him say, 'Better stay skinny for me' as she was eating a bowl of pasta and then smacked her butt. Like, he thinks he's being funny or trying to play off his rude comment as a joke. But I heard the tone in his voice; it was nothing but condescending. Most of all, Brodee, it's my gut. I feel it. He's no good for her."

I was praying the cake was a one-time incident, that Peyton would be smarter than that. It's not like her to let anyone make her feel embarrassed for what she eats or how much she could eat. Peyton needed all that food to feed her energy, to fuel all the gymnastics and surfing. She could out-eat me any day. I once witnessed her eat an entire pizza. Not a personal pan size, but a large, feed-an-entire-family kind of pizza. It was impressive.

"I tried talking to her at the wedding, but she brushed it off, said he was trying to help her keep her weight goals for the wedding," I tell Harper. "The gentleman that he is, he was trying to help her out so there didn't need to be extra alterations to her wedding dress."

"That's such…" Harper let's out a string of expletives. "She doesn't see it, Brodee, but he's a controlling codfish. Almost like he wants to change everything about who she used to be, so she can be his Barbie doll and no one else's."

A sudden wave of nausea knocks me in the gut. "Is he physically abusing her? Has he ever hit her? Because I will kill him."

"No," she says with certainty. "At least not that I know of. I don't think she'd stick with him if it got that bad. But just because he's not physically abusive doesn't mean the mental or emotional manipulation is any better."

"No, of course not. I just want to know what we're dealing with. How much control does he really have?" Her physical appearance, clearly. "Is there anything else I should know about?"

"Do you know how many times I saw her last year?" Harper doesn't give me the chance to answer. "Twice. I needed my best friend and maid of honor to help me plan the wedding, but she just couldn't manage to get a single weekend away after Skylar and I got engaged. Does that sound like Peyton to you?" *Not at all.* "He wouldn't let her come home on the weekends or visit without him. She'd say it was because he was busy with school, and she didn't want to leave him behind, but I know it's because he wouldn't let her come. He doesn't want her out of his sight. He's so possessive, to the point that it scares me, Brodee."

I can't see straight.

Harper continues, "Even if it's not physical now, what if it becomes that way? Whipping her into shape to be the picture perfect family. Did you know that after he graduates, they're staying in North Carolina to be near his family? And while things aren't great with Olivia and Nick, I know Peyton would much rather stay close to home. But it's like he wants to isolate her, keep her from everyone who knows and loves her. And maybe he's not overly controlling yet, but I see him inching in. Every time I talk to her or see her, it's worse. I think Peyton's been with him for so long, he's slowly dug his claws into her, and she doesn't even see how she's changed for him."

"Have you talked to her about this?"

Harper sighs. "I tried once, but as soon as I started to hint at his controlling tendencies she got defensive, told me I was being ridiculous and jumped down my throat, throwing out instances where Skylar has said something controlling to me. Skylar couldn't be controlling if he tried." I snort. If anything, the roles are reversed, but I don't dare say that to Harper. "I don't want her shutting me out more than she already has, so I've kept my mouth shut."

"So, it's not like Peyton's crying for help. She doesn't even see it or want to believe it," I conclude.

"I just thought maybe you could try talking to her. I know things have been a bit strained between you two, but if she'll listen to anyone, it's you."

"What am I supposed to say? You've been with her more than I have. Peyton and I are just beginning to gain our friendship back."

"Do you still love her?" I exhale and choose not to respond. I think I'll love Peyton for my whole life. She's my first love. It won't be a choice. Like the ache after losing someone, the grief never leaves, but it ebbs. Other people in life may become bigger parts of the heart, while a first love inhabits a protected corner—secluded—but never forgotten.

"I'll take that as a yes," Harper says, because I don't respond. "Use that to your advantage. Woo her away from him with your love."

"Harper," I groan. "It's not that simple. I'm with Brooke. I'm in *love* with Brooke. I'm moving to Boston with her, and I'm not going to screw it up. I can't just go throwing around the L-word with Peyton. I'll talk to her, but I'm moving on. I have to."

"What does it matter if you love Brooke? Peyton needs to know you love her, too."

"She does know, and it doesn't matter!" I regret snapping as soon as the words are out of my mouth. "I'm sorry," I say with a lowered voice.

Harper is silent for a moment. "Have you told her recently?"

"No, but she knows. I'll never stop loving her." I shake my head, pinching the bridge of my nose. "But that changes nothing. I asked Brooke to come to Boston with me. Peyton made it clear that nothing will ever come of us. And I'm okay with it. I want a fresh start with Brooke. I deserve happiness, too."

"Okay," Harper accepts. "Then, at least as a brother or a best friend or whatever you're calling yourself, talk to her."

"I will. And it's best friend. I'll let you know how it goes."

"I'll be waiting. Don't take too long. Tyler is supposed to come visit next weekend. Talk to her before then."

Why can't he just stay in North Carolina? "Okay."

The Day I Confronted Her

IT'S BEEN A couple days, and I'm still thinking about my conversation with Harper. Tyler will be here in two days, and I haven't figured out the best way to approach Peyton. Any way that comes to mind makes me sound jealous or insane. Maybe I'm both. I don't even know anymore. In no way can I allow her to think I'm jealous of Tyler though. I'll have to call her. This won't work in person.

"Hey," she answers on the first ring. "Is everything okay?"

"Yeah. Why wouldn't it be?"

She pauses. "You just haven't called for no reason in a long time. And since I'm right next door, it's weird. Why didn't you just come over?"

Because I don't know how to do this. Our dynamic is all screwed up. I don't know how to talk about this in person. I'd have to look her in the eye to tell her Tyler isn't good enough for her. In person, I can't hide facial expressions and reactions. I don't come up with a good response fast enough.

"Brodee? Is there a reason you called?"

I also hate that I have to have a reason. We used to talk just to talk. Now I can't even call her without getting the third degree. "Just wanted to chat. See how the wedding planning is going."

Honestly, I'd rather gouge out my eyes with a hot fire poker than hear her talk about the details of her upcoming nuptials, but I'll have to suck it up this once.

"Oh." She isn't buying it. "Really?"

"You set a date yet?"

"April 9th."

I nearly choke. It's January 6th. Three months. She wants to get married in three months? "You weren't kidding when you said it would be a short engagement."

"Yeah, well, Tyler begins dental school at the end of April, and we want to get married before that so..."

"Right. Can't mess around. I bet Olivia is freaking out trying to get everything put together."

"Yeah." She laughs, almost getting pleasure out of Olivia's pain. "Kind of. But like I said…it will be a small wedding, so she doesn't have to worry about much. And Tyler's mom doesn't have a daughter, so she's more than willing to get in on all the wedding planning. They've split a lot of the preparations to get it done."

"That's cool." I try to think of something to add. "Harper and Skylar's wedding give you any ideas?"

"That wedding was very Skylar and Harper, let's put it that way." She laughs.

"So you have the what-you-don't-want list."

Her amusement continues. "Definitely, yes. Though Harper did have some good ideas, I don't want to copy her. Our wedding should reflect us, not Harper and Skylar."

I agree, which might be the best segue into the conversation that I'll get. "You know, when I first saw you I was really shocked. It took a second to realize it was you. Why did you decide to cut your hair?" *Subtle, Brodee.*

"Harper talked to you, didn't she?" There's no question in her tone. *How does she know?*

"Why would that be something Harper talked to me about? I just realized I never asked you. You've never had short hair before, so I wanted to know what sparked the change."

"Gosh. She's such a drama queen. Would you tell Harper to cool her jets and worry about something that actually needs to be worried about."

I start back peddling. "This isn't about Harper, Pete. I noticed a change in you. I just wanted to talk to you about it."

"Why wouldn't I have changed? It's been four years, Brodee. It's called growing up."

It's not that she changed. There's nothing wrong with changing, as long as she's doing it for herself and not for him. "Sure. Everyone grows up. But why did you cut off all your hair and dye it white?" I ask again. After our surfing trip, I feel like we're closer to where we used to be, that I could be a little more evasive. Even if it means I'll piss her off.

"Because I felt like it, okay? I've never had short hair. I wanted to know what it would be like. Yes, Tyler liked the idea, too. But I came up with it."

"Makes sense. No need to jump down my throat."

Peyton sighs. "I'm sorry. Harper just has it in her head that Tyler is this controlling boyfriend, err…fiancé. And he's not. He's really not, Brodee."

"Okay. I believe you." I don't. I really don't. But I don't feel like I can argue any further. I have no claim to her life. Nor have I been there for any of their conversations. She could very well be telling the truth. For all I know, Harper might be building this up in her head. It doesn't mean I think he's good enough for her.

"I'm heading to Isle of Palms tomorrow morning. You up for it?"

She pauses before answering. I imagine her sitting on her bed, wanting to say no just to spite me, but she can't resist the waves when they call to her. "Yeah. Sure."

"Meet me at six in my driveway?"

I hear the smile in her voice. "I'll be there."

The Day I Wish She Didn't Ask

BROOKE DOESN'T SURF, and I haven't taught her how yet. It felt disrespectful to introduce her to something Peyton and I shared. I'm not sure why, considering I know Peyton goes with Tyler. When she told me they surf all the time, I wasn't expecting to feel offended. *Why wouldn't they go surfing together?* He's her fiancé. I can't expect to hold her to the same standard when she's no longer mine. I'll have to teach Brooke when we get to Boston so she can go with me. I'll need a new surfing buddy.

We're walking back to my car after surfing when Peyton asks, "Will you give me away?"

I'm confused at first. Those five words are not words I would expect Peyton to say to me. And then when I realize what she's asking, I nearly have a coughing fit. She can't be serious. I tighten my grip on the towel around my neck. "You want me to give you away to Tyler?" *Oh, the irony.*

"You'll be coming to the wedding, right? I mean, with your new job, I wasn't sure if you'd be able to come back."

I hadn't thought about using that as an excuse. *Duh.* It's the perfect out. She doesn't have to know the thought of watching her say 'I do' to him makes me want to jump in the ocean and feed myself to the sharks. But the look of hope in her eyes severs that thought. She's still my best friend. If the roles were reversed, she'd be there for me no matter what. "Yeah, of course. Like I'd miss your wedding day."

She nods, satisfied. "I know it might be weird since you're not the biggest fan of Tyler, but will you give me away anyway?"

Her request might be taking it too far. Being a guest and being a part of the wedding are two very different things. If I'm in the audience, camouflaged among the people, she's not looking at me; she's focusing on the groom and the officiant. If I'm walking her down the aisle, I won't be able to mask the regret in my eyes when she has me hand her over to Tyler. *Could I willingly do it?*

"After my dad died," she says, like she knows I'll need convincing, "I thought once that I'd ask Nick, but there's no way I'm asking him now. And I'm still not in a place where I'm ready to ask that of my mom. You're the closest thing I have to family. I really want you to do it. Say you will. Please, Brodee."

I remind myself we're beyond this. I've moved on with Brooke. I can handle walking Peyton down the aisle toward Tyler. I can handle passing her off to him when the time comes. When the officiant asks me, 'Who gives this woman to be married to this man,' I can say, 'I do,' without grimacing. *Right?*

No, I can't.

But, I can't tell her no. "If that's what will make you happy, okay."

"You will? Thank you." She sets her surfboard against my trunk and throws her arms around my neck, resting her chin on my shoulder. "Thank you so much." I lock my emotions in a cage. Then I toss a cover over the cage to conceal them for good measure. Hugging her shouldn't make me feel like this anymore. I have to love her like I would a best friend. That's it. But when I wrap my arms around her, the cage explodes. My emotions fly like shrapnel through the layers of my heart. I let go of her and step back.

I smile to conceal my uneasiness. "Anytime."

Boston can't come fast enough. If my apartment were available to move into tomorrow, I'd be there.

The Day We Agreed

"SO, TYLER CAME and went and the wedding is still on."

"How is it that you and I talk more than Skylar and I do?"

"I'm serious, Brodee." Harper clearly isn't amused. I try not to laugh.

"Harper, I tried talking to her, but nothing I say is going to make her see reason. In case you just met our friend, Peyton, she's a little stubborn. Once she has something set in her mind, that's it. She's going to have to figure it out for herself."

"What if she doesn't?"

I toss my hands in the air, even though I know Harper can't see me. *I can only pray she does.* "I don't know what to tell you. It's not our life. And maybe you've read the situation wrong. We've been hanging out, and she still seems like the old Peyton. She might come to her senses."

"Psh…That's because she doesn't have him hanging around. Did you spend any time with them when he was here last weekend?"

I'd rather swallow a gumball covered in thumbtacks. "No. I was busy helping my mom with stuff around the house."

"Well, Skylar and I went on a double date with them. You want to know what Tyler said to her while we were walking into the restaurant?"

I don't think I want to know.

"'*Those jeans are looking a little snug, baby,*'" she mimics him. "Her butt looked amazing in those jeans, by the way. And then when Peyton decided she wanted a burger and fries instead of something from the low-calorie section, he asked, '*Baby, are you sure you want to do that?*' If Skylar weren't there to hold me back, I would've lunged across that table and strangled him. *Baby?* I'd scratch out the eyes of any man who thought he could call me 'baby.'"

I laugh against my better judgment. I would've paid to watch Harper lunge across that table at Tyler. She'd be able to get away with it. I'd end up in jail for assault. "What did Peyton say back to him?"

"She told him it was her cheat day. Why did she have to justify it to Tyler in the first place? And since when does she have a freaking cheat day?"

Never. She doesn't need one. Her metabolism is that of a teenage boy going through puberty. "Did you say something to her?"

"I gave her a look, and she averted her eyes."

"Skylar didn't say something?"

"He was too busy trying to decide what he wanted to eat to hear the conversation."

As much as I hate the way their relationship works, I still don't feel like I can do anything about it. Not because I don't want to. If it were up to me, I'd punch the douchenugget and send him packing, but I know Peyton won't listen, and now that we're starting get back to what we once were I don't want to risk losing that.

"I know neither of us want this wedding to happen, but I'm not in a position to try and talk her out of it yet. I haven't been around Tyler enough. When I did try to call him out on some stuff, she immediately knew you and I talked. After that, anything I said wasn't going to be heard."

"I hate him," Harper mutters.

"Well, we can agree on that."

When Harper and I hang up, I look out my bedroom window and see Peyton walking around her room. It's dark out, so the light inside her room draws my attention. Her window is closed, but her white curtain is pulled back. I can tell she's arguing with someone. Her arms are all over the place, and she's pacing. We're opposites in that aspect. When she's angry, she paces. When I'm angry, I can't focus on anything aside from my anger. I pace every other time of the day.

Peyton chucks her phone onto her bed. She looks out her window and spots me watching her. Caught. I might as well lift my hand to wave. She walks to her window and pushes it up. I open mine.

"Why do men insist they're always right?"

"I think you have us confused with women."

"You better watch your tongue, Fisher."

I laugh, but ask, "You okay?"

She exhales through her nose. "Yeah, it was just a stupid fight about where we're going to get married. Tyler thinks we should get married in Asheville because of our family." She motions between the two of us. "He thinks it would be better to have the wedding where there's no awkward drama, like our hometown wouldn't come to the wedding because they judge our parents. And apparently his parents belong to some country club where he wants the ceremony to be."

Of course he does. And to think, I didn't think it was possible to hate him more than I do. "I take it you don't want to do that."

"No, I don't. So things are a little weird here, but if our parents can hold a holiday party and have a full house, I don't see why a wedding would be any different. And I don't want a country club wedding. How pretentious is that? But it's important to their family status in his community or something. I don't know. It's stupid. I'm not a country club kind of girl. This wedding should be about us, not how he wants to portray us." *Maybe she does see what Harper and I see. She just doesn't realize it yet.* Peyton sighs and lays her head against her arms folded on the windowsill. "He doesn't understand why I would want the wedding in my hometown."

Tyler seriously doesn't know her at all. "Maybe give it a couple days. He might come around if he realizes how important it is to you."

"Yeah. Maybe." She doesn't seem convinced. "I thought we could get married on the beach and do a casual dinner on the shore. Does that sound like such an awful wedding?"

Not at all. It sounds like Peyton.

"You want to come watch a movie? Get your mind off it. We can watch *The Proposal*." I know how much she loves Ryan Reynolds. "Or if you ask really nicely, I'll watch *Singin' in the Rain* with you."

A laugh bursts from her. "I think it'll be another ten years before I'm ready to watch that movie again. It still haunts my nightmares."

It's hard not to laugh with her. "*The Proposal* then?"

She hesitates. "Not tonight. I think I just want to sleep. You check the surf for tomorrow?"

"Yeah. It's not great, but we can go if you want."

She shrugs. "Nah. But I wouldn't hate heading out to Sullivan's and getting some Beardcats."

"In need of some gelato, huh?"

"In the worst way."

I smile. "Let's do it. Call me when you wake up."

"Okay." She smiles back. "You know what would really make my night?"

"What?"

"Your Chewbacca impression."

I should've known. I don't think twice as I open my mouth to release the guttural sound.

She giggles, and her face lights up. "Thanks, Brodee. Goodnight."

I tip my chin to my chest. "Night, Pete."

The Day She Didn't See It

BROOKE CALLS EVERY day with more places she wants us to explore in Boston. We've added The Freedom Trail, Harborwalk, and some swan boats we're supposed to ride in the public park. And now she's dying to go to the Boston Museum of Fine Arts. I'm pretty sure she has booked every weekend for the next year.

"I started packing up my things last night and my mom started to cry."

"She's not taking this move well, is she?" I ask.

Brooke chuckles, but it's not malicious. "Not really, but then I showed her all the cool stuff she could come and do with us, and it softened her a little bit to the idea."

I hear a knock at the front door.

"There's someone at the door, and I'm the only one home. You mind if we talk later?"

"No, go ahead. I've got to do some more packing anyway. Can't wait to see you next week!"

"Me too. Love you, Brooke."

"Love you more."

We say our goodbyes right before I answer the door. Peyton is holding *The Proposal* and a popcorn bowl with some kernels and oil in it.

"What say you?"

My smile spreads. "As long as that popcorn is meant for me."

"Like I'd come empty-handed with a chick flick."

I let her pass by and get a hint of her coconut shampoo. I forgot how much I love coconut. She's wearing black leggings and a sweatshirt that says, *Trust people who like big butts. They cannot lie.* I wonder if Tyler has seen her wear it before. It makes me think she's wearing it in defiance, and I can't help but feel proud. It's so passive aggressive. And so Peyton.

She heads for the kitchen and makes herself at home, pulling out the popcorn popper from below the stove. "Your mom here?"

"No. She went grocery shopping, and then has some Pound class."

"Huh?" Peyton turns and sets up the popper on the counter.

"I don't know. It's this new workout she's trying. They use drumsticks on the ground or something." I shrug and sit on the barstool across from her. "She loves it."

"Well, bummer. I know how much she loves *The Proposal*, too. I guess more popcorn for us."

I'm proud of myself. We've hung out several times over the last couple weeks and not once have I had the urge to kiss her. Of course, now that I'm thinking about it, it's all I can think about. The only makeup Peyton is wearing is some pink, glossy stuff on her lips, and she's pinned her hair back, but since it's so short, some pieces have fallen around her freckled face. I want to remind her that she doesn't need all that makeup to look beautiful, but I don't. Her natural hair color is starting to peek out. Though I know it's not very dark, it looks black compared to the whiteness of her dyed hair.

"What?" Peyton asks me. "Do I have something on my face?" She rubs her hand under her nose and over her mouth.

Crap. I was staring. *You're making her uncomfortable.* "No. I think I just zoned out. Sorry."

She pours the popcorn into the popper. "Tyler called me this morning and apologized. The wedding will be here."

The Tool does have some common sense. Who knew? "See. I told you it would work out."

"I'm sorry about last night." She's embarrassed that I saw her chuck her phone across the room. Been there, done that. "You caught me in the heat of the moment. He really is good to me, you know." I almost say, 'I know,' just as an automatic reply, but Peyton gives me a look, and I bite my tongue. It would be the blackest lie. "There are good days and bad, as I assume you and Brooke have. But isn't that what relationships are? You have to pick your battles and compromise and find a rhythm that works for you. What works in one relationship doesn't necessarily work in another."

But how many compromises has he made? Does the rhythm work because she doesn't choose many battles to fight for? Is she content giving in? This is a Peyton I don't understand.

I nod and keep my thoughts to myself.

"Tyler used to bring me flowers at least once a week. The first time he brought me calla lilies I finally had to tell him about my dad and the funeral. He was so mad at me for keeping that from him that summer. But, from then on, he brought every other kind of flower, but mostly tulips." She smiles reminiscently.

He probably did something he felt he needed to make up for with flowers, if he brought them that frequently.

"And even though I have a car, he used to take me to class and pick me up when he could, so I wouldn't have to worry about finding a parking spot. Ugh, parking was such a nightmare."

Or maybe he just wanted to know your whereabouts at all times so he took it upon himself to be your personal chauffeur.

"And when I complained to him about my wardrobe, he helped me clean it out, and then took me shopping. He helped me pick out all new clothes, and I didn't have to worry about a single dime. It was every girl's dream." She laughs. "He was like my own personal stylist."

All I hear is, he bought me clothes that he wanted me to wear.

How does she not see it?

So, you compromise your hair and body for sporadic acts of supposed kindness, the way I compromise by overlooking how Brooke eats Kit Kats and hates mornings. It's a good thing I don't say that out loud, no matter how much I want to.

"It's good you've been able to find a balance." I'm so full of it and she knows it, but doesn't say a thing. She used to call me out on all my bullcrap and force me to tell her what was really on my mind. Now she doesn't bother. She's too afraid of what I'll say.

Peyton finally turns on the popcorn popper, and halfway through *The Proposal* my mom gets home and plops on the couch to finish watching it with us.

The Day It Took an Instant

FIVE YEARS AGO

I'M DOING PHYSICS homework in my bedroom when my mom comes to tell me about Jon. Her face is tearstained and blotchy. She tells me to get in the car, that we're going to the hospital. My heart races. I don't really know what to think.

He had a brain aneurysm? How does that happen? What causes it? Can you survive a brain aneurysm?

My dad drives the four of us to the hospital. He remains the picture of calm and collected, while my mom sobs in the passenger's seat. He reaches over to take her hand and doesn't let go. Carter tries asking questions, but they don't know enough to give him any answers. I stay silent in the back seat, anxious to be with Peyton. She's probably a mess.

When we enter the waiting room, Peyton is there with both sets of her grandparents. She looks up as we walk in. While she looks sad, she's composed, but when our eyes meet, she crumbles. Like her tears were waiting until she couldn't hold it together anymore to release. The dam collapses when she sees me. She stands, and I rush to her. Though she has no strength to hold me in return, I tightly grip her to keep her from shattering.

It's not long after when Olivia comes to us to tell us they had to take him off life support. Just like that.

Peyton and Olivia cry and hug. It feels like our little world, the one where we were safe and nothing bad could ever happen to us, ceases to exist. It's the first time I realize it only takes an instant for change. One second and we could all be irrevocably altered.

The Day of Regrets and Acceptance

I'VE WONDERED IF, on the day Jon died, my dad thought, "This is my chance." It's a selfish, horrible thought, so I'd like to believe he didn't. I saw him that day. I remember his grief well. My dad lost his best friend, and it hit him hard. Tears were shed, and days were taken in solitude. I'd like to think he mourned the loss of Jon first, that he didn't think of pursuing Olivia until that summer, but I don't think highly enough of him to give him that kind of credit.

PEYTON AND OLIVIA are out searching for a venue that is willing to take them on this close to the wedding. Peyton will most likely get her beach wedding if they can't find one. My dad and I are having a guy's night. When he asked if I would come over for burgers on the grill and *Die Hard*, I couldn't turn him down.

The movie is queuing up when I ask, "When was it that you knew Olivia was who you wanted?"

My dad slowly turns his head. He doesn't look upset that I'm asking, merely confused as to why I'm asking now. "Are you asking me when I first knew that I loved her, or when I decided to…stray?" Meaning, one question he's willing to answer, the other not so much.

"At what point did you decide you wanted to spend the rest of your life with her?"

I can tell he's not sure how to answer this, or if he's not sure he wants to tell me the truth. The truth can be sharp and bitter on the way down.

He clears his throat before answering, "I'm not sure that there's a specific moment. It built up for years, but it was put on hold for quite a while until that summer."

"Why didn't you fight for her? If you loved her before you loved Mom, why didn't you fight for Olivia before you met Mom?" Then all of this could've been avoided.

"I wasn't man enough." I'm surprised by this answer. Not because he wasn't man enough, but because he's willing to admit to it. He's come a long way from the man who refused to apologize for loving another woman. "I was scared, too worried if she turned me down my pride would be damaged forever."

"So, you let another man fall in love with her and marry her?" I can't imagine loving her that much, yet being so willing to let her slip through his fingers.

"I knew Jon was a good man. And she loved him. Once I realized how much she loved him, I knew I was too late. She wasn't marrying someone who didn't deserve her." I think he's caught on to what I'm getting at. "If I had even the slightest inkling that Jon wasn't good enough for her, I wouldn't have given up until she chose me."

I nod. "If you could do it all over again, would you do things differently?"

"If it meant I didn't get to be the father of you and Carter? No. Not in a million years. I want you to know that, even if I could've had Olivia, I wouldn't choose her over you. Don't ever question that. But if it meant I could keep you, yes. I'd never have let her go."

I hope he never tells Mom that.

"Do you regret the affair?" I'm not asking to cause contention, and I think he realizes that now. I just need to know.

"I regret what it did to us." He looks pointedly at me. "I regret how it hurt your mother and Carter. How much damage it caused to so many people." It almost looks like he might cry—making it the first time I've seen him show this kind of emotion through this whole thing. "But I can't regret Olivia. I love her." He's says it so matter-of-factly. It's a simple truth he can no longer deny. "She's my first love, the love of my life."

The Day She Found the Lyrics

THE MOVE TO Boston sneaks up on me. I'm heading out first thing in the morning to make my way to Durham, so I can caravan up the coastline with Brooke. She planned out a route that will give us pit stops along the way in Baltimore, Philadelphia, and New York—places neither of us have ever been. It'll take us a few days, but I'd much rather have breaks along the way than drive the fifteen hours straight. I'm still not finished packing, so Peyton is taking a break from the wedding planning and helping me clear out the rest of my bedroom.

Peyton and I have been spending most of our days together, surfing and wandering around downtown when the surf isn't good enough. We've lived in Charleston our whole lives and rarely explored downtown. So, when Peyton called me *bored out of her mind*, we decided to do all the things we'd never done before. The Battery, Rainbow Row, Waterfront Park, The City Market. Conquering Charleston one cobblestone street at a time.

Every day with her has been refreshing. We managed to see each other almost every day without the past looming over us. She doesn't bring up Tyler again after the movie night, and I only bring up Brooke when Peyton asks. I have to wonder, if we only get along when we're not talking about our significant others, how we are going to manage when they're permanent fixtures in our lives?

There are no cheesy pick-up line challenges, which is harder than I thought to stop. I've had a few come to mind and kept them to myself. We make new inside jokes and memories to push us forward, not draw us back.

Now we're separating the things I'm bringing to Boston with me, things I'm throwing out, and important things I'm leaving with my mom so I don't end up losing memories she's made a point to save.

"I can't believe you kept these."

I look over to see Peyton sitting cross-legged on the floor by my open closet door with one of our old yearbooks in her lap. It's got some notes she used to give me during passing periods.

I forgot all about those.

I walk over and hover over her shoulder. She opens one that's yellow around the edges. "Oh my gosh." She laughs. "This is from freshman year." I see my name written in bright permanent marker at the top of the note. I'm pretty sure she spent more of her time in class writing my name in intricate designs than actually writing the note—or paying attention in class for that matter.

"You used to make my name all cool."

"Geometry and Spanish were so boring. I had to do something." She laughs to herself. Peyton finds another yearbook with more folded notebook paper. I kind of just shoved some of her old notes that had designs I thought she spent a lot of time on in each yearbook.

I watch her skim through them one by one. "In this one I was complaining to you about Brock Weckerly." She covers her mouth to suppress her laughter. "Remember when I dated him our junior year? He was such a jerk." She shakes her head as she folds the paper back up.

I forgot about him. He never opened any doors for her or paid when they went out on dates. I wasn't his biggest fan, either. Her track record with boyfriends isn't the greatest, I guess.

I let her continue separating stuff in my closet while I search under my bed. Missing socks. Old candy wrappers. Books I forgot I even had. I was such a slob. *How did I not clear this out before college?*

I'm crawling out from underneath my mattress when I hear a quiet intake of breath. I twist around on my hands and knees to see Peyton is still sitting in front of my closet. Her hand is pressed against her mouth, but she's not stifling laughter this time. When I get closer I see my handwriting scribbled across some notebook paper. I know exactly what it is the moment I see it, and it's not a note. It's the makings of the lyrics for the song I wrote her that summer. But she's not seeing the final lyrics. She's seeing what they used to be, what I never sang to her.

When you're here with me,
There's no other place I'd rather be.
Then he takes you away,
And I can't think straight.

What can I do

To deserve you?

I'm so broken,

Without you near.

What can I do

To deserve you?

I'm so broken,

Won't you be with me?

My Peyton.

On cold Hatteras nights,

He holds you so tight.

Then I stare into your eyes,

And that's when I agonize…

(Chorus)

Be with me.

So, I wrote this song,

For you.

I wrote this song,

For you.

I wrote this song,

To tell you,

I need you.

(Chorus)

I can't believe I thought those were good lyrics. Granted, for an amateur lyricist, I think I did pretty well. *Why did I keep those?*

"When did you write this?" Her voice is barely above a whisper.

My mouth feels like I've been in the desert for days without water. It's so dry.

She turns to me. "Brodee, when did you write this?" I can't tell if she's mad or sad, but her jaw is clenched, and she looks like she's getting ready to cry.

"A couple weeks before the party at Marcus's house that summer."

That eases the furrow in her brow, making me think she thought I'd just recently written the lyrics. Peyton looks away, back at the sheet of crumpled paper in her hands. She releases her grip so she's no longer wrinkling it. "Before?" It's a rhetorical question, so I don't answer her. I'm not sure what the right move is here. *Am I supposed to comfort her? Or explain how she had ensnared my heart as soon as Rylie dared us to kiss?*

"That's why lucky and Peyton didn't rhyme in the chorus," she concludes. I can't believe she remembers any of the lyrics I wrote the second time. I only sang it for her a few times in Hatteras. "When you said the lyrics weren't quite ready, you were still trying to find a better word to rhyme with my name."

"Peyton isn't the easiest name to rhyme with, surprisingly enough." I crack a smile, and she lets out a breath of laughter.

"I think we need a break from packing," she says, getting to her feet, cutting the tension. "Dinner?"

"Good idea."

AFTER WE EAT and pull into my driveway, she uses her thumb to point to her house. "I'm going to head home. I need to call Tyler, and my mom had some things she needed my help with before the end of the day."

This is it. The last time I'll see her before I'm gone.

"You're leaving in the morning, right?"

"Five o'clock. Bright and early."

Peyton reaches out and hugs me. "Drive safe."

I inhale and wish I hadn't. I'm blasted with coconut and memories. The hug lengthens, and it feels like she needs it as much as I do. We hold each other. I don't know what the exchange means, but it hurts. It's more than a goodbye. *What are we doing to ourselves?* She squeezes me tightly before she drops her arms. I should've let go first.

"See you at the wedding?" She smiles, but it falters.

"The wedding," I breathe with a nod, my lips tightening.

"Let me know when you get to Boston, so I know you're safe."

I salute her. Not sure why. But it happens. "Will do."

"Goodbye, Brodee."

"Bye, Pete."

The Day We Moved In

BROOKE AND I walk into our empty apartment and she squeals. "Oh my gosh, I love it!"

It's a one bedroom, open floor plan. I got lucky and was able to rent a corner apartment of the building, so we've got lots of windows. The kitchen is right off the entryway and has exposed brick walls. Brooke runs her fingers over the red brick by the door.

"It's not much, but it's what we could afford."

"It's ours. It's perfect." She kisses me and smiles. "Wait. We have to make our first kiss in our first apartment memorable."

I pick her up and Brooke makes a noise of surprise as she wraps her arms around my neck. I walk us out of the empty apartment, and then walk back through the doorway. She's giggling when I bend my head down to kiss her the right way—long and thoroughly. Her hands find my face and hold my mouth in place.

After I pull back, she licks her lips and grins. "That will do."

"Well, the boxes aren't going to unpack themselves. Shall we go retrieve them and get started?" I ask and set her down.

"Yes! Let's do this."

Before I walk out the door I shoot Peyton a text.

Me: Safe and sound.

Pete: Thank you! I was beginning to worry.

Me: Nothing to worry about. We're going to unpack and get settled in.

Pete: Send pictures when you're all done!

I send her a thumbs up emoji.

"THAT'S THE LAST BOX!"

Brooke flips on some music and jumps onto the couch. I can't believe we've unpacked the last box. I thought it would never end. We've spent all day moving, and since we haven't been grocery shopping we ordered take out twice. We now have Chinese and pizza boxes all over the kitchen, but it looks right. Lived in.

The apartment could hardly hold the boxes we brought, but now that everything is out and found its place, I wonder what filled up so many boxes. We've set up a white bookshelf with our combined collection of books in the main room. Brooke's placed everything carefully on the shelves with bookends and sculptures. We've got a kitchen table that looks more like it belongs in a dollhouse, but it's perfect for the size of our kitchen. She got some pictures of us framed and made a few collages on the walls in our living room. Our couch is a tan futon, but at least it serves multiple purposes.

Home sweet home.

Brooke dances in her tank top and a pair of old, black gymnastics shorts. I know they're gymnastics shorts because Peyton used to wear the same ones to her gymnastics practices after school. Brooke flashes her beaming green eyes at me. She laughs like she's never been happier. We bring that out in each other. She grabs my hand and pulls me onto the couch to dance with her. We're going to break this thing before we even use it. Her off-key singing begins, and I laugh because I love the way she sounds. Carefree and unapologetic. Her happiness has the ability to make up for what I lack.

The Day Chewbacca Stopped

EVERY WEEKEND SINCE we moved to Boston has been jam-packed. Brooke hasn't left time for anything but tourism. Which is great if you're her and don't work during the week yet. I understand she's ready to explore and get out of the house by the time the weekend comes. By Friday, I'm exhausted. I need a veg day, but I don't say a word. I keep a smile on my face, and do what I can to make her happy.

She's applied for several different engineering positions around Boston, but hasn't had any offers yet. I know she's getting discouraged. Not having a job means not contributing to our living expenses. Every day she tells me how she doesn't want me to think she moved here with me so I could pay for everything. *I'm not a mooch.* I know that, but she's stressed about it nonetheless. It's my job to reassure her and tell her a position will come along.

AND THEN, ONE day in early March, Brooke jumps up and down in the middle of our living room after she gets off the phone. "I got the job at Dewberry!" She bounces over to me and throws her arms around my neck.

"Babe, that's awesome! I knew you would."

"That interview process was so intense, though. I applied, what, like a month ago?"

"Yeah, but it worked out." I hold her waist, keeping her close to me. "When do you start?"

"On Monday."

"See." I kiss her lips. "I told you it would all work out."

"I know, but you know how much it means to me to be able to stand on my own."

"I do. It's one of the things I love about you." I yawn, and for some reason Chewbacca comes out.

Her eyebrow rises. "What was that?"

"Chewbacca," I say incredulously. Please tell me she knows who Chewbacca is.

"No, I know who it is. I just don't understand why you did it."

I shrug. I'm not even sure when I learned how to make the sound. I really only used to do it to make Peyton laugh. "It's just a fun sound to make."

Brooke nods, but she's looking at me like I'm crazy. I guess I won't do my Chewbacca impression around her.

"So..." I let go of her and walk into the kitchen to grab a drink, "My mom's birthday is next weekend. I'm thinking of surprising her."

"Well, dangit. Now you tell me. I won't be able to get time off to go with you!"

"I know, but it's okay. My mom will understand. You getting that position is more important than coming home with me."

The Day She Told Me

MY FLIGHT INTO Charleston gets in around eight o'clock. After I see my mom, I decide to go say hi to my dad. When Peyton opens the door in a yellow sundress that matches her hair, I'm taken aback. Her lips are glossed in pink. She smiles warmly. "Brodee!"

It's all it takes. Like a riptide, she pulls me back in. She can't help it. She doesn't even mean to do it. It's just who she is. Peyton. My riptide.

I smile back at her. "Hey, can I come in?"

"Yeah, sure. Come in, come in." She opens the door wide. "What are you doing here?"

"I came to surprise my mom for her birthday. The big fifty."

"Oh yeah, I forgot the dinner was this weekend! This wedding planning is frying my brain. I don't know how many cells I'll have let by the time I'm done. A month, Brodee. That's all we have left. So much to plan with so little time, but I only have myself to blame."

I follow her into the kitchen where she sits at the square table with

Olivia. Magazine clippings cover the entire table.

"Well, look who it is." Olivia's face lights up. I'm reminded where Peyton gets her eyes.

"Hey, Liv." I sit down with them.

"We're trying to decide on a cake," Peyton says and shuffles some clippings.

I look closer and see that's all that's on the table. Cake. I didn't even know you could decorate a cake so many different ways.

"Sounds exciting."

"It's really not." I'm sure there's some organization here, but I can't decipher it. "There are so many different themes to choose from, and the more I find that I like, the more confused I get. I hadn't realized I was such an indecisive person until I started planning this wedding."

"Ha. I'm sure you'll figure it out."

She looks up from the cakes. "Did Brooke not come with you?"

"Nah, she couldn't get off work."

"Well, that's too bad. I was hoping to hang out with her at the dinner tomorrow."

"Yeah, she was bummed, but only working at Dewberry for a week didn't give her much leeway. She didn't feel like she could ask for time off."

"Totally understandable. What is she doing?"

"She got a structural engineering position, and she loves it already."

"Good!" Peyton is overly enthusiastic. It's weird. She turns her attention back to the magazine clippings. "The job market is so hard to get into right now. I'm so glad she was able to find something so quickly."

"Me too. Is my dad around?"

"He had to work late today, so he won't be home until after ten," Olivia says.

I nod. Though, as much fun as this is, I have no desire to pick out wedding cakes with them, so I stand. "I just wanted to come and say hi. I'll let you two get back to the planning."

"Oh." Peyton gets up. I can tell she was expecting me to stay longer, but this is a lot more difficult than I thought it would be. Seeing the wedding planning is different than hearing about it. "I'll walk you to the door."

"What are you doing tomorrow before my mom's birthday dinner?" I ask when we reach the front door. "Maybe we can go get some lunch or something?"

"Don't forget about your appointment at ten, Peyton," Olivia hollers from the kitchen.

"Yeah. I know, Mom." Her eyes roll as she sighs. "Thanks for the tenth reminder."

"You've got to meet with a wedding planner or something?"

Olivia walks in and looks pointedly at me. "She has a doctor's appointment. She hasn't told you?"

"Mom," Peyton warns.

"He's family. He deserves to know, Peyton."

I look between the two women as they have an argument with their eyes. It doesn't seem like an argument I want to get between, but I want to know what Peyton is hiding from me. Doctor's appointment. *Oh hell.* She's pregnant, isn't she? I can't find my heart. It sank deep inside my chest. I lost it.

"What's going on?" I press. She can't be. Please tell me my brain is overreacting. I'm just getting used to the idea of their marriage. A Peyton and Tyler baby is not something I want to even imagine.

"Tell him," Olivia directs, her finger pointing at me like Peyton needs to 'fess up to a crime. She must be getting pointers from my dad.

"Mom," she hisses.

Olivia gives her The Look. I've seen The Look many times. It's Olivia's no nonsense face. If Peyton doesn't tell me, Liv will.

Peyton exhales heavily and looks at me. Before she says it, I know I'm not going to like this appointment. I'm going to hate this appointment with a passion. "I have an appointment with my oncologist."

It takes me a second to remember what an oncologist does. An oncologist is not an obstetrician. So, she's not pregnant. *Phew.* My brain starts to pick up again. Oncologist, oncologist… When I know, I feel my body collapse, but somehow I remain standing.

"I have ovarian cancer," she continues. "It's probably completely treatable. Nothing to worry about. Tomorrow I have an appointment to discuss the form of treatment we're going to proceed with."

I clasp my hand over my mouth before I let out a cry and exhale. "Peyton, why didn't you say something before?"

Olivia slowly retreats back into the kitchen, understanding this is now a conversation only between Peyton and me.

Peyton waits until she's gone and calmly says, "Because it's not that big of a deal, and I don't want people to treat me differently."

"Not a big deal? It's definitely a big deal."

"This. *This* is why I didn't want to say something." She points at me like I'm the one to blame for her condition.

I speak as normally as I can manage with every part of me screaming on the inside. "I'm sorry. How bad is it?"

"I don't know yet. The doctor seems to think we caught it early enough, but that's what the appointment tomorrow is supposed to help determine."

I'm having difficulty finding the right words. I don't want to cry in front of her. That won't help matters. "You shouldn't have kept it a secret from me."

"I've kept it from everyone, Brodee. I haven't even told Harper. So, don't you dare go blabbing your mouth to Skylar. I mean it. My mom, Nick, and Tyler know. That's it. This stays here until I know more. I want to give people good news."

"Peyton." The way I say her name says everything. I can't lose you like this. I hate cancer. I'm so scared. *Please don't leave me.*

"I would have told you eventually," she says softly.

"When? After you were treated or have surgery or whatever? Or once it got worse? We both know you were never going to tell me."

Peyton's eyes shy away from me. "I would have figured out something before then." I know she's lying.

"How long have you known?"

She scratches her temple. "About a month. When I went to see my OB/GYN for an annual visit, they knew something wasn't right. They referred me out."

A month? So, the whole time I've been in Boston living life and traipsing around the city sites, she's been here suffering. If I'd been here…

"Tyler isn't here to go with you to this appointment?" I know I sound judgmental, but if she were my fiancé, I wouldn't miss one single appointment with her oncologist. Not only for support, but for fear that she'd leave something out. Because clearly, she's good at keeping secrets.

"He's busy in North Carolina. Something happened at his dad's office that kept him there. He couldn't get away. But it's fine."

I'd risk losing the job before I let her go without me. His dad has to understand. And so I decide. "I'm going with you."

"Brodee, it's fine." Her reassurances mean nothing. "I don't need you to come with me. I told you, it's a simple appointment. I'll tell you all about it when I'm done."

"I'm going." I open the front door before she can keep arguing with me. "And if you even think about leaving without me I'll just ask Olivia where and who it's with. She'll tell me. I'll be there no matter what."

"Fine," Peyton snaps.

"Fine." I close the door behind me.

I didn't leave so she couldn't give me no for an answer. I left so I could rush home, to hole myself away in my room. When I shut my bedroom door, my body falls against it. My legs give out, and I slide down to the floor. It's then that I cry. My head falls into my hands, and my body shakes with each strangled breath that tries to leave my lungs.

The Day I Let Her Be Human

PEYTON SETS HER hand on my knee. "You're making me anxious. Stop it." I hadn't realized I was even bouncing my leg. We've been waiting for the doctor in a tiny treatment room with posters of lady parts and diagrams plastering the walls. It's not that seeing the female organs makes me uncomfortable, but I've never seen them in so many different forms all in one place.

"Sorry." *Hold it together, Brodee. You're supposed to be the rock for her, not the other way around.*

I know we've probably only been waiting for five minutes, but I swear it's been hours.

There's finally a knock at the door, and a man with salt and pepper hair walks inside.

"Peyton," he greets and shakes her hand. "How are we doing today?"

"Doin' good!" An automatic response, of course. *How do you think she's doing, Doc?*

"And you are?" Dr. Levanstine—as I read from his white coat—looks to me.

"I'm her best—" I say at the same time that Peyton says, "This is my brother, Brodee." She's never referred to me as that before. It sounds so wrong coming out of her mouth. I want to take the words and burn them to ashes.

"Oh, wow. You must take after different parents. You look nothing alike."

Ha. You could say that. "Well, we're *step*siblings," I say, correcting Peyton.

"Oh," he chuckles, "then, that explains it."

They talk a little about her medical history. It's weird the things you can learn about a person during a doctor's appointment, things I probably could've gone my whole life without needing to know.

Dr. Levanstine states, "Right now, in order to see how far the cancer has spread, I'll need to go in and take a look. If the cancer is confined to one ovary, we'll be able to do a unilateral salpingo-oopherectomy, which essentially means I'll remove one ovary and one fallopian tube. If the cancer is confined to one ovary, I'll be able to harvest your eggs from the other one."

He carries on, giving Peyton all the different surgery and treatment options. I try to take it all in, to understand what it will mean for her. Everything is starting clog up my thought process.

"And there's a possibility that it hasn't spread far enough that I'll need a hysterectomy?" she asks.

He pauses. "Yes, there is a strong possibility. As far as your tests have shown, you're in stage 1, but I won't know the severity of the cancer until I get in there. It's likely we'll be able to avoid it."

"And what if it hasn't spread that far? Would you still suggest a hysterectomy?" she asks.

The look on his face tells me he hates answering this question with patients. "You're so young, Peyton. I'd hate to suggest something that's so permanent, irreversible. It's your body. Cancer can be aggressive. Even if you think you have it all, it could come back. It could be lurking in places you don't suspect." He sets his gaze on her. "Ultimately, it's your decision. Only you can decide what is best for you."

Wait. Hold on. What did I miss? Why are we talking hysterectomies?

"Okay."

"Okay?"

"Do what you need to do," she says. "Take the eggs from the other ovary and get rid of everything else if it becomes necessary. Better to be safe than sorry."

I don't know how she's acting so brave. I feel my emotions getting the best of me, and she's not even mine. It's not my children she might not be able to carry.

"There's always adoption, right?" she says, a sad smile tugging on her lips. I take her hand and squeeze. She's not being optimistic enough. She won't need to adopt because everything is going to work out. Dr. Levanstine will take care of everything. I push my positive thoughts through my fingers, hoping they'll infuse into her skin.

"Are you sure you don't want to take some time to think about this?" I ask. She made that decision without nearly any thought. Maybe she's in shock. "That's a huge decision, Pete."

"I've done my research, Brodee. My aunt had ovarian cancer. I don't want to go through what she did. I'll do whatever I can to nip it in the bud."

I nod, trying to accept her answer, but I feel like there has to be another way.

"I promise I will do everything in my power so it doesn't come to that," Dr. Levanstine says.

After they set up everything for the procedure, we walk to my car in silence. She doesn't speak when I start the engine or when I stop for gas. She doesn't sing or hum along to my radio. She doesn't say anything until we're five minutes from home. Even then it's not words.

Out of the corner of my eye I see Peyton's head bow, and a gasp is yanked from her lungs. Like she feels the grief deep in her bones, she curls in on herself. I pull over onto the side of the road and stop the car. I don't think. I take her into my arms, pulling her across the console to hold her in my lap. To hell with her fiancé, she'll always be my best friend. Her face presses against my shoulder, and her fingers dig into my back. I feel her tears on my neck as she sobs.

"I'll never be a mom," her muffled voice cries.

"Peyton, yes you will." I run my hand over the back of her head. "He said there's a high chance one of your ovaries can be saved. That's positive. We need to be positive."

"But if it can't…" her voice fades.

"You said so yourself. There are other ways."

"But they won't be my blood."

I don't know what to say to that. I've never thought of having children who weren't my blood. It never occurred to me that I might not have children of my own. I doubt it's a thought most men have. Has Tyler ever wondered about these things? Will he be supportive of her even if she can't have his children?

As I rock her, there's a part of me that mourns, too. If we were to ever have children, they might not have her face, her smile, or her laugh. What a tragedy that would be.

When her tears subside, she pulls away and apologizes about getting my shirt all wet as she tries to dab it out with her long sleeves.

"Stop it." I grab her wrists. "I don't care about some tears on my stupid shirt."

She nods slightly as her eyes travel from my damp chest to meet mine. The sadness and vulnerability punctures my heart. There's nothing in the world that I want more than to take away her pain. Even if it means I feel it for the rest of eternity, I'd take it on so she wouldn't have to.

Her gaze drifts down to my mouth. And suddenly, I'm aware that we're only separated by inches. It's hard for me to breathe. Neither of us moves. My self-control is quickly depleting. Her hair made of coconut falls in her face. I'm instantly filled with nostalgia. I feel homesick, but that doesn't even make sense. I am home.

Peyton can't be immune to what's building between us. Her body language and her eyes tell me her shield is down, if only for a few minutes. She's been a bottle of sealed emotions for so long I nearly forgot what it feels like when she looks at me like she wants me. I let go of one of her wrists and grip the back of her shirt, then think better of it and latch onto my steering wheel. If I don't hold onto something aside from her, I'll do something she'll later make me regret. I watch her swallow, then blink and quickly crawl out of my lap, sitting back in the passenger's seat. I finally let out a deep breath.

"I'm sorry I'm such a mess." It's a broken whisper.

"I don't want you to ever apologize for suffering." It comes out more harshly than I intend. I try to soften my tone. "There's nothing wrong with letting yourself feel your emotions. It's okay to be human. Let yourself be human."

It takes her a minute, like she needs to let my words find a place to live, but she eventually says, "Okay," and I start my car.

"HOW'D THE APPOINTMENT go?" my mom asks when I walk in the front door. I know Peyton didn't want me to say anything, but when she found me in my bedroom after Peyton broke the news, Mom wouldn't let it go.

I drop my keys on the side table just inside the door and drag my hand through my hair. *How did the appointment go?* I'm exhausted just thinking about it. *Please don't make me think about it.*

"Brodee," she presses.

"Everything the doctor said sounded promising. She has to have surgery, but he sounded optimistic."

"Then why do you look like you just signed her death certificate?"

I bite my trembling lip and take a deep breath. "Peyton's not taking it well. The doctor might have to do a hysterectomy. The thought of not being able to carry her own children is hitting her pretty hard."

My mom rests her hand over her heart as a layer of tears covers her eyes. I can't handle seeing her cry, too. One woman I love a day. That's all my heart can handle.

"Oh, Peyton…She'll never…I just…I thought…" I can tell she's not finishing her sentences because she's hiding her thoughts from me, not because she can't put into words what she's feeling.

"Just say it, Mom."

Her lips quiver. "She'll never be able to carry your babies."

I know I've already had that thought, but hearing it said out loud somehow makes it worse. I bite back my sadness. "She was never going to carry my babies anyway, Mom. They're going to be Tyler's. It's time we all accept that. And Dr. Levanstine said he might be able to save her eggs if one of the ovaries hasn't been affected, but he'll have to go in to see what's going on first."

She swallows, brushes away the wetness on her face, and folds her arms over her chest. "Well, at least there's that."

"Yeah." Somehow it doesn't make me feel better. "At least there's that."

I MADE RESERVATIONS for fifteen at my mom's favorite restaurant downtown called Poogan's Porch. A couple of her close friends, as well as Carter, Peyton, Skylar, Harper, and Skylar's parents were invited. I asked her if she wanted me to include Dad and Olivia, but as soon as she hesitated, I decided that it was a bad idea. It's hard to decipher when it's right and when it's not with her, but I figured it was better that I decide not to include them rather than her.

Poogan's Porch is in an old, yellow restored Victorian house on Queen Street. When my mom and I get there, Peyton is laughing with Carter on the sidewalk in front of the house, this morning's appointment washed away from her features. When she sees us she smiles, tucking her hair behind her ear, and waves. Peyton is wearing a cream sweater over a long, light blue dress that brings out her eyes. It's like she's trying to torture me. Stay in love with me, she says. Never lose sight of what we had. I should be yours. *Shut up, brain.*

Carter breaks my haze when he says, "How is it that I'm here before you guys. I'm never on time. I should get a gold star for this."

"How about an ear flick instead?" I reach out and make contact.

He rubs his ear and laughs. "Ouch, doofus."

Mom hugs Carter and pets the back of his head. "Hi, son. You do deserve a gold star, but I'm fresh out."

"Happy Birthday, Mom. You don't look at day over thirty."

"Suck up." I snort.

Mom grabs Peyton by the shoulders and appraises her. She's trying not to cry. *Hold it together, Mom.* "You look so pretty, honey."

Peyton blushes, and it makes her look even prettier. "Thanks, Tate. Happy Birthday."

My mom takes her into her arms, and Peyton looks at me over my mom's shoulder. The grip she has on Peyton is deeper than a normal hug. I can tell Peyton is having a hard time getting air. She knows I told my mom, and she's not happy with me.

"Anyone else here yet?" I ask, slipping my hands into my pockets.

Peyton pulls away from my mom and answers me, "Harper and

Skylar are trying to find a parking spot. I'm pretty sure his parents drove with them."

"Well, let's get in there so we can get seated."

The dinner is delicious. Mom is happy, which is all I wanted out of the evening. Peyton is carefree. She laughs with everyone and pretends nothing has changed. For the night, her sickness is forgotten. Though I wonder when she plans on telling everyone else, I don't ask. That's her decision, and I'll respect it as much as I hate to.

As we all leave, filing out of the restaurant, Peyton finds her way to my side.

"Thank you for not say anything tonight," she whispers close to my ear.

"Don't mention it. I'm sorry I couldn't keep it from my mom."

"It's okay," she forgives me. "I get it. And I'll tell the rest of them. I promise. Just not yet. Let me process it first."

I agree with a nod.

"I know I didn't seem like it, but I really appreciated you being there this morning. It meant a lot to have you with me."

For a second I look at her. I absorb the sincerity in her eyes and breathe it back out. "You don't need to thank me, Pete. I'd do anything for you."

She smiles, close-lipped. This is our life now. Meaningful gazes and words unspoken. "It was really good to see you."

I tip my chin down. "It's always good to see you, Pete." I wink and offer my mom an elbow. The riptide that Peyton is, I have to get back to Brooke.

"You ready to go?" I ask my mom.

She thanks everyone and takes my arm. As we walk along the road toward her car, she says, "Peyton looked really great tonight."

I nod and keep my gaze forward.

"She was keeping high spirits." She's trying to sound encouraging. "That's good, right?"

"Well, she was also putting on an act since she's refusing to tell anyone what's going on."

She slowly nods and heavily exhales. "I take it she asked you to keep it a secret."

"She needs time to process it before anyone else knows, and I promised I would respect that. So, that means you too. I wasn't supposed to tell you."

"Mum's the word."

The Day She Was Going to be Okay

ON MY FLIGHT back to Boston I try to distract myself with an inflight movie, but I find my mind wandering back to Peyton. Halfway through the movie, I still don't know what it's about. So, I try reading a book—one of Peyton's dad's books—but I can't get my brain to focus. I've read the same sentence at least five times. And it's the opening sentence of the first chapter. All I want is be in Boston with Brooke and immerse myself in our life together. I need our piece of happiness now more than ever.

"HOW WAS YOUR visit?" Brooke kisses me when I walk through the door. I wrap my arms around her waist and press her again my chest, desperate never to let go. "Oh, hey there." She chuckles.

"Peyton has cancer." It tumbles out. I don't even think to gently deliver the news. Though I don't think there is a gentle way to deliver that kind of news. It plagues even the shortest sentence. It's all I can think about.

She pulls back. "What?"

I move Brooke to the futon and recount my visit, from the moment Peyton told me about it, through her appointment, and my mom's birthday dinner.

When I'm done Brooke says, "Well, hopefully one of the ovaries will be salvageable. She'll be okay."

I nod and try to lift a smile. It doesn't feel right on my face. I shouldn't feel this upset. It's treatable. She's not going to die. She's going to have surgery and be just fine. Somehow my heart doesn't believe that.

"I'm going back for the surgery in a couple weeks."

"Do you want me to come with you?"

"If you want, but I don't even know how much time I'll be able to get off work. It may even just be a day. It might not be worth it for us to both worry about buying airline tickets, especially with your new job."

She nods in understanding, but something tells me she's not happy about it.

"Are you hungry?" Brooke asks and heads toward the kitchen. "I've got some dinner in the oven. Should be done in about twenty minutes."

I'm not hungry at all, but I say, "Yeah. Sounds great. I'm gonna go take a quick shower."

"Good idea. You'll feel better after you've washed the travel off you."

The travel. Yeah. That's what's wrong with me.

Once I'm in the shower, I turn the water as hot as it will go so I can feel something aside from sadness. The steam fills the shower and fogs the glass. I want to burn the agony and fear from my body. My mind chants over and over.

Peyton is going to be okay.

Peyton is going to be okay.

Peyton is going to be okay.

The Day I Needed a Distraction

A LOT OF my days are spent going through the motions. I wake up. Go to work. Come home. Spend time with Brooke. Go to bed. Repeat.

Brooke has been patient with me. I can tell because every time she talks to me, it's like she's talking to a child, trying to pull answers out. It wasn't apparent to me that I was acting any differently, but every day she asks me how I'm doing and if there's anything I want to talk about. I smile and tell her I'm fine. Because I am. Peyton's not.

When my thoughts drift to Peyton I might as well call it quits for the day. I can't get my anxious thoughts to shut up. What if her condition is worse than Dr. Levanstine thinks it is? What if something goes wrong during the surgery? What if I lose Peyton in every sense of the word? Then it feels like I can't breathe and nothing helps to bring me back.

So, I haven't let my thoughts deviate from my daily life. I redirect them to numbers and reports and Brooke. She can still bring me peace.

I look at Brooke sitting at our tiny dinner table in our tiny dining space across from me. We're eating the chicken parmesan she cooked for us, and she's looking at me like she's waiting for a response.

What did I miss? Did she ask me a question?

"Did you hear me?"

I have my fork halfway to my mouth. *Crap.* She was talking about work and a girl named Gabi, who has been trying to make her job hell. But that could've been five minutes ago, for all I know. *Was she still talking about work?* I can't fake this one.

"I'm sorry, Brooke. I spaced out for a second. What was that?"

She calmly sighs. "I asked if you gave more thought into getting a dog."

Wow. I was way off. A dog. Yeah. A dog might be nice to have, but neither of us are home enough to take care of one.

"I don't know if it's such a good idea when neither of us is home for the majority of the day. We can't leave a puppy to fend for itself."

"Well, what if we got a rescue dog? One that's already been house trained, that just needs a good home. I'm not far from work. I come home most days for my lunch breaks anyway. So I could feed and walk the dog then. Just think of how fun it would be!"

I can't think beyond work and Peyton right now. The stress of a dog to take care of would be too much. Or maybe it would be exactly the distraction I need. If I'm not focused on Peyton, my days might go more smoothly.

"Okay, yeah. I think it would be good for us. You want to go look at the shelter this weekend?"

Brooke jumps up and wraps her arms around my neck. "Ah! Yes! I'm so excited! This will be so good for us, something for us to take care of and do together." She pulls back and kisses my cheek. "And I think it'll help put a smile on your face again."

What's that supposed to mean? I smile. I smile all the time. Maybe it's been hard to find a reason to smile recently, but I've only been back from Charleston for a week. I've only had a week to try and process what Peyton's going through. It's hard being so far away, helpless from a distance. I can't do anything for her from here. My brain tells me I wouldn't be able to do anything even if I was there. The fate of her life is out of my control.

"I'm sorry if I've been out of it," I say and pull her into my lap.

"It's okay. I know you're worried about Peyton. It's understandable, but everything will work out." She runs her fingers through my hair. "You know?"

When Brooke looks at me, I feel like she really sees me. I'm not sure she'll like what she sees once she exposes all of me.

I nod because I can't do anything else. Then I kiss her and help clear the table.

The Day I Couldn't Tell Her

THE NEXT DAY a package comes in the mail from my mom. It's a cardboard box of memorabilia. Some old photo albums she thought I might want to keep with me as well as my diploma from Duke. *Am I supposed to frame it, or…?* I'll probably just put it in a box in my closet.

Brooke sits in our living room on the futon, flipping through the old pictures.

"Look at that bowl cut." She giggles, almost squealing with delight. "You were such a lady killer. Oh my gosh, and that fanny pack!"

I come around the futon to sit beside her and peer over her shoulder at my neon orange fanny pack strapped around my waist. "What can I say? All the ladies loved me."

"Is that Peyton?" Brooke points to a picture of us sitting on a tire swing on the next page. We couldn't have been more than six years old. Peyton's arm is wrapped around my neck, nearly strangling me, but we're both grinning at the camera.

"That would be her." It's crazy how long ago that feels, and yet I remember like it was yesterday. She's wearing shorts overalls and a jean jacket. So much denim. She's got big bangs and her hair is braided in two.

Brooke flips to the next page and there are more pictures of Peyton and me. My seventh birthday party. It was Spider-Man themed. We're wearing Spider-Man birthday hats and I'm wearing a Spider-Man T-shirt. There's another picture of us inside a fort we'd built out of sheets and kitchen chairs and pillows in her living room.

"When you said you grew up together, you literally meant you grew up together."

"Since we were born," I reply.

Brooke gets quiet. "Did you and Peyton ever…" She doesn't finish, and she doesn't have to. I've done everything I could so Brooke would avoid asking this question, but I'm still surprised it took her this long. Technically, Peyton and I never defined what we were, so I could get around it. But somehow that makes me feel like a liar, and I don't want to do that to Brooke. Labels mean nothing to Peyton and I, but we had something.

Brooke keeps flipping through the pages, avoiding eye contact.

"The last summer before college, but it didn't last long."

"Wait." She looks up. "So, you and Peyton *did* date."

'Date' makes it sound so juvenile, so insignificant. "I wouldn't say that we dated per se. We tested the waters, but it didn't work out."

The wheels churn. Brooke begins to see it. The pieces are falling into place, and I wish they weren't. Her eyes turn down at the corners. "Because that was the summer your dad and her mom started having an affair."

I nod once, curtly. I don't want her to push any more. This can't end well.

But I can't end the conversation. It'll only give her an opportunity to ask more questions later. We just need to get it all out there and be done with it.

"So, when you say you tested out the waters, what exactly does that mean?"

How can I even begin to describe that summer? It was the summer we fell in love. It was the best and worst summer of my life. It was the summer that changed us.

"Did you love her?" she asks when I don't answer quickly enough.

I can't deny it. "Nothing ever came of it, Brooke. I remind her too much of my own father. It would've been weird. Nothing will ever come of that relationship."

Her hands grip the photo album. "Brodee, you two are grown adults now. Your families may have been close, but you weren't raised as siblings. You love her. What's stopping you now?"

Whoa, whoa. I turn toward her and take the photo album from her clenched fingers, set it on the coffee table, and clutch her hands in mine. "None of that matters, Brooke. I love *you*. I'm with *you*."

Her eyes remain glued to mine. She searches for answers. *What more does she want from me?* "But if your parents weren't married, if that summer never happened…"

If that summer never happened…

I would never have let Peyton go. I don't answer Brooke. I don't have to. She knows. My face gives it away before I can cover it up. *Suck.*

"Oh my gosh." She breaks away. Her fingers clench the roots of her hair as she stands. "Oh my gosh."

"Brooke…"

"Don't. Don't say my name." She spins around. "You *still* love her."

"No, stop that." I stand. "It's not like that. I came to Boston with you. *You and me.* We're going to start our life together here. All of the adventures that we talk about, we're going to live them, side-by-side. I love *you.*"

She stares at me, searching my face. "You didn't deny it." Tears pool in her eyes, an ocean of hurt ready to overflow.

Because I can't. I can't lie. I'm a horrible liar. I can't lie to Brooke. But I can't lose her, too. "Peyton's my best friend. I'll always love her. But you're my future, Brooke Whitaker. This. Here. Us." I motion between us. "This is what I want."

She's pacing the floor, avoiding eye contact. Her voice is a tangle of hysteria. I don't know what to do with a hysterical Brooke. "It's all so clear now. Why you hate Tyler so much, not just because he's a complete jerk who doesn't know how to treat women. And the way you look at her when you think no one is watching. All the pictures you've kept of her. Why this cancer is tearing you apart. Gosh, I'm so stupid. How could I be so stupid? That I fell for it all. To think you could have a best friend as gorgeous as Peyton and not feel a thing for her."

"Brooke. Brooke…" I try to soothe her as I cautiously approach. "Brooke, look at me. *Look at me.*" My hands carefully reach out to her. When they make contact with her shoulders, she lifts her head. "You're not stupid. There's a reason I never said anything. Please will you sit down and let me explain? Please."

Without a word, she exhales and makes her way to the couch like I'm about to deliver the sentencing at her trial. *I'm* the one on trial.

Do you love her? Guilty or not guilty?

Okay, fine! I'm guilty!

I sit beside Brooke and begin.

"Peyton was my world. I'm not talking about love and devotion. I mean…we did *everything* together. Our families hardly did anything separately. We had dinner together on the weekends and sometimes during the week if one of our moms didn't feel like cooking. We attended each other's games and recitals and parties. We vacationed in Hatteras every summer." I could go on, but Brooke doesn't need to know about the late night conversations at our bedroom windows or sleepovers when Peyton was mourning. She doesn't need to know about how we used to go surfing nearly every weekend or how I helped nurse every one of Peyton's broken hearts from elementary school through high school.

"Our families were never separate entities. When people referred to us it was: The Fishers and Parkers. It was never one or the other. It was always both. Our families were a package deal." I squeeze her hands. It feels like I'm enlightening myself more than her. A miniature me sits attentively in the back of my brain, waiting to see how I'll explain to my heart what I've longed to decipher. "So, yes. When Peyton and I spent our last summer together before we went off to college, things shifted. We couldn't imagine our lives without the other because we never knew what it was like to live separate lives. We started to feel things we never had before because our lives were changing for the first time. And yes, we fell in love, but it wasn't meant to be."

It wasn't meant to be.

It wasn't.

My heart slowly, gradually, irrevocably accepts it.

Brooke trails her fingertips along my jaw. "I believe you." Her lips brush a whisper of a kiss across my mouth. "But I see now. We're not meant to be either."

"Brooke…Please. I love you. I love you so much. Don't you see that?"

"Even if you've let her go, I'll never feel like your first choice." She shrugs and tears slide down her cheeks. "I'll always be second because if nothing was standing in your way, you would be with her right now. Not me."

My eyes close hard, and my fists clench. She's right.

Her voice is a broken mess. "You can't tell me I'm wrong."

I want to. There's nothing more I want in this moment. If it were up to me, I'd make Brooke first. I'd tell her all the things she wants to hear. How Peyton means nothing to me, and Brooke is the only one I see, my soulmate. We could continue living blissfully ignorant in Boston and forget my family. But…I fear that would only make me my father.

If I were to marry Brooke, move to some suburban neighborhood, and have a family with her, would I still love Peyton after all those years? Would I give it all up if I had the chance? The sinking feeling in my gut tells me I might. I'm not strong enough. I thought I could be. *What am I doing? What am I thinking?* Brooke might not be my wife, and we might not have children, but if Peyton were to show up on our doorstep and confess her feelings, I wouldn't think twice. *I'm already my father.*

I'd rather die alone than be him. I might not be able to lie to Brooke, but I sure can believe my own lie, making myself believe I could actually be free of Peyton Parker.

I open my eyes. "I'm so sorry. I *do* love you." Because I do. I just love two people. I have to let Brooke go. I have to stop this now.

"I wish that were enough."

And I stop trying to fight for her. I understand why she's letting me go, which only makes it hurt worse. I'm the one to blame. I'm the reason she's crying. I hate that I couldn't be enough. I hate my heart for not allowing me choose.

With the finality of her words, I want to hold her in my arms one last time. For the first time I feel the need to ask her permission, but I don't. When I take her into my arms, pulling her close against my chest, she comes willingly—instinct. I squeeze my remorse and love into her, knowing it's not enough, but needing to do it anyway. Nothing else is said. There is nothing more to say. We don't stay that way for long. Brooke pushes off my chest without sparing me a glance and walks to our bedroom, shutting the door behind her.

Brooke decides to move back to Durham the next day, and I feel more emptiness than ever when she's gone. I can't tell if it's the loss of her or because I lost her for something my heart can't control.

The Day I Felt Heartless

WHEN I WAKE up, it takes a moment for me to remember she's gone. It's the first morning without her. I stare at the empty sheets. I feel incomplete, but not hollow. I miss Brooke, but I no longer feel the overwhelming heartbreak. *That should mean something, right? Am I heartless?* I've been with her for over a year and yet, it hurt more to lose Peyton, someone who was only mine for a month four years ago.

I reach over to my nightstand and pick up my phone to text Peyton. With the surgery next week, I'm hoping she's filled in a few more people about her condition. I hate to even think the word. A word shouldn't terrify me as much as it does. It's only six letters and yet it has the ability to devastate me with two syllables.

Me: Did you tell Harper?

Pete: Yeah. She's not happy with me.

I can't imagine why. But I understand to an extent why Peyton wanted to keep her illness a secret. I wouldn't want people treating me differently either, and I wouldn't want all the questions and consoling looks like I might die. Peyton is not going to die.

Me: When's the surgery?

Pete: Monday

Me: What time?

Pete: 11am. Why?

I have a meeting first thing that morning, but I can make it work. As long as I'm back in Boston by Tuesday.

Me: I can't be there for the surgery, but I'll be there when you get out.

Her next text tries to talk me out of coming, but it sounds more like she doesn't want me to feel obligated. It's not a question of obligation. I need to be there. What if there are complications? What if Tyler decides last minute there's an *emergency* at work that can't wait? No. She can pretend that the surgery isn't a big deal and act like she's fine, that she doesn't need the support, but she's lying. I know she is.

Me: I'm coming.

Pete: Thank you

The Day We Grieved

WHEN I ARRIVE at the airport on Monday morning my fight is delayed. By an hour. I check the time on my phone. At this rate I won't get to the hospital before three. Hours after Peyton will be done with the surgery. *Dangit!*

Once I make it on the airplane I can't keep my leg still the entire flight. It bounces so much that at one point the person next to me asks me if I hate flying. Nope. Just counting down the hours until I can see that Peyton is okay.

My mom picks me up from the airport and drives us straight to MUSC Hospital. I used to love to look out the windows on drives and count trees as they flew by. South Carolina is so green. I love the green. I've missed the green. Right now I can't even stop thinking to appreciate it.

"Have you heard anything yet?" I ask.

"Olivia said Peyton is in recovery. The surgery took a little longer than they anticipated. Apparently, there were minor complications, but she's doing fine."

"Complications? Like what?"

"She didn't say. Just that Peyton did really well."

"Did she say anything else?"

She shakes her head no. "We'll find out more when we get there. It's okay, sweetheart."

My gut feeling tells me it's not.

When we arrive, Peyton has been moved to her own room. The anesthesia has worn off and she's talking. My dad shows me to her room. I knock once before opening the door. Olivia's back is facing me. She looks over her shoulder at me and offers a sad smile. She bends down to kiss Peyton's forehead before she squeezes my arm and leaves the room. Olivia must know, but she doesn't say a word to me.

Peyton slowly twists her head to see me walking farther into the room. Her face is wet and blotchy. "You made it," she rasps.

I rush to her side and sit down on the chair closest to the hospital bed on the other side of the room. "Nothing was going to keep me away." I take one of her hands in both of mine.

"What happened?" I ask. "They said there were complications."

She tries to swallow. "It was worse than Dr. Levanstine thought. He couldn't save my ovaries." Peyton shuts her eyes tight and her lip quivers. "He had to do the full hysterectomy." Nothing else comes but her tears. Her head bows. She doesn't make a sound. The pain even takes her voice. I scoot closer and wrap her in my arms.

"Oh, Peyton. Where's Tyler?" I ask.

"He ran back to the house to get his laptop," she utters.

"Before or after you found out?"

"Before."

"Does he know?"

She whispers, "Dr. Levanstine talked to him…as soon as I got out of surgery."

Tyler knew. He knew, and he didn't wait to be there for her when she heard the news. If there were ever a time for me to step in and tell her to call off the engagement, it would be now. He doesn't deserve her. The selfish, narcissistic waste of air.

But I say nothing. I sit by her side and take on her heartbreak. The tears come, flowing relentlessly down her face. I do the only thing I can. I hold her and smooth down her hair. I whisper words of commiseration and comfort. Though I'm sure it means nothing, I pour my heart into my words and my grasp, and grieve along with her.

When some time has lapsed, Peyton pulls away. "What if Tyler doesn't want to get married now that I can't have his children?"

"Then he's even more unworthy of you than I thought." I cocoon her right hand in my hands. The fact that she even questions it spirals me into a silent rage.

She laughs lightly and winces, drawing her other arm around her stomach. "Don't make me laugh. It's hurts."

"I'm sorry. I wasn't trying to be funny." Without thinking, I press my lips to her knuckles. I hold her hand there, looking up at her. When she peers over at me, a sheen of tears glazing her eyes and a sad smile crossing her lips, I don't think I've ever loved her more.

I'm about to say as much when Tyler walks in with the laptop under his arm. He stops when he sees me leaning close, Peyton's hand still in mine. For her sake I pull away and stand. Now that he's back, I no longer fit here. I can't be the third to their two wheels. I refuse to be.

"Brodee." It's the first time Tyler's greeted me without coming to slap my hand or spouting out some stupid nickname. When he's not smiling, I hate to say it, he's kind of intimidating as he towers over me.

But that doesn't deter me. He might be tall and threatening, but he's still a prick. I can't fathom what she sees in him. "Tyler, I was just leaving." I squeeze Peyton's hand before letting go. "Rest, okay? Call me if you need me." I bend down and kiss her forehead.

"You're leaving already?"

"You've got Tyler now," I say in all sincerity, not out of spite, but I hear how my words come across when her brow pinches together. She nods apprehensively and watches me go.

"Take care of her," I murmur as I brush past Tyler.

At first I can tell he's not sure how to respond, then he says, "I will," like I insulted him, as if he wouldn't know how to take care of her. I meant it that way. He doesn't.

Peyton calls my name as I'm about to walk out the door. "Thank you for being here."

I nod and close the door to give them privacy.

WHEN WE LEAVE the hospital, I ask my mom to take me to see Harper and Skylar. They're waiting for an update, and I want to tell them in person.

"Oh, Peyton." Tears trickle down Harper's cheeks. "I need to call her."

"Give her a little bit of time. I know she'll call you when she's ready."

"Where was Tyler for all of this?"

"At our parents' getting his laptop."

"I'm sorry. What?" Harper screeches, aggressively wiping the wetness from her face.

I mutter, "My sentiments exactly."

"I could kill him." Her face turns red. "She's so blinded by her love for him she doesn't see what a buttwipe he is. How can love make a person *that* blind? Were you there when he came back?"

"Yeah. I couldn't stand being in the same room as him, so I left."

Harper's teeth grit together as she shakes her head, fuming. "If she marries him, so help me, Brodee, I don't think I can go to the wedding."

"If I have to, you do, too."

"Maybe Tyler and I need to have a little chat," Skylar says from beside Harper on the couch. "If it comes from Brodee, it'll sound like jealousy. Maybe he needs to hear from me that I'll beat some sense into him if he doesn't get his crap together."

"I doubt that would make a difference, babe, but good on you for thinking it would." Harper kisses his cheek. "You're a good man, Skylar Dalton."

"Well, it would make me feel better. Maybe I'd get a punch in there before he beat the crap out of me for thinking I could take him. One punch might be worth it."

I laugh. "I've got to get back to Boston. I just wanted to say hi and bye before I headed out."

"You came to see her for the surgery, and now you're heading back?"

Harper asks.

"I've got a redeye to catch. I have to be back for a meeting tomorrow afternoon, otherwise I'd stay longer. My mom's waiting in the car."

"Does Peyton know that?" she asks.

"I didn't mention it, no. But it's fine. I was here for what I needed to be here for." At least I could be there when Tyler wasn't. "She has Tyler now."

"That's like having the comfort of a sack of rocks."

I know what Harper is getting at. "She's made her choice, Harp."

"It's the wrong choice. And so is yours."

"What choice is that?"

"Picking Brooke."

Ha. I guess I should let them in on the news. "Well, that's over now. So…"

"Since when?" Skylar asks.

"Since a few days ago."

Harper interrupts, "And you're still just going to walk away. Now that you have no commitment to another woman, you're just going to let Peyton marry that douchenozzle? After all of that?"

I groan and pinch the bridge of my nose. "Do you know how many times I've tried to tell her how I feel?"

"What about recently?" she presses. "Does she know you broke things off with Brooke?"

"Technically, Brooke broke things off with me, and no. It hasn't come up in conversation yet."

"It's simple, Brodee. You just come out and say it. Peyton, 'Brooke and I broke up.'"

I stand up from the corner recliner. "Right now, I think Peyton has more important things to worry about. And I have to go or I'm going to miss my flight."

Harper opens her mouth to say more, but Skylar stops her. "He's gotta go, babe."

"Fine," she spats, "but I'm not letting this go. We love you. That's the only reason why I'm pushing this so hard. Have a safe flight. Text us to let us know you landed safely, will you?"

I smile at her request and nod. "I love y'all, too. And I will." I realize, as I walk out of their house, no matter the family you were born into, sometimes family chooses you.

The Day It Worked Out the Way It Was Supposed To

I CALL PEYTON to see how she's recovering. She's pretty tight-lipped about how she's feeling, so I know she doesn't want to talk about it. I have a feeling it will be a while before she will.

"You didn't stay long," she says.

"I'm sorry. I had a meeting I couldn't miss." I don't tell her that I shouldn't have even taken that day, but thankfully my boss understood since it was a family matter, and it hasn't affected my work.

"If I'd known you were only coming for a few hours, I would have told you not to waste your time."

"And that's why I didn't tell you."

Silence. "We had to push back the wedding a little bit."

"I figured you would until you recovered. When's the new date?"

"April 24th. Tyler starts school on the 28th, so we're cutting it close, but it'll still be enough time. And since it's not like we're renting out a space, and instead getting married on the beach, all the vendors were pretty understanding when they found about the circumstances."

"Well, that's good. They better."

"How's Boston?" she asks, changing the subject. "The job? Everything going good?" Of course, Peyton's diverting the attention from her.

"Work is good. Boston's great. It's kind of cool living in the city. It's nice to be so central to everything. There's so much to do. No time to get bored."

"And Brooke? How's she doing? Does she like Boston?"

I don't know why, but I don't want to tell Peyton about Brooke yet. It somehow makes me feel like I failed. I tried moving forward. I tried loving another woman. But I'm not built to love anyone but Peyton. "Umm…she moved back to Durham. We didn't work out."

"You broke up?" The fact that she's stunned makes me wonder if what Brooke and I had was real. I know it was real, but was it worth trying to salvage? Why would I let someone as amazing as Brooke go?

"Yeah."

"Mutual?" she questions.

"You know…I think she broke up with me."

"You *think*?"

"Well, she didn't take it too well, either."

"I'm sorry, Brodee," Peyton sympathizes. "I know you really cared about her."

"I did. I loved her. She was really hurt when she left. She didn't even let me try to fix it. She moved back home the next day." It's horrible timing, but my eyes begin to water. I squeeze them shut to cut it off. I made the right choice by waving my white flag. Fighting for Brooke wouldn't have made a difference. She'd never fill my whole heart. It would always be too crowded for her to fit.

"Do you remember when we were little," Peyton begins tenderly, "and I fell off that tire swing you guys used to have in your backyard?"

It's weird that Brooke and I were just looking at that photo. "I cried like a baby and couldn't stop."

"You cried *for me*," she corrects. "*I'd* gotten all scraped up, but *you* were the one who cried because you knew I was in pain. I've never known a more empathetic person. You feel so deeply for others. It's one reason why I'm so lucky to have you as a best friend. You never let me hurt alone." She pauses. "Don't beat yourself up over Brooke. It's life. She'll move on. You'll move on. Life will work out the way it's supposed to."

I hate that phrase. Supposed to. So, my dad was *supposed* to cheat on my mom? I was *supposed* to lose Peyton? She was *supposed* to get engaged to Tyler? I was *supposed* to break Brooke's heart? I don't believe that for one second. Life is all about choices. Life will work out the way we choose. My dad *chose* to cheat on my mom. Peyton *chose* to get engaged to Tyler. I *chose* to lose Brooke. I could've tried harder.

Right now, I don't like the choices that have been made.

The Day She Went Missing

"SHE'S GONE."

"Well, that sounds rather cryptic," I say to Harper.

"Peyton. She took off."

I scoot onto the edge of my couch, and lower the volume on the TV. "Where? Took off where?"

"I don't know. Olivia won't tell me. Peyton turned off her phone, so I called Olivia to make sure everything was okay, and she said that Peyton just needed to get away before the wedding."

"Isn't she supposed to be recovering for two more weeks?"

"I guess she's going to recover wherever she went to get away."

"And Olivia didn't tell you where she went?"

"Where would Peyton have gone to hide away for a couple weeks?"

There's only one place, but no. She wouldn't have. We haven't been back since that summer. She vowed never to return. Though Peyton's track record for keeping promises isn't great.

"I'm guessing by your silence you know it's Hatteras."

"I can't imagine why she would go there." Peyton used to say Hatteras heals, but she stopped believing that a long time ago.

"It's the whole baby thing. She's having a really hard time coming to terms with it. I've tried talking to her, but I don't know what she's going through. Every time I try to say something to help her, she brushes me off. And clearly Tyler isn't very helpful. He left just after you did, and he hasn't been back since. Not to mention, you've clearly given up on her."

I sigh heavily. "I didn't give up on her. I'm giving her space. Maybe that's what she needs. She knows where I stand."

"No. What she needs is for you to go to Hatteras."

I run my hand down my face. "I've already taken too much time off work. I can't just up and leave again. I'm too new. They won't take lightly to an employee who isn't dedicated to building his career. They've been lenient enough, as it is."

"What's more important, Brodee? Peyton or your career?"

"That's not fair, and you know the answer to that, Harper. But if Peyton shut off her phone, she obviously wants to be alone. And we don't even know for sure that she's in Hatteras."

"Where else would she have gone to *heal*?" Harper says dryly.

She's right. There's nowhere else she would've gone. But if she wanted company, she wouldn't have kept it a secret. But if she wanted to keep her healing a secret, she wouldn't have gone to Hatteras.

"Go, Brodee. Go to her. If you don't, you'll regret it for the rest of your life. It's your last chance to win her over before she's married to that dirtbag. And I'll never forgive you."

The Day I Returned

I DON'T THINK twice like I probably should. I'm on the next available flight out of Boston the following day. I fly into Norfolk International at four o'clock and rent a car to drive three straight hours to the beach house.

This is crazy, I know, but I don't talk myself out of it. The weather is horrible. It's pouring rain. The road is nearly impossible to see. I drive cautiously, but I don't want to take my time. It's possible she's not even there, and I wasted my time and probably lost my job.

My parents have always taught me to work hard for the things I want. If you put in the time and dedication, it will pay off and the rest will fall into place. If only love worked the same way. Loving Peyton—giving up everything for her—doesn't mean that she'll have to love me back. It's all risk and no guarantees. But if it means she'll be mine, no matter what I lose in the process, having her will be all the reward I need.

I breathe a sigh of relief when I pull into the circular driveway and Peyton's white Civic Tyler bought for her is parked front and center. Grabbing my backpack from the front seat, I bolt through the rain and up the front steps. Running doesn't help. I'm drenched. I attempt to wring out my clothes, but it's useless. I don't have a key, and I don't want to freak her out by trying to open the door in case it's locked, so I err on the side of caution and knock.

It takes a couple minutes, but she finally appears in the doorway. Her short hair is tucked behind her ears. She's makeup free and in her pajamas—black yoga pants and one of her dad's oversized T-shirts. I should say something, but I can't. The sight of her makes me stop and stare.

"Brodee," she gasps, "How did you…? What are you doing here?"

"I took a wild guess. And…" I've had seven hours to think about my answer and never once thought to. "I figured it was time to come back. Someone needs to keep you in line while you recover. I'm here to make sure you don't try to surf."

She snorts a laugh and opens the door wider. "Shut up. C'mon. Get out of the rain."

I close the door behind me and set my backpack at the bottom of the stairs.

"You hungry for dinner? Or did you stop on the way?"

"I could eat." I try to shake the water from my hair. There was no time to stop for food. It didn't even cross my mind.

"There's a pepperoni pizza in the oven. Should be done in like ten minutes, if you want to go and change out of your wet clothes. If you're lucky, I'll share."

I come back downstairs in dry lounge pants and a hoodie, towel drying my hair. Peyton is taking the pizza out of the oven. I rush to her side to help.

"Is it such a good idea for you to be lifting stuff? Don't you need tc wait like six weeks or something?"

"First of all, it's been four weeks already. And this weighs like five pounds. I think I'm okay." She offers a little smirk.

"Just lookin' out. Don't need you tearing anything while we're all the way out here. It would be such an inconvenience to have to take you all the way to the hospital. I just got here."

"I should punch you for that comment."

"But you might pop some stitches." I dodge the punch and laugh.

After dinner we sit on the couch, leaning against the armrests, and face each other with our legs outstretched.

"So…it's gone, right?"

"Cancer. You can say it, Brodee."

She makes me feels so foolish for fearing a word. "Yes, the cancer. Your doctor got it all, right?"

She nods. "Dr. Levanstine said the surgery removed the cancer, but he advised me to go through one round of chemo to make sure it's gone."

"When do you do that?"

"After I'm recovered from this." Peyton points to her stomach and sighs. "So, I guess sometime next month."

She can't catch a break. "Scared?"

"Wouldn't you be?"

I nod. "Will you lose your hair?"

"It's possible." She shrugs. *Shrugs.* It's the most forced nonchalance I've ever seen. "It's just hair, right?"

Her hair doesn't make her who she is, but it's a part of her. If she loses re thing the cancer will have taken from her. I chew on my ıst hair, yeah."

"Did my mom ask you to come?"

"Huh? No. Why? She wasn't okay with you coming alone?"

"No." Peyton shakes her head and takes a sip of her Dr. Pepper. "She wanted to come with me, but I told her there was no way that was happening."

I laugh. "I'm surprised you came at all."

There's a far off look in her eyes. "It was the last place I felt close to him. Our home is full of Nick now. This is the only place I can still feel my dad."

I hate that for her. One more thing my dad ruined. "Was it as hard as you imagined it would be to come back?"

She straightens her back. "Actually, no. I was scared at first. But it was surprisingly easy because I knew, or thought, I'd be alone. That I could make this house what I want it to be without them spoiling it. When I opened the door I wasn't assaulted by memories of our last couple of days here. I was filled with all the memories of my dad. Him coming in soaking wet after surfing. Him writing on his laptop in the corner chair." She points to the recliner by the window that covers nearly the entire wall behind me. "Or playing Rook with him at the kitchen table. There was a burst of warmth that I haven't felt in so long. I'm grateful that they couldn't take this away, too." Her eyes meet mine briefly before they look back to the large window.

"Was it as hard as you imagined?" she asks me.

I honestly didn't even think about it. I knew she would be here, and that's all that mattered. And seeing her silhouette standing in the doorway when I first got here erased the possibility of any reservation that might have surfaced.

"I didn't even think twice when I heard you were here."

Her head snaps in my direction. *Did she really expect anything less?*

I can tell she doesn't know what to say so she diverts her eyes back to the window. I hear the rain and wind beating the glass. "It's a good thing you got here when you did. It's getting really nasty out there. The waves are out of control."

It's the ocean, grieving for us, and what we may never be.

"You can't marry him, Peyton."

It's like she knew this was coming. Her gaze calmly turns back to me before she asks, "And why not?"

"Because he doesn't deserve you. Where has he been when you've needed him? Shouldn't he be here with you now?" I look around the house. She starts to answer me, but I stop her. "I don't want his stupid excuses. They mean nothing to me. And I can't believe you think any of those excuses are valid. The Peyton I used to know knew what she wanted. She didn't let people walk all over her. She might have put others first, but she did it out of love, and she didn't let it compromise who she was."

"Change is a good thing, Brodee," she counters. "Compromise is what makes relationships work."

I lean forward and bend my knees. "Not when it means losing the best parts of you. He should love you for your imperfections—not try to change them. You're perfect as you are, but all I've seen Tyler try to do is form you into what he wants you to be. I can't stand by and let him distort all my favorite parts." I reach across the space between us and brush back the white, short hair hanging across her forehead. "How your sun-kissed, long hair used to tie up on top of your head when you surfed. Or how you could beat me in any pizza-eating contest. Or when I'd try to cheat in Hand and Foot, but you'd never let me get away with it, always trying to keep my honest. Or how you'd always speak your mind, even when you knew I didn't want to hear it. Your voice mattered, and you knew it, so you expressed it on more occasions than I appreciated."

Her eyes gloss over with unshed tears. I rein in the urge to take her in my arms. I need to say this. She needs to hear it.

"There are so many things Tyler loses by trying to change you. The worst one being your spirit. I don't even think he sees what the cancer has done to you. It's as though he thinks just because it didn't kill you, that everything is okay. He ignores the loss of light in your eyes because he doesn't know how to handle it. Rather than letting you talk through it and listening to your sorrows, he buries them so they can't tarnish the perfect life he wants to create. Newsflash: Life isn't perfect. If it were, it wouldn't be worth living. There would be nothing to fight for. And I will fight for you until you say 'I do.'"

Peyton reaches her hand up and presses it against my cheek. She shakes her head and looks into her lap. "And here it is. History repeating itself, except this time you're my mom, and I'm Nick."

"We are *nothing* like them," I argue, wrenching my face away. "You're not married with twenty years under your belt. I don't have a wife who recently passed away. We don't have two families who will be torn apart if we end up together. Us being together affects no one."

"But I'm with Tyler, and you've been weaseling your way into my life again, and I've been letting you. It was so minimal as first I didn't even notice it, but once you became a giant portion, I didn't know how to keep you out. I wanted you to stay. So, maybe that makes me my mom," she mumbles. "Because I let you in even though I shouldn't have."

I take her shoulders in my hands and shake her. "Never say that again. Didn't you hear anything I just said? We aren't our parents. We haven't done anything wrong. *You* haven't done anything wrong. You're not married; there's still time to call off the engagement."

She rips her shoulders from my grasp. "I won't do that."

I groan in frustration. "I'm only going to say this once because after tonight this ends one way or another. I'm not my dad. After you're married, I'll be done with us. I won't torment you or myself. I won't fight for you anymore. I'm praying you make the right choice before that, even if it's not me. Don't let it be him. Don't choose him."

She softly says, "I already have chosen him."

"But you love me, too. I know you do. We've had moments. I know you've felt them. You put up a pretty solid shield, but when it's down, I see our future in your eyes. Why can't you allow yourself to be happy with me?"

"Because I'm happy with Tyler, okay? We love each other, and it's uncomplicated and secure, and there aren't all these entanglements with the power to mess everything up."

"Are you really? Happy? Or are you just content? Does he make you feel the way that I do? When he kisses you, do you feel like the world would fall out of orbit if he ever stopped?" I pause. "Sometimes I think about never getting to kiss you again, and it feels as though I'll never breathe again, like the oxygen in my lungs is all I have left. The possibility of us is the only thing that keeps me going."

"Sometimes safe is a good thing, Brodee. Sometimes it's enough. It means stability and security."

"He's the opposite of stability! Who was with you for your oncologist appointment? Who was with you when you woke up after surgery and found out that you couldn't have children? He should have been there, Peyton!" I lower my voice. "He won't love you the way I do. I could give you those things. When have I ever not been your constant? I've always been there for you. Not out of obligation, but because I want to. I want to take care of you. I want to experience life with you."

She snaps. "It's not you I'm worried about. Don't you get it? It's this cancer. My useless body! It's our screwed up family!"

"This cancer *will not* kill you," I say firmly, so resolutely it has to be true. "You are going to be *fine*."

"You don't know that."

"I do because you'll fight it. We'll do everything in our power to make sure you beat this thing. And what more damage could our family possibly cause that they haven't already? We're already screwed up!"

"Exactly! You're my family, Brodee. If we want to get technical here—"

I shake my head. "Okay. Let's get technical. We are not actual siblings, Peyton. So what if a paper says we're related by law. It's nothing but a label. That paper means nothing. The only paper that will mean something to me is the one that makes you my wife."

"Brodee…" By the way she says my name, I know I won't like what follows, so I cut her off.

"So, we're a little unconventional. You think I care what anyone thinks? They don't have the right to judge us. You were mine first. I love you, and I only care what you think of us. Are we wrong? Are we twisted? Fine. So be it. There isn't anyone else in this world who I want to be wrong and twisted with more than you."

Her mouth curves into an uncertain smile like she wants to laugh. "I'm not really sure how to take that."

"Take it however you want. Just take it. Take my words. Take me. You already took my heart. Take everything else. It's yours."

She doesn't respond. Her eyes travel around my face like she can't decide what to focus on. Every time our eyes meet she shifts her attention, like making eye contact is too painful. "I can't take anything from you." Her voice shakes with indecision.

"I lost you once. I won't make that same mistake. I used to believe that that last summer tainted Hatteras. But when I look back, when I fall into the memories of this place and what it means to me, I don't think of the bad. I only think of you. I only think of the good because that's what you are. You are everything good in my life, Peyton. Be with me. Pick me."

Peyton stops her wandering gaze and looks me straight in the eye. "I can't, Brodee." It's the finality in her tone. Nothing has ever hurt me more than those words. "I can't."

I get up. There's no way I can look at her any longer. I go to bed and wake up the next morning before she does. I fly back to Boston. I won't fly back for the wedding.

The Day It Sucked

BOSTON FEELS MEANINGLESS. My apartment is empty. My heart is hollow. Everything sucks.

The Day I Chose to Avoid Insanity

I SEE HARPER'S name light up my cell on my desk. I think twice about answering it and calling her after I get off work, but she never calls just to shoot the breeze. That concerns me.

"What's up, Harp?"

"She called it off."

I'm not sure I hear Harper correctly. "What?"

"Peyton. She called off the wedding!" I can practically see her jumping up and down. Skylar is probably rolling his eyes and chuckling at her. "Well, technically she's postponing it again, but still!"

I fall back into the chair in my cubicle. My thoughts are like the metal ball in a pinball machine, ricocheting off the bone inside my skull.

"Did you hear me?" Harper's nearly shouting. "She's holding off on the wedding indefinitely. Are you going to come back?"

"Wait. Hold on. Hold on a second. When did she call it off?"

"This morning. He was here for the weekend for a final tux fitting. She cut the trip short."

"Did she tell you why?"

"She just told me it wasn't right yet—that she needed more time."

Why hasn't Peyton called me yet? Though, just because she broke off the engagement doesn't mean she did it for me, for us. "And that's it?"

"Well, I'd like to think it went something more like...*I'm done with you, you selfish scum-sucking pig!* But something tells me she was a little gentler. And sadly, it's not over yet; she needs just a little more to tip her in favor of ending it for good."

I can't think straight. She actually did it. But why?

"So, are you gonna go after her or what?"

"Did she tell you she wanted me to?"

"Well..." Harper hesitates. "No, but that doesn't mean she doesn't want you to."

I heavily exhale. "Harper, think for one second. She called off the engagement *this morning*. And she didn't even end it. She only postponed the wedding. It's not that simple. She needs to figure out what she wants. And I have to work. I can't just get up and leave everything every time you think Peyton is ready for me. I'm lucky I didn't lose my job the last time you told me to go and win her back."

"But this time there's nothing standing in your way! She just needs a little push in the right direction."

"Harper," I say sternly, but try to keep my voice low enough so the rest of the office doesn't hear me. "I'm going to say this once, and then you're going to drop it for good. I tried. Weeks ago, I poured out my heart in Hatteras, and she crushed it. She mutilated it. It's dead. Over."

"Okay. I get it."

"You don't get it. Otherwise you'd stop this. Stop coming to the wrong person. Stop trying to give me hope. Leave it alone. Peyton knows where I stand. I'm done chasing her."

"But—"

"But nothing. I have to go." I hang up before she can continue to argue with me. If I go after Peyton again, I'm nothing more than a fool. I can't expect a different outcome when I've tried the same thing over and over again. She's doesn't want me, and Harper needs to understand that.

"Fisher." I look to see my boss leaning around my cubicle. "Everything okay?"

"Yeah. Great." My smile is so fake it practically splits my lips.

He doesn't believe me. "Do you have the financial reports for me from last week?"

"Yes." I pull out my keyboard. "I'll email them to you right now."

"Good. Hey, listen," he comes around to the open doorway, "I know you've had some family emergencies as of late, but if you keep doing what you're doing—keeping up the good work—I see nothing but great things in the future for you. You just have to be present in order to show what you can do. Otherwise, I can't help you."

I nod respectfully. "Yes, sir."

"Okay." He nods once with a smile before he walks away.

I run my hands down my face. It's just my luck to have him show up when Harper calls. I'm blocking her calls from now on.

The Day It Had to be Enough

APRIL TURNS TO May. May turns to June. June turns to July. Months evaporate like clouds in the sky. I hear nothing from Peyton, and I make no attempt to contact her. It's the longest we've ever gone without speaking. Not even a text. My mom and dad filled me in on her chemo treatment in June. One round for precaution. That's it. She didn't lose her hair. And she's now cancer-free. I'm relieved. I am, but it's almost a win without victory because I'm not the one she's sharing it with. And now I feel like an insensitive prick for feeling that way. It makes me no better than Tyler.

Harper finally stops pushing the idea of Peyton and me having a future. I thought I'd be grateful for the day, but it only makes it feel more final. If no one besides me believes in us, there is no hope. There is no us to believe in.

I often wonder: if what we had was real, how is she okay without me? And why can't I be okay without her? I wonder if it was all a lie—something I created in my head because it was easier to believe a lie than to swallow the hard truth.

She never loved me.

There are days when I think of calling Brooke to check in on her, but it's for purely selfish reasons. I want to know how she's doing, but only to ease my heavy heart. I want to know that I didn't break her heart the way Peyton broke mine. So I never call.

Peyton called off the wedding, but for what? Clearly, since I'm still in Boston, alone and married to my job, it wasn't for me. And as far as I know, Tyler is still in the picture. I haven't heard otherwise. So, that's one other thing Boston is good for. I can keep myself detached from a world I no longer belong in.

I am grateful for two things: Peyton is cancer free, and she's still not married to Tyler. Maybe someone else will come along. Maybe there's a man better for Peyton than me. There's definitely a better man than Tyler.

At least she was mine for a summer. That will have to be enough.

The Day That Saved Us

WHEN I GET off the elevator on my floor, I trudge toward my apartment. It's been a long, tiring day. I had to stay and work overtime on a report my boss needed for a project in the morning. Of course, his request came in an hour before I was meant to head home.

I want to flip on the TV, put my feet up, and enjoy a beer. I stop in the hallway. There's a person seated outside my door, leaning against the wall. Her head is bent over her cell phone, blonde hair draped across the side of her face. When she hears me coming, she looks up.

"Peyton?"

"Oh, good." She grabs her purse and stands as I approach. "I didn't know when you'd be home. I tried calling you, but your phone sent me straight to voicemail."

"I forgot to charge it last night. It's dead."

"Well, that explains it." She's visibly relieved. *What is she doing here?* "I was hoping you weren't sending me straight to voicemail."

My lips purse as I shake my head. "Just bad timing." If she did try to call when my phone wasn't dead, I'm not sure what I would've done. I wouldn't have sent it to voicemail, but I'm not sure I would've answered it either. There was a time when I thought I could go back, that we could be best friends and live our lives apart. Now, looking at her standing in front of me, I know that's impossible.

"That's comforting." The corner of her mouth turns up, half-smiling.

"How long have you been waiting?"

"Not too long." She shrugs her purse up her shoulder. "A couple hours."

There's an awkward moment when we do nothing but stare at each other. Her hair is longer, less white, more natural. It lies below her shoulders in loose waves, like she just got done surfing. The closer I get, the easier it is to see the freckles gracing her face. She's not covering them anymore.

I unlock my apartment and let Peyton follow me inside, flipping the lights on as I go. I drape my suit jacket over the arm of my futon, loosen my tie and unbutton the first couple buttons of my blue button-down. *Is it hot in here, or is it just me?*

"Can I get you something to drink? Water? Beer? Dr. Pepper?"

"You hate Dr. Pepper."

I don't even know why I have it in my fridge. It's not like I was planning on her unexpectedly showing up. Or maybe I hoped.

I nod.

"Dr. Pepper would be great."

When I come back from the kitchen, she's still standing in the entryway, looking around like she doesn't know what to do with herself. I don't know what to do with her either. She must be able to tell I'm awaiting her explanation. I can hope, but for all I know, she came to apologize. Or maybe she just wanted to visit Boston. There's a first time for everything. If she wants me to be her tour guide, I'll have to pass.

After she takes her first sip, she says, "Your place is nice."

I look around. It's bare compared to what it used to be. My bookshelf has half the books it used to. There are no bookends or figurines, just books—disorganized and falling on their sides. And the pictures of Brooke and me on the walls are gone. The walls are empty. It's sad to think of what they once looked like compared to now.

"Brooke wanted it to feel like home, but she took most of the decorations when she moved out."

She nods. "It's got a bachelor pad vibe now." Peyton clicks her tongue, something she only does when she's nervous. "The night you played that song for me in your car, you remember?"

The night she told me she was going to marry Tyler and destroy any hope of us? *How could I forget?* I remember it all too well. I nod again.

"I wasn't listening," she says, and looks down at the soda can gripped between both of her hands. "My mind was wandering, trying to figure out how to tell you about the engagement. It didn't occur to me until yesterday that it was the words of that last song you wanted me to listen to, not just the music of the band." She lifts her gaze to me. "When I saw the album on Harper's iPod, I remembered how upset you were before I even told you about Tyler, so I asked Harper if I could play it. She hopped in the shower, and I sat down on her bed."

Peyton bites her lip. All I can think is, she wasn't listening?

"As soon as I heard the chorus, I started to cry. When I first saw you

I thought you'd moved on with Brooke. I pushed you away for so long I thought it finally stuck. It didn't occur to me that you were still holding out hope after all these years, that the song was your way of telling me everything you missed. I knew you wouldn't be happy about Tyler, but not because you were jealous or still in love with me. I know how much you hate him." She hurries on. "Then you came to me in Hatteras, and I thought I was your rebound from Brooke, someone who you'd always come back to because it was comforting, familiar. It's so easy for us to be around one another. And I saw how much you loved Brooke, and I completely understood because she is incredible, a real catch. It didn't make sense for you to give up on her so easily. You caught me off guard."

I try to interrupt her, but she stops me with a hand raised and sets down her drink on the side table next to the couch. Peyton takes a step toward me.

"When Harper got out of the shower and saw me sobbing on her bed, she sighed like she knew. And she did, didn't she? She's known all along what you felt." Peyton can see the truth in my eyes. "Harper looked at me and said, 'You dummy. How could you not know?'" Her laugh is breathless, like she can't believe she didn't put it together.

"Listening to that song…I was drawn back to that summer in Hatteras. Something clicked. Everything about Tyler became so clear. Everything you and Harper had been trying to tell me. And everything about you and me made more sense than ever."

"The first time you listened to the song was last night?" My heart flatlines.

She nods. "I hopped on the first plane I could this morning. If I hadn't,

I'm sure Harper would have had a conniption."

And like I've been jolted back to life, my heart starts racing. Every organ inside of me is bursting at the seams.

"Maybe if I'd stopped being so selfish for two seconds, I would have seen what I needed to from the start. I was so blinded by my bitterness toward Nick, so overpowered by my pride and what everyone would think. I so stubbornly wanted Tyler and me to work so I wouldn't see how much I was missing by pushing you away. I was too scared to give us a real chance. And then the cancer threw me a curveball. I don't even know how to play baseball." She laughs again, self-deprecating. "After everything we've already been through, I didn't want to put you through more. I couldn't expect you to take care of me, and I knew that's exactly what you'd have done. You'd have dropped Boston in an instant."

She doesn't give me time to respond before she's talking again. "I lied about why Tyler never came to my appointments with me and why he left after my surgery."

I don't understand why she would do that.

"I asked him not to come to the appointment. I asked him to stay in North Carolina." She takes a deep breath in a way that tells me she's ashamed. Her eyes dart around the room as she says, "He was never very good at consoling me. The words were always there, but they felt rehearsed. He was uncomfortable with my pain. Rather than taking it on, empathizing with me, he blocked it out."

I have to hold back my I-told-you-so expression. It would be poor form.

"You were right, and I knew it." Peyton finally sets her eyes on me again. "And after my surgery, Tyler told me he wanted the doctor to tell me the outcome. Can you believe that? What a coward. Why would I rather hear that kind of news from Dr. Levanstine? So I asked him to go home to get the laptop for me. I didn't want him to see me when I found out. It was *my* pain, not his. His presence would've only made my pain feel insignificant, as if I was being melodramatic, that it couldn't be as bad as I thought it was."

My hands roll into fists at my side. I hate how much he misunderstands her, underappreciates her. He has the best thing that could ever happen to him right under his nose, and he treats her like just another girl, not Peyton Parker.

She sighs and shakes her head. A humorless, short laugh escapes. "His life has been so cushioned; he doesn't understand loss. He doesn't understand what it's like to lose so much, so young. Within a year I lost my dad, my relationship with my mom, my second family. I lost my best friend." Her voice begins to shake, and all I want to do is hold her, but I can tell she needs to say this. "He never understood how much it hurt, how much it changed me. I tried time after time to make him understand, but it fell on deaf ears. There was nothing I could say that could teach him how to love me."

She shouldn't have to teach someone how to love her. How could loving Peyton not come easily, naturally? Loving Peyton is like breathing; I don't have to think about it. It's a part of me.

"I ended it."

I was waiting for her to say the words. They still knock the wind out of me. I want to say something, but I can't find the right words.

"Do you remember when we danced at Harper and Skylar's wedding?"

It's as if she thinks I remember nothing. I remember every moment with her. I answer with a nod.

"I lied to you."

"About what?"

"When you asked me if I ever think about that summer..." She gives me time that I don't need to recall that night. "Ask me again."

I blink. "Do you ever think about that summer?"

"Every day." Her voice trembles, clogged with tears. "And I don't think about the bad. I think about our first kiss. Not the dare, but the one on the beach, when you told me you were still here and not to leave you while you were still here. I think about the way you kissed me, the way your lips already knew mine. I think about how we danced in the rain and didn't care that we were soaking wet, how you sang to me and made me fall in love with you with one slightly off-key song. I think about the song you wrote for me on your guitar. I still hear it in my head all the time. When you're gone, and I need to feel you most, I sing it to myself because I don't know what I did to deserve *you*. You're *my* everything good. You know how to love me."

I close the distance between us and grab her face. I love her with my lips, with every brush, every nip. I love her with my hands and let them wander to places they've missed and craved to caress. I kiss her the way she deserves to be kissed. And when I can't breathe because my mouth refuses to leave hers, I kiss her harder and lift her off her feet. She smiles against my mouth, but I don't let go. Someone will have to pry my cold, dead lips off her because I could do this until the day I die. She gasps with me like it's the first time we've taken a breath since our last summer in Hatteras.

When we reluctantly pull away, her eyes shine with unshed tears. They smile at me.

"Little did I know the day I played you that song, it was going to be the day that saved us."

She lets out a breath of laughter. Then her face falls. "I can't give you babies, Brodee." She can hardly get the words out.

"Yes, you will." I keep her secure in my arms, pressing one hand against her cheek and rest my forehead against hers. "They might have DNA donors, but they will be ours. Our blood in their veins or not, we will love them more because of what we endured to get them. I will love them because you will help me raise them. You're *alive* to help me raise them."

With a smile, more tears come. "I was worried my speech wouldn't be epic enough. I've treated you so poorly for years."

Suddenly none of the time we've lost even matters. I feel like we've moved on from cheesy pick-up lines, so I try something new. "Like Tom had Renee at hello, you have me. All of me."

Peyton cracks a smile and wipes the tears from her eyes, never missing a beat. "Only if you're a bird. Because I'm a bird."

"So, that wasn't too corny?" I ask with a laugh.

"I'm looking for corny in my life."

I set her back on the ground and brush the back of my hand across her cheeks, catching some strays she missed. "Don't cry, Shopgirl."

"Is this our thing now? Romantic comedy references?" She laughs lightly.

"It seems to be the natural progression."

"You think you know enough to make a challenge out of it?" She dares me with her eyebrow raised.

"Will I seem like less of a man if I do?"

"Only if you can't beat me."

"You're on," I say.

"Shut up and kiss me," she says.

And so I do.

The Day He Was Right

WE DON'T SPEND the summers in Hatteras as a family anymore, but we take turns. Peyton and I get the beach house for a few weeks, and today is the first of our stay.

She stands at the railing overlooking the boardwalk and ocean. I brush her hair away from her neck and plant a kiss on her skin. Her hair is back to the way it used to be. Long and no longer white, but sun-kissed, as it was made to be. I loop my arms around her waist and rest my chin on her bare shoulder. She exhales and settles into my arms. Her freckles are featured under the sunlight. I want to kiss each and every one. And I can, because we have the rest of our lives together. So, I make that my new pact. To build Peyton up and help her love every flaw and imperfection that makes her who she is, that makes the woman I love.

"You know, my dad used to tell me something whenever life wouldn't go the way I planned."

"Oh yeah?" I tighten my arms around her and listen intently.

"He'd say, 'Peyton Jane, there's beauty in a new beginning. It brings the opportunity to create something more, something better.' And you know what?" I feel a contented smile brighten her face. "He was right."

ACKNOWLEDGMENTS

FIRST AND FOREMOST, I need to thank Michele G. Miller. She is the reason this book is in your hands right now. When my brain no longer wanted to give me words, she helped to drag me from the darkness.

Thank you, Madison Seidler and Samantha Eaton-Roberts, my editors, for cleaning up my messes and giving invaluable advice.

My sisters in fierceness, I think it goes without saying, but thank you for your awesomeness. Every day and always. Especially, Starla, for enduring the endless cover changes.

To Jessica, my alabaster doll, stay classy.

My work family who might as well be blood: Shawnna, Lisabeth, Laura, JJ, Stephanie, Cabell, and Lima, who put up with me daily at my "real" job and encourage me to pursue my dreams, even if it means not being "mentally" present every day. I love you guys so much.

As always, my family--both blood and through marriage--deserve the most thanks for your patience, consideration, support and all around love. And, of course, Ryan, the inspiration behind all my leading men. I love you. Thank you.

To my readers, it's a blessing to be able to begin an acknowledgment like that. I'm so grateful for each of you.

ABOUT MINDY

MINDY HAYES is the youngest of six children and grew up in San Diego, California. After attending Brigham Young University-Idaho, she discovered her passion for reading and writing. Mindy and her husband have been married for eight years and live in Summerville, South Carolina.

VISIT MINDY ONLINE

Website: www.mindyhayes.com

Facebook: www.facebook.com/hayes.mindy

Twitter: @haymindywrites

CPSIA information can be obtained
at www.ICGtesting.com
Printed in the USA
BVHW031252190420
577913BV00001B/109

9 781544 037851